Fall from Grace

A haunting novel, inspired by a remarkable woman's journey through life and her universal story of hope

Rob James

Copyright © Rob James 2023, Kapiti, New Zealand. First Edition.

ISBN 978-0-473-63558-9

Rob James asserts the moral rights as author of this book.

This work is copyright and all rights are reserved. No part of this book may be reproduced, copied, scanned, stored in a retrieval system, recorded or transmitted, in any form or by any means without the prior written permission of the author.

Designed by Precise Print & Design, Paraparaumu, New Zealand.

Sketches drawn by Rachael James.

Everyone it seems, has their share of dark secrets,
either their own, or buried in the annals of their family history.

This book is centred around some of those momentous secrets.

Secrets that, from the outset, threatened to rip a family apart.

Ultimately, they challenged the very spirit of human kindness,
hope and endeavour.

Foreword

We all go through change at many points of our life. Some of the change is by our own choosing, while often it's because of decisions made by others and we live with the consequences. When you look at your own life, you'll see decisions – big and small – that fall into each category.

It has been said that despite the source of decisions, we have the possibility of living life from two perspectives. One is from the point of view of Love, the other Fear.

When we choose to live from Love, we notice things in a different way. We see our lives through a different lens and we begin to understand that what we do matters. It matters to those we love, causes we love, and extends out to our love for our community and the wider world. Love is enriching, while Fear is depressive.

That's the message I learned from reading Fall from Grace. It's a book about Love.

The book tells the story of one woman's life, the decisions she made and decisions made for her, that was to unfold in a most unexpected and surprising way.

Set in rural Northern Ireland, the story – and the way it's told – reminds me of a fine fabric that is woven with rich patterns of colour and fine stitching, to produce a cloth that is both beautiful and heart-warming. The writing evokes a warmth that will have you fall in love with Grace, and perhaps see something of yourself in her.

While this story is about Grace and her family, it is located within a particular historical context. Woven throughout the narrative are important events that provide critical texture to the fabric of the story.

When I read the book, I could not put it down. It carried me along, wanting to know more, and wondering how it finally worked out for Grace. It also filled me with hope for the future.

Dr David Keane, PhD

Author of *The Art of Deliberate Success: The 10 Behaviours of Successful People*

Contents

Preface 9
Family Trees 11
Prologue - Oh Mammy, Mammy 13
Chapter 1 - The Liberty Bell 19
Chapter 2 - The Sheltered Lake 31
Chapter 3 - The Great Freeze 39
Chapter 4 - The Claim 53
Chapter 5 - The Bitter Seed 68
Chapter 6 - The King of Spits 77
Chapter 7 - The Orange & The Green 85
Chapter 8 - The Trade 93
Chapter 9 - Sam 102
Chapter 10 - Mad Maude 113
Chapter 11 - The Untimely Grim Reaper 126
Chapter 12 - Bury My Heart 139
Chapter 13 - Shelter From The Storm 148
Chapter 14 - The Blessing 161
Chapter 15 - The Choice 173
Chapter 16 - Lies Laid Bare 183
Chapter 17 - The Escape 192
Chapter 18 - The Curse 201
Chapter 19 - A Test of Time 214
Chapter 20 - Abandonment 221

Chapter 21 - Living In Exile 232
Chapter 22 - When Speaks The Heart 247
Chapter 23 - New Beginnings, Old Issues 256
Chapter 24 - The Crow is Born 267
Chapter 25 - The Cow's Tale 279
Chapter 26 - Fractures 287
Chapter 27 - Mourning The Mournes 300
Chapter 28 - Leaving The Heights 313
Chapter 29 - To Call Myself Beloved 326
Epilogue 332
Appendix 1 - Acknowledgements 335
Appendix 2 - References 337

Preface

Fall from Grace is a novel, greatly fuelled by my imagination, but inspired by an incredible true story, spanning nearly seventy years. That story is informed and enriched by an array of hazy, half-buried memories and hand-me-down tales, especially those about Grace. Grace was an ordinary woman from a time gone by, who chose to live an extraordinary life, filled with hope and love in the face of extreme adversity.

The truth of some things will forever remain a mystery, but Grace herself did reveal parts of her early life story some years before she passed on. Family and friends helped add to that from their own memories, long after the events. Amidst all of that there is much speculation on my part as to what actually happened, and especially as to why things happened in the way they did.

Growing up in the countryside in Northern Ireland was a glorious and privileged experience. I spent a bare sixteen years there, departing that fair land in 1966 with my parents and some of my siblings. We stepped into a very different world in England to the one we had left behind in Ireland. That seems so long ago, yet the places and the memories of the genuine warmth of the people of

Ireland never left us. There is a lot of truth in that old adage, "You can take the boy out of the country, but you can't take the country out of the boy."

The aim in writing this book is to remember Grace, and to take you, the reader, on an uplifting and enjoyable journey through some of her incredible story, even if that journey gets more than a little dark and bumpy at times.

We all share the dramas of life in one way or another, but through Grace, I've come to learn that we can also draw deeply on the joy and inner beauty of the places and people around us, whatever our circumstances. While Grace's story is set in Ireland, her message of hope and love is universal. Where the story does get a little dark, it may help to remember that people usually do things, sometimes awful things, for an underlying reason. Their reasons may be simple, or complex and profound. Sometimes they are just downright unfathomable.

However, in the process of writing this book and in seeking to understand, for me at least, it gave credence to another old idiom, "Before we judge, first walk a mile in the other person's shoes." Even if we never quite agree with their reasons or course of action, we might then at least begin to understand their underlying motives a little more.

In a similar vein, the odd peppering of historical events has been included to give context to the influences on, and underlying deep-seated culture of the characters in the story. To state the obvious, Ireland would not be Ireland without all that rich and varied history.

A family tree has been included to help keep track of the characters in the story. (All of the names used here are of course fictitious.)

Net proceeds from sales of this book are donated to charity, including Women's Aid.

Family Trees

Beth & Riley's Children
Grace · Dottie · Toby · Wendy · Gwen · Gloria · Myrtle · Olive · Daniel

Liza & Bob's Children
Bert · Harry · Jacob · Valerie · Freda · Lucy · Clive · Hazel

Maude's Children
Pearl · Nan · Donna

Grace's Children
Elizabeth · Vicky · Hugh · Ted · Joy

Pearl & Jeff's Children
Anna · Joe · Ruby

Prologue

Oh Mammy, Mammy

*If you begin to be what you are you will realise everything,
but to begin to be what you are, you must come out of what you are not.
You are not those thoughts which are turning, turning in your mind;
you are not those changing feelings; you are not the different decisions
you make and the different wills you have; you are not that separate ego.
(Shri Shantanan(n)*

Saturday 22nd December 1962

Outside, the light snow was already beginning to fall, like some gentle warning of what was to come. The icy cold wind gathered pace and tore away the last remnants of leaves on the trees as the dark Winter night wore on. Inside, the house was still and silent, except for the faint whispering resistance of windows and doors against the wind. The children, all eight of them, were gently wrapped in the warm embrace of deep sleep. The mother, Grace, was not so fortunate.

Once again, her sleep was uneasy, fragments of the dream starting to percolate through her troubled mind. Slowly at first, the trickle of long-buried memories began to slither silently past the relenting barriers of daytime resolutions. On they came, a faint image of unwanted recollection here, a dark shadow of remembrance there. Increasingly they came, ever hastening, her resolute will no longer present to restrict or contain them. Amassing now, pushing aside the walls of reality and reason, until they could no longer be suppressed. Grace writhed uneasily in the bed as the dream shifted into the awaiting nightmare.

All too real the flooding formation of those painful long-ago memories resurfaced and pulled her in. Now immersed, she was once again in the familiar hiding place, a cold and stark small outside toilet. It offered an unlikely temporary sanctuary for the young girl inside. The stomping of heavy footwear approaching on cobbled stone made her draw in a tight breath. She tried not to make a sound, praying she would not be found. The sudden hammering on the locked door sent jolts of fear raking through her. The angry shouting outside, threatening, bullying, and yet somehow familiar.

Inside, the young girl's fear was mounting, her whole being overtaken by rising terror. Her inadequate hiding place was discovered, and her heart sank as the demonic voice commanded her, demanding she come out. The angry hammering grew louder still, the voice seemingly all around her now, assailing her senses. It was more than the young girl could bear. A feeling of hopelessness swept over Grace. The icy fear, all too real in the midst of the nightmare, gripped her. The compelling power in the voice stealing all hope from her.

Grace's mind, acutely pained, rebelled against the half-memory, desperately seeking escape from the terrifying nightmare. Once again, another voice forced its way upward. Rising from the depth of her despair, up from the realm of the dream state, finally breaking through the bonds of sleep into the light of consciousness. Shattering the silence of the night, this time Grace heard her own pained voice cry out its all too familiar wail.

"Oh mammy, oh mammy, mammy, please! Please no, please don't!"

The cry echoed loud along the bedroom corridors. The woeful wailing filling the three upstairs bedrooms of the small overcrowded terraced council house. The man beside her was startled awake and sat bolt upright as sleep was snatched from him. In the other rooms some of the children began to stir.

"For God's sake Grace, not again! Wake up! You have to be quiet woman; you'll wake the whole house and the neighbours!"

Too late, Grace realised the dream for what it was, unreal, just another dark nightmare. With growing awareness, she made the shift from persuasive illusion to present reality, and abruptly fell silent. Several of the younger children, by now half-awake and already beginning to become familiar with this odd night-time routine, were slowly drifting into her bedroom and clambering half-asleep into bed beside her. She sighed resignedly, and did her best to make room for them alongside her.

It would be another cramped night, but gradually they would all drift off peacefully to a kinder sleep. "They're not real," she told herself, "just nightmares, just some shadows of a worried mind." She paused, reflecting. "It is what it is, and it's just the way of things," she told herself, as the children snuggled against her. There was some small comfort in that after all.

Grace smiled inwardly as she anticipated what the morning would bring. There would be the same little ritual of playful mocking voices from the children as they gathered early for breakfast. "Oh mammy, mammy, mammy!" they would echo in imitation of her. The younger children would squeal with delight as they tried to outdo each other's playful mimicking. This, and the crisp cold light of dawn, quickly dissolving any lingering power of her nightmare. She would laugh and join in with them, making light of it, making a game of it. And yet, like the elder children, young adults now, never quite immersed, never fully joining in. Their game would last a few passing playful moments. Then, when his patience had been tested, the man would call out, "Enough!"

She looked again at the faces of the children already asleep peacefully beside her. "Hope", she mused, "it doesn't just spring forth with the darkness and fade with the dawn, as some might have us believe. No", she thought, dimly remembering her scriptures. "Sometimes it has to go far and away beyond that". The morning light would soon rise and ease aside the veil of darkness for a new dawn. Another day would begin.

Tomorrow the man would go out hunting so they would have something to tide the family over for Christmas. He would take their eldest son out with him, a belated birthday treat. Grace would rise early to prepare some sandwiches for them. It was another little ritual, a simple necessity, yet somehow comforting.

Grace sighed deeply. For her sanity and for the sake of her children, indeed for everyone's sake, she was well aware she had to let go of the bitterness and darkness of the recurring nightmares and not allow herself to dwell in the past. With quiet affirmation of her faith, she resolved afresh to meet the new day with hope still in her heart. "Let it come," she thought, "all that is asked of me is that I meet it trying my best, and while I can still draw breath, I can surely still manage to do that."

There were those who might describe Grace as an ordinary woman, and indeed in many ways she was just that. She was still quite attractive even in middle age, with dark hair and swarthy skin, a look somewhat akin to the ancient 'black Irish' gypsies. She was after all just another hard-working housewife, struggling to raise a large family on a barely adequate income. Yet, for the few who knew her well, there was something more about Grace. Something of a subtle intangible quality; a kind heart that reflected a warm ready smile. She had seen more than her share of sorrow, but had learned from it too.

It had made her all the more determined to look for, and deeply appreciate, the joy of life, and not to be consumed by its sorrows. So, Grace chose to live her life as if it mattered, and, in her own unassuming way, to try to live it for the good of all others. One of many small examples of this was that she resolved she would try to meet and treat everyone as friend, whatever their background. That was not an easy thing to do in a country with an entrenched religious divide, and she didn't always get it right, but she persevered. Gradually, making a conscious choice to live her life as if it mattered had a subtle effect on Grace herself. In a sense it was beyond mere words, and not always obvious, but somehow recognisable at a deeper level.

For all that, Grace was very much a humble Northern Irish woman with a strong Protestant faith. Like many living in Ireland in the early 1960s, she leaned heavily on her faith. And like many, it was reinforced from an early age, depending upon which religion one was born into. Grace did her best to live up to hers daily, not just on Sundays.

There was something else about her too, a defining hope, if not quite a belief. Deep down she felt that her compassionate God would surely not put into someone's life more than was their unique ability to handle. For Grace that was significant. It meant hope, even if sometimes she might be taken to the edge of the precipice. Even if sometimes she had to draw upon the last vestiges of her strength just to cope.

As she slowly slipped once more back into sleep, Fate it seemed, had heard her internal resolution. Grace didn't know, could never have guessed, just how much the hand of Fate would continue to test her resolve, again and again.

Inside, the house settled back again into a temporary quiet. Outside, the icy wind eased a little, as if resting and readying itself for the ominous onslaught soon to follow. In a few more days the heavy snows would start in earnest. Soon after, the temperatures would continue to fall, all as had been forecast. But even the best, or worst, predictions would fall woefully short of the magnitude of what was to come that Winter. For it was no ordinary Winter storm that was slowly stirring. Nature was preparing to unleash an awesome power. A power, the like of which history would record, Ireland and its people had not seen in more than two hundred years.

Chapter 1

The Liberty Bell

There are places I remember all my life,
Though some have changed
Some forever, not for better
Some have gone and some remain
All these places have their moments ...
And I know I'll never lose affection
For people and things that went before
And I know I'll stop and often think about them
(In My Life – John Lennon & Paul McCartney)

1914 – 1920 (First World War Era)

In some ways it all began when brother and sister married brother and sister. Yes, it could be said that's where Fate really started to toy with their lives, from the time of that double wedding. Of course, some might argue it only really began in earnest with that other fateful event, some seventeen years later. Still, we are all creatures of habit, and very much more subject to those habits we unconsciously form than we might care to think. So perhaps it was indeed the double wedding, that triggered the land transactions, that in turn set the wheels in motion for those other catastrophic events which were to follow.

The two young couples were married not long after the Great War of 1914-1918. Against expectations, and heated protests, the weddings went ahead and brought together two long established staunch Northern Irish Protestant families. The families, the Maddens and the Wilsons, had hated each other with a passion for as long as anyone could remember. Their feud was said to have stemmed from a dispute over land, but no-one really knew any more, only that they disliked each other intensely. That was, until two of their offspring, a brother and sister from each family, married a brother and sister from the other family. Like elsewhere, ingrained feuds in Ireland don't usually disappear overnight. However, the double wedding obliged the families to cool off somewhat, or at least to find something else to argue about.

The young couples had all become well acquainted years ago through regular attendance at the local large Presbyterian church, naturally enough. The old stone and timber church stood tall, surrounded by large oak trees and well-manicured grounds, and the inevitable graveyard. Harlborough Presbyterian church was situated at the centre of the little fortified township of the same name, and at that time was indeed very much the centre of the local social scene.

The parents of one family owned some stock and a small farm. The parents of the other, having run aground many years past on hard times and never quite recovered, owned precious little other than the small house they occupied. Daniel Madden was the son of the family with the land. He was to inherit most of it, along with the south-facing stone farmhouse that sat boldly on top of a hill overlooking the farmland.

A long dry-stone wall ran along the country road that sprang from the main track just over half-way between Dromana and

Harlborough. Following the wall north for a couple of miles along this road, just past the green gate in the wall, ran another narrower lane branching to the right. This lane ran straight into the heart of the lush Harlborough countryside. After another mile and a half, it gently rose upwards for the last half mile, leading directly to the imposing white-washed house that stood out on the skyline like a monument.

Set out around the white house were large white-washed stones, forming a perimeter boundary for the gardens laid out at the front. To the west ran a small single-track lane leading away from the house and down through the fields surrounding it. On that west side too was a deep covered well that provided all the potable water. Behind the house were the out-house stock buildings, including a byre, barn, poultry houses, and pig-sty, all similarly white-washed, as well as a toilet for the house occupants.

The property was called The Liberty Bell and was well known around the area. In a country of small farms of less than fifty acres, The Liberty Bell was a fine farm, though admittedly among some of the smaller ones. Yet, this house and the farmland around it, would lie at the root of much of the troubles and nightmares in the years ahead.

Curiously, The Liberty Bell had originally been a country schoolhouse. It had been purchased by Daniel's parents and renovated into a house and farm around the turn of the century. On a whim, it had been named after the famous Liberty Bell in America. At that time the bell itself had reached considerable fame, having rung out a hundred years of independence for the American people, many of whom were of Irish descent.

It was understandable therefore that Daniel, and his new wife, Rose, considered themselves fortunate indeed. The Liberty Bell farm required a good deal of upkeep and careful management, but it was more than an adequate inheritance for a young couple starting out together in the North of Ireland farming community.

Beth and Riley were not so lucky. Beth had finally agreed to marry Riley Wilson shortly after her brother Daniel had announced his engagement to Riley's sister, Rose. Riley had made no secret of the fact that he was keen on Beth from the beginning. However, it was not an obvious match. Beth was astute, determined and forceful, some might even say stubborn. She was decidedly strait-laced and very much her own woman. Riley, although a likeable young man and a year older than Beth, had a tendency to be whimsical at times, and Beth did not suffer fools gladly.

In his favour, Riley was a regular church-goer and very accepting of Beth's strict views on religion. He did his best to try to endorse and support her staunch and outspoken views whenever in company. That seemed to impress Beth and it would be fair to say that it helped Riley's case with her. Also, though Beth may have been unaware of it, as a big intimidating man, Riley was not slow to discourage, or indeed frighten off, any other would-be suitors from the scene.

Whatever the reasons then, Beth was finally persuaded to accept Riley's proposal. She did so in time for it to be a double wedding with Daniel and Rose. In the end, she had no regrets about marrying Riley. She found that she liked him much more than might have been expected, and over time grew to cherish him. Riley, for his part, clearly loved Beth from the beginning and was always ready to do whatever she asked to keep her happy.

Riley had never known any wealth to speak of and therefore never missed it. Beth, though her family had never been what could be called 'well off', had at least sampled a little of home comforts in her early years. It was not much, but just enough to fuel her ambitions for more of its fruits. Just enough, but then the years of the Great War and the Easter Uprising had taken the edge off all that.

The war to end all wars had stolen her older brother from their family. There was only Daniel and Beth left now, and a father and mother who were broken-hearted and not in good health. Just as the war was coming to an end, her father had felt obliged to sell off the lower part of The Liberty Bell farm to the Jessman family, who had a larger farm close to it. Beth was very much against the sale, but despite her loud and passionate resistance, her young female voice had been ignored. She had loved that lower area of the farm where there were rich green pastures and the ford crossed over the small stream. It meant so much to her that Beth had wept to see it go. Her tears dried up soon enough, but the grudge that she continued to carry did not.

By the time of the double wedding Beth's parents no longer felt able to look after The Liberty Bell. So, when Daniel had announced his engagement, they had decided to give it to him as his early inheritance and wedding gift. The aging couple then moved into a small cottage near the farm to see out the rest of their days. They had offered to share their little cottage with Beth and Riley until they had found their own place. In addition, they had managed to arrange a brief honeymoon stay for them in a simple little bed and breakfast hotel in the nearby seaside town of Castlewellan. The gesture was gratefully accepted by Beth and she and Riley enjoyed their first days of married life together relaxing by the seaside.

It was a few days after their return from honeymoon, and in the early hours of the morning, that Beth's feelings of anxiousness had begun to surface in earnest. Returning to the little cottage with almost nothing of their own, they learnt that Riley's work had run out. Worse still, there seemed little prospect of him finding another job in the area anytime soon. Beth had come back to the reality of a marriage with them sharing her aging parent's cramped little cottage, as well as the worrying prospect of a slow descent into poverty with children at her feet. It had a profound effect on her.

She could not help but contrast her present situation with what it had been, and might have been. Her frustrations and anxiety played on her mind, as her resentment grew at losing her place on the farm. That morning her bottled up emotions crept up on her. She had long since learnt not to be soft, to push through hard times, and rarely if ever wept now. Try as she would though, the overwhelming feelings swept over her, until finally she could no longer hold back the flood of her tears.

Beth had felt much anxiety and resentment before, especially over the past few years. Things were not always the way she felt they should be in the world. Immersed as she had been for most of her young life in hopes and religious zealousness, it seemed to her that a myriad of god's punishments on the world had unfairly spilt over onto her. Beth had kept a mental list of those infringements locked up inside her. It was a long list, and, like the links in the infamous Jacob Marley's chain, would in time come to weigh heavily upon her.

For a start, during the surprise 1916 Easter Uprising, she had felt a deep seething anger at the rebels in what many of the people of her church had called 'the betrayal of Ireland'. Britain was doing its utmost to survive in the Great War when the Irish rebellion, if it could be called that then, had first erupted. Beth could not, nor did she want to, understand any of what was behind the events of that one week of violence in Dublin. For her, it was all plain enough. The predominately Catholic Irish rebel forces had simply tried to take advantage of a country in the grip of a colossal war, and to her mind, had quite rightly had come unstuck.

Beth, like many other Irish Protestants, identified strongly with Britain and supported it in the war effort. She saw the uprising in Dublin as an act of treason, and agreed with the rhetoric that it was plunging a dagger into her nation's side when it was most vulnerable. She was glad when justice was meted out. The rebellion was put down very firmly and resolutely by the British, with swift and severe punishments and a series of executions.

Yet somehow, despite the severity of the harsh reprisals, or perhaps because of them, the Easter uprising had become a catalyst for further widespread rebellion. It garnered first empathy, and then the active engagement and support of many Catholics, who up to then had been only mildly sympathetic to the so-called Irish Republican cause. The uprising, and the severity of the British response, were the political sparks that focused public attention and ignited a growing rebellion in the South of Ireland. In time it led to a complete political divide, raking through all of Ireland in just three short years, polarising more and more people, stretching right up into the North.

Beth had also felt anger and resentment within her at the onset of the Great War itself in 1914. As the war wore on, she found her feelings of anger more and more directed against the German people. As an outspoken teenager, she cared little if the German people were active perpetrators, or unwilling participants. To her, they were just as guilty for joining in, or working in factories and tacitly supporting it, or simply standing by and allowing it to continue. It was a view held by many of her teenage friends at the time, but for Beth it had quickly hardened and consolidated when the war took the life of one of her brothers and several other young men from her town.

That Great War had left 20 million dead and a similar number of soldiers and civilians wounded or maimed, mentally as well as physically. To Beth it was just another sorry indictment that all was not well with the peoples of the world.

Yet, even all of that must not have been retribution enough

on mankind, or so it seemed to Beth's hurt and deeply ingrained religious mind. The atrocious war conditions, and the vast movement of people at the end of it, ensured a colossal spread of the lethal Spanish Flu. Like the Black plague centuries before that, which had killed over 100 million people, and the other plagues in the interim, Beth felt sure that her God had sent this latest great dark plague upon mankind as punishment for the Great War they had just waged. No doubt Beth felt justified in her views, for the Spanish Flu more often cut down many young soldiers in their prime, taking the lives of 50 million people, more than double the number killed in the Great War.

Finally, there was that one other very significant hurt that Beth carried within her. A hurt that burned her more than she would ever acknowledge.

In Beth's eyes, while it was her brother, Daniel, who had inherited the farm, it was her sister-in-law, Rose, who through her marriage, usurped Beth's place upon it. The Liberty Bell was now Rose's gifted start to married life, when it was Beth who loved it and had spent her young life growing up there. As a young woman in those times, all Beth was expected to do was to cast her lot in with whoever chose to marry her, and then raise their children.

Beth did not hate Daniel and Rose for what had happened. No, it was more the injustice she saw in all of it. She had felt the bile taste of wrath arise because, with one act of marriage and the resultant transfer of land, she Beth, had to forfeit everything, while an outsider, Rose, could gain it all on the instant.

It had all left an indelible mark upon Beth, shaping and hardening her for the future that awaited her. She had learned to form more of those habits of hardness, slow to forgive, quick to take offense – even when none was given, firmly holding and nurturing a grudge in mind. All the while, thinking they were not unreasonable habits of self-protection in a world where she felt women had no rights.

Beth kept it all at bay, mind closed, refusing to acknowledge the extent of influence the stored-up accumulation of hurts had upon her. Yet there it all lingered nevertheless, a rampant hungry wolf within her. It gnawed at her, and from time to time as Beth dwelt upon all her perceived grievances, she fed the hungry wolf.

Even then, a small voice of reason in Beth's head had whispered to her to let it all go. It echoed the ancient wisdom of the slave Epictetus, that there was little point in worrying or harbouring bitterness about things over which she had no control. Beth chose to ignore it.

So Beth harboured hurt and anger, storing it within her, fermenting it quietly, ready to explode some other day. Though she knew it not, the day would come when all her bottled anger and resentment would explode. When it did explode, it would come crashing down upon all of them, like a bomb, causing unimaginable havoc and harm.

Yet, she almost escaped that particular destiny. To her credit, Beth realised early on that she and Riley could not endure staying in her parents' small cottage home for any length of time. There was nothing here for them, and certainly nothing could be expected by way of support from Riley's family. No, they were on their own now, and they would have to make the most of it. They needed to move, to move on, and soon. Riley, she knew, would follow her to the ends of the earth if she asked him.

She remembered hearing from friends that there was a call for Irish workers at high wages over the water in Newcastle-on-Tyne. It would mean taking a ship to England, and being out of Ireland, but they could still earn good money there. "Yes," she thought, "we can raise a family and make a new beginning of it over there. Who knows, maybe we can even learn to forget The Liberty Bell and leave all this behind us when we are gone once and for all."

Beth's idea quickly began to take shape as she planned for a fresh start. To her surprise, the prospect lifted her spirits and she began to feel happier and more relaxed than she had done in a long time. She determined that they could sort things out quickly and make arrangements to go in just a few weeks. It gave her purpose and a new hope, an escape from a troubled destiny in Ireland.

The next morning, she spoke to Riley about it. Enthusiastic young man that he was, he jumped at the idea of the adventure like an excited child. Yes, of course they would go to Newcastle! Yes, of course it would all work out for them! Yes, finally he and Beth would get to leave the shores of Ireland and seek their fortune in a foreign land. They could do this together! It would be a great adventure! A grand adventure! Even if that foreign land did have to be over the seas in heathen England!

Three weeks later they were on a boat to Newcastle-on-Tyne. They were fortunate to find work easily enough. Riley picked up a job in a heavy engineering and construction firm down near the shipyards within the first days. Not long after, Beth was able to get an office cleaning job there too. It was hard work and long hours for both of them, but the money was good and they were even able to start making some savings. Though Beth still thought of it affectionately sometimes, soon enough Ireland, and The Liberty Bell, were no longer uppermost in their minds as they set about building a new life in the new country. For the moment at least, Fate seemed to be smiling on them.

Their tiny bed-sit accommodation sufficed for much of that first year. Then Beth realised she was pregnant. When they started to look around, they found they could afford something a little bigger in preparation for the coming baby.

In the late Spring of 1920, in one of Newcastle-on Tyne's fine modern hospitals, Beth gave birth to a dark-haired, swarthy-skinned, beautiful baby girl. It was a straightforward birth. The baby was healthy and blissfully happy and brought joy into their world. They named her Grace.

Nature's Magic

Chapter 2

The Sheltered Lake

Your enjoyment of the world is never right
till every morning you awake in heaven ...
and look upon the skies, the earth and the air as celestial joys,
having such a reverend esteem of all.
(Centuries of Meditations – Thomas Traherne)

Sunday 23rd December 1962

The boy saw it first, catching his breath at the rare sight.

As boy, man, and dog trudged their way together across the frosty snow-covered expanse of rolling Irish open countryside, he spotted it. Quite a long way below them and to the left. It was moving slowly along the top of the ditch line that curved around the edge of the little glen. Even in the cold half-light of early dawn, its natural colours stood out boldly, camouflage hampered by the near whiteout.

The big male fox was a magnificent sight. A simple, yet minor miracle of nature's design. Its face, muzzle and ears were dark, with amber eyes bright and watchful. The fox's dark red bushy tail, white tipped, was held confidently high, gently swaying as it walked. A rich fur of fiery red covered his neck, back and flanks. Much less common, a dark silver line, almost black, ran the length of his back, to meet another similar line crossing over his shoulders. The cross extended on down to darkened legs and undersides. The unusual colouring was the result of a silver fox joining the red fox ancestral gene pool somewhere back in his lineage. With the distinctive cross marking, such a fox was indeed a rare sight. This one, wild and majestic, at ease in his natural realm, sniffed the snowy ground as he moved, ears set and eyes ever watchful.

Letting his breath out slowly, the boy nudged his father's elbow and whispered, "Dah, look!"

It was enough. The man, acutely attuned to the natural landscape around him, noticed the slight movement of the fox on the instant. The dog, at his heel, picked up his master's reaction, and was similarly alerted. The trio stood still and watched.

The man whispered, "That fellow is up early. Probably out hunting for a meal for him and his family."

"Like us," the boy whispered back.

They remained still, simply watching, enjoying the moment.

Suddenly the fox stopped, turning its head up in their direction and sniffing the air. The boy gasped and tensed, fearing they would be seen. His slightest movement too was enough. With senses and instincts honed through centuries, as both hunter and hunted, the fox perceived rather than saw or heard the danger. Its lithe body whirled and swiftly blurred into action. Leaving nothing to chance, it raced away. In another instant it was gone.

The boy had watched the fox quickly disappear along the ditch line and into the glen. Without realising why, he felt saddened.

"Hope those damn red-coat pansies and their pansy fox hounds don't catch him." he muttered.

The man overheard him and smiled. "No, they won't," he said, consolingly. "Some other one perhaps, but they won't catch that one. Not today, nor any day. He's far too quick and cunning for the likes of them to get anywhere near him."

Inwardly, the man hoped he was right. It was one thing to hunt game to feed a hungry growing family. It was quite another to make a silly game of the hunt. He had always been careful to take only what was needed, not killing just for the sake of it. To do otherwise made no sense to him. Especially the hunting game played by some of the local gentry. "Grown men," he thought, "and nowadays even a few women, all dressed up in their finery and galloping their horses and howling hounds over hill and dale." They churned up the countryside, upsetting many of the country folk wherever they went.

Aloud he muttered, "And what's it all for anyway? A colourful show maybe, a spectacle to make a point of some sort? Surely not all that to catch a poor damn fox."

The Winter wind was cold and the man and boy had a way to go to reach their destination. The man started onwards again and boy and dog followed. They had no time to waste.

The man had been thinking about Grace and her recurring nightmares. They always seemed to plague her more often around Christmas and her birthday. There was a reason for that of course, which he knew now. He sighed and looked up at the skies. Intuition, merged with long experience, told him that the radio weather forecasts of a big storm coming soon might well be right, and perhaps not too far off.

The thought of the storm led him to another thought, this one closer to home. He sensed that other storm was slowly building too, only this one had nothing to do with the weather. This one was between him and Grace. Far out there on the horizon, simmering, waiting for him, but it was there, that was for sure. He grimaced inwardly. Two big storms on the way. He knew which one he feared most.

At a glance, the man's attire that morning was deceptively simple. Thick socks, sturdy wellington boots, heavy trousers, course shirt and layered woollen jumper, short waterproof jacket, and traditional flat cap were usually enough to keep the cold at bay, but not this morning. This morning they needed to keep on the move to stay warm.

The unhinged, well-polished shotgun lay open in the crook of the man's arm, ready to be snapped shut for use at a second's notice. The old leather and canvas hunting bag hung over his shoulder and rested at his waist. Its familiar game smell wafted to the boy's nostrils as he walked just behind, his head bobbing along at the same height as the bag.

The boy, copying his father, was dressed in similar style. He however, carried a short stick instead of a gun, and his small bag contained the egg and cheese-filled sandwiches that Grace had made for them. She had insisted they take plenty. The boy was already hungry and cold but much too excited to even think about stopping to eat. He knew where they were going. This was not any of their usual hunting locations. This was special, this was a treat.

They walked on through the frosty fields, gradually descending towards the bog in the valley below. The bog ran along the lower end of a particularly large field. Unlike some of the larger peat bogs much further south that provided fuel for much of the Irish countryside, there was no usable peat in this bog. The locals called it a bog, but it was little more than a big marshy swamp. For the most part it was covered in isolated shrubs and plants, heavy mosses and a variety of tough tussocks and clumps of tall grasses. A few large bull rushes eked out an existence along its outer edges. Just past them, ice-covered stagnant water saturated the grasses and gathered in isolated patches. In some places it was ankle-deep, muddy, murky, and hard to avoid, even when using the clumps of tall grass as stepping stones.

Further into the bog, the tough sprawling grasses grew denser and more difficult to pass through. Still further in and towards the centre on a slight grassy rise, there was a copse of trees. From a distance they looked dark and foreboding, seemingly rising out of the middle of the bog. The narrow paths across the bog to the copse had long since been abandoned. As seasons passed, they were increasingly hard to find. A small stream curved and twisted its way through the bog but offered little by way of direction.

The almost impenetrable boggy terrain was usually enough to keep most people out. Not surprisingly, only a few even attempted to cross it. Fewer still actually managed it, or knew what lay within the shelter of the little copse. The man was one of those very few who did know.

He had been to this particular oasis many times. As instructed, the boy and dog followed close behind in the man's footsteps, while he, trusting his instincts, carefully led their way through. It was not easy, but they persisted, pushing onwards, assured in the knowledge it could be done. Finally, the ground started to become a little firmer again as they reached the edge of the little wooden copse in the centre. In just a few more minutes they were clambering up and over the gentle grassy slope and down the other side as it descended slightly and merged into the undergrowth beneath the trees.

Walking slowly inwards towards the centre of the copse, they found it. A small lake of dark, rich water, long nourished by the little stream that flowed through it. With ice around its edges, nestled amidst the surrounding trees, it was another hidden gem of nature, tucked away from the hustle of the outside world.

Keeping just clear of the icy edges of the lake the trio found a small clearing amidst the overhanging bush. Man, boy and dog, quickly and quietly settled down to rest and eat. The boy knew what was expected of him. He sat still and silent, waiting patiently, feeling a little cramped and cold, not quite knowing how long they would need to wait. After the initial flurry of flight and bird alarm calls, as they had entered the clearing, there was now a watchful and eerie silence. Time passed slowly for the boy at first, but gradually the little glade started to come alive again with sounds and movements, as the inhabitants of bush and lake began to accept the strange visitors hidden among them.

The cold was unrelenting and the boy was tired from the trek and the pre-dawn start. He was beginning to regret not putting on the extra jumper and woollen socks when the first faint calls of their awaited visitors reached him. Duke, the big old black Labrador, had already perked his ears up, but was not about to give up his well-earned resting place quite yet. The Duke, as he was more often called, had been a constant companion on many hunting-trip adventures over the years, but of late his old bones welcomed more rest.

The distant sounds echoed the strange mixture of joy and sorrow that nature had somehow distilled into the haunting call of the wild goose. The noise increased in urgency and intensity as they came nearer. Soon the air around the trio was filled with the energetic calling and honking of geese. It was a skein of small pale-bellied Brent Geese arriving in numbers, to feed on and around the lake. Then suddenly, the whole lake was a cacophony of sound and movement, as a host of the resident moorhens, ducks, coots and even a few greylag geese hastily scattered out of the way of the rapidly descending masses. Duke sat up, by now very much awake and fully alert.

The boy watched in awe as the Brent Geese came flying down to the lake, only a short distance from the cover of his ringside seat. Closer and closer, lower and lower they came, their wings open, their dark feet splayed out like water skis ready to touch down, urged on by the loud calls of those queuing up behind them. For the boy, it was an incredible acrobatic aerial display. Each Brent Goose in turn would land, slide and spray up the water, before coming to a graceful stop. The trio watched the air show in silence, until at last the regroupings of the birds on the water were complete and finally the lake settled to a quiet stillness once more.

For a few moments the trio continued to sit in silence, absorbed in the sanctity of the lake and the simple solitude of their surroundings. Here was a connection with nature that could not be taught. It could only be experienced in the magical moment. The silence continued.

"Do we need to take any of these, dah?" whispered the boy.

The man noted the tone. He glanced at the boy, then out again at the peaceful scene on the lake. The small black and white Brent Geese would likely have come with many others all the way from Canada or Iceland earlier in the Winter. Most of the breed had already spread out into many other coastal parts of Ireland. The little lake and surrounding grasslands would be a temporary shelter for this small group that had ventured a bit more inland. It would be several months yet before they would begin to gather together in large numbers to make the long arduous journey back towards Iceland and Canada. The larger greylag would be here a while yet too. He looked back at the boy. There was time.

"No, not today," he said. "Today we'll just sit here a few minutes more, then we'll be on our way again."

On the way back from the bog, they detoured around the little glen, but this time the silver cross-fox was nowhere to be seen. At the edge of the glen the boy watched as the man passed up the opportunity to shoot a large buck rabbit sitting tight on the ground. It would have been an easy stationery target, in full sight and easy range of the shotgun. As was his way, the man chose to wait a moment longer until the dog had flushed it out. Then, as the well-trained dog dropped and waited, he took the harder shot as the rabbit raced away at full pace. Close to the limit of the range, a single shot rang out. It was all that was needed. With the slightest of gestures from the man, Duke retrieved the buck.

A mile further, along the edge of the woodland, they came across another rabbit, and shortly after that, a plump wood pigeon obliged by flying low overhead. All were gathered into the shoulder bag. Man, boy, and dog had done their work that morning.

"That's enough for now," the man said. "We can all manage to get through Christmas on these. It's been a long morning. Let's get home and see what Grace can do with this lot." The boy nodded eagerly in agreement, already anticipating the prospect of his mother's delicious pigeon soup.

Chapter 3

The Great Freeze

*Man finds happiness only in serving his neighbour.
And he finds it here because in rendering service to his neighbour,
he is in communication with the divine spirit that lives within them.
(Leo Tolstoy)*

Christmas 1962 - March 1963

Grace's rich pigeon soup was legendary. That is to say, it was legendary with her family and many of her neighbours in the Heights, with whom she sometimes shared it. None of these it seemed, praised her soup more than Bill, the popular confirmed bachelor and owner of 'Bill's Little Shop', across the road from where Grace now lived.

Initially, it was something of a mystery how Bill, quite an ordinary man in many other respects, had an uncanny ability to know just when the soup was being made. Of course, Bill would only say that he had a nose for good soup. He simply smelt it whenever it was cooking. That might well be so, but nevertheless it was still a bit odd, for Bill would need outstanding olfactory receptors.

For a start, there was the distance involved. Somehow the faint aroma of pigeon soup would have to waft through the open windows of Grace's house, cross right over the road, drift through the open front door of the little shop, find its way over to the counter where Bill would be serving customers, and there to be divined by his keenly perceptive nostrils. Uncanny no doubt, miraculous even. Yet who could argue with him? As soon as he smelt the soup, Bill would boldly announce it on the instant to his customers.

"Can you smell that? Grace is making pigeon soup again, so she is! Oh my, that smell, that is so delicious!" Eventually there was no doubting the plain fact. When it came to detecting Grace's pigeon soup, Bill's prominent protuberance was never wrong!

Naturally, Bill's acute sense of smell only heightened his desire for the soup. He did his best to be subtle, but his efforts fooled no one. Just the same, his frequent compliments on the wonderful aroma of Grace's pigeon soup, and his far from subtle comments on how delicious it must be, were enough to have the desired effect. In short time it became customary for one of Grace's children to take a bowl of her pigeon soup over to Bill's shop on every occasion it was made.

Bill was an ever appreciative and generous soul and reciprocated in kind. The child soup-bearer would often return beaming, carrying a huge bag of treats from one of the large glass jars on display in his shop, or some freshly baked baps. All were gifts from Bill's shop to share with the rest of the family. It was a fair trade, with each enjoying the underlying trait of human kindness it conveyed. More than that though, it was one of many examples of how things were often done in the Heights. Despite occasional differences, and irrespective of religious beliefs, the people of the Heights seemed to make a conscious effort to be good neighbours.

'The Heights' was the shortened name adopted by all who lived there. It was a little estate of forty-seven properties, basic and simply constructed white pebble dashed council houses, perched on one of several hills surrounding the small marketing country town of Dromana, in the north of Ireland. The town had a long and colourful history, having been largely destroyed during the Irish rebellion of 1641. Dromana still had the rare distinction of having ancient stocks in the market square. Having long outlived their original purpose of temporary imprisonment, the stocks now served as a notable monument, and a popular attraction for inventive teenagers' stunts.

Near the town centre was preserved the derelict remains of an old Norman castle. A once fierce fortress from a bygone time. Further up on a hill on the outskirts of the town, stood a large motte and bailey, now the ideal picnic spot for the fit and adventurous. Through the ages Ireland had a long history of many invaders, including the Vikings, Spanish, Normans, and even the Scottish when Robert the Bruce sent his brother Edward to the Emerald Isle. Yet it was the centuries old Norman relics that so often prevailed as visible landmarks scattered across the country. The dark stone remains of one of these still stood proudly in Dromana.

Ireland had long been a nation of country dwellers and small farming communities. It was only in recent times, partly prompted by the two world wars and evolving industries, that more and more people became town dwellers. Grace had become one of those. The council estate where she lived was roughly oblong in shape. It had been built some seven years previously, sited on one side of a narrow road that stretched up from Dromana and on into the surrounding lush countryside. The newly built houses in the Heights had been quickly occupied as soon as they became available.

Like Grace, many of the people of the Heights had long been on council housing waiting lists, living in near poverty in rough, run-down, cold stone houses scattered in and around the area. Most of these old country houses did not have running water, gas or electricity, or indoor toilets. So, for Grace and many of the others with large young families, the move to live in the Heights, with their indoor facilities and amenities, was a seen as a godsend. Consequently, their new homes, though simple, were much appreciated and generally well cared for by their grateful occupants. It was this focus on what they had, rather than what they lacked, that helped everyone get along well together.

The houses were a blend of two-bedroomed bungalows and three-bedroomed two-story terraced houses, with a handful of small flats. Most of these backed onto each other and had small front and rear gardens. The rear gardens were used extensively to grow vegetables to help feed young hungry mouths. Around the back of the estate there was a car park. As very few families could afford cars, it doubled perfectly as a playground and place for many enthusiastic youngsters to enjoy a game of football. With the close proximity of the homes, scant fencing between them, and the numerous children playing together, neighbours were given frequent opportunity to meet and greet each other. This they did, and often!

When Grace had first moved into the Heights, much to her amusement and that of a few of her neighbours, her man immediately went about covering all the windows with bedsheets, even in broad daylight. In the beginning she had asked why he felt the need to do that.

The man had sighed, then spoke. "Look Grace, the neighbours are fine enough, but sure they are all right on top of us and can see straight in here plain as day through those big windows. Sure, they already know all of our business and every hole in my underpants just by looking at our clothesline. If we don't cover these windows, I won't even be able to have a cup of tea or go to the toilet without everybody out there knowing all about that too."

Grace had smiled and nodded. She knew he was not accustomed

to having any neighbours living so close and, with windows larger than they were used to, she could see why he felt they were constantly being observed. She guessed it was also partly due to his blackout experiences in the war, so for a while she indulged his whims. The bedsheets stayed up all day and every day, until she found time to make curtains to replace them. Over time, she was gradually able to open the curtains a little more each day, until the man had grown accustomed to his new surroundings.

The people of the Heights found they had much in common. From the outset they quickly grew into a close and supportive community. They welcomed new families into the fold and shared in each other's cares and celebrations. It seemed this sense of unity surfaced naturally when their interdependence was acknowledged and accepted, and efforts made to set differences aside. Certainly, everyone seemed to know everyone else in the Heights. Not only that, but for the most part they took more than a passing interest in each other's welfare. Bill's little shop was a good deal more than just a convenient source of supply for all sorts of handy provisions. It was an essential communication centre, the trading post and casual meeting place for frequent catch-ups on the comings and goings of the folk on the Heights.

That's not to imply that the tensions and divisions between Irish Catholics and Protestants were not still simmering beneath the surface, as they had done everywhere for centuries past. The roots of that protracted division were still strong, long, and deep. By the end of that decade, they would of course erupt like a volcano into the terrible 'Troubles' that were to divide and destabilise Ireland, especially in the North.

Those 'Troubles' were coming alright, but not for a few years yet. For now, Ireland and the people of the Heights were busy trying to cope with the astounding power manifested in that harsh Winter of

1962/63, aptly named the 'Great Freeze'.

It had begun to show a little of itself in the days before Christmas. The man, boy and dog had felt the early tugs of its tentacles when they had been out hunting. Nature, with all its latent powers, had slowly begun to stir and stretch. In doing so it had flung out a wide covering of frost and a flurry of fine powdery snow. This snow and frost had combined to make a very cold white Christmas. For a short while some welcomed the white Christmas and the fairy tale look that it brought to Ireland. But that welcome was short-lived, for in reality it was but an ominous portent of things just ahead. Nature, all too frequently taken for granted, was readying herself for an immensely powerful show of strength to shock and awaken the unwary.

Just after Christmas of 1962, Nature's icy-cold Scandinavian winds were unleashed. Called the 'lazy winds' by some, because it felt like the winds tore clean through the being, rather than go around them, these winds raged across the Irish countryside. They swept aside trees and even some buildings in their path and created havoc and turmoil everywhere. Harsh, cold, and relentless, they spared no-one, young or old.

In the last days leading up to the New Year, Nature belched out great blizzards of freezing cold snow. Carried on her ice winds, they came with a frenetic fury. Billowing white curtains draping down from the skies, swiftly smothering everything that stood in their way. They heralded a very different promise for the New Year of 1963.

For two full days and nights the blizzards roared and roared. The 'Great Freeze' swiftly spanned the width of the countryside, changing not only the landscape but the very pace and face of normal life. In the north of Ireland, as elsewhere, the smaller towns were the most vulnerable. They ground almost to a halt under the weight of waist-deep snow. Traffic stopped, and cars were abandoned and quickly buried under its relentlessness. Roads and paths were left all but empty. Rural roads disappeared under a sea of white.

The fierce winds pushed the snow drifts higher and deeper still. Hedge rows and low buildings became barely visible landmarks, taking on odd, peculiar shapes as the white tide spread ever onwards. Telegraph poles became white totems with sagging strands, eerie out of season Maypoles rendered silent by the snow. All around it seemed that strange white monuments were arising in homage and testament to a display of majestic power that Ireland had not witnessed in centuries.

The Great Freeze was everywhere, foreboding and enduring, an all-powerful Midas with a deathly frost-white touch. The mightiest of rivers and lakes succumbed to it. Defying history, the river Shannon froze for the first time in living memory. Across the Irish sea in England the great river Thames fell to the same fate. A few brave, or foolish, adventurers ignominiously took to riding bicycles and driving small cars and other vehicles over it.

Nestled in the centre of five of the six counties forming Northern Ireland, lay Lough Neagh, the largest fresh water lake in the British Isles. As if in further homage to the power of Nature, the giant lough froze solid and turned into a strange and unlikely skating rink for many unbelieving revellers. Even the very seas froze. In great grey-white monoliths, like a vast barricade around the sieged frozen lands captured within, sea ice stretched for miles out from shores. The coldest January in recorded history was biting deeply into the very psyche of Ireland.

During this coldest of Winters, there were a great many joys and sorrows. Many, especially the frail, succumbed to the prolonged icy cold, while others seemed to welcome, even relish, the challenges posed by it. Grace's neighbours, in the face of this common adversity, tended to help one another get through it all with numerous small acts of kindness. It was just their way, a natural trait, somehow brought more to the surface by the fierce storm.

Two things were notable for Grace and her family that icy Winter. One, was the sad passing of old Duke. The other was the flying expulsion of a gob-stopper that brought some unwanted fame to Grace's youngest son, Ted.

Young Ted was a precocious nine year-year old, but even so, that's still quite an early age to be drawing attention to oneself. However, as Grace would later nod and smile if asked, at the time there was not one jot of ego involved in Ted's attention seeking.

A group of children had been playing on the compacted snow and ice along 'the Steps'. The Steps, as they were known, were in fact a group of about a dozen broad low steps rising gently, before continuing up as a sloping paved walkway. They stretched from the lower end of the Heights to the upper end, forming an easy access to and from the front to the back of the Heights. With a field to the bottom left of the Steps, and an unfenced grassed garden area at the bottom right, and a single lamp-post, the Steps were a popular gathering place for children to play in the day-time. They were also a quiet and convenient place for would be romantic teenagers to converge under starry skies in the evenings.

The combination of angled slope, and the deep compacted snow and ice that now covered and smoothed both pathway and steps, made it a perfect area for long fast slides for many children and young adults alike. Some of the young men had promised to clear away the snow and ice from the Steps. Somehow though, for reasons that might well be guessed, those same young men never seemed to be in any hurry to get on with it. In any case, it was on that particular day, young Ted had been one of the children playing on those icy slides at the Steps.

After an hour or so, having worn himself out, Ted ambled off around the corner to his home, in search of food and the next form of entertainment. His mother, Grace, was enjoying a cup of tea with her next-door neighbour and good friend, Kathy, sharing stories about the difficulties of finding good honest and reliable husbands for the girls in their families.

Ted came in the back door, made himself a jam sandwich, then sat down in their midst idly seeking to listen in on their conversation. Kathy, who always seemed to have a lot to say about a lot of things, gave him a glance, then carried on full steam regardless. Grace however, was not at all keen on Ted listening in on this particular conversation. She suggested to Ted that he might like to play outside for another twenty minutes until she finished her chat with Kathy.

Even at that young age Ted was not slow to recognise an opportunity when it was right in front of his face. He put on his best practiced smile and promptly asked, "Alright, I'll get out of your way mah, but maybe I could have some money for sweets, eh?"

Against her better judgement, Grace relented and sent him on his way to Bill's shop, with strict instructions to buy some fruit with the single coin she gave him. Ted had other ideas. He had been Bill's first ever customer in the little shop when it opened a few years previously. Not one to miss a trick, back then the youngster had emerged with a free bag of sweets, courtesy of his new friend Bill. Now as he ran across the road, coin firmly in hand, Ted had no doubt whatsoever that he could handle a little bit of negotiating with Bill to get another bag of his favourite sweets.

Kathy and Grace settled down to resume their chin wag. Ten minutes later Grace heard the urgent banging on her front door. Leaving Kathy alone in the kitchen, she raced to open it, already sensing something was very wrong. Two of the older children of the Heights had come to fetch her. The eldest, Thelma, blurted out. "Oh missus, please come quick! Your wee Ted is sitting in the middle of the road and he looks like he's gonna die!"

The girls moved aside and gestured wildly towards Ted, who sure enough was sitting folded over double in the middle of the road in front of the house, holding his throat and struggling for breath. A few other children, having seen what was happening, were already crowding around him, yelling a barrage of incoherent instructions. Grace ran out immediately and took hold of Ted by the shoulder, bringing him upright. In an instant she saw that his face was drained and she thought he might faint at any moment.

A frantic Grace yelled out, "What's happened to him!? How did he get like this!?" A jumbled mass of frightened voices, told her that Ted was choking on a sweet. Not knowing quite what to do, Grace tried to slap Ted's back several times to try to free the sweet from his throat. It didn't work, and worse, the boy's face was now turning blue.

Bill and his customers had heard the loud raucous and came out to see what was happening. Grace was getting desperate but felt helpless. Something had to be done and fast before Ted choked, but nothing she tried seemed to be working.

She was about to slap Ted's back again, when Kathy, who had just joined the growing crowd, saw immediately what was happening and pushed through to intercede. "Give him to me and get back all of you! Give me some space here, now!" she shouted. Without waiting another second, Kathy quickly stepped in front of Grace and grabbed Ted from behind. Wrapping her arms firmly around him, with a mighty heave she hoisted him high into the air. With Ted held fast, and her fists clenched tightly into his midriff, Kathy half released him, then using his falling as momentum, gave a swift almighty squeeze into his abdomen.

Several things happened at once. The sudden exhalation from Ted's lungs sent the lodged sweet hurtling from his windpipe like a bullet from a gun. The half-consumed gob-stopper projectile flew out a full ten feet at high speed. It was only stopped when it whacked into the face of one of the young women who had gathered around to see what the commotion was about. Startled, she screamed, and the terrified child in her arms immediately launched into a fit of crying. Another small boy saw his chance. Ducking between adult legs, he promptly retrieved the evidence from the ground and, giving it a rudimentary wipe and casting a furtive glance around him, at once stuck it into his own mouth.

Kathy meanwhile put the now furiously wriggling Ted back down as he cried and gasped in air, colour slowly starting to return to his face. Grace took him in her arms and was so relieved she didn't know whether to scold him, or to cry herself.

In the end Grace did neither, but ensuring Ted was alright, she then threw her arms around Kathy and thanked her, as the watching audience, clearly relieved, spontaneously applauded. Ted was taken back home and confined there for the rest of the day with strict instructions not to eat any more sweets. Meanwhile, Kathy remained outside Bill's shop, making a few token gestures to shrug off the compliments from the admiring bystanders, and all the while savouring every moment of it.

Grace was grateful that her good friend and neighbour had been on hand when needed, and that her youngest son was safe and well. Things could certainly have turned out very differently, but Grace had learned enough to count her blessings when they came her way. It was just a little thing, but she noticed too that young Ted kept well away from Kathy, and gob-stoppers, for a quite a while after that.

Eventually, well into March 1963, the great thaw gradually

pushed aside the last remnants of the Great Freeze. Improvised hot water bottles, endless blankets and coats on beds, candles, primus stoves, woollen mittens and cardboard lined shoes and boots, even a few old Tilly lamps, could finally be put away as nature allowed the gentler temperatures to return. Nevertheless, the Great Freeze had left its mark and taken its toll. Hundreds of people had died and thousands of animals had perished under its spell. Sadly, one of these had been the old dog, Duke.

The man's younger brother, Clive, lived about twenty miles away on the outskirts of Belfast. Clive was well aware of the Duke's reputation as an excellent gun-dog. Having seen him in action on a number of occasions with his brother, and witnessed first-hand the almost uncanny understanding that they had between them, he admired the dog all the more. He had asked to borrow the Duke many times but the man had always refused. On this particular day, and following much promising on Clive's part to take very good care of the old dog and not work him too hard, the man had finally relented.

Clive had borrowed the Duke to go on a day's hunting over farmlands near the foot of the Mourne mountains with a couple of friends. The big old dog had served him well that day, and Clive and his friends were suitably impressed. Even so, Clive noted that the Duke was quite a lot slower now with age, and did not cope so well with the cold. They had stopped for food and a drink on the way back, and stayed longer than planned. As it was getting late, instead of taking him home as promised, Clive had taken the Duke on home to Belfast with him. After feeding the dog, he had put him out in a shed for the night, intending to return him to Grace and his brother early the next morning. That however, was not how things worked out.

The old Duke did not understand that he was to be taken back the next day. He only knew he was being kept away from his home and family, and he sensed he needed to get back there, especially now.

Before the dawn of the next morning, the Duke had jumped onto the workbench and then half crashed his way through the open window to the outside world and freedom. With some minor cuts and bruises he had loped slowly away to begin his long journey home. The dog was unfamiliar with towns and cities. Nor did he know how to negotiate the back roads of Belfast or any of the other country towns that lay ahead of him on his journey. He only had the ancient instincts of his kind to guide him, and the pull of home and his family.

It was several days later, in the evening, that they found him. He was huddled against the side of a thick grassy ditch, looking cold, thin and exhausted, barely alive. Some children had discovered him as they were walking in the country lane, just a little way from the Heights. They recognised the Duke instantly and ran off to tell Grace. The man had come at once and seeing the poor state the dog was in, picked him up and carried him home in his arms.

Grace wrapped him up in an old blanket and the Duke spent that night and most of the next day huddled up in his favourite spot by the warm fire, hardly moving away from it. He was stiff and sore and the cold seemed to be set into his very bones. Even so, his tail wagged frequently in happy response to all the fuss and attention he was getting from his family. He was clearly very happy to be back home.

They found the Duke in the same place early next morning. He looked content, but the essence of life had left his body. Duke was like a part of Grace's family and as they crowded around him they all felt the loss. Some of the children cried, and even the man seemed shaken at the loss of his old best friend. Young Ted, overcome with emotion as he hugged the body of the lifeless dog, whispered. "Poor old Duke, ach sure I'd rather have died m'self."

His father smiled and gently laid his hand on Ted's shoulder. Then, as much to himself as to the children, he said. "The Duke has had a long and happy life, but all that is born dies." Sensing the need, he added consolingly, "Some dogs know when it is near their time. The Duke must have known too and wanted to make his way back here, to die in peace, at home with his family. He was able to do that, and die happy. What more could he ask for?"

Chapter 4

The Claim

*Our homes are such unwieldy property
that we are often imprisoned,
rather than housed by them.
(Henry David Thoreau.)*

May 1963

The nightmare assailed her, the half memories haunting Grace, once again tormenting her unguarded mind as she slept.

The young girl was trapped and terrified. The angry hammering and banging on the door grew louder and louder. A dark gloved hand tried to reach through the narrow slot and around the lock. The commanding voice demanded the door be opened. Terror had seized her, ripping at her heart. The hopelessness fell on her like a suffocating heavy weight, bearing down on her young body, edging her ever closer to submission. The temporary refuge of the small outside toilet no longer offered the protection she so desperately needed. Instead of being her shelter it was now her prison. Trapped, confined, the terrifying nightmare was unshakeable.

"Come out! Come out here to me now!" the demonic voice bellowed.

The young girl screamed in the dream, "No, I can't, I won't". Then pleading, "No! please, please no!"

Impossibly the dark hand was reaching through the door, stretching, straining to reach her. Black, crow-like eyes glowered in at her through the small gap. She recoiled instantly, pressing herself hard against the back wall of the toilet, trying to melt into it. It wasn't enough. The angry booming voice now ringing in her ears, threatening. The grasping hand inching forward, almost upon her, relentless. Her heart was pounding, her terror unbearable, but her escape impossible.

The young voice screamed out even louder for help, as her mind rebelled against the crushing nightmare. In fear and desperation, again the scream of the dream reached ever upwards, penetrating, crossing over into the realm of wakefulness, again tearing asunder the silence of the night.

"Oh mammy, oh mammy, mammy, please! Please no, please don't!"

Once more Grace's screaming voice woke the man beside her. Once more she herself was awakened, abruptly quietened, reassured, rescued. Sweating, trembling, breathing heavily but finally subdued, she regathered and calmed herself.

The little drama of the morning began to unfold itself much as before, as the children again readily played their parts. Grace did her best to shake off the residue of the nightmare and be light and easy with the children as they went through the little ritual.

The young children knew nothing of their mother's pain. They knew nothing of what lay behind her nightmares. They knew only that by the morning she was herself again. That she would be there to help them through their own bad dreams if they needed it. That she was there and would provide for them, and care for them. It was enough for now.

What they did not know, and could not then have understood, was the reason for their mother's nightmares. That as much as she dragged herself free of them and clung to hope in starting each new day, at times Grace herself wondered if they would ever end. Wondered in despair if her past life would forever haunt her.

1924-1934 (Some 30 Years Earlier)

Grace was only four when the first big change came into her young life. Even in those early years it might be said that much of her life's path was already being forged by the choices and action of others, especially her parents. Fate, or karma, may well have had a strong hand to play in Beth and Riley's life and in Grace's too. It was as if it was somehow locked into their DNA, despite their new life and environment in Newcastle-on-Tyne. Yet, perhaps that is not the whole of it. For surely their destinies were just as much shaped by the choices they made back then, and repeatedly in the years that would follow, whether made consciously or otherwise.

At four, Grace had little concept of the future, but the letter that came to her parent's house in Newcastle-on-Tyne that day was about to change everything. Beth opened the letter from her brother Daniel in the kitchen and started to read it as they were having tea. For a moment she was quiet as she began to take in the contents of the letter. Then, standing up so quickly that she knocked over her cup, Beth gasped out at Riley. "I can't believe it! Daniel and Rose are selling The Liberty Bell and moving to Ontario, Canada! They're asking us if we might be interested in buying it!" She sat down again to reread the letter aloud to Riley, slowly digesting what she had just read.

For Beth and Riley, the news was stunning, right out of the blue. Yet, when they thought more about it, they could see that they should not have been quite so shocked. Daniel had spoken often of that vast far away country and the early development opportunities Canada offered. It had long held an attraction for him, especially so after the war.

Daniel's letter indicated he had taken to the farm well enough, but had never felt really settled back into Ireland after the Great War. The loss of his brother and some close friends in that war, the undercurrent of political and religious tensions in Ireland, especially the recent contentious division of North and South, had all served to make him feel Ireland was too steeped in an old history of strife. He believed Ireland was still carrying that past history into its future, stifling opportunity to grow and prosper. It all served to cause him concern for the ongoing welfare of his family and their Protestant way of life.

So once decided, Daniel had written to tell Beth that as soon as he could sell the farm, he and Rose would be on their way to Canada. Over the past year he had been in regular correspondence with their uncle who had gone out to Canada when Daniel was much younger. His uncle had reassured him that, for those ready to work, Canada was indeed a land full of opportunities. His uncle was also very willing to help Daniel and Rose get started on their new life out there. That was enough for Daniel. He didn't need any further encouragement. He and Rose had talked it all through and decided Canada was the place for them to raise their family together. They were making plans to go as soon as possible and selling The Liberty Bell.

By 1924, when Beth and Riley received the news of Daniel's immigration plans, they had already given young Grace another sister, Dottie, and more recently a baby brother, Toby. Their life in

England was busy but it was flourishing and held promise for the future. Riley was handling his job well and earning good money. There were indications he would even get a chance to work on one of Newcastle's biggest ever projects, the massive new steel Tyne Bridge, that was being planned.

With three children, Beth had not been able to do much paid work, spending more time at home to look after their young family. She was a strong and formidable woman and had already made sure they fitted well into life in Newcastle-on-Tyne. With a growing family, and Riley earning good money, they had been ready to make England their home for the foreseeable future. Yet now, with the receipt of this letter from Daniel, all that changed. Now they might just have an option to go back to Ireland and lay claim to The Liberty Bell.

That night Beth barely slept. Old memories of life on The Liberty Bell farm resurfaced. The possibility of her and Riley owning it, of her living there again, kept stirring up in her mind, rekindling half-forgotten thwarted dreams. Through it all, one thing became abundantly clear to her. Beth realised she still loved that farm, her forfeited heritage, with a burning passion.

She began to wonder if, with their savings and a mortgage, they could scrape together enough to buy it from Daniel. Riley was not a skilled farmer, they both knew that, but Beth convinced herself that it didn't matter. He could learn soon enough and together they could manage the place. The longing to possess The Liberty Bell had never left Beth. Pushing aside any further doubts or trepidations, the idea of owning it gradually grew more and more compelling, until it dominated all her thoughts.

Beth began to the see the letter from her brother, not so much as a letter, but more as a message and an opportunity that had been delivered to her and Riley by Divine providence itself. She saw it as a chance for redemption that she could not let pass by.

"Yes," she said enthusiastically to Riley, "this is our redemption, this is meant to be. It will all be possible if we just have faith and want it enough, and Heaven knows, there's nothing I want more than to get back The Liberty Bell."

Riley, as ever, was easily convinced that they could leave England behind and go back to Ireland to make a go of running the farm. He was still ready to follow Beth wherever she went. So it was not long after that they shared their own plans with Daniel. For his part, Daniel was delighted that ownership of The Liberty Bell might yet remain within the family. In a matter of weeks Beth and Riley had sorted out the financial arrangements with Daniel and Rose. A few weeks after that they took possession of The Liberty Bell, full of dreams to make a happy and comfortable living off the little farm.

Beth and Riley had staked their claim, but ownership of the Liberty Bell had come at a high cost. Riley was not a strong negotiator and found it hard to secure the level of mortgage they needed. Feeling pressured by Beth to find a suitable loan somehow, he had finally settled in haste on an arrangement with a money-lender at less than favourable rates.

In the short term the loan helped them secure the farm, but it was ill-timed, ill-advised and ill-managed. That loan would later spiral into a weighty ongoing debt. The repayment of it would remain a heavy financial yoke for Riley and Beth to bear for many years. So much so, that at times it would drive them to despair and to make unwise decisions. The hand of Fate that had so readily offered them opportunity to gain the farm, did not do so without taking something else away.

In the first few years on the farm, it became increasingly clear that it was going to be a much harder job managing The Liberty Bell farm than either Beth or Riley had imagined, but they were healthy and well and stuck to their task. Their family continued to grow, as Beth had anticipated it would, and that meant more mouths to feed. As the woman of the house, and full-time mother of their children, Beth gradually became a little more limited in what she could do in the daily care of the farm. As it was, she still worked long and hard managing the house and gardens, and raising their children.

She readily applied herself in the home, cooking, baking bread and scones, making buttermilk and butter and fruit jams and preserves of all sorts. Often too, especially with Riley overstretched at harvest time, she was called upon to help out with milking their cows and feeding and tending to their pigs and poultry in the outhouses. They worked hard, but there was much enjoyment too for them, especially in those first few years on the farm. Riley was very willing but had much to learn. He was certainly not a natural born farmer and had many mishaps and misjudgments, especially in those early years.

Fortune played with them. Once in a while there was the odd surprisingly successful venture which turned out well for them. On one such occasion, a befuddled Riley had come back from the market having purchased a dozen shaggy looking sheep. He had only gone to the local market to meet a friend and look over some dairy cattle, not intending to buy anything. So, when he arrived back with the sheep it was a complete surprise to Beth. An exasperated Beth soon let Riley know how she felt about his purchases.

"Dear Lord, why on earth did you go and buy sheep Riley? Sure we know nothing about raising sheep! We can hardly afford to look after the cows and pigs and poultry, without you bringing home sheep to add to our troubles, you daft fool!"

Riley, one might say sheepishly, confessed that he had never intended to buy the sheep in the first place. "Yes, I know, I know.

I made a mistake Beth and I'm sorry! But sure, I never intended to buy the damn things in the first place. I just felt sorry for old Tom, the auctioneer. With no-one wanting to bid, I thought I could give him a hand and put in a wee bid, just to help him start them all off like. Well it worked at first, but then I got a bit carried away and next thing I knew I was the only one bidding, so I was stuck with them."

Beth shook her head in disbelief at her husband's naivety. She was about to tell him so, but seeing the look of sheer embarrassment on his face she decided to let it go at that. There was no taking the sheep back, they were stuck with them alright. Fortunately, that Spring all the ewes produced lambs and the whole flock thrived. The sheep went surprisingly well for quite a few years after that too, delivering better than expected results, in contrast to many poor ones elsewhere on the farm.

As the last of the roaring 1920s gave way to the early 1930s, the world economic depression and rising unemployment hit hard everywhere. Ireland was not spared. Small farms especially, like The Liberty Bell, felt the pinch. Within just a few short years they were all finding it extremely difficult to keep operating under depressed competitive markets.

Sustainability and survival called not only for prudent farming decisions and shrewd business acumen, but often some luck as well. Although he continued to work long and hard, Riley had none of these attributes in abundance. Like many others, he was just an average farmer giving his best, but barely coping. With Beth's help, and through their sheer hard work, they continued to scratch a living for themselves and their growing family.

In those very tough early years of the 1930s, increasingly it had turned into a long hard slog for both of them as they sought to maintain the repayments on the farm and keep their heads above water. They were just barely getting by and making do on the edge of poverty. This was a far cry from the life Beth had been hoping for when she and Riley took on The Liberty Bell. Despite all their efforts, her dreams of a happy and successful farm life were turning sour. She was becoming more tired and irritable and much less patient, worrying increasingly about how she and Riley could manage to keep up their mortgage repayments and feed their large family on the limited income of the small farm.

Grace, like many children at that time, had left school on her fourteenth birthday. Within a few days she had taken up a job at a large linen factory in nearby Dromana. She cycled the five miles to and from work each day, dodging the heavy trundling delivery lorries on the way. More than once she had to take swift action and pitch bike and all headlong into the roadside ditch to avoid them. She kept up her daily chores on The Liberty Bell, starting in the early morning before she left, and continuing in the late evening when she returned home. Grace handed over her mediocre pay packet unopened to her mother at the end of every week, with just one notable exception. Sometimes Beth gave her a shilling or two for her own spending money, sometimes she didn't.

Perhaps it was in an effort to maintain more control over events, that a distraught Beth sought to impose ever more strict disciplines with her family. She was often in turmoil over it, for she was a devout Christian and also wanted to rule her family from a position of love. However, because she considered Riley to be too soft, she took it upon herself to be the disciplinarian. Practice in time turned into habit, and the habit of very strict, sometimes unduly harsh disciplines, gradually became the new norm. Beth was not alone in that. This harsh discipline was an increasingly common factor in so many households in Ireland in those stressful years.

Grace had just turned fifteen when Beth gave birth to her ninth child and second son. He was called Daniel, after Beth's brother, now settled and doing well in Canada. Young Daniel was to be Beth's last child. As was needed, and expected, the older children were obliged not only to help on the farm, but to help with the care and upbringing of the younger children.

It was around that time that Grace had made the unfortunate mistake of not handing over her unopened pay packet to her mother. It was the one and only time she ever chanced to do so.

Some of Grace's friends at the linen factory had planned to go and see the highly acclaimed all talkie movie, King Kong, that was on at the nearby Picture House that Friday night straight after work. They had all been so excited about it and they insisted that Grace should go with them. Grace had never been to see a movie before. She longed to go, despite her misgivings about how her mother might react. With much persuasion from her friends, she had finally relented and gone along with them. It was a completely new and amazing experience for Grace. She had loved the excitement and wonderful realism of it all, and like her friends, the young Grace had wept when the great ape was shot down and fell to his death at the end of the movie.

As she cycled home, much later than usual, Grace had tried to think how best to explain her lateness and opened pay packet to her mother. She decided to tell her mother the truth and hope she would understand. If not, well she would just have to face the consequences.

Beth had not known where Grace had been, nor why she was over three hours late. In her already tired and frazzled state, she had been pacing about the house, wondering what on earth had happened to Grace. Her eldest girl had never been this late before and Beth worried that she had been in an accident on the dark road home. Maybe she was lying hurt in a ditch somewhere, or worse.

When Grace finally arrived home, Beth's initial relief quickly turned to anger when Grace explained where she had been. Beth was not just cross, she was absolutely livid!

To learn that far from being hurt, Grace had been out spending money going to the Picture House, that God-forsaken den of iniquity, only added fuel to Beth's anger. With the farm debts rising, as far as Beth was concerned, they were all now in survival mode. There was no room for this sort of outright disobedience and petty self-indulgence by her eldest daughter. She was caught up in her own frustrations and worries and began to vent her anger on Grace.

"How could you be so stupid and selfish?! You know full well we all have to do our best to keep this farm afloat, and there you are, out squandering our money in that heathen place with those young sluts! What sort of example is that for the other children?! Well, I'll make an example out of you, my girl! Let's see if spending the night out with the pigs doesn't make you change your rebellious ways."

When any of the children had been misbehaving, Beth had often warned them that she would put them out in the boar's pen unless they mended their ways. She knew it would frighten the living daylights out of them, but did not expect the boar to actually harm them. Up to now it had only been a threat. One she had not yet resorted to carrying out because so far, the very thought of being shut up with the pigs, especially the big boar, so terrified the children that it had been more than enough of a deterrent to sort out even the most wayward of behaviours. Now, as Grace faced that prospect in the dark of the night, she was even more scared.

The huge boar was a fine cross-breed pig, a blend of large white and some other local mix. From end to end he was the length of a tall man, more than half his height, but well over three times his weight. A dirty off-white colour, he had a big broad hairy back, a small wiry tail, and long floppy ears that draped around dark human-like eyes. Due to his sheer strength and stubbornness at times, the boar had largely been left to Riley to deal with.

Grace was crying and pleaded with her mother. "It was only once mother. Please, I won't do it again. Please, I promise." An angry Beth ignored her pleas and half-dragged the frightened Grace by the arm to the pigsty. Despite Riley's protests too, she pushed Grace inside the boar's pen. "Right! You can stay there and don't move until I come back to let you out. Maybe that will teach you not to disobey me!" Beth slammed the door shut, locked it, and walked off, ushering Riley back to the house with her.

Grace stood as still as she could in the corner of the small dimly lit concrete pen. As she was being taken out, Riley whispered to her, "You'll be alright if you just stay still and leave him alone. He won't bother you as long as you don't bother him. I'll come out and fetch you in an hour or so after your mah has cooled off a bit."

His words helped Grace, but only a little. An hour or more locked up with a huge boar would still seem like an eternity to anyone when they are terrified of what was going to happen to them. Especially a fifteen-year-old girl.

The big boar came over and stood in front of her, lifting his massive head up so that he could look directly at her. Grace trembled and shut her eyes tightly so she would not have to look back at him. Burying her face in her hands, she hoped and prayed the boar would leave her alone and wouldn't hurt her. Even with her eyes closed, Grace could still smell his presence and hear his laboured breathing. She waited, praying and softly crying. The stiff bristly hair on the boar brushed her sides as he leaned in closer to examine this intruder. Grace pressed her back tighter against the wall, holding her breath, hoping she would be safe if she just stayed still, as her father had told her.

Sometimes Providence can be kind. After a few more sniffs and snorts to determine just who his visitor was and to enquire if she had brought any food, the boar turned around and went off to lie down in the opposite corner. Grace gratefully opened her eyes again and let out her breath as she heard the boar lying down. The boar continued to watch her, looking out with his intelligent round eyes, as if perhaps wondering why this young human was also imprisoned in his tiny pen.

Still tense and worried, a sniffling Grace continued to stand in the corner of the pen, all the time keeping a close watch on the boar. After about fifteen minutes of this, she began to relax a little as she realised that the boar was not bothered by her presence. In fact, as he had determined she wasn't a threat and didn't have food, he didn't seem particularly interested in her at all. While he himself looked fierce and threatening when he stood up, lying there on the ground the boar seemed more docile. He was just like any other big animal, enjoying having a bit of a lie down.

Grace was naturally fond of animals, and after a while she found enough courage to try talking softly to him, as she had often seen her father do. As she spoke a few words, every now and then the boar moved his head and flicked his big ears, as if perhaps listening to the sound of her voice. Encouraged by the boar's response, Grace spoke a little more.

By the time an hour had gone by, Grace was sitting down on the ground nearer to the boar, tentatively scratching his side and talking away to him. Sometimes the pig, a species with far more intelligence than most realised, would give a soft grunt of satisfaction, as if the little human had just scratched a particularly itchy spot.

A short time later, Grace heard Riley calling to her as he was coming to let her out. She felt it prudent to resume a more cowering remorseful attitude, so quickly jumped back up into the far corner.

As Riley came in, Grace sniffled a bit more for good measure.

Walking back to the house, Riley whispered. "Are you alright Grace? I thought I heard someone talking a minute ago. That couldn't have been you talking to that big pig now, could it, eh?" Grace decided to keep her head down and say nothing.

"Nah, nah, course it couldn't," Riley continued, as if answering his own question. "I'm the only one around here daft enough to do that aren't I." He put his arm around Grace and grinned. "Must just have been you crying, shut up in there with that big old boar, right Grace?"

As they entered the house Riley quickly took his arm off Grace's shoulder and in a stern voice said, "Here she is now Beth. Yes indeed, I think she's been taught a lesson right enough! Stop your crying now Grace, and get off to bed with you. And just remember what your mother told you. If you don't ever want to be shut up with those pigs again, just bring your pay packet straight home and stay well away from that heathen Picture House."

It was indeed a lesson well learnt, and perhaps in more ways than one. Through all of it, their very strict disciplines and religious upbringing, their scarcities and frugal measures, the long hours of physical work, Beth and Riley's children fared relatively well. They continued to survive. Mostly they were resilient and they bounced back to meet each new day anew in a cheerful manner, for they knew nothing else. Mostly they did, but not always. Some things undoubtedly left their mark.

As is often the case too, somehow the children grew closer together as a result of the hardships they faced. Out of necessity, they came to rely upon each other from an early age. They were their own best friends and supported each other. Like all children, they had their squabbles, but amidst their hard life on the little Irish farm, they forged the bonds of a strong love for each other that was to endure all their lives.

It was perhaps because of their close loving relationships, that what was yet to come was so appalling and unexpected.

Serendipity

Chapter 5

The Bitter Seed

As the plant springs from, and could not be without,
the seed, so every act of a man springs from the hidden seeds of his thought,
and could not have appeared without them.
(James Allen)

Early Spring 1936

By 1936 tension was mounting throughout Ireland and Europe. In Ireland, religious and political divides were again bubbling to the surface and becoming more prominent under the dominance of British rule. Over the water, the mighty British monarchy itself was in turmoil, brought about by the influence of a strong, twice married woman, Wallace Simpson. Rigid in its traditions, and set against her becoming the consort of the king, the monarchy had been rocked to its foundations by the abdication of King Edward VIII, and resultant rapid ascension of his younger brother, the new King George VI. Remarkably, he was the third king to sit on the British throne that year.

Further afield in Germany, events were becoming much more

ominous. Hitler, the rising Chancellor and now also President, was earning praise for the firm measures he was taking to pull that country up out of the world-wide economic depression. At the same time, the Führer was building vast and powerful new armies. His Mein Kampf book, written over a decade earlier whilst he was in prison for treason, had become the popular guide to his ideology for the German masses. Worse yet, he had embarked on an extremist approach to develop racially superior humans, his so-called strong and pure Aryan race.

The ancient and highly controversial practice of selective breeding had been brought to the scientific foreground by the cousin of Charles Darwin, Sir Francis Galton, in the late nineteenth century, labelling it the doctrine of eugenics. Even America had already dabbled in a form of the practice in the early twentieth century, purportedly sterilising an estimated 64,000 people over the thirty states in which it had been made legal. Infamously, the German Chancellor would later embrace this concept and, in his growing madness, would incite a maelstrom of unbelievable cruelty that would in time lead to the mass killing of millions of the Jewish people.

So as 1936 rolled on, and a fanatical Hitler was beginning to urge his adopted nation to restore lost pride and create his so-called superior Aryan race, the seeds of wrath were being sown for yet another cataclysmic confrontation of major powers. Meanwhile, the rest of Europe was slowly waking up to the fact that the present state of peace, after the war to end all wars, might be much more tenuous than they had imagined.

While on the macro scale, Europe was on a slippery slope slowly heading towards a second war, much closer to home, the seeds of an assault of a different kind were also being sown.

Riley and Beth received an unusual visitor in the early Spring of that same year. Their visitor was Jessman, the owner of the farm that was close to The Liberty Bell. He was the son of the same family that had bought the lower piece of their land from Beth's father some twenty years before. This particular Jessman was just a few years older than Beth and Riley, but although a neighbour, was a very infrequent visitor. In past years, following the death of his parents, even his visits to their local church had become less and less. Since then Jessman had run the farm mostly on his own, apart from a few casual hired hands at harvest time.

He also had a much younger brother, Sam, who had Down's syndrome. Some said Sam had a mental age of perhaps ten or twelve, but no-one knew for sure. Certainly he was an exceptionally capable, strong and very likeable young man who willingly helped around their farm, though he was almost totally dependent on Jessman for his needs.

Burly from working on the farm, Jessman was of average height, with ginger-red hair, a ruddy complexion, coarse features and brusque coarse manners. He was comfortably well off, but clearly socially awkward. After a few half-hearted attempts at courtships in his earlier years, he was now a confirmed bachelor. Not much used to children, he was decidedly uncomfortable when around them. Grace and her siblings were polite, as bidden, but for some reason were wary of Jessman and stayed well clear of his few clumsy attempts at friendship.

Soon the reason for Jessman's unusual visit became clear as they sat around the kitchen table drinking a cup of tea, and eating the large buttered scones that Beth had baked. Jessman casually announced that he was aware that Beth and Riley had been struggling to make ends meet on The Liberty Bell, particularly over the past few years in the difficult economic climate. Jessman hurried on to say that he was very much a business man as well as a farmer, and a shrewd one at that, and he thought he saw an opportunity that might benefit all of them here, if they would be prepared to hear him out. Beth and Riley glanced at each other, then back at Jessman and nodded warily. Seizing the moment, Jessman launched into his proposal.

He began awkwardly. "Look, I'm not saying that The Liberty Bell isn't a fine farm, but God knows it's just not running efficiently at all. Besides, it's hardly big enough for the pair of you, never mind supporting all those wee children you have. It's no wonder you're barely getting by and running up debts all over the place."

Riley spluttered and coughed loudly, bits of his scone flying out as he did so. He was about to interject, when Beth placed her hand on his arm, and quietly asked Jessman to go on. Jessman didn't need to be asked twice. Pressing his luck, even less tactfully, he blundered on.

"You should sell the farm off now, while it's still worth something. The sooner the better, for it's only going from bad to worse. It's as plain as day. If you don't sell up very soon you'll be in debt up to your eyeballs and your creditors will just take it from you. "

Seeing Riley getting increasingly agitated and fidgeting in his seat, with Beth now taking a firm grip on his arm, Jessman rushed on to ask the question that had been on his mind from the outset.

"Look, I'm your neighbour and I'm a very fair man. Why don't you sell the farm to me and I'll give you a fair price for it?" As if it was an afterthought, he casually tossed out such a low figure that to Beth and Riley it amounted to no more than an insulting offer. For a moment there was stunned silence as they just looked at him and then again at each other.

Poor Riley did not know what to think. He was both embarrassed and outraged, a dangerous mixture of emotions in the big man. His thoughts were racing, propelling his rage. How dare this pompous excuse for a neighbour imply that he was making a poor job of farming The Liberty Bell. How dare he imply he could not afford to feed his own children. They had spent years toiling long and hard on The Liberty Bell farm and it was far from easy raising nine children. A small faint voice in Riley's head started to whisper that in truth maybe he could have done quite a lot of things better, but he angrily squashed it down. His pride was now at stake and another, louder voice of bruised ego was roaring in his head. He was not about to be told that he was doing a poor job by this arrogant ass, neighbour or no neighbour.

Riley's face was dark as thunder and he could hold back no longer. The veins around his thick reddened neck stood out as suddenly he clenched his fists, and brought them slamming down like heavy hammers on the table. In one motion he clambered to his feet, towering over Jessman, his chair knocked flying across the floor as he did so. Alarmed, Jessman rose quickly too, almost falling off his chair. Struggling to maintain his balance, he swiftly backed away. For a split second it looked like Riley was going to punch Jessman, or throw him out of the house, or both.

Beth had seen immediately where things were headed and had also jumped up swiftly to her feet. She pulled hard on Riley's arm, momentarily holding him back. Then, stepping deftly between the two of them, she hastily thanked Jessman for his offer, quickly guiding him a little further away from the fuming Riley as she did so.

Loudly, so Riley could not possibly miss it, Beth said, "Look Mr. Jessman, we have no notion of selling The Liberty Bell! So, let's just leave it at that for now and not waste your time and ours discussing it further." Then, in a slightly more conciliatory manner, she added, "If we ever consider changing our minds, well you can be sure you will be the first to know."

Riley started to interject with loud defensive comments about the state of affairs at the farm and then began throwing out insults at Jessman's offer and suggestions. Recognising that things could only get worse, Beth told Jessman that it was probably best that he should leave now, and quickly, while he still could. The next instant she was gathering up Jessman's coat, hat and gloves, and ushering him out of the door and on his way. A confused Jessman found himself swiftly bundled outside, still wondering what had just happened. With Riley still growling and becoming ever more incensed, Beth slammed the door shut behind Jessman, keeping it firmly closed with her back to it, and breathed a deep sigh of relief.

As soon as he was gone, Riley erupted again. He reeled off a host of names for Jessman. A cunning, calculating, condescending, conniving crook, soon escalated to a wider repertoire of much more unsavoury names that would not bear repeating. Beth let him rant on for a few moments to let off steam, before reining him in by gently chastising his un-Christian like behaviour.

Gradually Riley calmed down as she reassured him that there was no intention of selling off The Liberty Bell. Then, almost like a final reprimand to both herself and Riley, she added that there might be something useful in what Jessman had said, so they should not dismiss him completely without at least thinking about it.

Later that night, with Grace and the other children finally settled in bed and Riley out doing final checks and closing up the yard, Beth sat at the kitchen table again and went over in her mind all that had transpired earlier with Jessman. He was a dogged and stodgy farmer, and yes, maybe calculating and conniving too, but all the same he was successful. He had managed to do well even in very difficult economic times. His farm was several times larger than The Liberty Bell and she had heard nothing but good reports of it. Perhaps Jessman had made a valid point. The Liberty Bell was simply too small to support all of them now. Perhaps they should consider selling up after all.

As that thought surfaced, she felt her buried anger rise again with it. She and Riley had nothing but a heavy mortgage and other debts to show for all their years of hard work. All too well Beth recalled how her father had sold off The Liberty Bell's rich fertile lower pastures and outbuildings to Jessman's father, all those years ago. She had objected back then and was still acutely annoyed, for those pastures were an integral part of The Liberty Bell and could have made all the difference to the farm's viability now.

She and Riley were doing their best, but they were stony broke, heavily mortgaged, and going nowhere. They now had a large family to support, and would have to do so for some years yet. Jessman was right, it was an uphill task in their current circumstances. The thought of it weighted down upon her shoulders. At that moment it all seemed hopeless. She felt they had hit rock bottom and soon would have to sell anyway, or lose the farm to their creditors. What would happen to her and Riley and the children if that happened? Would they all end up in some back-water rental cottage, or worst still, out on the street and some of the children put in a home?

Then, with these last thoughts, came a new clarity. Beth realised, despite everything, she did not want to sell up. She did not care how bad things were right now, the farm was still her destiny, it was pre-ordained. She had grown up on The Liberty Bell. It was her farm, her home, and she had poured her life into keeping it going. No! She was not about to give up on it now. No! She would not let it go. They would survive, all of them. Somehow, they would survive on The Liberty Bell.

The long-suppressed anger that she harboured within her was awoken, smoldering, urging, again finding its way to the surface. Pained and frustrated, she exclaimed aloud, "Damn Jessman, and his stupid offer! It's mine, it's our home, and I will not part with it, not one inch of it. No, not for him, not for anyone!"

The words echoed around her head and the house like a prophetic proclamation of some bold intent. A line drawn in the sand from which Beth would never retreat, not at any price. Though right at that moment, she knew they were in a desperate state. She could not see any other option or any other way. Beth went to bed, weary, tense and still incensed by what Jessman had said, even if much of it might be true.

It was in the middle of the night, as she lay awake, that the idea first came to Beth's mind. That desperate, searching mind, set on retaining her farm at any price. Rebuking herself, Beth quickly dismissed the idea on the instant and tried to get back to sleep. To her annoyance the thought crept back again later and again she chose to dismiss it. In the early morning it surfaced again to harangue her. This time she indulged it for a while longer before dismissing it again.

Each time the conscious choice that she made to dismiss the idea took a little longer and more effort than before. Unknowingly, each time Beth indulged the thought she was again choosing to feed the hungry wolf. Each time the door was left a little more ajar for its return. Finally, the idea was allowed to return and dwell too long in the fertile ground of captive attention. Nourished, the bitter seed took hold. Flourished, it took form.

Beth said nothing at all to Riley about it. She did not know how. Yet the idea was formed, and held fast within her, waiting for the moment when it would surface and manifest into being.

That moment came a little closer when less than a fortnight later they received the final overdue notice. The debts on the farm had been sliding out again and again, and had now gone far beyond their ability to make the repayments. They had been ordered to bring their affairs back into order or face foreclosure. Despairingly Beth and Riley had gone through all the motions, trying everything they knew. There were last minute meetings, promises on promises, and passionate pleadings. Despite it all, there was no reprieve in sight.

There now seemed to be no way they could possibly make the payment to avoid forfeiting the farm. Beth felt there was no alternative. Her next step was not inevitable, but the wheels had already been set in motion with the seeds planted in her mind. She convinced herself it was for the greater good, yes, surely it was for the greater good. She decided to tell Riley that evening.

When evening came and Beth finally spoke the fermented idea aloud into words, her words chilled the air. Even her devoted Riley was stunned into disbelief. "Dear God, woman! No, we cannot do that! We cannot do that!" But Beth was resolute, and she knew her Riley. She knew that it would take time for the idea to settle, to take hold. That Riley, however revolted or resistant, would come around in time and eventually accede to her wishes.

Chapter 6

The King of Spits

A human being is part of the whole that we call the universe,
a part limited in time and space. He experiences himself,
his thoughts and feelings, as something separated from the rest –
a kind of optical delusion of his consciousness.
(Albert Einstein)

Early July 1963

The King of Spits was never going to be beaten. At least not this day, and certainly not by this lanky, red-haired, squint-eyed, arrogant, thirteen-year-old snot of an excuse for a would-be gang leader, who didn't have a decent spit in him.

The Summer after that Great Freeze of 1962-63 was kind and the children of the Heights were frequently out and about making the most of it. Having grown up in the countryside like many of the other parents living in the Heights, Grace encouraged her children to play outside and explore nature in what was a relatively safe environment all around them. Of course, what some of the growing children got up to in that expansive playground often remained a mystery to Grace and the other parents. On balance, perhaps that might well have been for the best.

The boys had assembled on the Mound for the contest. It seemed fitting. There they were, the two groups of young lads, standing atop the huge ancient Norman grassy green earthwork motte and bailey on the outskirts of Dromana. It had been constructed by John de Courcy's army during the Anglo-Norman conquest in the thirteenth century. The great Mound stood tall, one of the largest and finest in Ireland, with a circumference of over six hundred feet at the base. From the base it towered up with sloping sides, rising like some alien sculpted giant cone to a flat top of some eighty feet across.

The top offered splendid views all around, overlooking Dromana and the river Lagan that curled around the lush green countryside as it journeyed on its way. From the top it was also possible to see the ancient ruins of the Norman castle that had been preserved in the town. More importantly for the lads, the high flat platform, with its slight elevated ridge around the top, gave them just enough privacy from any prying eyes down below to sort out the important matter at hand. Namely, was the King of Spits about to be taken down? It was the perfect setting for this very different sort of battle that was about to take place.

As the current King of Spits and representing the Heights gang, young Micky knew this challenge to his prowess had been coming for a while. Beatty, the sullen red-haired snot, had made it clear days ago that he was going to challenge Micky for the leadership of the Heights gang and the coveted title of King of Spits. Beatty was already leader of the neighbouring Maypole Park gang, and looking to expand his gang empire. Of course, not everyone might consider it to be an empire. After all, there were only four boys in his gang, and one of those was his younger brother. The younger brother, being only ten, had not been accepted at first. However, when he had cried and complained to his mother, she told Beatty in no uncertain terms that if his little brother could not be in the gang then there would be no gang. On reflection, Beatty had agreed that perhaps he had been a bit hasty and that his little brother did meet the entrance criteria after all.

Micky was a neighbour and best friend of Grace's eldest boy. Honour was very much at stake when a formal challenge for King of Spits was issued. The wager was for leadership of both gangs and was simple enough. It was just that there was also another little caveat. A not very pleasant penalty for the loser.

He was a lean lad Micky, despite his penchant for thick jam-filled sandwiches between meals, and hordes of plain biscuits with endless cups of tea. He was fit and tall, similar in height to Beatty, though a year younger at twelve. However, his manner was a complete contrast. Beatty could be a bit of a bully, with a tendency to be forceful and sometimes sullen. Micky, on the other hand, was easy-going and well liked, with a sharp wit and pronounced sense of humour that drew endlessly from a bottomless pit of terrible jokes.

After the savage Winter just passed, Micky and his friends had revisited many of the old favourite haunts left unattended during the Winter months. The big spy tree, the lower glen and old viaduct, the swimming areas at the river Lagan, and more especially, the Rocks. It was at the Rocks some days ago that Beatty and his gang had overstepped the mark. The Rocks were, as the name might suggest, a tall rocky outcrop, that rose up in one of the many expansive open green fields surrounding the Heights. It was a special place for the Heights gang. Indeed, it was revered as their sacred ground.

The gang had been busy fortifying an old hut there when Beatty and his Maypole Park gang had come prowling around the Rocks uninvited. It had almost turned into a fight in the first moments they were spotted. After the initial bit of blustering and posturing by both sides, Micky had calmed things down. Eventually Beatty and his fellows had agreed to return to more neutral territory, but only after Beatty had loudly issued the challenge to Micky and it had been accepted.

Now, here they stood, both gangs of young boys atop the Mound, these would-be knights, ready for the event. It was an ideal day for it, with barely a breath of wind to give anyone an unfair advantage.

Spitting was naturally frowned upon by Grace and the other parents. Few of the boys had escaped the lectures. "Spitting is a disgusting habit that spreads germs and diseases. Don't do it!"

The warning may have worked well enough around the home, but had less effect when the boys were out and about in the open countryside. Besides, it was this unsavoury pastime that provided a relatively peaceful means of settling disputes between some of the groups of younger boys around Dromana. Unfortunately, the aggressions of gangs of lads in their later years were not so easily reconciled.

The two contestants lined up at one side of the flat-topped Mound, with their gang members forming a line stretching out in front of them into the centre. Between the line was the general target area in which the spit saliva was to fly. It was to be a best of three efforts. Beatty, who had been secretly practicing intensively since issuing the challenge, until his mother discovered him and gave him a firm clip around the ear, was first to go.

Limbering up with some jogging on the spot and with some deep huffing and puffing, he stepped up to the line. Then, reaching up to his full height, he swished a great glob of saliva around the inside of his mouth, sucked up air to swell his lungs, arched his head back and with a sudden release, let fly up and into the sky. The spit landed a good seventeen feet away, a fair start. Amidst loud cheers, it was instantly marked with a stick by one of his gang, closely watched with growing apprehension by Micky's supporters.

There was an art to getting the spit to be just the right amount and just the right viscosity. It had to hold together and not spray out like a fountain in wasted effort. Micky had it down to a fine art, but clearly Beatty did too.

Micky, still looking calm, smiled and stepped up to the mark to take his turn. He had an unusual style, curling the tip of his tongue back to cradle the spit, then leaning back and, like a cock crowing, flicking it out with a sharp forward jerk of his head and quick release of air from his inflated chest. It looked effortless, yet was highly effective, and sped out to land well over a foot ahead of Beatty's mark. He was not called the King of Spits for nothing. Micky's supporters cheered him on, and this spot too was marked with a stick. Then, rather unfairly, they began taunting Beatty. That was a mistake.

As he stepped up to the mark for his second go, Beatty was really riled up. He was so cross at being mocked and ridiculed, even if it was mostly in fun. Being mocked and ridiculed had happened way too often in Beatty's young life for him to dismiss it easily. Right now, he wanted so much to beat Micky. That would shut them all up for good.

On his second attempt, Beatty surpassed himself. Lungs absolutely full, and with face reddened and looking ready to explode. He stretched back his neck, and then lurching swiftly forward, he let fly the spit on a great barrage of air with an almighty swoosh. It flashed up and out, then landed a full two and a half feet ahead of Micky's attempt. Beatty's supporters roared their approval and marked the spot with gusto. They pumped fists in the air, clapped Beatty on the back, and congratulated him on what was a truly awesome effort.

It was as far as they had ever seen anyone spit. Then they all looked expectantly towards Micky. The tables were turned, and this time it was Beatty's gang that began to jeer and heckle. Then, as one, they gave Micky an ominous thumbs down sign.

For the first time Micky began to look uncomfortable. He rarely contemplated defeat, but now that prospect was staring him full in the face, as Beatty's gang noisily reminded him. He stepped up to the mark for his second attempt. This time it was released with a little more strain, and not quite the same finesse. Although marginally further than his first attempt, it fell well short of Beatty's mark. Micky's supporters looked downcast, perhaps for the first time realising that the impossible might happen, and dreading the implications of defeat.

Beatty's confidence had grown, as had his arrogance. His third and final monumental effort landed even further ahead of his previous mark, both now well in front of Micky's attempts. As his gang cheered, Beatty jumped into the air, yelling in his excitement. Fired up and feeling triumphant, he turned to Micky and shouted with contempt.

"There now, you dirty fenian git, I told you I was going to beat you!"

The intensity of the slur slashed through the air and silenced both groups. Instantly it laid bare old festered wounds between feuding Catholics and Protestants that had spanned the ages. Long cultivated wounds, old histories, all of it, pulled out of the past and hurled into the present by Beatty's careless insult. A focus on differences, obscuring the underlying unity of mankind. In an unguarded moment of exultation, Beatty had crossed the line. It was a mistake and they all knew it. Beatty knew it too. He wished he hadn't said it, but it was out now and he was not about to back down.

Micky's two best friends, David and Grace's eldest boy, started forward towards Beatty, ready to make him pay for his insults. Micky quickly saw where it would lead, and stopped them.

"No, leave him. It's not over yet. I've still got my turn to come."

Micky felt he had to show him, show them all, he couldn't just leave it like this. He looked over again at the still glowering Beatty, who still had the lingering traces of arrogance and contempt in his eyes. It was right there and then, in that instant as they looked at each other, that the King of Spits knew he was not going to be beaten. Not this day, and certainly not by this ignorant, arrogant snot.

Micky went up to the line with renewed determination. There were no distracting nerves, tension, nor doubts this time. Composed and with total focus he filled his lungs and curled his tongue back around the spit in readiness. Then propelling himself high into the air and arching back like a jack-knife, his body whiplashed forward. Air, spit, and tongue were unleashed all in one powerful harmonious movement. He let fly for all he was worth.

It was perfection of the art. The spit hurtled ever upwards and forward. On it sailed over the heads of the watching boys, on and on, finally landing way beyond Beatty's best mark. It was massive, over twenty-five feet, absolutely unbeatable, a spit to behold, a king of spits, and one perhaps never to be repeated.

Stunned, the boys raced to fix the marker in the ground, then looked back in awe over the distance. Shouts erupted and Micky was hoisted onto shoulders and declared the outright winner and still undisputed King of Spits. It was too much for Beatty and his gang. With begrudging respect, they acknowledged Mickey as the winner. They knew they were well beaten and what was to follow. The penalty was after all a matter of gang honour, and the part of the rules of the challenge. There was no choice but to see it through.

"Alright then, that's it, you've won," Beatty grumbled. Then more gamely, "Let's get on with it, we may as well get the damn penalty over with right now and be done with it."

Later, there was a fair amount of laughing and joking as Micky and his friends made their way home to the Heights. After the challenge the two gangs had gone down to the river as planned. With its grassy banks and cool, clean, calm waters, the river Lagan in those halcyon days was an idyllic place to swim and relax. As was often the case on a warm Summer's day, a few other young people were already making the most of the good weather and enjoying a swim by the ever-popular Gib-stone.

The Gib-stone was a great rounded rock embedded in the river bed that rose to just below the surface of the deepest water in the middle of the river. It was out of sight from the river bank, except in a severe drought when the water was very low. Yet, like folklore, knowledge of the great Gib-stone had been passed down to children for generations. They still came to jump or dive off it as they had in centuries past.

Most of the boys who came to swim wore swim shorts or some kind of underpants appropriate for the day. Not Beatty, he had to do something different if honour was to be restored. With a posse of lively young boys yelling and laughing behind him, Beatty, to his credit, sprinted full tilt down the grassy slope to the river and with a huge jump he plunged straight in. Then, amidst much cheering, he scrambled atop the Gib-stone, stood there for a second, before boldly executing a wonderful swan-dive back into the river. As the penalty required, Beatty was completely buck-naked.

Chapter 7

The Orange & The Green

This illusion is a prison for us, restricting us to our
personal closeness and affection for only the few people nearest us.
Our task must be to free ourselves from this prison by widening
our circle of compassion to embrace all living beings and all of nature.
(Albert Einstein)

12 July 1963

About a week later, on the 12th of July of that year, the day of the Protestant's annual celebration of the Battle of the Boyne, a seemingly trivial incident happened just outside Grace's house. Trivial perhaps, yet in some ways profound and reflective of the situation then prevalent in Northern Ireland,

The Battle of the Boyne was a highly significant historical event and for many lay at the heart of all that was Northern Ireland. It's 300-year legacy has had an astonishing and complex influence on Irish history and culture, touching countless Irish lives throughout the ages. Even today, many staunch Northern Irish Protestants still like to celebrate it.

Particularly for people living outside Ireland, it is difficult to understand why on earth so many of the Protestants in Northern Ireland, primarily the Orange Order, would continue to celebrate the victory of an imported Dutch Protestant, King William of Orange, over an English Catholic one, King James II of England, Scotland and Ireland. Especially, as it was a battle fought way back in 1690. Especially, as many would view that battle as being much less about Ireland, though fought there, and much more about preserving England and its Protestant British crown against an emerging Catholic dominance.

By way of a brief background, just a few years before the battle, King James had visited his cousin Louis in France. He had been convinced to convert from his Protestant faith to become a Catholic. This was alarming enough, but when James took a much younger Italian Catholic girl for his bride, Protestants began to fear that their hold on the British crown was slipping. Finally, when James began ousting Protestants from key political positions and replacing them with Catholics, it sent shock waves through his Protestant British realm, especially in the north of Ireland. Protestants reacted by persuading James' son in law, Dutch King William, to overthrow James and usurp the throne, which he finally did. At first it was a relatively peaceful coup, as James fled. However, when James tried to recover his crown again at the ensuing Battle of the Boyne, it resulted in the famous victory for Protestant 'King Billy'.

Of course, arguably the real root cause of the religious problems in Ireland began 150 years earlier, when around 1540, King Henry VIII, began to establish a Protestant administration in Ireland to solidify his recent switch to a controversial Protestant rule.

Born and raised as a staunch Catholic, King Henry had at first firmly rejected Martin Luther's emerging Protestant reformist ideas, instead rigorously defending his Roman Catholic faith. However, later when he wanted to divorce his first wife, Catherine, to marry Anne Boleyn and improve his chances of begetting a male heir, the Pope refused to approve the divorce. Henry, not to be denied, promptly turned to the Protestant faith and made himself head of the Anglican church.

In effect, it was Henry who turned the Catholic British monarchy into a Protestant Anglican one, all so that he could have his divorce. It was a little ironic in many ways, but perhaps then again, there could have been many who might have sympathised with Henry's marital predicaments.

There was even irony in the selection of the Republic of Ireland's tricolour flag, when in 1848, in the midst of the Irish famine a group of French women presented the flag as a gift to Irish leaders. The flag was designed to symbolise the healing of the age-old 'religious' divisions. The green representing Catholics, the orange representing Protestants, and the white representing a long-lasting peace between them.

It was a bold gesture, though the divide was a very long way from being healed back then. Three decades of 'Troubles' that were to follow in the latter part of the twentieth century more than demonstrated that. Whatever the reasons then, Northern Ireland, and the Orange and the Green, remained a troubled country and a political hot potato.

As part of a Catholic minority living in a largely Protestant area, Micky, the intrepid young gang leader, was naturally all too familiar with the folk-lore around the Battle of the Boyne. He was also already well accustomed to seeing some of the Protestant Orangemen and other organisations gathering together for their annual Twelfth of July celebrations of it. Union Jack flags, the symbol of Protestant British heritage, hung from almost all the Protestant houses, and a flurry of red, white and blue flags lined the streets. The parades of well-dressed bowler-hatted, orange-sashed men, and the gaily coloured men and women in Scottish bagpipe, flute and brass bands, always attracted large crowds and provided much delight and entertainment at locations all around Northern Ireland.

Grace loved it too, well for the most part anyway. She also had her reservations about it, especially when it went late into the day and dragged on a little too long for her liking. That year, Dromana was included as one of the locations for the parades, almost on their doorstep.

On the day before the celebrations, Micky had come around to spend time with Grace's eldest son. As he munched his way through yet another of his favourite jam-filled sandwiches, Micky mumbled that he might just go along to have a look at the parade. Grace had overheard the lads talking as they sat at the kitchen table. She felt a tinge of apprehension and felt she should just give young Micky a brief word of caution.

"If you want to see it Micky, then go in the morning. After that you can go on off home for lunch and just leave them all to it in the afternoon. Understand?"

Micky nodded, but looked a little puzzled by her instructions. Grace just smiled at him reassuringly and did not elaborate further. She knew full well how the afternoons tended to go when the alcohol started to flow after lunch and at tea time, especially if the weather was hot. Though the majority of revellers were well enough behaved, there were also of course many exceptions.

That was when some over-indulged. That was when for some an otherwise steady rationale could evaporate and behaviour begin to deteriorate. No different from many other social events perhaps. Except that at this event the focus was on a long-ago Protestant victory over Catholics. A victory over a 300-year-old Catholic foe that was rejuvenated every time it was celebrated in the present. It was not hard to see how quickly that particular theme could be taken too far by some of the rowdier drunken celebrants. That was the time for curious Catholic youths to stay well clear.

At the Heights, Grace's boy and his father were getting ready to join the parade that morning. The man was a pipe major, a leader of a much-respected local pipe band. The boy was particularly excited. For the first time he was considered old enough and able enough to join the band on public parade with the other pipers. He had been practicing and looking forward to this day for quite some time. He was only allowed to join in on some of the easier tunes, but it was a start.

Man, and boy, began to don their band uniforms, unique to their pipe band. That was no simple task. At first glance, the carefully laid-out ensemble was bewildering. It included shirt, tartan kilt, doublet, braid shawl, sporran, brogue shoes and tartan socks, spats, belts, glengarry hat, broaches and a dirk, not to mention a set of bagpipes. If dressing up in all this was to be done well, they needed help.

Grace was adept at helping the man to prepare, but in recent times one of her good friends and close neighbour, Jane, would also come over to lend a hand. Jane's help was always appreciated, for she had quite a knack for making the person in uniform look their very best. There was a certain irony in this too. Jane was a Catholic. Yet, here she was, willingly doing the good neighbourly thing by helping her Protestant neighbours dress up. She knew full well it was so that they could go out to celebrate a centuries old battle and a Protestant victory over Catholics. It hardly mattered to her. For Jane, friendship came first. There was no reason for any division or any resentment to surface between them just because of some parade. Unfortunately, that was not the case with everyone.

Shortly afterwards, some of the other band members arrived in a van and stopped outside Grace's house to collect the man and boy for the parade. As they gathered together the contents for the journey and placed them on the footpath beside the van, a few of the neighbours and children of the Heights came around to watch the proceedings and join in on the banter. Micky was among them. Jane had gone back to join her husband, both standing at their open doorway, watching too. Pipes and drums and the various oddments were all laid out to be rearranged in the van, along with the revered symbol of the Protestants, a Union Jack flag. It was rolled up on its long wooden pole and propped at an angle resting against the low garden wall.

The boy was standing by the van, having just talked with his friend Micky. As the boy was still busy helping, Micky moved a little way off, to stand near the flag. Everyone was busy helping to sort out the van contents or chatting. Everyone it seemed, except Micky. The boy glanced up just in time to see Micky raise his booted foot, and grinning up at his Catholic neighbour, pretend to bring it crashing down to smash the Union Jack flag. It was a simple boyish gesture. A trivial act as a bit of fun, done on a whim, with no real harm done. Apart from the boy and Jane's husband, no-one else had noticed it, but the effect of Micky's gesture on the boy was profound.

He had been so looking forward to this parade. It was a special day for everyone to enjoy. So he was all the more shocked that Micky, his best friend, would even think of breaking the Protestant's sacred flag. That doing something like that, to sabotage or ridicule the parade, might be his friend's idea of fun. That Micky should think somehow his Catholic neighbours might share in this secretive inside joke. To the boy's young mind, Micky was mocking their whole celebration. Why would his best friend do that? It felt like a betrayal.

And then, watching Micky, still standing away from the others, an inkling of the truth began to dawn upon the boy, and he felt saddened at the realisation.

Everyone had grown accustomed to the recurrent jibes that took place between Protestants and Catholics from time to time. It didn't seem like much, but there was always some trace of that around, that division. The recent episode on the Mount with Beatty was just another example. His mother, Grace, had always taught the boy that everyone was equal, whatever their beliefs. "Don't think you are better than anyone else, and don't think anyone else is better than you", echoed in his mind. But perhaps not everyone saw things that way.

Though the boy did not then understand the rationale or the subtle nuances, somehow this simple little incident went deeper and touched a nerve. The reality was that his good friend Micky was not a part of this celebration. He never could be. He was a Catholic, and feeling excluded. He could not possibly join in, even if he wanted to. An accumulation of thorny jibes must surely have their effect over time. A focus on all their differences, could only result in an attitude of 'them and us', rather than the unity.

Of course, that was never articulated. That was never the intention. It was simply a Protestant celebration. A celebration of a momentous historical event, meant to honour the heroes of the past. It had been going on for years and had grown into a traditional day out for the men and their families. Of course, many came simply to enjoy the bands parading, their magnificent marching and their colourful costumes, all displaying their wide range of talents. It was hugely entertaining for the people that came to watch and add their support. Surely there was no harm intended, nor any disrespect to present day Catholics. Many Catholics were close friends after all, but just not in this parade. How could they be?

And yet, seeing his friend's reaction at the colourful pageant, the flags and the banners, another vague memory echoed within the boy. It was his father's words that came floating back to him as they had watched the beautiful fox disappear and his father had spoken disparagingly of the hunt. "And what's it all for anyway? A colourful show maybe, a spectacle to make a point of some sort?" Did Micky, like countless others, feel he was, in some ways, just part of the present-day fodder for these celebrations? If so, no wonder he had tried to make a joke of it all.

A Division of Colours

Chapter 8

The Trade

*When anger and fear, and pleasure and pain,
and jealousies and desires, tyrannise over the soul,
whether they do harm or not,
I call all this injustice.
(Laws 864 – Plato)*

May 1936 - (27 Years Earlier)

In the late Spring of 1936, still in the midst of the Great Depression, the long-anticipated day of Grace's sixteenth birthday arrived. Along with some of the other older children she set about her early Saturday morning chores before breakfast.

It was a beautiful bright May morning on The Liberty Bell. The morning sun had started to rise up from the horizon, its golden touch warming all it fell upon. The pastures for the cattle were now a long lush green, growth flourishing in the warmer earth and extended sunlight. The blue and white hydrangeas at the front of the house were in full bloom again, neatly cordoned off at the base by the large carefully placed white-washed stones. The last of the trumpet daffodils that ran along the side of the lane had long since given way to a host of other colourful wild flowers, as Nature granted each in turn their due measure of days in the sun. Even the Liberty Bell house and out-houses were looking immaculate, bright and impressive after Riley had finished white-washing all of them just a few days prior.

A glorious, wonderful day to be sixteen, Grace thought. She noticed Riley had quickly set about milking the cows, but this morning he had a long scowl on his face, for some reason. She had also seen that Beth had busied herself sorting out the younger children and preparing breakfast. Only the other children seemed to share in Grace's excitement about her birthday. Beth had looked particularly tense that morning, passing it off brusquely as a headache. With Riley already in a sombre mood, there was a sense something was amiss.

It was not unusual. Of late they both seemed to be constantly on edge for some reason, with hushed conversations and frequent rows. In the past few days, it had been as much as Grace could do to keep the children well out of the way of the overspill of her parent's tense and volatile emotions. Something was brewing, that was for sure, but Grace did not know what. She guessed it must be more money problems, as it frequently was.

Over breakfast, as they sat around the long old wooden table, Grace received the mandatory warbled rendition of 'Happy Birthday' from her siblings. It was a tradition of sorts. A little off-key and out of sync, but Grace readily accepted it all in good humour. She got the usual few presents from the older children too, in the form of hand-made cards and a few sweets and small treats. Among them were a few crayons so she could perform her little party trick. Grace was left-handed but had been obliged to learn to write with her right hand at school. In fact, she could write and draw with both hands, at the same time, hence her party trick.

The presents weren't much, but it was not in Grace's nature to complain. They had all learned to make the most of what they had. Besides, it was their company she valued, beyond the few little presents. Grace felt a great joy and closeness with her siblings and they in turn looked up to her as the elder sister.

So when Riley and Beth presented her with a number of unusually generous gifts, a brand-new dress, light cardigan, gloves, socks and even new shoes, Grace was surprised and delighted. She had never had so many nice new clothes at one time. She was full of gratitude, brimming with joy and filling up with tears. Fifteen just yesterday, but all this now that she was sixteen. She felt that sixteen was just the best age to be, and couldn't wait to try them all on.

Before she could begin to do so, Beth quickly announced that they all had to finish up breakfast and clear it away first. Then, a little tersely, that the whole family were to get dressed up after breakfast as they were all going out for a special occasion. She would let them all in on the surprise outing when everyone was dressed and ready.

Grace could hardly wait, but it was nearly mid-morning by the time the family was fed, washed and dressed, and all sitting around the kitchen table again, awaiting news of their outing. Even Riley was wearing his one and only Sunday best suit and tie. He was sitting back from the proceedings in his old armchair in the corner, the remnants of his early morning scowl still with him. Beth, was also in her Sunday best. She had her hat with the feather in it ready by her side, best black sturdy walking shoes, dark dress, with long elbow length matching gloves, and light shawl. Grace had donned her new clothes and, looking a picture, was sitting with a beaming smile, expectantly.

Beth, hesitated for an instant, then, silently admonishing herself, resolved to see it through. She drew a deep breath. "First, there's one more present," she said.

Without further preamble, Beth reached over and handed the final present to Grace to open. Grace, still smiling, took hold of it and began to open the loosely wrapped present. She held it up, for all to see, though she was not exactly sure just what the flimsy black garment was. She checked the packaging again and read aloud the label. She was puzzled and a little surprised to learn it was from their reclusive neighbour, Jessman.

"What is it? And why is old Jessman of all people giving me a present? I don't want anything from him, I don't even like him."

Beth, replied simply, "It's just a negligee." Then more determinedly, "Jessman is giving you a present, Grace, because today you are going to become his wife. He is coming over here in his car shortly to collect you, and we are all going together to the church to see you get married to him. Your father and I agreed you would marry Jessman, and for that he is going to help us keep the farm. It's all been arranged and it will all be fine."

For a second, the words bounced around Grace's head without traction or conveying any real meaning. Then slowly fragments of understanding began to seep through to her mind. There was an incredulous idea that she was to get married, that very same day. Married, her, on her sixteenth birthday. She hadn't even had a proper boyfriend yet. Married, to Jessman, but how could she marry Jessman? He was as old as her parents, older maybe. It didn't make sense.

She was shocked and repulsed at the prospect. Uncharacteristically, Grace's protests erupted in a series of loud emotional outbursts that rang through the kitchen. "What? No, no, no!! I'm not going to marry that weird old fart Jessman! Not today, on my birthday! Not on any day! Not ever! You can give him back his stupid present. I don't want it!"

"See," said Riley, finally finding something to latch onto, "I told you she wouldn't."

The hot anger flashed up in Beth, unused to being spoken to in such a rebellious way by her children. It was fuelled in part by the challenge she perceived in the outspoken disobedience of her daughter, and in part by what she saw as Riley's disloyal and spineless attempt to side with Grace, against her.

Beneath it all was also a much older anger, long buried unresolved hurts, held onto from her past. Ignited now by Grace and Riley's words and the underlying fear of being denied her carefully laid plans. Plans made in desperation to retain The Liberty Bell, that had begun seeding in her mind from that first visit of Jessman's many weeks before. Plans she could not deny then, and would not now. The Liberty Bell was her true heritage and must remain so, for all her family's sake, whatever the cost.

In an uncontrolled rage, Beth lurched forward and grabbed Grace fiercely by the arms, shaking her as she thundered out the words close into Grace's face.

"I've told you; you'll marry Jessman today, and marry him you will! Whether you like it or not! We have no choice girl; don't you understand, can't you see that? Just as you have no choice!"

Then, seeing Riley's looks of alarm, she thrust Grace back into the chair and turned away, at last recognising that the true source of her fears and anger was not Grace.

The force of Beth's wrath and words hit Grace like an unforgiving hurricane, hammering the harsh message home, removing any last semblance of uncertainty of intent. Grace knew only too well the dominant iron will her mother possessed when angry and obsessed, as she was now. Grace was just a sixteen-year-old girl, a child long conditioned to obeying her mother's forceful commands. There was no question of choice, not any more. The exuberant youthful euphoria she had felt just a short while ago had been snatched mercilessly from her. The beautiful, joyous morning of her sixteenth birthday, had been rent asunder in mere moments.

With a new reality, the thoughts of marrying Jessman again assailed Grace's mind. Jessman, as a forever husband, to live with, to spend all of her life with. Old Jessman, who sent her that scanty negligee as a birthday present. Her mind ran on, and her unwanted thoughts revolted her. She began to feel physically sick, gasping for air, waves of nausea rising, dizziness pulling at her. In a daze, she bolted for the sink and threw up among the few remaining breakfast dishes. Appalled at herself, and still in a state of shock, she withdrew and slumped to the floor, sobbing loudly.

Dimly she heard Beth shouting something behind her about cleaning up the mess, and not dirtying her brand-new wedding dress. Then Beth's voice, firm again, resolute, telling Grace to pull herself together. Repeating the ritual. Telling her again she had to marry Jessman so they could keep the farm. Telling her again she had no choice. Telling her she was going to get married today whether she liked it or not. And then more quietly, urging her to stop her crying as Jessman would be there soon to collect them.

Half turning, Grace glanced in desperation at her father. He caught her look and turned his face away holding his head in his hands. Compliant now, he said nothing to defend her. Hurt and humiliated, he shrunk further into the chair for refuge. "Oh, please no, not even my own father," Grace sobbed, then she too turned unsteadily away.

The tearful sobbing continued to flood through her. Her young mind still struggling, still resisting, unwilling to accept this hideous idea. Several of the children were crying too, some unsure what was wrong, but sensing the shock and trauma that their sister was experiencing. Suddenly, springing up, Grace ran out of the back door and into the yard, seeking air, seeking escape, any hiding place of refuge. Anywhere, just as long as it was away from here.

Half blinded with tears, unable to think straight, she ran back and forth. Then, in a panic, she ducked into the small outdoor toilet. Slamming the door closed behind her and bolting it, she sank down onto her knees, holding on tight to the handle with both hands to keep out the world that had turned on her. If she could just hide here, maybe no-one would find her. Maybe she might wake up from this nightmare. Trying now to quieten her breath, trying to stay out of sight. Hoping that somehow this impossible thing would just go away, if she could just stay here hidden out of sight for long enough. She could not get the fear of marrying Jessman out of her mind. No, she could not do that, no matter how much they wanted her to.

It was then that she heard them. The heavy, menacing footsteps approaching on the cobblestones. Coming closer, somehow sensing where she was. Mind tyrannised, body shrinking away, Grace retreated further into the back of the small toilet, squeezing herself against the wall, trying to melt into it.

The sudden urgent hammering on the door jolted through her, as if banging onto her own frail body. For a moment, she saw it all as if outside of herself, floating above it, the young girl trapped within, frightened mind desperately seeking escape. Then it was real again, her mother's frustrated angry voice ringing out, breaking through the flimsy veil of her mind's feeble attempt at self-protection.

Grace felt the weight of her mother's authority in the loud commanding, compelling voice. She felt her own hopelessness rise with it. Caught now, the black hooded crow-like eyes piercing through her feeble shelter, holding her captive, frozen in terror.

Grace could only watch helplessly as Beth's gloved hands sought to reach around the door lock, seeking a way through to prise it open. It was too much for her to bear. The scream rose within her, and at the top of her voice Grace wailed out her last desperate plea.

"Oh mammy, mammy. Please mammy no, no, please don't! Please, no!"

In the moments that followed, Beth had prised open the door and pulled her roughly from the outside toilet. She had dragged Grace back into the kitchen and pushed her limp body down into a chair. There, in front of Riley and the other children, a furious Beth had launched into a tirade, repeatedly scolding Grace for her disobedience, browbeating her eldest daughter into further submission. Riley had tried to interject, explaining to Grace more gently that she had to marry Jessman so he would pay off their debt, or they would all lose the farm and worse, the children could face starvation or be put into separate homes.

Beth angrily dismissed his gentler, more reasoned approach, instinctively sensing that way might lead to a different outcome and failure. Instead, she resolutely held firm, extolling the virtues of the marriage as the only solution, and a sensible business arrangement, now that Grace was of age.

With some satisfaction Beth revealed that in return for marrying Grace, Jessman had agreed to pay off nearly all of their debts. At her insistence, he had also agreed to return the lower pastures that his family had acquired those years ago. The Liberty Bell would again be what it once was. Grace's few numbed, mumbled protests were quickly dismissed. At the last, making it plain there was no alternative, Beth announced sharply that there was no longer a place in her home for Grace if she did not go through with the wedding.

In the low sobbing silence that followed, Beth, in an almost conciliatory tone, said, "He only seems old to you now because you are so young." Then, pulling herself back into the safety of her firmness, "You'll be marrying into wealth. Just be a dutiful wife Grace, and maybe one day when he's gone, that whole big farm of his will become ours."

The simple church wedding later that day was a quiet, dull formal affair. There were only a handful of invited attendees as witnesses. The shortened service was hurried and stale, both in setting and execution. Grace was subdued and resigned, mechanically going through the ceremony and the various administrative functions, until it was all official. The whole thing was in many ways an anti-climax after the terrifying events of the day.

Later, amidst all she had heard earlier that day, one thing resonated above all others in the mind of sixteen-year-old Grace. It was not in any of the many lecturing words of her mother, but in the few spoken by her father. What stayed in her mind, was that the fate of her brothers and sisters was dependent on her marrying Jessman. In going through with the wedding, she held tight to the hope that she might indeed be helping them. It was a fragile raft of hope to cling to in a churning sea of despondency and despair, but Grace hung grimly to it.

So on that fine day in May 1936, young Grace became Mrs. Jessman. The sixteen-year-old bride, and the groom, three times her age, became just another bland statistic in the records of the old parish church.

Chapter 9

Sam

All of us are born for a reason, but not all of us discover why.
Success in life has nothing to do with what we gain or accomplish.
It's what we do for others.
(Danny Thomas)

1936 - 1938

Whether Grace's marriage might later have been contested as a marriage contract made under duress, and possibly even invalided, mattered little in the way things were eventually to transpire. For the present, Beth's bitter trade had carried the day. The way Beth saw it, her trade had secured a larger and now more viable Liberty Bell for her and Riley and the children for the foreseeable future.

Jessman, a lonely mid-life bachelor, could certainly consider himself lucky to have gained such a lovely young bride for the sacrifice of a few acres of pasture land and some savings. Beth had even managed to secure significant wealth for Grace, with a rich husband into the bargain. As for love, well that was another matter altogether. Beth felt Grace might do well to remember one of her own favourite old sayings. "If you can't marry the man you love, then love the man you marry."

There were other viewpoints too of course. For unlike Beth, it was not this particular kind of wealth, nor indeed this kind of man, that young Grace treasured in her heart.

It is doubtful that Beth ever suspected that the consequences of the marriage trade she made that day would have such far-reaching effects. She thought she was acting in their best interests. She could not have foreseen that her trade would in time touch the lives of so many people in so many different ways, and the pain it would cause her own family. She did not know that she was, in a sense, opening Pandora's box, releasing a surge of harmful dark spirits that would come out to blight them all in one way or another. Perhaps it was in some ways fortuitous then, that alone of all these spirits, it was the great spirit Hope that did not flee from the opened Pandora's box. That it was Hope alone that remained.

Yet Beth did have fair warning of the consequences of her actions before she made her choice. It came in the shape of the telegram she received from her brother Daniel just before the wedding. Unbeknown to Beth at the time, Riley, perhaps burdened with feelings of guilt, had written to inform his sister, Rose, in Canada, about Beth's plans to marry Grace off to Jessman so they could retain the farm. When Rose told her husband Daniel, he was appalled that his sister Beth could even contemplate doing such a thing. He had immediately sent a telegram to Beth, begging her to call off the wedding. In his telegram, Daniel had made a passionate plea to his sister, as much for her own sake, as for that of Grace.

"As you seek ever to lead a Christian life sister, I beg you to re-examine your motives. You love your family dearly, but I fear your love of The Liberty Bell is blinding you. Mark my words well, no good can come of a marriage based on ill-intent. There is always a bigger price to pay."

Late that night, after the wedding was finished, a troubled Beth had long since retired to bed but was still unable to sleep. Her thoughts returned to her brother Daniel's telegram warning and the awful numbed look on Grace's face as she had gone through with the wedding ceremony.

"I did what had to be done for all our sakes," Beth whispered consolingly to herself. "It was the only way and there's no going back on it now. What's done is done."

It was indeed. Not very far away, in Jessman's house a young Grace was circling the kitchen table, brandishing a kitchen knife. Her brand-new dress was torn, her face and arms were bloody and bruised. For the present, at least, she was bravely managing to keep at bay the brutish approach of her drunken husband, impatient to collect his part of the day's trade.

It was inevitable that Jessman would not be kept at bay indefinitely. Over the course of the next few months, Grace was repeatedly beaten and raped. She fought against him, but he was much stronger than she. More often than not the assaults would happen late in the evening after Jessman had been drinking. He would sometimes apologise afterwards, promising to treat Grace better, if she would just love and accommodate his wants.

Instinctively, Grace did make efforts to find a better side to Jessman, to find the kindness and good that she felt was in everyone. Some days she tried to talk to him and gently encourage him to treat her as an equal, with equal rights. Sometimes it seemed that she was making progress, and things did improve a little. Often enough though, it was only a means to an end for Jessman, and he would revert to bullying habits when it suited him. Like any marriage, it needed the absolute commitment of both of them to make any real progress. Without that, there was little chance of moving forward to any sort of a sharing and caring based loving relationship. But as it was, they both held something back.

Grace held something of herself back, because she still feared him and, in her heart, wanted youth and love. As a bruised and battered young woman, she could not help but see Jessman as an unsavoury old man, with traits she could not condone, never mind grow to love. He held something back, because he saw her as just an immature young woman, little more than a girl, and more akin to his property now than his deserving equal. Like some universal law, in the holding back, nothing was given, so nothing much changed. The divide remained an unsurmountable chasm for both of them.

Her husband, Jessman, was after all simply a much older man who had been caught up in the fringes of an uncertain time of inequality. He failed to recognise that he was putting perceived male rights ahead of gentleness and respect, power ahead of moral justice, and lust ahead of love. While Grace, a once happy and high-spirited girl, was too often reduced to a fettered, bruised and battered young woman, paying the price that had to be paid.

It was, much as Daniel had foretold in his telegram, a marriage based on ill-intent. Grace might have run far away, escaped from the purgatory she was facing, but she could not do so. Young as she was, she held onto hope, recognising in some way that her family were dependent upon her, that somehow, she needed to endure her living hell for the sake of her young brothers and sisters.

As it was, on the few weekends when she was allowed to visit her own family, she could say little. Her mother would hear none of it, repeatedly rebuking her for not being a better wife, and she could not bring herself to tell her father. So, for the most part, Grace suffered in silence.

She might have become bitter and hardened with the kind of life she was now living, but Grace did not. She never lost her faith. Gradually, as she endured, and out of necessity, she recognised the need to let bitter and overwhelming thoughts go. Instead, in order to preserve the faint spark of joy and hope within her, she began to look for something in each day for which to be grateful. This simple practice became a habit with Grace that was to last a lifetime. It was part of her nature too that she would still try to consider the welfare of others. Paradoxically, it was in doing this, helping someone else in need, that paved the way for help to come to Grace from such an unexpected source.

Sam, Jessman's much younger brother with Down's syndrome, still lived in the house with them. At first Grace had little to do with Sam, as Jessman took care of his basic needs and, from long established habit, kept him largely at a distance from anyone else. Sam was encouraged to work outside as much as possible, and he seemed to enjoy and thrive on that. Grace knew very little about what people mistakenly referred to as the stigma of 'Mongol' children, other than the misguided empty rumours that she had heard from others. She considered Sam must have been fortunate to have managed to avoid being put into an institution when born, as she understood that was the usual way of things in Ireland.

She also wondered how he had managed to be so healthy and live so long, as again she had heard stories that many such children in institutions died quite young. It was hard to tell, but she guessed Sam must be at least in his late-twenties. Perhaps that might be a fair age by some standards. Yet, there he was, a bit on the small side, but sturdy and stocky and full of life. He was actively engaged on the farm, and this seemed to help keep him healthy and happy. He did his jobs willingly and he clearly felt that he was useful and needed, which of course he was. The active farm life in the open air certainly seemed to agree with him.

Sam was always very polite to Grace and it was only natural that Grace would gradually start to take more of an interest in him and get to know him better. She found he was much brighter and more insightful than she first thought. Grace had plenty to do around the farm herself, but somehow Sam helped to lighten up an otherwise dreary existence. His bright and cheery disposition and slightly quirky sense of humour, were all in contrast to the staid and sullen Jessman. Grace began to make more enquiries about him with Jessman too, and over time started to develop a better understanding.

Jessman's mother, a schoolteacher, had given birth to Sam late on in her life, when she thought she was no longer fertile. Despite pressures from her doctor and her friends, she had resolutely refused to send Sam to an institution. Instead, going against the societal norms at that time, she had directed all her efforts into looking after him in her own home. It was a brave yet far from easy task.

Sam had been a difficult baby and a very slow learner as a child. With unflinching perseverance over the next decade, his mother had managed to teach him to talk and function reasonably well. To the surprise of many, Sam had managed rudimentary reading and writing skills before his mother had passed away, a couple of years after his father. Sam's brother, Jessman, had made his mother a promise on her deathbed never to put Sam in an institution but to always look after him. To his credit, Jessman had kept his promise over the ensuing years.

By the end of her first year with Jessman, Grace had begun to step more and more into the role of taking care of Sam. She prepared all his meals, sorted out his clothes, and had insisted he wash himself much more often. She had noticed too that working outside so much, and unkempt, Sam would often have lice in his hair. It soon became a ritual that Grace would set Sam down on a regular basis and thoroughly wash and treat his hair. Even Jessman succumbed to her constant haranguing and gradually improved his own personal hygiene.

In their second year together, not only was Jessman's house clean and tidy beyond recognition, but both its male inhabitants had far better standards of hygiene, and no doubt, were much healthier as a result.

The friendship between Grace and Sam continued to grow as the months continued to pass. Having taken the trouble to find out a little more about him, Grace had found there was much more to Sam, the man-boy, than met the eye. He was sturdy and awkward, but also an able and genuinely caring person, and she really liked him. At his request, she started to read to him most evenings. It was not long before she was helping him with his own reading and writing again. Grace began to look upon him as part of her family, another of her siblings that she cared for and loved. As for Sam, he thrived under Grace's care and attention. He learned to love Grace too, though he looked on her more as a surrogate mother than as a sibling.

Sam had seen Jessman on many occasions bully Grace and physically assault her. When Jessman told him to go into his own bedroom and stay there, Sam would obey, lying on his bed or sitting on the floor, hands covering his ears, unable to keep out the shouts and screams completely. Though it disturbed Sam immensely, he would do as his older brother directed and did not interfere. Over time these situations became increasingly difficult for Sam to endure as his friendship and indeed love for Grace blossomed.

One evening everything changed. Jessman had just returned from an evening out, having had quite a few drinks. Like many men of his generation, too much alcohol not only made him drunk, but often belligerent and unpredictable too. As the evening out had progressed, and the alcohol flowed, he had started an argument with one of his colleagues. There had been a bit of a tussle, and Jessman had been sent home by the pub owner and told to go to bed and cool off.

Cooling off was the last thing on his mind, and once home he set about taking out his anger and frustrations on Grace. Sam was told to stay in his room. He lay on top of his bed, ears covered by his hands, trying to shut out the frightening raucous. Even then Sam heard Grace cry out, "No, get away from me!" Followed in another few seconds by what sounded like furniture being knocked over. Then, "Leave me alone, you're drunk!" As the barrage of blows reached his ears, Sam frantically buried his head in his pillow, but Grace's panicked scream still reached him. "No, stop please, you're hurting me!" Then in desperation, "Sam! Sam! Oh Sam, please help me!"

Sam, like his biblical namesake, could not ignore the repeated calling of his name. Tossing his pillow aside, he came hurtling into their room. He was just in time to see his older brother wrenching at Grace's clothes while trying to hold her. Then with a wide swing of his arm, Jessman punched Grace hard in the face. She buckled, dropping to the floor, blood streaming from her mouth. In an instant, Sam was at Grace's side, strong-arming Jessman and bundling him away from Grace. A drunken Jessman snarled at him savagely, "Mind your own business you half-wit! Go on, get back to your room now!"

Sam ignored him and just for a moment, turned his back on his brother to help Grace to her feet again. Angry and not thinking straight, a drunken Jessman rushed forward and lashed out at Sam too, knocking him aside. Once more he grabbed roughly at Grace who was still sobbing in pain. She wrestled and pushed past him to find shelter behind Sam as he righted himself. Sam turned back again to face Jessman. This time, where once fear of his brother had subdued him, a fury now rose in Sam as he saw close up the harsh injustice of Grace being bullied, beaten and abused.

For the first time in his life, Sam launched into a furious attack on Jessman, pushing him back with all the force he could muster and rapidly slapping hard at his face as he propelled him away. The bully confronted, Jessman was stunned and cowered away, arms trying to protect his pummelled face, as he was backed up into a corner. At last Sam stopped, panting with the exertion, holding Jessman rigid against the wall with one arm. Pointing the index finger of his other hand into the face of his brother, Sam shouted at him.

"No more! No more you hurt Grace, never ever again! You hear? Never again!"

The power and intensity in Sam's voice was immense. It had the desired effect. Jessman, overcome by Sam's strength and fury and brought abruptly into a more sober awareness, saw that Sam meant every word. His face reddened and sore from Sam's hard slaps, Jessman did not want to invite further onslaughts. He succumbed meekly and silently nodded his agreement.

After that eventful episode, Grace found that her married life became a little more bearable. Jessman was just as surly and difficult at times, but he begrudgingly gave Grace a lot more space and even a little more respect. His bullying assaults and coarse attempts to assert his rights of marriage, while not entirely forfeited, were no longer such an ever-constant frightening threat when Sam was around. The generous hearted Sam, a most unlikely of protectors, had made sure of that.

Grace's spirits lifted a little more from that day onwards. Slowly she started to regain some of her self-confidence which had suffered enormously at the hands of Jessman. It was not an easy journey back from being a young bruised and battered housewife, especially while she still had to live with Jessman under his roof. Nevertheless, she slowly improved, resigning herself to spending her life being the wife of a man she did not love, for the sake of her family.

She was also resolved to make of her marriage what little she could, to try to broker some kind of friendship level between them, and to see it through as best she could, though without any great expectations.

Grace was consoled in some measure by the knowledge, from the occasional visits Jessman permitted her to The Liberty Bell, that life for Beth and Riley and her siblings had improved significantly. Again, to his credit, from the day of their marriage Jessman had kept his part of the bargain and paid their debts for them, as he'd promised. He had also legally transferred ownership of the lower pastures. He had even given Riley some advice from time to time on how to manage The Liberty Bell farm, which unfortunately Riley would often choose to ignore.

As Grace's marriage rolled into its third year, the trade that Beth had orchestrated seemed to be playing out as planned, and looked like it might do so for the foreseeable future. As it happened though, the imminent onset of war and the birth of Grace's baby girl, Elizabeth, a couple of years later, would soon change all that.

A Time to Remember

Chapter 10

Mad Maude

By the time we are five, much of our personality has been formed. By then we've developed some fixed beliefs about ourselves and the rest of the world. Some of these beliefs we hold onto consciously, and others are buried in our subconscious. Having formed these beliefs, they rule us.
(Andrew Mathews)

1936 – Boxing Day, December 1938

Grace barely knew Mad Maude. That is to say, Grace didn't know her well, but then again few did. Certainly, when she first met her, Grace did not have any inkling of how much her own life would come to be impacted by this wild and impetuous young woman.

Mad Maude was not always known as Mad Maude. In fact, as far as she could recall, it was only a nickname given to her as a wayward child, that somehow seemed to stick. Maude first gained the nickname through her rebellious nature, and particularly, her love of fairgrounds. Her lack of fear of heights, recklessness, daredevil antics on even the most frightening of fairground activities, meant that her friends called her 'mad'. 'Mad Maude' had an easy ring to it, and in the beginning it was said with a certain awe and respect.

Nick-names, or labels, often attributed in early years, are mostly a passing thing. Given in the moment, sometimes they endure for a while, then fade with time. Sometimes, as in Maude's case, they endure longer. Whatever their nature, as we progress through teenage years and beyond, at times the label can take a firmer hold, especially when the bearer starts to identify with it. It is then that the nick-name can evolve to become a self-label. Reinforced by our own beliefs it may embed itself ever deeper into the heart and psyche of the bearer.

Maude relished her Mad Maude daredevil label. With a little encouragement from her friends, she sought out more and more opportunities to live up to it. Opportunities to act outrageously, to appear to be wild and reckless, free of all responsibilities. The 'Mad Maude' tag grew with her. In time, she forgot it was just a nick-name and began to believe it was true and a part of her. In a sense, her self-label began to assume a power all of its own, pushing the boundaries ever closer towards behavioural oddities. Driven by Maude's deepening belief, and choice, it clung fast to her like some kind of shell, a hard crust of those behaviours that helped define it.

In the beginning her Mad Maude persona had been an easy and benign kind of mutualistic symbiosis. It blended in well with her natural adventurous self, if anything even boosting her confidence. Slowly that had begun to change as a more parasitic nature started to surface. That was when she started to feel her actions more driven, she obligingly going along for the ride.

The person who had begun simply as Maude was receding. The practiced behaviours that became habits evolved and expanded. In combination they culminated in the personality of Mad Maude, and more often dominated. In just a few years they had become a fixed integral part of her. This chosen self-image had, in effect, become her new norm.

By early 1936, when Mad Maude was in the last year of her teens, she had already established her reputation as a brash and rebellious, slightly odd young woman, with a devil may care attitude and wild nature. During the latter part of the depression years of the 1930s, this was in stark contrast to how most other women behaved. It was a time when women, who had not long gained the right to vote and enter parliament, were generally expected to be reticent and demure, remaining in the background. A time when, in the eyes of many, women's primary role was to become reliable housewives, cooking and cleaning, and raising children, while their husbands went out into the world to do the real work. Mad Maude did not fit into the role of that compliant woman at all easily, nor indeed did she want to.

As it was, this rebellious and not unattractive young woman, who seemed to care little for societal norms, had a certain magnetic appeal to many young men of that era. Finding that she had quite a choice when it came to it, Maude was not slow to learn how to manipulate and use this to her advantage. The haughtier and more aloof she behaved, the more fascinated and intrigued the young men around her seemed to be by her outlandish behaviours.

As part of her exuberant role playing, at times Maude took to parodying her film screen idol, Marlene Dietrich, especially in her portrayal of the notorious and sultry Shanghai Lily. It was all still part of an act, like slipping on a coat. A coat that was Mad Maude. In keeping with her practiced act, she kept her feelings for these young men on a superficial level, her emotions at a safe distance.

Though she may not have known it back then, Maude would turn out to be less of a sultry Shanghai Lily, but much more a cold hard Estella to a captivated Pip. Maude would have laughed haughtily at the comparison to Dicken's heartless Estella of course, but in many subtle ways that likeness might have been a little closer to the truth than Maude would ever have cared to acknowledge.

In time, and in some ways inevitably, one young man in particular did catch Maude's eye. He did not chase after her like some, but was more reserved. The young man was intelligent and dark and handsome, with a quiet manner that she found was an appealing contrast to her extrovert forceful nature.

As was Maude's way, it was a whirlwind relationship, that she largely orchestrated. She was attracted to this young man from the beginning. He was different to most others and she thought with him she might find the happiness and contentment that had up to now somehow eluded her. She determined to make him hers.

The young man seemed every bit as smitten by Maude. Indeed, although more reserved than most, he was besotted by her. They were both swept along, excitement and fun, alcohol excesses and hangovers, and all too quickly it led to the inevitable and predictable obligatory wedding. Before the year was out Maude was a married woman, and just like Estella's besotted Pip, the young man had become very much Maude's young man.

Despite their hurried race to the alter they began well enough. They shared dreams of an exciting and happy future, building a home and a life together. It would all be so easy. They would chart their future together and nothing would stand in their way. They had only a vague awareness then of the unrest that was building in Germany, a country spurred on by a deluded vision-driven Chancellor. At the time, though it made them a little uneasy, it did not hold much interest for them. They had no inkling of the dramatic effect it would have on the world around them. Or just how much it would impact on them personally.

They managed to rent a small stone cottage with a thatched roof, not too far from where Maude's in-laws lived. It wasn't much, small and in need of repairs like many other country cottages, but it was a start. The young man was a highly skilled carpenter and coach-builder, who could turn his talented hands to almost anything. He readily applied his skills to making items of furniture and repairing their little house. Maude made it comfortable enough inside, a place they could call home.

The shifting hormonal changes that came with her first pregnancy had a strange effect on Maude, very much more than might have been anticipated. Somehow for the young woman the advancing prospect of motherhood was both terrifying and wonderful at the same time. At one moment gloriously happy, the next depressed, apathetic and listless. She dreaded the looming loss of her independence and freedom. At times the thoughts of staying home, feeling trapped into a life of cooking and cleaning, looking after a small baby, slipped out of control and sent her head spinning.

The reason for these recurring thoughts and her grief was complex. To her confused thinking and conditioned perspective, they often foreshadowed a kind of life style that would clash endlessly with a free and easy Mad Maude way of living. While a part of her wanted a family, at the same time another part did not want to give up the freedom and abandonment of responsibilities she was enjoying as a young woman. A woman, she thought, daring to live a care-free reckless life in a man-biased world.

Try as she might, these conflicting and encroaching thoughts, particularly of her perceived loss of freedom, would not cease. At times these thoughts threatened to overwhelm Maude and she felt suffocated. It seemed like wave after wave of them came, thrashing against a sea-wall that was the shell of the persona she had built around herself. And yet, despite all this, there were also more peaceful softer moments too, when the waves quietened.

In those few quieter moments, a lingering, deeper part within Maude yearned for motherhood and the baby that she knew she would love. It was something Mad Maude's outer shell could not completely obliterate. Something that was still able to send a glimmer of hope through her for an acceptance of this new way of living.

Mad Maude's first baby girl was born in the Summer of 1937. They named her Pearl, their treasure. Pearl, like her namesake, was a treasure indeed. She too had, in some ways, been formed like a valuable pearl within the soft centre of a shelled mollusc. But this baby would never be like the hard pearls of nature. No, and it would not be too long before, in an uncommon act of kindness beyond her early years, the child's simple gesture would demonstrate the warmest of hearts.

Pearl was an easily contented baby and gradually with time Maude found that her earlier dark thoughts and fears had largely subsided. She enjoyed the novelty of motherhood and taking Pearl out and about in the pram to show her off around the neighbourhood. Meanwhile, her young man's work at a local firm was going well and his skills were much in demand.

Their marriage, which had been more than a little turbulent at times, seemed to be settling and to be on a better footing as Winter days started to give way and signal an early Spring of 1938. They made time some weekend mornings to walk together in the surrounding countryside, the young man even taking a bold turn once in a while to push the pram along. Sometimes they detoured to pick a few cheerful sun-touched yellow primroses or some startling white snowdrops, emerging from the grassy hedgerow banks. Sometimes they strayed along the edge of a small wood, where they might also pick a few early daffodils and some brilliant bluebells to brighten up their home.

For many years, when Maude would look back, it was the fragmented glimpses of these simple memories that she would hold most dear, and during these quiet times that she would feel she had been most content and at ease.

It was as they advanced through their second year together that Maude found she was pregnant again. At first, they were both delighted, even though it was very soon after Pearl. While they looked forward to their second addition to the family, a familiar pattern started to emerge. As her hormones began to churn with the pregnancy, Maude's erratic mood swings again became more noticeable.

As Spring advanced towards Summer, Maude could do little to resist the inner swing of wayward thoughts and strange feelings that were again arising within her along with her advancing pregnancy. It seemed that her feelings and emotions were being tossed up and down, out of her control, like some small dinghy, bobbing unpredictably in a wild turbulent sea.

This time, with this second pregnancy, her inner turmoil was more acute. Her thoughts of being entrapped, isolated, growing as the weeks passed. She started to dwell on things more, often trivial things, sometimes allowing her mind to project irrational images. She slept more and more. Fitful at first, then gradually descending into a heavy slumber. A slumber that clung to her when she finally awoke, making her feel groggy and incoherent.

Sometimes a sleeping Maude would imagine herself surrounded by hordes of weeping children. Only to find, as her waking senses returned, it was just Pearl, needing her attention. Maude felt increasingly driven to seek relief in medication or alcohol, but instinctively held back as best she could, given her pregnant condition. As it was, she began to let herself go, and was putting on an excessive amount of weight, far beyond the needs of her pregnancy.

Not surprisingly, it was as this second pregnancy progressed, that Mad Maude's relationship with her young husband again began to falter. There had always been disagreements, but usually the young man relented for the sake of peace and let Maude have her way. Now though, fuelled by Maude's aggressive mood swings and increasingly irrational thinking, the rows became more frequent. It was as if Maude would arise from one of her long dark and sombre moods, and deliberately find something, anything, to argue and fight about.

The young man was at a loss as to how to cope. He could not recognise the patterns of what in later years might be called bi-polar illness, and possibly even some elements of lingering postpartum depression, nor even that Maude might be in need of more specialist attention. Instead, he sought avoidance and time out. He started to spend more time at work and out of the home, away from Maude, avoiding her. It began as a temporary respite, but such habits are easily formed. In turn Maude was left more alone with Pearl and her thoughts, inadvertently fuelling her own worst fears of isolation and entrapment. As the pregnancy advanced, and tensions mounted, inevitably it put more pressure on their relationship and their marriage.

Maude's second baby was born just over a year after Pearl in the late Summer of 1938. She was fortunate to have another healthy and happy baby girl. They named her Nancy, Nan for short.

By the time Winter of that year had come around, a weary Maude had again started to surface from the worst of her erratic mood swings. It had taken a little longer this time around, and though much improved, she was still susceptible to them. Maude was now more often withdrawn and wrapped up in her own little world. A world of fantasy she wasn't much inclined to share with her young man.

It was not that Maude had made any sort of explicit decision to withdraw from her husband or family obligations. Rather, it may have been more a reflection of bi-polar tendencies that she was so often just plain bored with family life. She would daydream and drift endlessly along with her fantasies of some other more exciting life. At times she recognised that things were not quite right, but she did not know why.

Maude's erratic tendencies and withdrawals remained outside the field of her young husband's understanding. So, as was the way of many young men, he returned to his earlier habit of spending more of his evenings out of the house, drinking with his friends in the local pubs. The more this habit became entrenched, the more his escape from the home was exacerbating the situation. Once again, Maude was finding herself too often left at home alone with the children. Left alone with her wandering thoughts.

That Christmas came to their rescue, or at least partly so. Somehow the season gave them the much-needed time together and impetus to take a fresh look at themselves and their relationship. They were both still young and new at the practice of marriage, but they both still wanted to make their relationship work. With just a little more opening up on both their parts, they resolved anew to try to make more of an effort on their marriage.

They were due to spend Boxing Day of 1938 with the young man's parents, a long but manageable country walk away. They had wrapped up warm, for there was a chilly light breeze, though fortunately the yellow-white Winter sun shone out bright from a clear blue sky. The bracing mid-morning walk, alongside the still frosted hedgerows and through the narrow country lanes, surrounded by sparkling green countryside, again helped to lift their spirits. Nature, the great healer, was offering her gift of slow gentle healing to those who could make time to embrace it.

They laughed a little on the way as Maude responded positively to the surroundings and the light exercise, linking arms and pushing the big pram along with Pearl and Nan snugly tucked inside it. For a while they could put aside all their cares and just enjoy this time walking along this country lane together. There was something special about it, as if for a few moments Nature had swept aside their human troubles and held them contented in her arms. They both felt it and neither of them seemed in any hurry to reach their destination.

Their destination at Maude's in-laws lay just a little way ahead of them. It was to be a large family gathering plus a few invited friends. The young man had three brothers and four younger sisters. The two older brothers, Bert and Harry and their wives would be there, each with a young daughter. His four sisters, Valerie, Freda, Lucy, and young Hazel would also be there, and of course his younger brother Clive.

There had been a bit of a gap to the birth of young Clive and his youngest sister, Hazel, neither of whom had yet started school. Liza, their mother, had joked that when her youngest daughter had arrived, her three eldest brothers had promptly decided it was high time they left! For they had indeed all left home within just a matter of weeks of Hazel's birth.

It was a quirky family too in some ways. Of the eight children, three pairs of siblings shared the exact same birthday. When for example, the youngest daughter, Hazel, was born, it was on a Christmas Eve, the same day that the eldest daughter, Valerie, celebrated her birthday.

Liza was an able mother and a very kindly wise woman. She was astute, and knew well how to manage her home and large brood with the right blend of mirth, gentleness and firm guidance. Liza was well regarded in the neighbourhood too. She did not seek to interfere in the lives of her neighbours, but often found herself being sought out by them for wise counsel.

Being a good listener, she did not usually offer advice unless it was requested. Then, in her calm and caring way, she could usually find the right wise words for those who were ready to receive them. As often as not, her few well-placed questions helped to draw out into the light even the thorniest underlying issues. It was little wonder Liza had an enduring reputation as a good and charitable neighbour in the area.

The father, Bob, was an intellectual of sorts, who now worked in education. His role was to encourage and cajole Ireland's thousands of wayward child labour to attend schools. On the face of it he was a well-respected and outwardly pleasant and sociable man. However, behind that façade was a man of many mixed emotions, and understandably so.

Bob had been an army Sergeant Major, one of the youngest in the first World War, and was a decorated hero. He had fought for Britain in France against the Germans, and had earned medals for outstanding bravery in the death-trap trenches during the Battle of the Somme. The 36th Ulster Division was among the first sent into the Somme and had acquitted itself exceptionally well, but with eight out of every ten of these young men of Ireland ending up as casualties in the war, they had been nearly decimated.

Not surprisingly, Bob rarely spoke about it, for those were memories that could not be shared. Like many other survivors, he kept the horrors of war to himself, but he had not escaped it unscathed. How could he? He had seen far too many of the men under his command terribly maimed, or die violent deaths alongside him in the muddy, rat-infested trenches. His younger brother had been one of those, mortally wounded in one of the many attempts to push back the Germans. It was all an impossible situation that

Bob had to endure. Like many other survivors, Bob died a little inside with each new atrocity that they suffered.

Hero he might be, but Bob had long since carried the pain of the awful memories of war with him. He had suffered post-traumatic stress for years, and yet compared to some, he was considered to have been one of the lucky ones.

Although now very much improved with the passage of the years, there were still times when Bob could not shake the depression. Like many others deeply disturbed by the atrocities of that awful war, in desperation he would try to drown his memories in alcohol. During some of those heavy drinking bouts, he could at times become confused, lose control and get aggressive. While alcohol may have temporarily helped him to escape the traumas, as with many such remedies, it came at a heavy price.

Bob's occasional lapses into drinking caused his family much stress and worry. It also allowed the in-built propensity for alcohol addiction that ran through Bob's genes to surface and take hold more often. Liza did her best to help him cope and keep his forays into aggressive oblivion to a minimum. This she did exceptionally well. Indeed, it was largely due to her stoic efforts that for the most part, they were still able to enjoy a relatively happy and stable family life together. However, it was no coincidence that having seen how it affected their father, her two eldest sons completely abstained from alcohol of any kind.

As Maude and her small family group arrived at the country cottage and knocked on the door, they were immediately welcomed inside with open arms by a jubilant Liza.

"Come in, come in! Ahh, it's so grand to see you both again, come on in and make yourself right at home. Ohh, Good Lord, sure would you look at the size of those two wee youngsters! Oh, aren't they just lovely!"

The rest of the family were just as welcoming. There was a good fire burning and the house was already warm and bright, with many colourful decorations and a large Christmas tree on display. Everyone seemed so happy and relaxed and able to get on well together from the outset, as some families do experience, especially at Christmas time. Even the house itself seemed to have such a convivial atmosphere, that it was almost possible to feel the warm friendly nature of its kindly matriarch radiating from the very walls.

Liza had invited an additional guest along for lunch that Boxing Day. They had become good friends when the young woman, a neighbour, had on occasion helped Liza to look after her two youngest children. Now she and some of Liza's other family members were busy helping Liza to finish the preparation of the food in the kitchen, and beginning to serve up the generous Boxing Day lunch.

The young woman wore a wedding ring and looked to be in her late teens. She was unassuming and reserved, yet had a composed calm presence that belied her young years. She had such an easy relaxed way with the younger children that they in turn seemed drawn to her. Her hair was jet black and she was slim and attractive, with swarthy skin, dark eyes and a warm smile. She introduced herself simply as Grace.

Chapter 11

The Untimely Grim Reaper

Our dead are never dead to us, until we have forgotten them.
(George Eliot)

Boxing Day 1938 - December 1940

It had been a fitting end to that Christmas of 1938. One that both Maude and her young man would look back on with fond memories in the troubled war years that lay just ahead. As they had walked gaily back home from Liza's cottage that Boxing Day evening, Time Magazine's 'Man of the Year', the little German Chancellor, was about to bring havoc into their lives, and indeed millions of others.

Like many of their friends, they had heard of how Hitler had ignored the Treaty of Versailles and built a powerful army, intent on recovering German lands that had been confiscated after the Great War. He had seemingly worked economic wonders and restored the national pride of the German people, even if he was increasingly leading them towards conflict with the rest of Europe. Everyone it seemed had heard the rumours that foretold of a coming war, but largely chose to ignore it, for as long as they could.

Yet, it was not just the war with Germany that was to cause Maude to make her heart-wrenching choice in just a few more years. A fateful and painful choice that would reverberate through the ages to come and haunt her until she was finally laid to rest. No, it was not just the war. Maude's choice would be predicated on a much more personal level than the strife of war.

It would seem that universal laws of cause and effect play out in our lives and continue unabated, whether or not we are able to recognise the patent or latent connections between them. For Maude and her young husband, it was perhaps one dreadful event in particular that would tip the balance and finally culminate in Maude making the choice that would change the course of their lives forever.

As Maude walked briskly along towards home that Boxing Day, huddled up together with her young husband, Pearl and Nan once again obligingly fell asleep in the pram. The young couple were enjoying the walk in the crisp but clear moonlight evening. They were feeling full and well contented, having eaten a hearty Boxing Day lunch, and then stayed around long enough to finish up the leftovers for a wholesome late afternoon tea. It had been a thoroughly enjoyable day, a rare event for the two of them in recent times.

There had of course been the few awkward lapses, especially when Maude had become a bit more opinionated and talkative than necessary, aided more than a fraction by the luncheon wine and her changeable moods. Things could have taken a turn for the worse, but their host, Liza, with her usual tact and diplomacy had managed to lighten things up easily enough, with an adroit change of subject here, and a few gently spoken reminders of the season there. She kept the peace and the conversation moving along on an even keel. The rest of her family, particularly Liza's eldest daughter, Valerie, had readily picked up on Liza's cues.

All in all, it had been a very cordial and successful family day together. As Valerie had whispered quietly to her brother as he was leaving. "Our dah was blessed with knowledge and intellect. But did you notice how it's our mah who draws upon the deeper well of wisdom when it comes to dealing with people and keeping the peace?"

She was right of course. Without effort, Liza who was so observant and attuned to the people around her, could readily pick up on their feelings, and if needed, could gently guide the play of the orchestra in front of her. It was a talent she had developed over the ages and had once again used to good effect that day.

There was something else too about that day that had intrigued Maude's young man. It puzzled him, yet in an odd sort of way it also felt like a kind of unfettering. In another slightly disturbing way, it also carried with it an uncomfortable sense of foreboding. As he had sat and talked, sometimes looking around and observing the unfolding interactions of the children and Maude and Grace and all his family members about him, it was as if something had subtly shifted. Something over which he had little or no control.

He had wondered idly if it was perhaps just something to do with the congenial atmosphere that always seemed to pervade his mother's house, in stark contrast to his own. Certainly, that homely contented feeling he sensed so acutely there that day, was very different to the colder disconnected feelings he could sometimes experience at home. He said nothing of it, for it was not something he could yet understand or put into words.

Something might have also have stirred in Grace too back then at that memorable Boxing Day lunch at Liza's home in 1938. For Grace everything was still a little new, especially being in Liza's home with her family that day. A little unsure of herself at first, she had just tried to be herself. She had found, that somehow that was often the right and natural response to most things.

Grace was still a flowering young woman, mature yet not quite in her prime and only gradually becoming accustomed to the company of adults. As she relaxed and joined in with the festivities, Grace found she had thoroughly enjoyed the day. Liza and her family had made her feel so welcome. It was odd, but she felt that she almost belonged there with Liza and her family that day. It was a feeling of being at home much more than in her own house or even in The Liberty Bell.

Throughout that Boxing Day too Grace could not help but notice Maude. She saw that Maude could often be so abrasive when the mood took her. Maude's barbed little sarcastic comments were not reserved for anyone in particular, but a number had come Grace's way. However, Grace had chosen to let things pass and not to let Maude's problems steal her own peace of mind or spoil her day.

She noticed also that Maude's husband seemed to sense the discomfort that Maude could cause around her and that he and his sister Valerie, and of course Liza, had quickly intervened to lighten things up again when needed. Grace had appreciated their kindness but wondered why it was that Maude could be so moody and caustic for no apparent reason.

The Winter months quickly passed into Spring and Summer and eased gently into Autumn. By the time the inevitable war with Germany was finally declared on 3rd September 1939, Britain had already accelerated its preparations on both the home-front and in the armament factories. Although conscription was not enforced in Northern Ireland, some fifty thousand able-bodied men and women, aged between eighteen and forty, volunteered to join the fighting forces. Many thousands of others, while not actually joining the fighting forces, went into supportive work service of one kind or another, all as part of the civilian war effort. Life in Ireland was about to change.

Despite a slow, sluggish start, the people of Northern Ireland soon became a vital part of a massive campaign to build ships and planes, munitions and armaments of all shapes and sizes. Changes flowed through the country, touching everyone. Much of the land was already taken up with arable farming, but now even more was ploughed up as the country took on the role of supplying food to help feed the burgeoning British troops.

Flax production increased six-fold as the linen factories in and around a vibrant Belfast, aptly dubbed 'Linenopolis', churned out vast arrays of Irish linen products. Among these were immense quantities of parachutes and literally millions of shirts for soldiers. Mighty Harland and Wolff, makers of the Titanic, had for some time been directed to focus on the critical production of modern war ships, to further supplement Britain's formidable navy. In the Belfast shipyard areas too, the rope factories were producing enough hemp netting and rope to wrap around the globe many times over.

Maude's young man was part of the war support effort to keep Britain's pilots supplied with air-worthy planes. In the beginning, he found himself assigned to the busy city of Belfast, putting his much-needed skills to good effect in the production of component parts and the assembly of planes. This meant spending a bit more time away from Maude, as with the long working hours and demands of work, he was sometimes obliged to spend nights in Belfast. He was apprehensive of the effect the war and the added stress of his temporary absences might have on her, and more to the point, on their relationship and young family.

To his surprise, he found Maude seemed content to stay at home in those first months of the war. She looked after the two children and fortunately found plenty of things to do in the neighbourhood to keep her occupied. Even as the long dark nights of Winter crossed over into the new year of 1940, the war was still something of a novelty for Maude. Its deadly scythe had not yet touched Ireland's shores, but was largely confined to the continent.

Although Maude helped locally with some perfunctory civil defence preparations for the war, somehow it did not yet seem at all real for her. To Maude it was still just another exciting diversion, just something different, a welcome temporary escape from the normal routine of everyday life.

During these first months Maude and her young man made a point of visiting Liza regularly when he was able to get back home, taking their children, Pearl and Nan, with them. Liza, partly out of concern for the welfare of her growing number of visiting grandchildren, and partly as an excuse to see more of her family, had asked her son to make oak fire surrounds and screens for the two open fireplaces in her house. Maude's young man had duly obliged, spending the few spare hours he had at his mother's house, attentively crafting functional fireguards that were also beautiful works of art.

On a few of his visits Liza had managed to gather together other members of her household who also happened to be available. Having survived one war and fearful of what might yet happen, Liza knew the value of family gatherings. She and Bob, a battle-scarred husband, knew only too well why war, the untimely grim reaper, was called the robber of youth and breaker of hearts.

So for them, especially in times of war, every single opportunity for family gatherings was to be appreciated and treasured. Fate rarely chose to announce which was to be the last appearance of one or more of them. All that would be left would be the many little things, the favoured empty chair, the photograph on the mantlepiece, the hat left on the hook, and the worn shoes by the doorstep. A hollow emptiness, yet somehow these little things still echoed the wordless words of the loved ones who had left them.

Liza had already begun to look upon her young friend and neighbour, Grace, as part of her family now and included her when she could. For her part, Grace had readily welcomed the opportunity to become a regular visitor. She now looked upon Liza not only as her trusted and loved mentor, but in many ways as her surrogate mother.

To Grace, Liza's home was a heaven-sent sanctuary, offering her the solace she so badly needed. Needless to say, it was no wonder she visited regularly. It was a place where she was always made to feel welcome, where she was consistently treated with kindness, as an equal and with respect, in contrast to her lowly status in her own home. For that, Grace would be forever grateful to Liza and her family.

It was not long before the eerily quiet start to the war on the home front in Britain and Ireland began to change. The phoney war was about to give way to the onset of the real war. Hitler's well-prepared war machine had begun to gather momentum and increase its reach over Europe. By mid-1940 Germany had brushed aside Belgium, Holland and then France, having already easily taken Denmark and Norway. France had fallen all too quickly. Despite its lauded mighty forces, the French army was out-manoeuvred and ripped apart by the blistering speed of the blitzkrieg invasion of the drug-fuelled German ground troops.

Acutely aware that it was England's turn next, Churchill, the newly elected Prime Minister, searched his biblical readings of the Psalms, for something to rally his nation for the coming onslaught. It turned out to be his magnificent 'finest hour' speech.

As expected, Hitler had paused only briefly after taking France. Then he had turned his gaze across the English Channel towards Britain. His aim was simple; wipe out the British air force with Goring's formidable Luftwaffe, and when the skies were cleared, mount a massive unstoppable invasion by land.

Just before the fall of France, Maude's young man had been transferred from Belfast to the newly built Hawker Aircraft factory at Langley, on the western edge of London. He was helping to build, among other things, the Hurricane airplanes that would play a crucial role in the Battle of Britain and the rest of the war. At first it was a busy but untroubled transition for him. He was working long hours with a fine group of conscientious men, but in the early stages was still very much on the periphery of any real war action.

He took to writing letters to Maude in the late evenings, and it soon became a regular routine for at least one censored letter to find its way through to her in the week. She looked forward to reading them as he kept them light and simple. Interestingly Maude also appreciated the beautiful handwriting on the page. Somehow, even in his absence, the regular flow of the carefully measured script and the reassuring words helped to soothe Maude in a way she could not explain.

On 10 July 1940, the aerial war in Britain and Ireland began in earnest. The Luftwaffe commenced their reign of terror with an assault on the ships protecting the English Channel. For the next four months the British Summer skies hosted the aerial battle that was both hauntingly spectacular and utterly savage in its intensity. As historians have recorded, it was a pivotal battle in the war with Germany. At stake was everything that the British people knew of freedom and their way of life.

Soon enough the tone of Maude's young man's letters began to change. As the brutal war in the skies reined mercilessly on, he, along with millions of others, started to realise the harsh reality of what was already happening and what could lie ahead. Almost daily it seemed, there was the loss of more and more pilots and planes. As the race to repair or replace them became critical, his work was becoming ever more demanding and urgent. Like those around him, he too was becoming noticeably more tense and stressed as the war gradually began to eradicate any semblance of normal life.

When he did get the odd half a day off work, he would go into London, just a short train ride away. He and a few of his work mates would seek out somewhere to let off steam and get drunk. Even if only briefly, it was their temporary escape from the intensity and pressures of their working days. Then, while they still could, they would stagger back into Langley in the evening, only to begin the cycle all over again the next morning. When he was permitted a couple of days leave, he would go back to Ireland and his wife and family. Maude and his two young girls would be there to greet him. Depending on how the mood took her, sometimes it was a warm and welcome greeting from Maude, sometimes it was not.

In September 1940, in a massive retaliation for the bombing of Berlin, Hitler shifted the focus from day-time aerial battles to night-time bombings of British cities. This was another significant turning point in the war. No longer a battle waged mostly in the air between armed forces, it now brought the bloody war right to the doorstep of thousands of civilians. Many lost their lives as their homes and workplaces were destroyed by the unseen enemy in the night. Hitler's blitz of British cities would continue for months to come, right through the Winter of 1940 until late Spring of the following year. With homes no longer the safe haven they had once been, the British way of life was being undermined, if not quite eroded.

It was also around September 1940, that Maude found herself

pregnant again. Once again, a similar pattern of rollercoaster emotions mirrored her previous pregnancy. The temporary elation of having another child was quickly replaced with irrational worry and depression. She fretted that she would become even more house bound and have yet another mouth to feed on scarce wartime rations. She worried about losing the war and her life being cut short. Most of it began with a thread of truth, but then her emotions would shred that truth and run riot.

As Maude's pregnancy progressed and her emotional turmoil grew, their home became less and less a safe and stable retreat in the country where her young man could find peace and rest on the few home visits he was permitted. They did have their moments when things went well of course, but once again their relationship was becoming strained.

Perhaps with the added stress of war, they found it was more difficult to bring themselves back from the edge of looming arguments. Even their occasional visits to Liza's house, normally a sanctuary for all who came there, started to lapse into just another forum for venting bitter discontent with the world at large and each other.

By mid-November of that year, after Germany had carried out its massive 'Moonlight Sonata' bombing blitz on Coventry, leaving its beautiful old cathedral in ruins, Maude's third pregnancy had already begun to show. Some of her friends noticed her changing state and for a while it became the topic of their enquiries. Often it was just innocent enquiries, such as, "Oh, Maude you're so lucky, another wee baby on the way. When is it due? Do you want a boy or a girl?"

Sometimes a moody Maude would just ignore them or reply bluntly, "It will be born early next year and I don't give a damn what it is as long as the little mite is healthy." If Maude happened to be in a better mood, she might add, "Well, if you must know, we have two girls already and so it might be quite nice if we had a son this time." What she didn't share with them was that she had already chosen a name if it was to be a boy. In fact, once or twice she had dared to call the growing life within her, Jack.

It was just a few days before Christmas 1940, when she was entering her third trimester, that Maude had her miscarriage.

There had been few warning signs, other than a little cramping and a few spots of bright red blood. It happened in the very early hours of the morning while her two girls slept and Maude was alone. She had been woken by the cramping and early pains, only to realise with horror what was happening. Her waters had broken and her body was in the beginning stages of labour.

For the next few hours Maude wept and screamed her way through the whole long excruciatingly painful process. That pain was made all the worse knowing that her unborn child was already lifeless, or very soon would be. Maude felt utterly helpless to stem the tide as her body went through its time-honoured ritual of expelling the rejected foetus within her.

Desperately her mind sought answers for why this should be happening to her, and why now. She could not think what she might have done wrong, and anyway all that was futile now. Then once more she succumbed to the all-pervading agonising pain. As the cycle carried remorselessly onwards, and she neared the point of exhaustion, she had a vague sense that for some reason she was being robbed of the miracle within her. At this moment there was no way to understand why.

When it was finally over, and the still born form had been expelled from her body, Maude was emotionally drained and exhausted. She could not bring herself to do anything at all, other than just lie there on the bed sobbing and staring at the ceiling. All the while she averted her eyes from the blood-soaked bedclothes and anything else that might reside there. Afterwards she began to feel numb and cold, physically and emotionally. Then, for a while she fell still and silent, almost trance like, body immobile and mind deliberately obliterating the sea of red that surrounded her.

Later, when young Nan's awakening cries rang out from the other small bedroom, something within Maude responded and urged her mind back. Slowly she arose from the side of her bed. Painfully she pulled off the remains of her bloody night garments, and somehow managed to pull on some clothes. Then, not once looking back at the bed, she closed the door tight behind her and staggering along went to see to the needs of her two children.

It was not until quite some hours later that Maude found the energy to wash and change into a fresh set of clothes. Returning to her bedroom and still carefully avoiding looking at the bed, she took what she needed and closed the door tight behind her once more. Alone with her two children in a small house in the country she somehow managed to get through the day, resting when she could.

That night she shared Pearl and Nan's little bedroom, finding sleep in fits and starts, body still slowly seeping and racked with pain, but at last beginning the long slow healing physical process. Her mind however, was still numbed by the whole awful experience. As she drifted in and out of sleep it yielded up a strange mix of thoughts and feelings. Uppermost was an acute sense of loss and disappointment. Just behind that, feelings of guilt and anger were beginning to mingle with the mounting apprehension of what still lay in the other room.

A Time to Forgive?

Chapter 12

Bury My Heart

Not to love is not to live, or it is to live a living death.
(Ralph Waldo Trine)

December 1940

Maude woke early next morning after a fitful night's sleep. She was still a little groggy. She moaned quietly as the reality of her painful miscarriage and the feeling of emptiness and loss swept over her. It was followed soon after by the dread thought of what awaited her in the other room.

An unreal bloody image had already imprinted itself on her disturbed mind and her irrational fear had been allowed to take hold. Growing, it had swept all her reason aside. Mercifully, Pearl and Nan were still sleeping soundly as Maude rose, knowing she must face the unbearable task before her. She carefully removed the crude wrappings from her body, washed away the still slowly seeping blood as best she could, then pulled on some fresh clothes again.

The small mirror on the wall caught her eye and she stared into it, hardly recognising the tired haggard face that stared back at her. She looked like some bedraggled mess. Maud stood, not proud and straight as she once had, but slumping forward with the lingering pain. The unflattering baggy clothes hung loosely on her baggy body. Her hair was a matted, sweaty entanglement, falling wilfully around her head and shoulders. Her eyes were dull and troubled, reflecting the inner as well as the outer state. All were testament to her neglected self.

"Oh Maude," she moaned to herself, "what has become of you?" The haunting eyes in the mirror held her gaze a moment longer. Then with a wrench, she turned her eyes away in disgust.

This was not the glamorous care-free beauty that the wild and reckless Mad Maude of old had so often imagined herself to be. No, this was the stark reality of an emotionally and physically drained young woman, trying to cope with the all-powerful touch of Nature. Trying to understand that which for the moment was beyond her comprehension. A universal Nature, that did not discern on the basis of individual dreams, needs or wants. The same Nature that is so often seen as bountiful and kind when the seeds of the earth flourished with life, and yet villainous and vile when it took them back to its own bosom.

Maude took a deep breath and steeled herself for what she must do before entering the bedroom. Beginning to confront her fears, she pushed the door ajar and took a small tentative step forward. Hardly daring to lift her eyes at first, she took another deep breath and slowly brought her gaze upwards to the bed.

Her eyes and then her mind took in the sight of the blood-stained bed and the small lifeless figure that lay limp upon it. Pint-sized, it was perfectly formed, this now discarded miracle of Nature. As Maude looked at its still form her mind saw what might have been. A baby boy, a little brother for Pearl and Nan, perhaps one day a fine young man, her son. Why had this dreadful thing happened? The deep despairing wail arose from her, of its own accord. If only, if only.

For a moment the surge of compassion welled up in her, as her eyes filled and her heart began to melt and open at the sight of this small beautiful frail part of her. Her aloof protective persona was faltering, beginning to give way to an inner more vulnerable and natural Maude. She could have let it all go right then. Let go of her fears, the underlying feelings of unworthiness. Unlocked the dam that held back her tears and pain of loss, so that in the letting go the real healing might begin.

Instead, the conditioned reflex began, the ingrained blend of anger-covered fear once more wrenching her back from the brink. Instantly her protective shell responded, clenching down on the brief opening, closing the door on any exposure to her vulnerability. She was Mad Maude, wild, reckless, unbreakable. She had to remember that, hold it fast. She could not allow herself to be otherwise. Yet somewhere still lingering in Maude's trouble mind, the faint echo of doubt remained, whispering that this tiny baby had lost his life because of some failure or inadequacy on her part.

The wave of feelings of failure and the sense of shame that followed, threatened to surface and overwhelm her. Her mind refused to carry this burden, this blame, alone. It sought a reason, justification, anything to make sense of this terrible reality that lay before her. Pained, her mind searched for someone to blame and inevitably found her young husband.

To Maude, her judgment and reason clouded and disturbed, he was the cause of all this. Where was he when she needed him? He should have been here! Here to do this now! Damn the war that took him away! He had abandoned her, left her to deal with all this alone! Damn him to hell! Once more the unguarded wail broke from her and once more she clamped it down shut, resolved in what she must do.

Angrily, she grasped an old newspaper from the small table at the side of the bed. Bitterly, she wrapped the small figure in layers of the newspaper and tore the sheets from the bed onto the floor. Shaking, she picked up the paper parcel and carried it out of the room. Committed, she walked into the garden and stuffed the parcel deep into the waste bin. Despairingly, she stood staring inside, eyes momentarily locked on what now lay inside this strange tomb. Numbed, she pulled herself upright and hurriedly slammed the lid closed. Emotionally exhausted, she staggered back to the house.

Maude collapsed into an armchair feeling sick and utterly spent. Her body bent forward over her knees, head clasped in her hands, she began rocking back and forward in uncontrollable spasms of sobbing.

A short while later, as the first awakening sounds of her children reached her ears, she sat upright and mentally dragged herself back from her brief moment of weakness. She could not do this. She was not going to allow herself any further remorse over this thing. She had dealt with it and that was that. It was gone. It was not even a legal person, just some 'it', just a thing wrapped up in an old newspaper and buried in a garden bin.

"I've done what I needed to do", she scolded herself. "I've dealt with it and that's the end of it". The hardened shell of resoluteness tightened around her, as she locked down on her heaving emotions. Mad Maude, alone with her pain, shutting herself off from the outside world.

Nan's plaintiff cries rang out. It was as if the small child had somehow sensed some discordant ripple in the ether around her and cried a warning to her mother. Pearl, now also wide awake, joined in the call out for her mother. As Maude slowly gathered herself together and set off to attend to her children, her face was grim, her mind was set, rigid in her resolve, blocking out any feelings about the recent events.

The faintest voice in her head again whispered to Maude's mind that something was not quite right. That maybe her actions could have been different. That maybe there was a more humane and loving way to deal with her loss. Maude angrily shredded it asunder, hurriedly wrenching it from her wounded mind.

Yet, the image of the bloody but perfectly formed foetus still haunted her mind, refusing to be cast aside. The unresolved fissures in Maude's mind remained and festered, worming ever deeper into her psyche. In time they would drive her to doubt her own ability as a mother and to commit that other awful act for which she could never forgive herself.

Knowing nothing of the situation across the Irish Sea in Langley, Maude's young man had managed to get a couple of days much needed leave so they could spend Christmas together. It was only to be a brief visit before he was due to return again to Langley and the madness of the war. He was looking forward to the break and eager to be home to see his children. He was also hopeful Maude's moods might have improved a little with her advancing pregnancy.

He arrived on Christmas Eve, a Tuesday, just two days after Maude's miscarriage. For the first few hours back in his home he did not notice anything amiss. After all, Maude's pregnancy had hardly begun to show when he left and he was distracted with the excitement of his homecoming. Besides, he was so happy too to see his children and to make a big fuss over them.

Maude was curt and tense, holding back from him as if still in the aftermath of some unspoken, unresolved argument. The atmosphere she created was so palpable that it was as if he had somehow intruded in his own home and was no longer welcome. Her coldness irked him but he tried to let it pass, putting it down to another of her many mood swings. So, instead he concentrated on the children and tried to be patient, hoping she would come around soon enough. As the late morning progressed, the warning signs became a little more apparent. Watching her, even dressed in her baggy clothes slowly the awful truth began to dawn on him.

He waited until after lunch and the moment seemed right. Pearl was playing by herself and Nan was having her nap. They were in the small kitchen, alone together for the time being. As he sat at the kitchen table sipping tea, he began warily, trying to be kind and gentle. "I've been away quite a while Maude. Are you sure everything really is alright with you and the children?"

Soft the words, but the long-conditioned protective shell refused entry. She snapped back at him. "Yes, you have been away quite a while, but we've all been fine without you."

Maude's repeated terse rebuttals to his various skirting enquiry attempts left him confused and frustrated. Gradually he became a little more direct, though still mindful of how she might be feeling. Finally, after a lengthy silence, and still feeling he had to know, he gently asked, "Maude, please tell me, are you still pregnant dear?"

Maude had her back to him, standing at the kitchen sink washing the dishes. Instinctively her hand tightened on the handle of the long kitchen knife. She knew the moment would come, had to come. Knew that awful question would arise sooner or later, had steeled herself for it. Braced as she was, for a moment the gently whispered question broke through the shell of her defences.

For an instant she was back in her bedroom, taking her first close look at the tiny foetus. The perfect beautiful form lying there on the bed, motionless. The fragile future that was stolen from her. The swell of emotion arose once more in her, tears again starting to fill her eyes. Maude might have been able to let it all go even then, opening up to the agony and pain of her loss with him, embracing and comforting each other, letting the tears flow. The wounds, the fissures in her mind, cauterised with the sharing and outpouring, perhaps in time beginning to heal, to live and love afresh.

For that split second, she teetered on the brink, sensing him rise to embrace her, the leap of faith beckoning them. Then something snapped within her, abruptly refusing the path that might have been. Again, the gates of her mind and heart slammed closed, tightly shut.

The moment was gone, the layered protective shell enveloping her into its cocoon of isolation once more. Her mind was intent on finding someone to blame. Angrily she lifted the kitchen knife and spun around to face him. Startled, he fell back into the chair. Glaring down at him, the perceived cause of her pain, she waved the knife menacingly in the air as she spoke.

"No, I'm not bloody pregnant anymore! It's gone, and no thanks to you, damn you! It's gone!"

The angry outburst was aimed directly at him. For a moment he was taken aback, shocked by the intensity of Maude's actions, her harsh words and underlying accusation. He tried to compose himself again, trying to see past the anger, trying to understand what had happened. Again, seeking information and understanding, he asked if she was alright. It did not come out quite as intended. To Maude's ears it sounded more like an inquisition, casting doubt on her sanity, rather than a caring enquiry. To her still traumatised mind the implications of blame rang out loud and clear in his questions.

Her stinging replies escalated still further, tainted by her own sense of blame and anger at the loss. The young man's defensiveness and reactionary attempts to calm her rising emotions falling on deaf ears. Instead of finding comfort in each other, their words were causing hurt and pushing them further apart.

At last, any restraint and attempt to remain civil were cast aside. Maude's chilling anger-filled words yelled across the wide chasm that now divided them.

"If you must know, it was a boy, a bloody little boy! He's gone and you weren't here! Where were you? You left me all alone with that thing! You weren't here damn you!"

As the avalanche of despair and rage quietened, her head and shoulders slumped down and her words trailed off. For just a second it seemed that she might break down, might falter and collapse into his arms to share their grief.

He stepped forward to offer solace and comfort, another chance to cross that slender bridge to reach each other, perhaps their last chance. Abruptly she looked up, met his eyes, then stopped short again. Mad Maude held herself in check, raising her head in angry defiance. Then casting herself adrift, she spat the vengeful words into his face like acid to burn him.

"I buried it in the bin in the garden! I cleaned up that dead bloody mess and shoved it into the bin out my sight! Is that what you wanted to know? Are you satisfied now?!"

Afterwards, when the children were settled down for the evening, in the half-light the young man retrieved the small parcel, placed it in a wooden box, then buried it deep in the ground at the foot of their garden. He put a small wooden cross on the earth to mark the spot. In silence the young man transplanted one of the rose bushes onto the site, gently bedding it in the ground above where the small body lay cold and still beneath.

Still, it lay, the small lifeless form of the boy-child, abandoned and rejected, then recovered and redeemed. The gift of life stolen from his tiny form before he could draw a first breath, before the wondrous light of day could first pierce his tiny eyes.

There was no name on the tiny grave, just three carefully carved letters on the wooden cross. He was not a particularly religious man but he felt the need to say a few words over the make-shift grave nevertheless. He did not weep, that would come later. Maude stayed inside all the while. Keeping out of sight she watched him through the window, her emotions still in a state of turmoil. The rift between them raw and acute.

The young man could not bring himself to visit his parents over that short trip home. When he left to return to Langley, Maude barely made an effort to bid him goodbye. Leaving her and the children behind, the young man felt the empty void in his stomach. It was a Christmas at home that he wanted to forget, but knew that he couldn't.

That night he reflected again on what had happened, hardly able to believe it. Over and over the thoughts beat at him. The accompanying emotions of deep sadness, tinged with anger, weighted ever more heavily on his heart. Roughly he used his sleeve to wipe the unbidden moisture from his eyes. He could not escape the overwhelming feeling that something had shifted between him and Maude. As a fitful sleep began to embrace him, he wondered if he had buried much more than his still-born son in that tiny grave.

Chapter 13

Shelter From The Storm

*This above all: to thine own self be true
And it must follow, as the night the day
Thou canst not then be false to any man.*
(Hamlet – Shakespeare)

February 1941

It was neither contemplated nor planned. Yet it was another of those critical moments in life where the hand of Fate is once again at work. In those special moments the choices we make can shape our lives forever. Grace certainly did not know back then how the course of her life would change so dramatically when she simply chose to follow her heart.

As Grace's visits to Liza had become more frequent, she freely helped Liza with the children and some housework from time to time. In doing so, she continued to find there the shelter and warm companionship of a loving home that she so treasured. Liza's family all seemed to accept her from the outset. Valerie, who was just a little older than her and in full time work, had soon become a close friend.

When Grace could not bring herself to elaborate much about her background or marriage to Jessman, she found to her relief that Liza and her family were considerate and did not try to press or intrude into her circumstances. The older ones only asked a few questions out of politeness then left it at that, and the younger children were too young to care.

Liza however, had noticed the little tightening in Grace's conversation when Jessman was mentioned, but she let it pass. She had also heard the rumours around the neighbourhood a few years ago about Jessman and a sacrificial young bride and she felt only compassion for Grace. Liza guessed that there was a hurt there that ran deep but it was none of her business, unless and until Grace wanted to share it with her. She knew too that Grace would need to feel completely safe and secure in their company if she was ever to share that particular burden with them.

Through Grace, Liza had extended invitations to Jessman to visit her home as well. Grace had reluctantly mentioned these to Jessman out of a sense of duty, but was relieved that he did not seem in the least bit interested. Jessman's main concern seemed to be that Grace looked after the house, provided his meals, helped Sam and did not neglect her duties around the farm. After that he did not seem to care much how she spent her free time.

For Grace, Liza's home was now very much her welcome sanctuary, a place where she could feel safe, relax and just be herself. She also knew in her heart that it would not feel the same for her if Jessman was to intrude upon it.

As the influence of the war began to seep into the lives and perspectives of the people, Liza's instincts started to prove right about Grace. Little by little Grace gradually felt more able to share pieces of her story with Liza. It was not an easy thing for Grace to reveal how, when she was but a girl, she had come to marry a man so much older than herself. Then opening up further on the bitter struggle of those first years, when she was simply trying to survive a bloody, bruised and battered existence with Jessman.

Even now, with Sam doing his best to act as her protector, it was still a difficult and oppressive existence that she felt compelled to endure. Yet she also felt she could not remain an island, locking all her secrets up inside herself.

Liza was a kind and patient listener, letting Grace unravel her story in her own time. As Grace slowly revealed more and more of her background to Liza, she realised the process was helping her and she felt so much better for having done so. Her circumstances were still very much her own burden to bear, but somehow now having voiced the suppressed pain and shared it with Liza the burden felt a little lighter.

For the first time in her young life, Grace had been able to tell someone the full truth of her past few years. Not just that, but that someone had given her their full attention and listened patiently with kindness and understanding. To Grace, it was as if she had received a beautiful gift from someone who genuinely cared.

She felt sure too in the knowledge that Liza would not betray a confidence, especially one that was ongoing. Grace felt that the bond between them had grown into a strong mutual trust, one that neither would willingly break. With that trust in mind, it was not an easy thing then for the still young Grace to acknowledge to herself that the growing friendship between her and Maude's young man, might be anything more than that.

That first day of February 1941, a Saturday, had started innocently enough. Jessman was making one of his monthly visits to Belfast to get some supplies for the farm and visit an old relative. As usual he was taking Sam with him.

Despite the bombing blitz that was tearing apart cities over the Irish Sea in England, there was still relative calm in Northern Ireland. For some reason it had remained sheltered thus far. That would all soon change when, in just a few short months, the deadly bombing raids of Easter 1941 would cause havoc and devastation in and around Belfast. For the time being though, while the country knew to expect the inevitable, Northern Ireland was still relatively safe from the bombing.

Jessman and Sam had started out early that Saturday. It was a cold and wet Winter's morning and Grace had prepared them well with a hearty breakfast and some thick cheese and onion sandwiches to take with them. With a gracious wave she bid them goodbye, then watching them go, breathed a deep sigh of relief. They were not expected back much before midnight. She was alone, but looked forward eagerly to having the peacefulness of the long day all to herself.

On his return Jessman would no doubt be troublesome. He would have consumed more than his fair share of drink, despite Sam's pleadings. She would have to be extra careful to avoid another of his crude assaults and an angry drunken beating. However, as long as Sam returned with him and could intervene, Grace could feel a little safer.

Come what may, Jessman or wild wintry weather, she saw no point in worrying about the things she could not control. Right now, the day was hers to enjoy. Grace was learning from the hard lessons of life and had long since decided she was not going to waste her life moping about in self-pity.

As usual, she made plans to use the morning to give the house a good clean and tidy-up while Jessman and Sam were out. Then, after an early lunch, she would usually go over to spend the day with her family. Beth and Riley were just beginning to feel their age and her brothers and sisters were growing up fast.

Today however, she planned to do something a little different. She would brave the mixed weather and take a leisurely walk over to Liza's house for a few hours. Grace enjoyed Liza's company and looked forward to helping her take care of young Clive and Ellen. There was of course that other reason too, though she didn't care too much to admit it, even to herself. Maude's young man was expected back on a few days leave and might be at Liza's over that weekend.

Even though Grace had only seen him a handful of times at Liza's over the past year, they had developed a warm, easy-going friendship. She enjoyed talking with someone closer to her own age and his calm manner and humour made such a pleasant change from her usual conversations with Jessman.

Of course, that was all in stark contrast to the unease and tension Grace sensed in Maude every time Maude chose to accompany her husband. Fortunately, Valerie had forewarned Grace that Maude had recently lost a baby when at least mid-term, and so everyone had been trying to make allowances for that, and the added effects the stress of the war was having on all of them.

Grace was pleased then, that despite the cold weather and odd shower, Maude's young man was already at Liza's when she arrived. On this occasion Maude was not with him. He had come mid-morning to finish off the kitchen cupboards he had been making for Liza. Maude was not feeling well and had chosen to stay at home. Given the uncertain weather, Pearl and Nan had stayed at home with her.

The ever-watchful Liza had already noticed the growing

friendship between her son and Grace and was all too aware of the current tensions with Maude. She had not spoken to him of Grace's background, other than to issue a gentle warning that Grace had endured a lot of trouble already in her young life and didn't need any more. Liza hoped that would be enough.

The weather started to worsen as the day slipped by all too quickly. By late afternoon it had already begun to darken outside. As the wind picked up, a light rain began to fall. With a good half-hour walk ahead of her, Grace told Liza that she was already running late and had better head off home before the weather got worse.

Liza offered to put her up for the night, but was not surprised when Grace declined and pulled on her coat and head scarf, getting ready to leave. It would not bode at all well for her if she was not in her own home when Jessman returned. Maude's young man was also on the point of leaving. He politely offered to walk part of the way with Grace as it was not too far out of his own way home.

They had set out together, well wrapped up against the weather. Their conversation was easy and light at first. The weather was quickly deteriorating as the icy February wind and driving rain increased in intensity. Soon they had almost to shout to make themselves heard against it. Linking arms and with heads down, they leaned into the oncoming weather, bracing themselves against it. They forged onwards, barely able to see in front of them with the combination of rain and darkness. Though it was difficult to make progress and both felt the cold bite and pull of Winter, yet in making their combined effort, they shared the close welcome presence of the other.

As they drew near the narrow road junction where Grace was to turn off towards her own home, Maude's young man called out that he would take her right to her door to see her safely home. Amidst the downpour and howling wind, they turned together as one.

When they arrived, he stood drenched on the doorstep while she opened the door and entered. With a look, a smile, then a hurried wave, he turned to go and resume his own journey home. Just as he did so, he slipped on the cobbled stones and fell awkwardly, barely managing to save himself from the worst of it with an outstretched arm. The downward force still sent him sprawling onto his side into the gathering puddles.

Seeing his plight, Grace quickly reached out to grab his arm and help him back to his feet, the door banging shut again behind her in the wind. He clung to her as he slowly staggered to his feet, still unsteady. Grace, supporting him, instructed him to come into the house to get dried and cleaned up. Sodden and embarrassed, and still a little shaken from his fall, he hobbled inside as she opened the door again and helped him through. Grace entered the house just behind him and pushed the door closed against the angry roar of the storm outside. Cold and dripping wet they found shelter inside.

She quickly lit the fire and hung up the outer layers of their clothes to dry. A couple of heavy woollen blankets and a pot of hot tea served to keep them warm in the meantime. Fairly soon the wooden logs were burning brightly as the fire's hungry yellow flames gradually devoured them and flicked out their radiant warmth into the room.

A Tilley lamp gave them enough light without being too intrusive. They sat on the floor near the fire to dry out and absorb the heat all the more. The initial light banter about the weather and their predicament slowly ebbed away. In its place came the comfortable long silences of two friends sheltering close together, watching the time-honoured dance of the mesmerising flames, while the wild weather raged outside.

Searching for a deeper level of communication, she gently asked him what life was really like with Maude. He glanced at her momentarily, recognising the question for what it was. Then looking back into the fire, he spoke quietly, as if sharing this as yet unspoken truth with himself as well.

"I've felt in awe of Maude from the very beginning Grace, completely swept along by her flamboyance and energy. Of course, I do care deeply for her and the children, but I can't fathom her changing moods, no-one can. Lately it's been getting worse."

As he stared into the fire, he began to speak of Maude's miscarriage and how it had caused immense pain for both of them. He related how he had buried the baby and how the way Maude had disposed of it broke his heart. Almost as an afterthought, he added, "It must have broken us too, for no matter what I do, Maude and me have been drifting further apart. I feel like a stranger in my own house and she's just biding time until I head back to Langley again."

The play of the flames held them in silence for a few more moments as the storm still rattled away outside. Then, feeling the question arise in him, for the first time he asked her what it was like being married to Jessman. Grace knew the question did not come from idle curiosity or simple reciprocation, but from a genuine concern for her wellbeing. She hesitated, then without holding back, she told him how she had come to marry Jessman.

The tears welled up in Grace's eyes as she told him. She shared it all, from how it started on her sixteenth birthday, her mother telling her it was the only way to save the farm and family, right up to the kind of tormenting life she was now obliged to lead. How her life had been a constant endurance of being raped, bullied and mistreated by a much older husband who clearly didn't have any loving feelings for her at all. How Sam had helped to keep him somewhat in order, but that there seemed little prospect of any real improvement in her life with Jessman. It all came pouring out of Grace, as the tears rolled down her face.

"I can't see any way out. Inside me I feel just as trapped now as I did as a young girl on my wedding day, when I was terrified and hiding away from my mother in a little outside toilet."

Even though he had suspected old man Jessman mistreated her, the young man was visibly shaken by Grace's words. He reached out to her and put his arms around her, to soothe her with gentle words. For long moments they sat together, wrapped in each other's comforting embrace. The pain of the other, the sharing and the caring, bringing them ever closer together. It was not explicit, this love, yet it reached across time and touched them, for who can bear to see a loved one suffer?

And it was not from passion, but through her sister, compassion, that the barriers of convention fell away. It was an inevitable journey then to find that greater love. A recognition of the true beloved in the other. A response honed through the eons of time itself. A silent irrefutable beckoning call of the heart that brings true soulmates together at last.

Afterwards the young man told her he had loved her from the first moment he saw her. Grace reflected for a second on his words, as their warm embrace flowed through her. Then she responded in kind, hearing the truth of her own love expressed in the sound of her voice as she spoke. She did not know how, but she recognised this feeling from the depth of her being, as if it had always been there, calling to her. She mused quietly, "Maybe real love does happen instantly, it's there right from the beginning, even if it takes time to unveil itself."

Following her train of thought, he too reflected for a moment. Then he told her that she had been in his thoughts from that first meeting at the lunch on Boxing Day, a little over two years ago. In a whisper he told her it was from that first moment he had heard her speak, saw her graceful movements, looked into her eyes and felt that strange connection. He told her he had felt something shift within him right then, but could not put words to it. Something about her that gave him a sense of being completely at home in her company, yet it was not until later he had realised it had nothing to do with any place of abode.

He had not fully recognised the depth of his feelings then. Indeed, he wondered if, because of his circumstances, his errant mind had refused any suggestion of anything more than a mild attraction and admiration for Grace. He had denied his own feelings through a mixture of guilt and other obligations. As Grace listened, she recognised the similar thoughts that had played on her own mind. "Yes, how could it be otherwise?", she whispered, half remembering her scriptures. "We must live our lives as strangers without hope, until the moment we truly see through the eyes of the heart".

The comfortable silence overtook them again as they remained in each other's arms and listened to the gentle purring of the fire. Grace had not known anything like this love for a man before, and certainly not for Jessman, her husband. This all too brief stolen time together was an escape from the ties of society and convention that bound them. It was as if they had somehow reached beyond their burdened reality to soar high in the sky, and for just a brief moment in time to touch the sun, intoxicatingly beautiful. An escape to another world, where she was free and safe.

Yet even now, like Icarus touching the bliss but perhaps sensing the inevitable, a part of Grace began to realise it could not last. All too soon that quiet voice of reason whispered to her that she could not avoid the painful fall back to earth and their separate existences.

Unconsciously Grace sat upright and wrapped the blanket tightly around her, habitually isolating herself again. Like the blanket, the long tentacles of obligations from the world she had temporarily escaped, slowly reached up and engulfed her. Tightening their grip on her, they forced her eyes to open as slowly they began to steal her beautiful dream away from her. Seeing the situation now for what it was she gasped deeply, the inevitable beckoning. Her courage was failing her, but unlike that other time years before, she would not seek to run and hide from this reality. She would face it, even if it took everything from her.

As difficult as it may be, they both had obligations to their spouses and, in the young man's case, to his two young children. As the log fire burned down and the weight of convention descended upon them once more, so did the cruel reality of their lives. This moment together was to be treasured, but like Icarus, now came the fall back to earth. They were married, but not to each other. They led separate lives. It could not now be otherwise.

Grace felt the unbearable agony of her predicament tearing at her heart. This short-lived moment of love and happiness could not be allowed to endure. She was part of a trade that she could not escape. Despite everything that had just happened, she could not just walk away from her marriage to Jessman. It was not just about her, there was also her younger siblings and her parents to consider. Now somehow, she must find the strength to make another sacrifice. She must forego her own chance for love. Her own needs must once again be placed secondary to her obligations to her family.

The cold realisation stealing away her hopes and beating her down would not relent. Married, but forever alone, a life without him. It was unbearable, her heart was bursting, yet it could not, must not be otherwise. Tears of overwhelming sorrow flowed from her as the fall to earth crushed her completely. There was no longer any hope in her mind that it could somehow be different.

As if reading and sharing her thoughts, Maude's young man, leaned forward and saw the tears in Grace's dark eyes. Recognising her pain, and knowing why they came, once more he held her tightly in his arms. Her head and jet-black hair rested against him. As he comforted her in the moment, he too was feeling the heavy burden of society weighing upon them. Their temporary sanctuary, a dream-like respite from the world outside, was just that, temporary. It could not last. There was no future for either of them here.

Gathering all her strength of will, Grace set aside the despair in her heart, searching for the courage to do that which must be done. To say that which must be said. The rhythmic ticking of the old clock on the mantlepiece counted down their seconds. She held his hands in hers, noting the strong straight fingers and tightly clipped nails. The hands of a gifted craftsman, measured and precise.

She took a deep breath and at last she found the courage and her voice. She whispered that she loved him but for them it was not enough. There could be no continuation for it would not be fair to each other or to their spouses or their families. It would be living a lie. That way led only to disaster. They must part and go their own ways, live their separate lives.

These were not the words of the deliberate destroyer, though in a sense they did that. Nor were they the words of the practiced persuader, though they did that too. They were simply the words of irrefutable truth, spoken out of necessity by Grace, as kindly as she could.

The words reverberated in his head, like a mantra that refused to release him, tormenting him in his own denial until finally he submitted to their truth. At last, like her, he did. There were no attempts to try to convince otherwise, no dissention, but even in the knowledge and unbearable pain of their parting, no regrets for their time together.

It had been but a stolen moment in time, a time out of time in a world that did not belong to them. A fleeting treasure that could not be lifted from the deep well of imagined possibilities into the light of day. They sat, wrapped tightly in the embrace of the other, hearts wanting it never to end, heads realising it already had.

The moment was passing, as all things must. Outside the storm had eased, its torrent spent for the present. As he stood holding her hands at the door and reluctant to leave, he tried to make a little light conversation to ease her pain before he left. As if to gently encourage her, he reminded her that at least she'd have wealth, for even though Jessman was a brute he was still one of the more important brutes in the area. Grace nodded, acknowledging his despairing efforts. "Perhaps so", she had responded, smiling kindly.

Then thinking of how a drunken Jessman would be on his return, Grace shuddered. Remembering one of Liza's many wise sayings, she murmured, "Well, we both know what Liza would say…. it's nice to be important, but it's more important to be nice."

For a long time Grace could not bring herself to go back to Liza's house after her brief affair with Maude's young man. She still felt the awful gnawing pain of parting from him and having to abandon any thoughts of a future together. Yet now there was something else too, a lingering sense of unease. It was just that she felt she had somehow betrayed Liza, if not Maude, and right now she could not yet bring herself to bear this secret in their company or to try to carry on as if nothing had changed.

Chapter 14

The Blessing

*Though we travel the world over to find the beautiful,
we must carry it with us or we find it not.*
(Ralph Waldo Emerson)

April 1941

It was the ancient Greek Stoic slave Epictetus who taught emperors and his many followers to question precisely what lay within their control and what lay without. For though we may seek to govern our lives through the conscious choices we make, yet what playthings of an unmoved and impartial Fate we are in the dance of life. While we may chart direction and think we alone steer our ship through the wide seas of life, even our conscious choices do not always determine which storms we will encounter, or which carefully hidden havens we may discover on our way. In the end, as Epictetus observed, all we can do is to choose how best we may respond to the circumstances of our lives.

When circumstances contrived to prompt Grace and the young man to reach out to each other that magical evening, it might perhaps have been seen as some random act of kindness by Fate. After all, they were both touched by the light caress of a timeless love that was far beyond anything they had ever known before. Yet it was that same Fate that, once having enabled their souls to find that rare yet abundant love that was their birth right, cruelly ripped it from their grasp before the evening was through. Even then, as Grace was soon to discover, Fate had not yet done with tossing her life around, like so much early blossom plucked from the trees by the Spring storms of nature.

Grace had wrestled with her conscience for several weeks after her affair, taking a fresh look at her life. She was still a young woman, not quite 21, but much stronger and more mature now than the young girl who was forced to marry Jessman. She had to stand on her own two feet, to get on with this marriage arrangement and make the best of it. At the same time though, she did not want to cut Liza and her lovely family completely out of her life.

Eventually, she set aside her reservations and made the effort to return to Liza's house, initially keeping her visits brief and her conversation light. Increasingly she found herself more comfortable in the company of Liza's eldest daughter, Valerie, and their deepening friendship continued to grow as they spent time together, now mostly away from Liza's house.

Grace also visited her own family more often now, spending time with her siblings and trying to improve her relationship with her parents. They, and her siblings, occasionally visited her, but Jessman's gruff sullen attitude was enough to drive even the most enthusiastic visitors away. So mostly she saw her parents and siblings at The Liberty Bell.

To her pleasant surprise, Beth and Riley seemed increasingly to acknowledge her status as a married woman and not just another child of their household. More often now she was able to ease into discussions with them on an improved, if not quite equal footing. It had required effort on her part but there had been a slow gradual transition, particularly over the past year or so. The shadow of the past still lingered, but with renewed commitment, Grace felt she could just try to be herself a little more around them.

Jessman, as was his way, rarely chose to accompany Grace to her parents' home at The Liberty Bell. That suited Grace, for even though she had been married for several years now, his very presence in their company still brought back jarring memories of that awful day for all of them.

Her siblings were growing up quickly too. Just a few months ago, the next eldest sister, Dottie, married a fine young man that she had met through their church. Grace had quizzed Dottie before the wedding, trying to satisfy herself it was a matter of free choice for Dottie and not a marriage of convenience as in her own case. She need not have worried. Dottie's man was a gentle giant of a man, respected and respectful.

With the farm doing a little better, some of it with Jessman's help too, and her parents no longer under the same strain of enormous debts, they had not interfered in Dottie's marriage at all. For them, as long as Dottie was marrying a good and staunch church-going Protestant, they were happy to go along with her choice of spouse. Happy that was, just as long as it was a proper wedding in a proper Presbyterian church with a proper minister.

The large white wedding had gone off without a hitch, bride and groom clearly very happy and the church full of well-wishers. Even Beth and Riley seemed to be relaxed and enjoying themselves. It was a far cry from the events of that other wedding day just a few years before. Seated there in the church Grace had watched it all intently, enjoying the service and the celebrations and feeling happy for her sister.

There were moments of sadness too of course, when Grace's wondering feelings of what might have been for her own wedding day still threatened to bring her to tears. Yet, for her sister's sake, she held them back and shared in Dottie's joy. Grace was grateful that at least Dottie, and in time her other siblings, were free to marry whomever they might choose. Though she would never dream of mentioning it to them, she reflected that perhaps they were now more able to make that free choice in part because of the sacrificial trade she had made in marrying Jessman.

What Grace could not know at the time, was that it would be many years before she could attend another wedding of her siblings. Fate, having deprived her of the happiness she might have experienced on her own wedding day, was about to intercede again and deny her further. Even the vicarious joy that Grace would have found in seeing her other siblings happily wed was soon about to be taken from her.

From the beginning of the war, Grace's brother, Toby, had become his father's right-hand man around The Liberty Bell farm. He was third in line of the siblings and eldest of the two brothers. Working part time in a hardware store in Marlborough, he had quickly matured into a bright and determined young man. He had become increasingly effective on the farm, recognising the family's dependence upon it and beginning to see it as his own future heritage, being the heir apparent. In consequence, he had not hesitated to push and prod his father, Riley, into making better farming decisions in an effort to keep The Liberty Bell on an even keel.

Unfortunately for Riley, young Toby's increasing influence around the farm was not to last long. In the aftermath of the Battle of Britain he could hardly wait until he was old enough to join the war effort against the growing threat posed by the German

Chancellor. Toby enlisted on his eighteenth birthday and left home to start training for the Air Force, not long after his sister Dottie's marriage. He didn't know it then, and it would not have deterred him, but statistically the chances of British pilot survival were at best 50%.

Toby would survive, but not without the scars of the war. Even years later he would be reticent to talk about it, except perhaps to regale a little about some of the many legendary pilot heroes he'd had the privilege to meet. One of those heroes would be the infamous Spitfire ace and youngest ever RAF Wing commander, Paddy from Dublin. Apparently, not only did Paddy shoot down an incredible thirty enemy planes, but he had been a mean poker player too, as Toby had found out to his cost!

Just a little younger than Grace's brother Toby, Wendy and Gwen, were next eldest of the family. Both had left school and were now also employed in local shops in Marlborough. As their mother Beth had long since decreed, each Friday night they deposited their pay on the table in unopened envelops and waited for their mother to give them just enough to see them through the week.

Beth was not easily persuaded that the individual needs of the girls should be put ahead of any needs of the farm, especially in times of war. Instead, she adopted a very frugal approach when it came to their allowance. Beth never hesitated to admonish their desires for material things, often quoting biblical verse when it suited her. Of course, from Wendy and Gwen's perspective, this restraint was stifling and completely ignored the important needs of young girls beginning the transition into young women.

As a result, Wendy and Gwen constantly called upon their father, Riley, to intercede on their behalf. When they were persistent, which they often were, poor Riley felt badgered from all sides. If he felt brave enough, or foolish enough, he would gingerly try to put their case forward and gently remind Beth that they were no longer small children and had needs. As often as not when Beth's mind was made up it did little good. Then, as he felt the wrath of his wife's tongue lashings and preachings, Riley would cringe and regret his foolish attempts.

"What do you mean they have needs? What needs do young teenage girls have that can't be sorted out by a bit of hard work around the farm? I'll have none of that stupid talk in this godfearing house about wearing fancy clothes and dancing. And you Riley should have more sense than to encourage them!"

However, in time and with a persistence born of necessity and stubbornness, perhaps mixed with a little foolishness, Riley and the girls would once in a while find a convincing argument and Beth would relent a little. Riley eventually noticed that their pleadings for new and fashionable clothes tended to be just a touch more successful when they emphasised the need to dress well on Sundays, ostensibly for family social standing and appearances in the community.

It was then a more natural follow-on to this argument to suggest that the girls might benefit from attending some church-sponsored event or other. Beth was very wary of suitors at the best of times. However, she knew that if the girls were to be married off, then at least through the church they had a better chance of finding a wealthy young suitor from the right family. That was, if the young men had not already raced off to war!

Grace's youngest siblings, Gloria, Myrtle, Olive and Daniel, were all still at school but now much more able to fend for themselves, or at least help take care of each other. Grace loved each and every one of them and spent many happy hours with them when she could. The three old battered bikes that were used for transport into town provided the means to cycle through the country lanes together, with this one or that one, talking all the way. Gloria especially was a lovely fun-seeking live wire and was always keen to spend time with Grace. Once in a while the old bikes also provided the opportunity for Grace to take Wendy and Gwen into town for an afternoon of freedom together. She treasured these moments of happiness with her family.

So it was that Grace began to let slip any thoughts of a future of her own choosing. She had long since accepted the idea that, for the welfare of her siblings, she must simply reconcile herself to the future that had been pre-ordained for her by her parents. Now, it was becoming more and more of a practical reality.

She resolved yet again to try to be more of a caring wife to Jessman, even if he did not seem to care much for her. That reasoning took her back again and again to the same place. If she must spend her future with him, then she would just have to make a go of their marriage and all that that entailed, for better or for worse. Whatever his nature and shortcomings, he was after all her husband and she was no longer a child. She didn't love him, but at least she could care for him, and try to salvage something worthwhile from their marriage.

With this quiet resignation, Grace might gradually have settled into a quiet life of mediocrity, even if it left her feeling empty, even if it was in many ways another life of quiet desperation.

However, sometimes life refuses to turn out as we expect it to. It was on one of Grace's visits to Liza's home that something happened to change everything. Something that upset all her resignations and plans. It happened during a conversation with Liza about the war, while they were busy preparing an early lunch together in the warm kitchen. It happened mid-sentence, without warning. Grace felt acutely sick.

The heat felt unbearable and the smell of the spicy food wafted over Grace causing her stomach to heave and churn. Waves of nausea flowed through her and upset her vision and balance. She stumbled and had to grab onto a chair to steady herself. Desperately she held herself back from vomiting on the floor, but try as she might, mother Nature was the more compelling.

With an effort Grace slumped heavily into the chair, bending over double as her senses betrayed her and her mind floundered around in a flurry of hormones in turmoil. She struggled to describe to Liza what was happening to her and how she was feeling. It seemed as if her voice did not belong to her, incoherent words somehow emerging from her mouth as the room swam around her.

Liza, already beginning to sense what was happening was quick to act. She steadied Grace in the chair before putting a cold damp flannel around her neck and shoulders, opening the windows to allow some cool fresh air to enter. Then she cleaned up the mess on the stone floor, keeping a watch out for Grace as she did so. Soon Grace was feeling a little cooler and a little better, sipping slowly from a glass of ginger ale that Liza had offered her.

The dark golden ginger ale was a disappearing legacy of its original inventor, Belfast's Doctor Cantrell. Liza had watered it down just enough to temper the strong ginger spice flavour, but somehow it and the cooler air seemed just the thing to help settle Grace's stomach. In a short while it was as if nothing had happened and she was quite herself again. Feeling somewhat foolish, she apologised to Liza for what had happened. Liza nodded but said little, brushing the matter off with a knowing smile.

A couple of weeks later Grace's doctor confirmed that she was pregnant. Grace was dumfounded, sitting down on the small park bench on that cold morning to think through her startling news. She was deliriously happy at being pregnant, at knowing there was a miraculous beginning of life growing within her. She knew beyond any doubt this unborn child could not be Jessman's. Her mind raced back to that magical Winter's evening, remembering, remembering. Grace smiled, there could be no doubt.

Then unbidden, her mind raced ahead, projecting dreams of what might be. How wonderful, how truly wonderful and fitting that their brief moment of love should gift them with a child. In that instance she felt joy. The joy of one who knows intimately the gift of life that springs within. It was beautiful. She sensed more than felt it within her, this beautiful presence of another being.

She sat in stillness, perhaps for the first time sensing this same gift of life in everything around her, hearing its expression in every sound and every movement in the park. Everywhere she looked it seemed she could see and feel life's timeless presence whispering to her. The beauty of it all touched her, swept through her, brought tears of joy to her eyes. Full of gratitude and feeling blessed in the splendor of the moment, Grace promised herself this special moment in Nature would never ever be lost to her. Never, till the day she died, should she live to be a hundred.

Time passed. Grace made as if to rise from the seat. As she did so, her perspective suddenly shifted and new thoughts swept over her. Shaken, she slumped back down onto the bench. All too soon this different reality of her situation gripped her, like an unbidden cold icy wind that sprang up to steal her dreams and breath away. Grace gasped, but could not avoid the rush of those other unwanted thoughts that suddenly swept over her. Engulfed by those pressing thoughts, she slowly began to realise their implications and feel the suffocating sadness they brought.

How awful, how appallingly awful. How could she possibly share this knowledge with the father of her child? She could not share this truth with anyone! What would happen to her if she did? What would happen to her family? They were all deeply religious people, all with strict family values and beliefs that governed their very lives. They could not condone what she had done, no-one could.

She was a married woman. If this truth surfaced it would certainly destroy her marriage, and possibly his too. She would surely be branded, called unsavoury names, like some outcast leper of society, forever to walk in the shadows. Even this blessed child would carry the stigma of it, the heavy yoke of broken social convention, another target for name-calling. How could she bring that truth upon them all? How could she bring that truth upon her child?

Once more feeling trapped with no way out and no alternative, Grace made yet another vow to herself that morning. It was a very different kind of promise to the one she had made only moments ago. Slowly she whispered the words to herself, as if quietly giving them voice would help bind her to them. "This is a truth that would surely destroy them all if I should let it come out into the open. I cannot do that. It must remain my secret, alone to bear. For all our sakes, I must bury that secret here now with me!"

Again, she felt the torrent of conflicting emotions within her. Despairingly she held her face in her hands to hide the tears that threatened to flow. As she sat there on the park bench, Grace felt utterly alone, swept along by the tides of Fate once more. What might have been one of the happiest of moments of her young life, all too soon stolen, torn from her. First her marriage, a mockery, her cross to bear. Then her chance for true love, found and forfeited, perhaps lost forever. Now even the discovery of this small miracle of life within her, this tiny gift of their brief moment of shared love. Even this must be shrouded in untruths to avoid bringing down pain and scorn on her and her family. She sobbed silently.

Instead of joy and love, in that moment Grace felt the heavy weight of the burden she must carry, must face alone. Though it went against all that she believed in her heart, to live this lie, she could not see any other way forward. Not only must she live without him, but she must keep this secret of their love-child within her. Filling up with unchecked anguish her emotions burst forth, spilling into the cries that escaped her mouth unguarded.

"Please Lord, how much more do you want to take from me? When will it ever be enough? Must I sacrifice everything that I hold dear in this life?" Grace wrung her hands in grief as her desolation swept over her.

The park remained silent, as if Nature might be ignoring her plea for an answer. Grace in turn, no longer seeing its splendour. The light morning wind picked up a little more, rippling and dancing its way through the nearby trees and bushes. A blackbird alighted on the ground near Grace. It was a dark brown female, oblivious of the inaccuracy in its name, though the male was indeed jet black. Nature had designed the female's bland colouring so it would be inconspicuous on its nest and blend in beautifully with its surroundings. Here it was, caring nothing for labels or misnomers bestowed by humanity.

Momentarily the brown blackbird looked directly at Grace, as if gently admonishing her for an uncharacteristic abandonment of hope and indulgence in self-pity. Then it hopped off to forage beneath another bush, continuing undaunted in its search for food for its young.

Above in the higher branches of the trees, opportunistic sparrows fluttered about from roost to roost, all the while surveying the scene below for an unwary grub or insect. The trees, in Spring blossom, swayed and bent gently to the will of the wind, allowing the turbulence of the breeze to pass through them, unresisting, undiminished. Nature, ever-changing yet ever constant, gently offering Grace whatever guidance or answer she chose to see or take from it.

Still caught in the paradigm, and her thoughts of how her situation would be viewed by society, Grace saw only her dilemmas and thwarted dreams. That might all change in time, but for the moment it was all she could think about. After a while she wiped her eyes and braced herself, rising wearily from the bench to begin the long walk home.

In Paradigm's Cage

Chapter 15

The Choice

Let choice whisper in your ear
and love murmur in your heart.
Be ready. Here comes life.
(Maya Angelou)

April – December 1941

Within days of Grace discovering she was pregnant, the Belfast blitz began to smash down upon the people of Northern Ireland with a vengeance. It was mid-April, in the Spring of 1941.

A few earlier token exploratory raids had shown Hitler that Belfast was ill prepared for an aerial onslaught. Having exposed its defensive weaknesses, it had not been long before wave after wave of the Luftwaffe's bombers rained ruin down upon the city. Expanding upon the destruction that had been wrought upon England for the past six months, the bombing assaults on Belfast were utterly devastating, showing the people no mercy.

A thousand lives were lost and a hundred thousand lost their homes as half of Belfast city was completely flattened. Hitler's radio stooge, Lord Haw-Haw, added further insult with his cynical jibes and talk of Easter eggs for breakfast as the bombs poured down. It was all designed to break the will of the British people and beat them into submission.

As was the case with many bombed cities, whether Coventry, London, Dresden, Hamburg, Belfast, or a host of others, the devastation of the air raids caused enormous havoc. However, in the midst of all the chaos, often the bombings seemed to further strengthen the resolve of the people who lived there, bringing them closer together with uncommon acts of courage and kindness.

In Belfast, staunch Protestants fleeing from the ruins of the Shankill Road, were welcomed into shelters in the Falls Road by equally staunch Catholics, temporarily setting aside their differences and uniting against a common enemy. In the South of Ireland, the leader, or Taoiseach, Eamon de Valera, urged unity with his all-embracing 'We are one and the same people' speech. Here, amidst the ravages of a bloody war, it was perhaps the nearest to being 'united' that the people of Ireland would experience for many years to come.

Through it all, the child in Grace's womb continued to grow and flourish. With an enthusiasm that belied its size, the small embryo began to make its fluttering presence felt as it kicked and stretched within its safe cocoon. Gradually, as the weeks continued to pass, the womb expanded in perfect harmony to meet the growing needs of its tiny occupant.

Grace found it increasingly difficult to hide the fact that she was pregnant and finally no longer bothered to try. Instead, she began to settle into the rhythm and joy of her pregnancy, as the timeless bond between mother and unborn offspring arose to strengthen and consume her. Even so, Grace tended not to speak of her pregnancy unless specifically questioned. For all the world about her it was simply a child of her marriage to Jessman, a natural consequence of their marital union. In her stilted approach, Grace was careful to say nothing that might persuade them otherwise.

In contrast to Grace's quiet reticence, Jessman loudly proclaimed his wife's pregnant state with gusto. He had quickly begun to anticipate the forthcoming birth of his assumed long-awaited son and heir with much elation and excitement. Jessman felt confident his status in the local community had improved as news of Grace's pregnancy spread around the neighbourhood. He went to church with Grace more often, primarily because it was another opportunity to show off his pregnant wife.

If previously he had been perceived as a rich and quirky, domineering old bully, now perhaps he had managed to garner a little more of their respect. He had not been that well in recent times and was certainly beginning to show his years. Now however, with more than a little gloating, Jessman felt he had proved he was still a strong virile man. Surely his few friends and neighbours would have to acknowledge that he was at least well enough to be capable of fathering children with his attractive young wife.

So as Grace's pregnancy gradually advanced, it provided Jessman with opportunities for drunken nights and much bragging of the sons and heritage that his young wife would provide for him. Grace did her best to ignore it all, or at least to say little and especially not to contradict Jessman or in any way to arouse his suspicions. All the while she was inwardly groaning at the accumulation of lies that seemed to be arising unbidden all around her.

As for Grace's own family, they were delighted, especially her siblings. They talked excitedly and incessantly about the forthcoming baby and how they might all be able to share in its care and upbringing. Her mother, Beth, was also delighted to hear the news of the pregnancy. However, Beth saw it much more pragmatically. To her it was of course a welcome event, and in some way further promulgation of the success of their arranged marriage.

Even Riley conceded that at it might bring about a consolidation and strengthening of the bond between Jessman and Grace. Though he didn't quite dare to voice his hope that it might even help them transition from a slightly odd married couple towards being more a family unit.

For Beth it was a vitally important natural progression. One that she thought was long overdue! Beth was convinced that if Grace could produce children for Jessman, it would forge stronger ties, not just between Jessman and Grace, but also with Beth and Riley and their whole family. That would help draw them all together in one big united family.

It was all very simple in Beth's eyes. She was still the matriarch after all and far from finished with dreams and ambitions for herself and her offspring. She knew Jessman's health had been slipping over the past year or two. He was not a particularly healthy man and did not appear destined for a long life. She considered his young brother, Sam, could not run Jessman's farm, even if he survived his older brother. So, perhaps in not too many more years, with a little careful planning and orchestrating, the day would surely come when Jessman's farm and wealth would fall into Grace's hands. From there it would be an easy step to have it all merged with The Liberty Bell. That of course had long been Beth's goal.

When Beth had thought to encourage her by saying that Grace might one day have ownership of Jessman's farm, Grace was not at all interested. "You know I don't care about all that stuff, mother. I'm not ambitious like you. Lord knows I've had to endure enough pain from scheming about land to last me a lifetime. All I want to do right now is forget about all that and just enjoy my pregnancy. If

I can bring a healthy baby into this world, I'll be wealthy enough." Beth had not bothered to respond further, other than to give Grace a dismissive look as if to say, "You just wait. You'll learn!"

Though Grace still saw less of Liza, her bond of friendship with Liza's daughter, Valerie, was firmly established. She found that when she was with Valerie she could relax and escape the oppression of home life with Jessman, even time out from her own mother. It felt good to have that little bit of freedom away from all of them once in a while and simply enjoy her pregnancy.

Grace did not actively seek news of Maude's young man, the father of her child, but Valerie had mentioned that her brother was so caught up in the war effort in England that he was rarely able to visit his wife Maude or family now. When Valerie started to share her concerns about his heavy drinking and the bitter rows between him and Maude when he did return, Grace was quick to steer the subject away from him to avoid yet more pain.

Valerie was her best friend, but Grace did not dare reveal the secret she held within even to her. Valerie, in character was so very much like her mother. She remained ever supportive and empathetic, sharing in Grace's joy and just being there when her friend seemed to need her. Valerie simply accepted as natural the mixed emotions Grace was exhibiting about the forthcoming birth. To her mind it was entirely understandable that Grace would have moments of worry and reluctance to bring a child into Jessman's home and be further bound to him. In that Valerie was only partly right.

The Summer of 1941 came and went, passing through to late Autumn. Grace drew ever nearer to the time when she would give birth.

It is said that the ancient Celtic feast of Samhain, around a massive bonfire at sunset, some 2500 years before on Tlachtga, in County

Meath, celebrated the end of harvest time and heralded in the start of Winter. In some ways, it was also seen as the birth of what, in much later years, would be called All Hallows Eve, or Halloween.

For those who farmed the land in Grace's time, Halloween certainly did mark a time by which the last harvests of Autumn would be stored up, before the onset of Winter. However, it was a much more intriguing event than just that. The celebration of all 'hallows' or all saints, was a blend of pagan and Christian rituals that have pervaded the ages.

In this odd dichotomy, Halloween is a prelude to a widely celebrated Christian holy day, while at the same time it is also a night of secrets, dark rituals, and costume disguises, in a long-celebrated pagan festival. There are many who even believe it to be a night when the veil between the worlds of life and death are at their thinnest.

Perhaps in some strange prophetic way, it was also a fitting night on which a beautiful child was born to Grace. And beautiful she was.

The child was born in Banbridge hospital, a converted former workhouse, that had been one of many designed by English architect George Wilkinson a hundred years before. Once a last resort accommodating 800 of the desperate poor, dying and destitute, the old workhouse had long since served its purpose. After almost 90 years it had been closed, renovated and turned into a modern hospital.

It was a welcome advancement, as the trend away from home births was very slowly being replaced by hospital births. The hospital was located just far enough away from Belfast to have escaped the bombing and had become a favoured and safe place for young first-time mothers in the locality to give birth to their babies. Grace was fortunate to be considered one of these.

The staff at the hospital had seen many children born there previously, all beautiful in their own way. However, few had seen a child quite like the beautiful baby delivered to Grace that night. From the outset she was so popular with the nursing staff, that they affectionally dubbed her "God's little princess." As it turned out, it was an oddly prophetic choice.

Her perfectly smooth skin did not have the initial slight purple hue that was a common trait of many new-borns. Her eyes, which would change a little over time, were an unusual shade of dark grey-green, mesmerizingly beautiful. As the infant gazed out at her strange blurred surroundings, it seemed to allow her beauty and poignant innocence to shine through all the more. During the few days of Grace's enforced rest and recuperation period, it was not uncommon for several of the hospital staff to make some excuse or other to visit her and want to hold the child, marvelling anew at the miracle of birth and God's beautiful little princess.

Jessman and Grace had quickly settled on the name of Elizabeth for the baby. Jessman had not really given any consideration to a girl's name, having fully anticipated a son. Though he made token efforts to hide his disappointment at not having a son, it was fairly evident in his reaction to the child.

Grace on the other hand had hoped for a girl. She was drawn to name the child Elizabeth for her own mother, but all the more so for the young man's mother, her good friend, Liza. To Grace, the name Elizabeth secretly reflected a sense of gratitude for this special gift of unification of their two families. Jessman knew none of this of course, but simply went along with the name that Grace had chosen, presuming it to be just for her mother.

As it was the custom of the time to give children more than one name, Grace added the name of Gloria, after one of her younger sisters. Gloria was herself growing into a beautiful young woman and, like all of Grace's siblings, had a wonderful sense of humour. However, it was more than just that. Perhaps out of necessity, Gloria had developed a special empathy, a kindness and understanding of people that seemed to go far beyond her young years. Grace admired these qualities and the additional name of Gloria seemed fitting.

We all enter this world free of names or identities, until they are bestowed upon us by others, but somehow the given name 'Elizabeth' rested particularly easily on the small child. An innocent, with beauty already radiating from her small form. A tiny infant who, unbeknown to Grace, would in a short time, wield the power to change the course of Grace's life forever.

In the initial few weeks that Grace returned to live with Jessman she had many visitors. Even in times of war, neighbours, friends and family came regularly to see the new mother and child. There were many who offered Grace help with the sudden life changes brought about by a new-born baby. At first Grace was pleased and thankful to see them all, and certainly appreciated their help. However, being the eldest of nine children, she was not entirely lacking in the experience of caring for young babies.

With her strength quickly returning, she was also thankful that as the novelty of the situation lessened, so did their visits, enabling her to have a little more time alone with her baby. It was a special time for Grace, just being with the child and experiencing each and every small progression in those first few weeks of her infant life. Understandably, it also brought with it considerations of the child's future, and what that might mean for Grace and Jessman as her parents.

Anchored to the house more than usual by Elizabeth's needs, the cold weather, and the long dark nights in the weeks prior to

Christmas, Grace was also in Jessman's company more than ever during the day. He could not spend as much time outdoors on the farm in the short daylight hours, and was bored and aimless having to spend more of his time inside the house. He tended to brood on the sorry state of the war and was often depressed. With a young baby disrupting his sleep at night and then in constant need of Grace's attention during the days, it was a recipe for increased friction. Even with Sam around, a fractious Jessman inevitably meant more bullying.

Despite her earlier resolve to build a better relationship with him, and despite her genuine efforts, Grace found that she was growing more resentful of Jessman's impatience and brutish ways.

Jessman did little to help his own case. He would seek his temporary solace in the pub and come home drunk. Grace was sure that Jessman would not knowingly harm Elizabeth, but sometimes in his inebriated state he was prone to behave more recklessly. On more than one occasion, when he could barely keep himself upright, he would try to lift Elizabeth out of Grace's arms and hold her aloft like some trophy he had just won. It was all Grace could do, with the help of Sam, to keep Jessman steady and return Elizabeth to safety. The incidents only served to make Grace all the more on edge and wary of him, not only for her own safety now but more so for her small child.

Her tension mounting, Grace found it harder to hold back her growing repugnance as Jessman drooled over the child increasingly while drunk, yet largely ignored her during the day while sober. Like most men of his era, Jessman participated little in the daily care of the infant, leaving everything to Grace. At the same time, he still expected his home to be kept tidy, his clothes washed and his meals to be ready for him on time.

The arguments between them became more heated, with Grace,

acting from a mother's protective instincts and putting her child's needs first, often suffering the brunt of Jessman's impatience and resentment. Sam as always had been sympathetic and helpful, despite his limitations, but even his attempted peace-keeping interventions did little to ease the palpable tension and bitter atmosphere that pervaded the household. No-one was happy in the circumstances, not Grace, not Jessman, not even Sam.

Grace, feeling more isolated, began to feel she could bear the situation no longer. She had accepted being trapped in this loveless marriage for the sake of her parents and siblings for nearly five years. Now there were other needs she had to consider. Surely Elizabeth would eventually start to suffer harm of some sort if things continued like this. She had enough insight to recognise that part of the problem was due to her own resentment of her bullying husband laying claim to her child. The more he claimed her the more it irked Grace. This beautiful child that was the only remnant she had of her brief affair with the man she truly loved. That was certainly not Jessman.

It was a difficult choice for a young mother in a time of war. On one level she recognised that if she was to maintain the marriage it was better that Jessman believed the child was his. Yet, she could not help her inner rebellion against that untruth for it betrayed something deep within her.

She felt caught in the suffocating web of the lie, knowing full well that if she did reveal the truth to Jessman it could be the end of her marriage and perhaps a kind of social suicide for her and her child. More than once she wondered what choice she really had in all this, how she could possibly survive without Jessman, how she could ever be able to provide for her child on her own.

Chapter 16

Lies Laid Bare

I would rather that the whole world should be at odds with me, and oppose me, than that I myself should be at odds with myself, and contradict myself.
(Socrates)

Christmas 1941

On Christmas morning of 1941, Jessman took Sam, Grace and Elizabeth to spend the day with Grace's family at The Liberty Bell. Half a day with Beth and Riley was about as much as Jessman himself could put up with, and it was much the same for Beth and Riley, though they managed to put on a brave Christmas face throughout. However, it came as no surprise and suited everyone when Jessman and Sam once more retreated to their own farm after a hearty lunch, with plans to return and collect Grace and Elizabeth late that evening.

Grace enjoyed the experience of being back at The Liberty Bell at Christmas, spending time with her own siblings and parents. She had been through a particularly harrowing few days and appreciated the chance to relax a little and catch up with her family. However, as the evening wore on a heavy tiredness had swept over her as she waited for her husband to collect her again. For some reason he still hadn't arrived as it was approaching midnight and by then only Grace and her parents were still awake.

As a tired Grace talked to her parents, she began to reveal a little more of what her life was like at Jessman's home and her concerns for Elizabeth. At first her conversation was light, but then more and more the truth of her unhappiness in the abusive relationship began to creep through. Perhaps it was being back in The Liberty Bell and her tiredness that had brought her bottled emotions to the surface, but for no apparent reason Grace found her unguarded feelings beginning to flow. All too quickly the trickle of repressed emotions started to gather momentum and pour forth as words from Grace. She started to let it all go then, the door of her heart opening a little to give it release.

"Look, you don't really know him. I've come to accept there is no love in our marriage, but it's worse than that now with Elizabeth around. Almost daily I have to endure Jessman's bullying ways. If Sam isn't there to protect me, or Jessman has sent him off somewhere, he takes the opportunity to get into a fight with me, or worse. There are days I'm so bruised, I'm ashamed to leave the house. With all his drunken antics around Elizabeth, I'm terrified she might get hurt too."

Riley, who had never liked Jessman that much anyway, bunched his fists and growled beneath his breath. Beth, already well aware of some of Jessman's transgressions, saw the signs and instantly recognised where Grace's outpouring might lead. She did not want Grace to have to suffer any significant harm at the hands of Jessman, but neither did she want to encourage any undermining talk about their marriage failing if the situation could be improved or managed. There was far too much at stake to allow that now.

Hurriedly Beth intervened to try to quell the storm. Once more she sought to brush aside Grace's outpouring as just some early marriage differences that would settle down again in time. Then, well-practiced at taking the high ground and thinking it might knock some sense into Grace, Beth again roundly scolded her eldest daughter for not being able to manage Jessman by now, especially as he was no longer a young strong man.

Seeing Grace's momentary hesitation and homing in on the weakness, Beth pushed it further yet, inferring that Grace might be bringing all her problems upon herself by not being a better mother and more attentive wife. Like a juggler deftly tossing another selection of carefully chosen words high into the air, she launched in again.

"You're a grown woman Grace. Surely to God you can cope with that rich old fool's manly needs for a few more years and hold this marriage together. One day that big farm will all belong to you! Can you not see what a wife and a mother is supposed to do? If you'd stop making such a fuss and just get on with it, then maybe Jessman wouldn't need to be such a bully!"

Beth's words were meant to convince and contain. Like so many spinning clubs, mesmerising as they reached their pivotal point, before descending again into the skillful juggler's outstretched hands. Except this time her words hung limpid, suspended in the air, motive all too transparent.

With a sinking awareness, Beth sensed she might have pushed too hard, gone too far. In trying to force down the situation, in brow-beating Grace, she had mistakenly added the ultimate insult to injury. She saw the dark look flash cross Grace's face just once, but it was enough. Like a host of fumbled clubs, Beth's persuasive arguments crashed and clattered all around her.

Her accusing words had pried open that age-old chasm of self-doubt that clouds the perspective of victims and withers their will to act. Left unchallenged, these self-doubts grow and take up residence in the very psyche of the vulnerable, becoming entrenched there as some kind of thwarted truth. With repetition they begin to become accepted, no longer questioned or challenged. "You brought all this upon yourself. You don't deserve any better. You deserve whatever punishment you get. It's all your own fault."

The words were not Beth's actual words of course, but the underlying implications were much the same. What was said and what was heard in the moment were two different things. What was heard was the beguiling echo of that internal voice of self-doubt that festers and grows, unless the vile weed is plucked out there and then upon the instant.

Beth's words staggered Grace, unbalanced her, but they did not break her. This was no longer the timid sixteen-year-old frightened child hiding in an outside toilet on her birthday, submitting meekly to a desperate mother's dominant will. No, and Grace was after all her mother's daughter. There was also another reason why Grace would not give in to self-doubt, or be cowed or silenced this time.

She was now a mother with her own child. Now with that child Elizabeth in mind, Grace found all the determination and strength she needed. Her sobbing ceased abruptly, her mind clearing with a fearsome steadiness. She looked directly at her mother and spoke the words quietly but firmly.

"Jessman's bullying ways are entirely of his own choice and his own responsibility. They are none of my making." With a resoluteness she confronted her own long-conditioned obedience and underlying fear of her mother. Again, she spoke out. "It's not just my own safety that matters now, there's also Elizabeth's. I have to think and do what's best for her."

Seeing Riley had tensed up and was about to side with Grace, Beth tried again to interject, seeking to keep the situation under control and somehow stop the rift that was clearly coming.

"He's just a new father, having a few drinks too many and boasting that he has finally been able to sire a child with his young wife! For goodness' sake Grace, can you not see that? The child is his after all, he has as much right to her as you do!" she finished forcefully.

Then there it was, out in the open. The lie laid bare. The lie that pierced Grace's heart anew every time it arose, had surfaced once too often. The lie that her beautiful child, conceived in sacred moments of stolen happiness, was fathered by an old bullying husband she could not love and who had continually abused and wronged her in this wretched marriage of convenience.

Every time she had allowed it, it was a denial of truth, but not this time. This time the smothered secret that Grace had long held back surged forth unchecked to reveal itself in the heat of the moment.

"No, he doesn't!" she yelled back at Beth. "He has no right to her at all! Jessman is not Elizabeth's father! He has no right to her whatsoever!"

There was a sharp intake of breath and a momentary stunned silence as Beth and Riley just looked at her, trying to take in the unconscionable. Riley opened his mouth to speak, then closed it again, shaking his head in disbelief.

The brief silence was shattered by the sound of the old car horn outside the house telling them Jessman had arrived and was waiting to collect Grace and the child. As she hurriedly gathered up Elizabeth from the make-shift cot to leave, Grace looked down to her parents still seated at the kitchen table looking aghast at her.

"I can't go on like this, living with this deception day after day," she told them. "I just can't bear to live with that awful man any longer. I'm going to leave him."

Beth, caught completely off guard, with her mind still in turmoil from the shock, pleaded aloud.

"Is this really true, Grace? Jessman is not the child's father? Surely that can't be true!" Then, as the shock began to abate, mind grasping feebly at the reality, almost in a whisper Beth's words spilled out. "No! You can't do this to us Grace! In the name of God girl, what have you done?"

Grace did not say anything more, there was no need. She turned her face toward them again momentarily and Beth saw the truth and resolution in her eyes. Then as Grace started towards the door, a host of dreadful implication upon implication began to dawn on Beth. Still reeling, she blurted aloud her fear-driven thoughts.

"You can't tell him, Grace, you can't! It will be the end of us all if this gets out. It will ruin us. For God's sake girl, just pretend it's his child, he won't ever know. He can't ever know! Stay with him and he can provide for you both, he can take care of you both. You must do that Grace for your sake, for all our sakes! Grace, promise me that!"

Again, Grace looked at them but said nothing, though her mother's words disturbed her. She chose not to respond for she did not want to cause them further grief. As she left the house and got into the old Ford car with Jessman to leave, she heard again her mother's voice in her head.

Jessman, irksome and tired from a long day had fallen asleep in his armchair and Sam had only just woken him. Still tired and irritable from being kept waiting even a few moments, he barely gave Grace and the baby more than a second glance and a gruff greeting. Oblivious to what had just taken place, he revved up the car and drew away into the cold dark night, focused only on the road ahead. Grace sat quietly in the dark, the sleeping child in her arms.

The gentle rocking of the car and sound of the engine as they drove slowly along the uneven road gave Grace a temporary solace. She worried what might follow if she revealed the truth to Jessman. What vengeance might he bring down upon her and indeed perhaps even upon Elizabeth? Yet, as she sat in the emptiness that surrounded them, she also wondered again what choice she really had. How could she possibly continue to live this awful lie and bring her child up in the home with this abusive and domineering man that she did not love and who clearly did not love her? Didn't the bible say something too about how the Truth would set you free? Would the Truth help set her free?

The car journeyed on into the night, ferrying them away in the darkness from The Liberty Bell and towards Jessman's farm not far away. As Grace tried to weigh up the impossible choices in her mind, she looked briefly at Jessman, who was intent on his driving. For a moment she again felt that conditioned fear clutch at her heart. This time it was fear of Jessman's formidable wrath.

The child stirred, perhaps sensing her tension, then settled down against her again. The small movement was enough to arouse the protective instincts in Grace. In that moment she felt again the touch of that all-powerful strength of purpose that Nature bestows on mothers. That power to overcome fear and confront the danger for the sake of their offspring.

Grace's life was wretched enough having to endure her marriage to Jessman, but now she had voiced the truth. She would no longer live this lie and raise her child in this corrosive atmosphere. A corrosive atmosphere that would in time undoubtedly overspill onto Elizabeth. No, she might suffer the pain of this marriage alone, but she would not permit Elizabeth, this beautiful innocent, this vulnerable child, to share in that suffering. Resolved now in her course of action, she knew that for the sake of this small child she would bear whatever vengeance Jessman might wreak upon her.

The car slowly wound its way up the long farm lane to Jessman's house, and Grace took a deep breath and readied herself to disembark. She knew she would need time and help in planning her escape from Jessman and this place. She would need to get far enough away that neither he, nor her mother, could find her. There was no point whatsoever in trying to run home to mother, she reminded herself. When she had tried that in the first few weeks of marriage, Beth had promptly brought her right back to Jessman.

This escape would not be easy for she would not only need to find a place to live but also a paid job of some sort to survive. Still, there had to be a way and perhaps her brother Toby could help her. Holding fast to her resolve, Grace entered the house with the child still in her arms. Looking around at her prison home, she grasped onto hope. Hope, that yes, there had to be a way.

Later, as she lay fitfully half-awake, having fed Elizabeth and settled her back into the small cot beside her, thoughts and worries floated around in Grace's mind. Her choice made, she tried to brush aside the doubts and allow herself the peace of sleep. Reassuring herself that somehow she would manage, somehow she would cope. As light slumber in time gave way to a deeper sleep, Grace was at last able to take her rest, her mind now fixed on a course of action she knew would bring a different kind of hardship, but one she hoped she could manage for her own sake and for the sake of her child.

Fate once again looked upon Grace as she slept, this young woman so resolved now in the path she had chosen, yet such a tiny plaything in the great cosmic game of chance.

Every once in a while, our journeys through life seem to take us to a crossroad. A major junction in the road where we recognise that there may be very different paths to follow. The choices we then make are often of great import, not just influencing our own lives, but sometimes touching the lives of those around us. Whether she recognised it or not, this was yet another of those momentous choices for Grace.

Very few women in those hard times could leave their husband, even if they wanted to leave. Even if some were being constantly abused. Even if that abuse spilt over onto their children. To Grace, all that mattered right then was the welfare of her child. For her child's sake she would endure Jessman's wrath for deserting him, and she would meet with fortitude whatever scorn society threw her way.

What Grace did not know then was just how far reaching her choice would be. For a far greater wrath than Jessman's awaited her on that chosen path. A wrath so bitter it would inflict upon her one of the deepest hurts any young mother would ever have to endure.

The Weight of Choice

Chapter 17

The Escape

> We need the possibility of escape as surely as we need hope.
> (Edward Abbey)

January 1942

As January of 1942 rolled in, Hitler, had already turned away from bombing Britain and expanded the war by turning his attention towards Russia the previous Summer. He had signed a non-aggression pact with Russian at the start of the war so they could carve up Poland. That done, he was quick to renege on the pact that had outlived its usefulness. His three million Axis troops had pushed far into Russia, threatening to over-run it. However, the bitter cold Russian Winter and dogged resistance of the Russians slowed their progress. Germany's swooping Typhoon pincer offensive had been stalled as the crucial battle for Moscow dragged on.

The fighting had spread elsewhere too. The whole world now seemed caught up in the war. In the Pacific, Japan's remorseless expansion had continued, perhaps somewhat predictably.

Japan had been Britain's ally in the first war, gaining recognition as a country of some power when her forces had managed to get the better of Russia a decade prior. President Roosevelt had intervened back then to broker a peace treaty between Japan and Russia that had earned him the Nobel Peace prize. After Japan had helped Britain in the first world war, as an ally, it had expected to receive more ready access to both Britain and America. However, when this was denied, Japan felt excluded and unfairly discriminated against.

Roosevelt's decree, that only 'white' people were permitted free access to America, did not help matters. Nor perhaps that white western powers such as America, Britain, France, Portugal and Holland, all held vast controlling Imperialist interests throughout the far away shores of South East Asia. It could hardly have come as any great surprise then, as western colonial powers fought amongst themselves in the second great war, that Japan might seek to exploit the fall of France and Holland to Germany by pushing her own presence further into the Asia Pacific.

When, as history records, Roosevelt finally decided to stop Japan's advancement by cutting off her vital oil supplies, against all probability, Admiral Yamamoto, took the audacious step of attacking America's assembled fleet in her far-flung Hawaiian base. As history also records, the devasting surprise attack on Pearl Harbour on 7 December 1941, not only dealt a major blow to America, it also propelled her into the war with Japan, and in a matter of days with Germany too.

In Northern Ireland the mobilising and arrival of thousands of American troops in January 1942 was a very welcome sight. Up to that point the outlook had been bleak for Britain. However, now there was more than a glimmer of hope that following the crippling onslaughts Britain had endured, and with the Americans at last joining on their side, the tide of the war might somehow begin to turn more in their favour. Hope was further fuelled by the recent signing of the Declaration of United Nations. This was a host of allied nations coming together so that they could be stronger. It was to be a pivotal year in the war.

It would also be a crucial year of change and hope for Grace. If Jessman had suspected anything at all that weekend he never mentioned it. He surely could not have known what Grace was planning or he would have squashed it all right there and then. Certainly, Grace would not have dared to tell him. A divorce was unheard of, and with the shame and stigma that accompanied it, rendered it totally out of the question. If she was ever to get away from Jessman, she knew it would have to be by quiet stealth.

It was the last Saturday in January 1942, one of those odd months on the calendar with five Saturdays. Jessman had taken Sam and they had gone out for the day to make another of their now infrequent trips to Belfast. Grace and Elizabeth had been left alone in the house. With the help of her brother Toby, who had been sworn to secrecy, Grace had been gradually making careful plans for some weeks, awaiting just the right moment.

Now the day had come. She would finally escape. Young Toby had offered her another life raft, when, through a network of friends, he had found some cheap rooms for long term hire in Newcastle on Sea, the popular little Irish holiday resort in County Down. Toby had gallantly offered to use his savings to pay for the first month until Grace found some sort of a job. Apprehensive as she was, it was all more than Grace dared hope for. A new start, maybe a chance to live her own life, if Jessman and the world would only let her.

She looked around Jessman's farmhouse one last time, silently acknowledging the many little improvements she had made to it in the five years she had endured there. She had tried to make things work here, really tried, but if she was honest with herself, her heart had not been in it. Then almost inevitably, she remembered that first day again. She remembered entering into this strange new world and her feelings of terror as she wielded a kitchen knife to try to keep Jessman at bay. She remembered Sam, poor dear Sam, for a while her only friend it seemed. How she would miss him.

Yes, she had mixed emotions about it all even now. It would be a difficult road ahead, she knew, but there was no turning back. She would leave this house and go without regrets. For if she was still being honest with herself then she knew that too. It was only a house and not a home. In so many ways it had been more akin to a prison.

Still, Grace knew she could not depart without leaving Jessman a note to explain why she was leaving him, along with a plea not to try to find them. While she continued to live with him Grace reasoned she could not risk telling Jessman that he was not Elizabeth's father. Now that she was fleeing from him it was different matter.

She felt she owed him that truth at least, but not out of spite. No, that was not in Grace's nature and she would not give in to it even now. In any case, she reasoned, if she told Jessman the truth perhaps he might be less likely to try to find them, nor to try to take Elizabeth away from her. Beth would be livid that she had told him, but that couldn't be helped now. Grace would continue to do her best to protect her family's name of course, but she would tell Jessman regardless. Then it would be their choice, Jessman and her parents, whether they wanted to keep it secret or not. It was no longer Grace's burden to bear.

Finding the right true, necessary and kind words to say in the letter proved difficult. How could it be otherwise for a young woman in those times trying to tell her abusive older husband that he was not the father of her child and she was leaving him? Yet Grace did her best to tell the truth in a kind way, even for Jessman. Then, trying to shed the last vestiges of self-doubt, with a flurry Grace finished the letter and left it in a prominent place for Jessman to find on his return. Taking a deep breath, she turned to leave.

Toby, hurrying her along, helped her to gather up the last few things for herself and Elizabeth. Somehow, she and Elizabeth squeezed snuggly into the little side-car and Toby kicked his reliable old Norton motorbike into life. Then, with a thumbs up signal followed by a turn of the throttle, the engine powered up and without another word they sped away.

Grace sat in the side-car with Elizabeth on her lap. After some initial squirming and wriggling and noisy objections from Elizabeth, both gradually settled down into the soothing swaying rhythm of the sidecar and the journey. Grace had been to Newcastle many times as a child on their annual Sunday School outings. For a while this trip brought back sweet memories of those times. Back then it had taken over an hour by bus on their annual excursions to the coast.

She had loved those outings with her friends. The early morning bus journeys would be filled with laughter and much singing on the way there, with endless excitement and anticipation. After a long and very full day out at Newcastle, the return journey in the evening would be much quieter. The enthusiastic bantering and sharing of tales would gradually cease and the children quieten with the encroaching blanket of darkness. The latter part of the journey home would invariably be an easy churning and turning of the engine, nudging most of the youngsters and even some of the adult chaperons into a sleepy comfortable silence.

Grace had shared the truth of her situation with Toby, and he had rightly realised that to escape she needed to get right away from everyone. She needed to find a safe haven, away from family, away from the bombing. He had known just the place immediately.

Somewhere far enough away, yet not entirely unreachable, so her siblings might be able to visit.

To some, Belfast might have seemed a likely choice, especially with the war effort still very full on and not too many questions asked of willing workers. Grace could certainly hide herself among the bustle of that city and leave the countryside, and Jessman, far behind her. Yes, Belfast was certainly one possibility, but Toby felt it wouldn't be quite right for Grace. On the other hand, Newcastle, now that did feel absolutely right!

Toby knew that Grace loved the little seaside town of Newcastle by the Mourne mountains in County Down more than any other place in Northern Ireland. In fact, more than anywhere. She grown to love it from occasional visits there in early childhood. Yes, for Grace it just had to be Newcastle.

The little town was said to have taken its name from an old sixteenth century castle, built by one of the powerful Magennis clan. It was rumoured that it was descendants of this same Magennis clan who had given their name, not only to the ancient castle, but more recently to a particularly well-known Irish stout. Many an Irishman had blessed that famous stout, but many too had fallen foul of it. Of even more renown, Ireland's primary patron saint, Welsh-born St. Patrick, was famously said to have stood atop Newcastle's surrounding mountains and banished the snakes from Ireland. Whether there were any snakes there in the first place was a matter of some debate, but whatever the reason, Ireland remains free of snakes nonetheless!

For Grace, Newcastle was a seaside holiday town unlike any other. It had the usual range of colourful little shops along the seafront and the endless swings, dodgems and entertainment rides in amusement parks. That had all been fun for her as a child of course, but there was so much more, so many other charms that drew people to Newcastle.

The little town had a wide promenade that bordered a long wide sandy beach that stretched all around the natural bay. Grace loved that promenade. Children raced along it, young lovers strolled along it hand in hand, older people too, all could enjoy this special setting, rain or shine. When the sun did shine, the clear waters of the sea reflecting a glorious blue sky above was a timeless sight that could take one's breath away.

Newcastle sat cradled at the foot of the dark granite mountains of Mourne, named after an ancient Gaelic clan. There, where the mountains of Mourne swept down to the sea, as immortalised in Percy French's haunting ballad, was a scenic beauty that had inspired a host of poets, song writers, and authors for centuries. It was this special sense of magic, a rare majestic ambience about the place that seemed to touch not only Grace, but all who visited there, if they but took the time to discover and embrace it.

As Toby and Grace began to draw nearer to the town, Grace noticed the long dry-stone walls stretching for mile after mile across the hillsides. The stone walls brought her memory back to The Liberty Bell and the wall she used to follow on her way home from school to lead her back home. Then, inevitably her thoughts, driven by early memories, turned again to her husband, Jessman. This was no Sunday school excursion she reminded herself. She was fleeing from Jessman and his farm with another man's child in her arms, seeking desperately to find a new life in this Newcastle.

She thought of how her own parents had also gone to live in that other Newcastle in England years before, probably when they were of a similar age. Grace had been born there in that other far away Newcastle after all. Of course, Beth and Riley had gone there under very different circumstances. Her parents weren't exactly escaping in the same way as Grace was now, but they had been seeking a kind of escape nonetheless. She smiled to think that perhaps Newcastle was indeed a special place for her.

As Toby slowed and wound the bike into the little picture-postcard coastal town, Grace's mind was filled with a mixture of joy and trepidation. "Maybe history doesn't just repeat itself," she mulled to herself, "though it does seem to have a strange sense of irony."

The rooms Toby had located were little more than a barely furnished bed-sit with a small kitchen off to one-side and a tiny bathroom on the other. It was very basic but sufficient for Grace's needs. The landlord was an elderly school master who had fought in the first world war and managed to return home safely, only to lose his wife to the Spanish flu within the year. Now he lived alone and no longer needed all of the house for himself. He had converted part of it to rent out for additional income.

He also needed a housekeeper, so the nominal rent and housekeeping arrangement suited Grace well. Toby had already explained some of Grace's circumstances and, as promised, had paid the first month in advance. The landlord seemed an amiable man and gave them a brief welcome and explanation of how things worked in the rooms. After making it clear that as long as Grace followed the rules, her circumstances were her own business, he had added that if she was no trouble she could stay as long as she wanted. Grace thanked him for his kindness. With a smile and a parting handshake the landlord left them to it.

Toby stayed around for a few more hours, helping Grace to settle in and get her whereabouts, before he set off. He pressed some money into her hand, warning her to keep her head low and be sure to stay out of trouble. With a smile Grace responded, as Toby had anticipated she might.

"Yes, I know, troubles rarely come alone and if you invite them in its very hard to get rid of them."

They embraced and she thanked him dearly for all his help. Toby bid her farewell, promising to return as soon as he could, though it might be a while. Grace stood on the doorstep and watched him ride away and out of sight, with a slightly anxious feeling rising in her heart. Then she heard Elizabeth's waking cries and her anxiety dissipated a little as she went back inside the rooms to see to her.

After Grace had cared for Elizabeth's needs, she sat quietly in the bedsit taking in her surroundings. Toby had already drawn her attention to a couple of part-time jobs in the newspaper that might supplement her income, one of which was caring for a young child with Down's syndrome. She hoped that with her previous experience with Sam, she had developed a better understanding of what was needed and might be found suitable.

Grace's thoughts once again turned to Jessman and what she had left behind. She had made the break, she had escaped, but now she had to make it work. She and Elizabeth were now fugitives, starting a new life, trying to survive on their own. It was a scary feeling, but exciting too.

Chapter 18

The Curse

The best people possess a feeling for beauty, the courage to take risks,
the discipline to tell the truth, the capacity for sacrifice.
Ironically, their virtues make them vulnerable,
they are often wounded, sometimes destroyed.
(Earnest Hemmingway)

April – May 1942

It was a few months before Toby was able to visit Grace in Newcastle again. By now Grace had settled into a workable routine with her job as housekeeper for her landlord. She had also been fortunate enough to be accepted as a part-time helper for the young child with Down's syndrome. While the job was at times challenging, having to manage Elizabeth as well, it helped pay her bills. It was rewarding in other ways too, and Grace was increasingly discovering she had been blessed with many skills in looking after young children.

When Toby arrived that weekend, he had brought two of their sisters along with him, Wendy and Gwen. Both had been sworn to secrecy and both were ecstatic to see Grace and baby Elizabeth. They spent the day catching up on all the news and cooing over Elizabeth, encouraged and delighted when the child responded with a smile or even a grimace.

As far as Grace could make out from their tales, it seemed that all hell had broken loose after her departure. Jessman had found the note Grace left and had raged about her leaving him, questioning everyone as to her whereabouts. He had angrily accused Grace's parents, Beth and Riley, of complicity and threatened to make them pay back all the money they owed him for paying off their debts. Beth, as expected, was seething at the news of Grace running away and it soon became evident even to Jessman that Beth and Riley had not helped her make the escape.

Beth had questioned all her family to find out where Grace had gone. Of course, until Wendy and Gwen's current visit, no-one knew anything anyway, apart from a tight-lipped Toby and he was often away for months on end with the war now. So, Beth and Jessman's efforts to locate Grace were frustrated. Even Jessman's enquiries with the police went nowhere. It was a time of war after all and the police had other far more pressing matters to handle than some old fart of a farmer's attractive young wife absconding, no matter how belligerent he might be. So Jessman was largely ignored by the police and his own efforts proved fruitless.

As the days passed into weeks, it seemed that rumours of Grace leaving Jessman had spread through the local community. What might have been juicy gossip for quite some time was soon curtailed as the news of the war continued to dominate. Though his efforts at finding Grace were stymied, Jessman however remained just as bitter.

Toby suggested that while Jessman may well still be fuming, he might also be in a quandary. Having boasted to all and sundry how he still had it in him to father a child, Jessman would not want to face the embarrassment of his neighbours knowing that the child he had boasted about was not actually his, but the result of his young wife having an affair with another man. He would surely want that kept very quiet, especially if he thought there was any chance at all of Grace coming back to him.

Wendy and Gwen insisted that Jessman was not the sort of man who would be inclined to forgive Grace and be ready to provide for another man's child by his wife. They felt that as time went on, he might be less inclined to want Grace back again and, if that was the case, then that might work out better for all of them. Naturally enough, it seemed they had all been discussing Grace's situation, and all had opinions on the matter.

One thing they all agreed on was that if Grace could just stay hidden and keep her head low for a few more months, things might well start to settle down. After that she would not have to be quite so much a fugitive and could come back home whenever she pleased. In the meantime, they all promised they would visit her often and help her keep things quiet and ticking along until the time was right for Grace to come out of hiding.

How wrong they all were.

Beth had been having her own sleepless nights. That draining, distorted sense of reality that tends to visit in the half-sleep was pursuing Beth. It caused her to worry that Jessman would not let up over the money they owed him now that Grace had run off. He was not without power in the community and she feared that power and what he might do.

What Beth held dear in her heart floated endlessly through her jumbled thoughts, making her feel vulnerable. Could Jessman somehow take that lower portion of The Liberty Bell away from them yet again in his bitter vengeance? The thoughts plagued her.

In that distorted reality all that Beth had worked so hard to gain over the years, was now becoming a burdensome fear of loss.

She felt that all her careful planning was coming undone. Just when things had seemed to be going better, all now placed in jeopardy because of Grace and her damned affair. Beth was distraught and her worries clung to her. She had to find Grace and knock some sense into that foolish girl. She had to make her go back to Jessman before it was too late.

Just like any mother, Beth noticed it almost immediately. Mothers sometimes have a kind of sixth sense when it comes to being aware of the comings and goings of their offspring. They may not know exactly what is happening of course, but Nature has gifted them with an uncanny natural ability. An ability to notice the little signs in their offspring that help them sense just when something is amiss or seriously out of sync. So it was with Grace's mother, Beth.

For the past few evenings after work, Wendy and Gwen had been having hushed talks in huddles, quietly discussing their visit to Grace and how they might help her. Beth could not hear them of course, but she felt it was more than just girl talk and certainly about something they were not inclined to share with her. Even when Beth confronted them, they had made up some lame excuse or tried to change the subject.

Yet Beth was no fool. Overhearing the odd hushed word, seeing the way they behaved, reading their expressions, she had quickly sensed they knew much more about Grace than they were letting on. She could try to force them to tell her, but they were fiercely loyal to Grace and might be hard to persuade.

Beth had spent years raising her large family, often barely scratching a living for them when the odds were stacked against her. While Riley was honest and hardworking, it was really Beth who had developed the guile to get by in difficult times, to help them all survive. She would call upon that same guile again now, in her time of need.

It wasn't too difficult as it turned out. On the Friday night, as Wendy and Gwen deposited their wage packets on the table for their mother, Beth had simply told them that she was aware they knew where Grace and Elizabeth were living and that they had been visiting her. When they tried to deny it, she told them that she and Riley wanted so much to see Grace and their first little grandchild again and to help them. Before long she had convinced them that they should all go together to see Grace the very next day.

Much of it was true of course. Beth did want to see Grace and her child again, and she did want to help them. Just not quite in the way that Wendy and Gwen anticipated. What Beth had omitted to mention was that she also wanted to persuade Grace to return to Jessman. As far as Beth was concerned, that was entirely for the best.

Therein was the problem. For who could really say what was for the best, and for whom, and what indeed was not for the best? Even when we may firmly believe what we are doing is for the best, our intentions may be tainted if our own self-interest is getting in the way and subtly clouding our judgement. So it was on the day that Beth visited Grace in Newcastle.

They arrived at Grace's rooms in the late morning. Toby was still away on duty, and Riley, Beth, Wendy and Gwen had all come by bus. A protesting Gloria had been left at The Liberty Bell to look after the youngsters. After the initial surprise and a certain amount of apprehension, Grace welcomed them all into her little home. She sensed the tension in her mother, especially when Beth declined to hold Elizabeth, but Grace did her best to put that aside and try to make her mother feel at her ease.

The weather was cold but dry, allowing them opportunity to venture outside a little later for a walk along the promenade. That helped ease the tension enormously and in a spirit of family conviviality, they were able to spend a pleasant couple of hours together enjoying Newcastle. From time to time they encountered some of the American troops that had now become a regular sight in the town and were typically met with wide beaming smiles and friendly greetings as they passed by.

By way of fitting in with the Northern Ireland culture, the troops had been instructed to give the locals a friendly greeting, but never ever to argue politics or religion with any of them, and never ever to boast. It was the second and third elements of these instructions that proved quite a challenge for the young Americans! Nevertheless, it was wise counsel and, for the most part anyway, had held the troops in very good stead. It certainly seemed that everyone in Newcastle that day was buoyed up by their presence, Grace and her family visitors included.

For a while then, the little group were able to leave their troubles behind them as they strolled along Newcastle's beautiful promenade. Riley bought ice-creams for everyone and when he thought Beth wasn't watching, he slipped Grace some folding money to buy a few things for Elizabeth and tide them over. The magical atmosphere and beauty of Newcastle seemed to be rubbing off onto all of them. For a short while they even escaped the turmoil of the war, and simply enjoyed a few hours in the quaint little seaside town.

It was not to last long.

Over afternoon tea back at Grace's rooms, less than an hour ahead of the scheduled return bus journey, the pleasant atmosphere began to ebb away. In its place, the earlier tension in Beth returned and filled up the two small rooms. Sitting facing Grace, Beth placed her teacup on the table, and sitting up straight announced that she had something important to say and it could not be put off any longer. Grace and the others looked at each other, each with their own ideas of what Beth might be about to say and each feeling more than a little uneasy.

Beth began quietly enough. She told Grace that she should be grateful for the time in Newcastle away from Jessman. That it must have been like a long holiday for her, but now it really was time for Grace to return to her husband and make amends. Then she added, that especially in a time of war, it was just not right for a woman to walk out on her husband, especially with a young baby in tow.

Grace's younger sibling, Wendy could frequently be outspoken. Now she interjected on Grace's behalf. "Well, can't you see she's doing alright here mah, and she's got a wee job and all. Sure, that old sod Jessman was bloody awful to her when she was there with him, so I don't think she should go back to him at all, even if the old bugger begged her!"

Beth gave Wendy a sharp look and told her brusquely to mind her language, that she didn't understand these things, and not to interrupt her again. Riley had been grinning and nodding his agreement with Wendy, but quickly took the smile off his face at Beth's curt words.

Grace had not expected the visit from her parents, but she knew her mother well enough to know she would try to persuade her to return to Jessman. She was ready with a gentle but firm rebuttal, briefly reiterating her reasons for leaving Jessman and explaining that she felt she and Elizabeth could survive well enough on their own.

The tension in Beth was clearly mounting. With the exchange starting to become louder, she tried again to persuade Grace that it was not in her interests to abandon the husband who had supported her and her child and helped them all keep The Liberty Bell.

"Look Grace, if you just come back and say you're sorry, I'm sure Jessman can be convinced to take you and Elizabeth back under his roof again, but it has to be very soon, before his patience runs out!"

This time it was Gwen who tried to intercede on Grace's behalf. She had only uttered a few words when Beth turned on her and told her to shut up and stay out of it. When Riley made a brief attempt to speak up too, he got a similar blunt response.

Beth was fixed on her purpose and would not be denied. All too aware of the growing resistance of her own family, and seeing that Grace was as yet unmoved, Beth was becoming more and more angry. She was like a bomb that might explode at any moment. A bomb that could inflict terrible damage if it did explode. As Beth rounded on Grace once again, she was increasingly threatening.

"Yes, Jessman may be a difficult husband at times, but you're just being selfish and naive. He has enough money and influence to be a very dangerous enemy to all of us! Especially when his wife has just left him to give birth to another man's child! God knows, our whole family will suffer the shame of that if it ever gets out, and Jessman may yet take the farm out from under us! Is that what you want?!"

Grace might have wilted beneath her mother's aggressive argument in bygone days, but now she had Elizabeth and she was determined she would not raise her beautiful child in Jessman's house. Once more she held firm and insisted that she would stay on in Newcastle.

In the face of Grace's determined resistance, and with the others siding with her, Beth could see her case was falling on deaf ears. Losing all semblance of control now, she rose to her feet. Pointing a work-hardened wiry finger over at Elizabeth, her voice roared out.

"This damn child could be the ruination of you, the ruination of all of us! If you're trying to think what's best for her then you should take her straight back home now before it's too late!"

Moving as if to stand closer to Grace, Beth spoke in that same booming voice she had used to command Grace to come out of her tiny hiding place just a few years prior. The words came out as an ultimatum.

"I'm telling you for the last time Grace, take her and go home to Jessman! If you don't then you and this child will be outcast from this family! Do you understand me girl, you'll be an outcast! Now, tell me you will do as I say!"

Riley and the girls again began to protest, until Beth in a white-hot temper told them all once more to shut up and wait for Grace's answer. Like a hawk circling above its prey, Beth crowded right in on Grace waiting for her answer.

Sensing a crucial moment had come, with some trepidation Grace stood to face this strong imposing woman that was her mother. This woman, this mother of nine children, who had inflicted upon Grace the pain of a loveless and brutal marriage to Jessman for a cause she honestly believed in, but which Grace now knew in her heart to be a mistake. Now, her mother had come here to find her, to demand that Grace and her child go back to that same marriage of misery, to make that same mistake again, for the sake of the farm and her family.

In that brief instant, as she stood and looked at her mother, Grace saw for the first time the long years of fatigue and insecurity behind her mother's burning eyes, the fear behind her anger. Understanding dawned. For that brief moment Grace saw not a fearsome woman, but a woman full of fear. Beth was a tired and worn mother, still trying to do what she thought was best for her family. Grace felt an outpouring of compassion fill up her heart.

Yes, of course Beth was being driven. However, it was not so much by ambition as it might first have seemed, but more out of a deep-seated underlying fear and concern for her family, their reputation, and their farm. Once again, out of that fear of loss and shame, she was ready to sacrifice the one for the many. Yet Grace could also see that her mother's actions were misguided, her decisions made in error, as decisions are wont to be when made in the grip of fear and anger.

This time, with a new understanding, Grace found the strength to stand firm in the face of the raging storm that was her mother. She shook her head and said gently, "No mother, I'm sorry. I am thinking of Elizabeth. That's why I will never go back to live with that awful man again. Never. Nothing you can say will ever change that."

The absolute power and certainty in Grace's quiet words brought them all to silence. Grace was immovable. In that silence it was as if the bomb, having landed in the room, had somehow been defused and failed to explode. Now the bomb lay there, for all to see, powerless in the face of Grace's quiet resolve, rendered inept.

The moment lingered on; the frozen silence stretching out, unbroken. Still Beth said nothing. Then slowly she began to move. This time it was her turn to move aside, to give way, bend and gather up her coat to leave. Her face was steely grey, gaunt, filled up with the years of repressed anger, hurt and pain. Her efforts to persuade her daughter to return to Jessman had proved utterly and completely futile. Grace would not be persuaded. Head bent, Beth took another slow step towards the door.

Then, ominously she lifted her head again and turned back to stand in front of Grace. She was holding herself in check, poised, almost shaking with rage. For a moment Grace thought her mother was going to embrace her, but suddenly Beth's hand lashed out, striking Grace full in the face and knocking her back down into the chair. Before anyone had time to react, she leaned over Grace, grabbing her shoulders, the curse beginning in a gruff whisper, ascending into a dark frightening fury. The bomb was ticking, about to explode.

"Listen to me you stupid girl! Listen now! If you leave Jessman we may lose everything! You'll condemn us all! So you'd better understand this Grace. If you leave him, then you also leave all of us – forever! We'll have nothing more to do with you. You are forever outcast from this family! Do you hear me? Forever outcast!"

Riley, shocked beyond belief, jumped to his feet to protest again, beseeching Beth to wait, to calm down, to give it time. It was too late. Beth would not, could not wait. Now, in the firm grip of uncontrollable anger, that venomous, vindictive, vehement anger, the bomb exploded.

Running amok, the destroyer of souls trampled the quiet voice of reason within Beth. The quiet voice that might have pulled her back from the brink. Too late, the dread curse of anger erupted from deep within her like burning lava to rage unchecked. Laying waste to that final barrier of reason, it ripped away the last shreds of compassion for her eldest child. Anger, fuelled by years of long-buried fears and frustrations, rising in rampant ascendency, to bring ruin. Beth's dread voice poured out the damning words.

"If you cannot go back to live with Jessman, then never, ever set foot in my house again, for you are not my daughter! None of mine will ever set foot in your house or see you again. I will see to that, damn you!"

"Go then if you must and take this bastard brat with you! Go live in that god-forsaken Crow's Nest with that other one like some harlot for all I care. But with every part of my being, I curse you,

Grace! I curse you! May you never find peace, and if you try to find it with that other one, may your children all be born black, black crows!"

Riley, in astonishment, begged Beth to take it back, pleading with her that no-one deserved to be treated so harshly, least of all their own daughter. Beth rounded on him, still burning fiercely. "You are either with me Riley, or you can stay on here with this harlot! She brings it on herself! There's no going back on this."

The loud angry voices had woken Elizabeth and she had begun crying. Wendy and Gwen, now also crying, tried to comfort their weeping eldest sister. With the room in utter chaos and destruction behind her, Beth stormed out, leaving them all totally devasted in her wake.

Destroyer of Souls

Chapter 19

A Test of Time

> *When we are pushed around among opposing chances*
> *and compulsions and strong assaults of passions possessing our soul,*
> *we acknowledge all these things as our masters and are enslaved by them*
> *and carried wherever they take us.*
> *(Plotinus 204-270)*

June 1942-1943

By June 1942, America had cobbled together her battered navy again after the disaster at Pearl Harbour only six months prior. Then, in a risky but decisive manoeuvre she had deliberately sailed her fleet into the carefully planned Japanese trap at Midway, Hawaii. In a fierce struggle that hung in the balance throughout, the American Forces finally managed to emerge victorious. It was a turning point in the war with Japan. Many other sea battles continued to rage throughout the Pacific, but Japan was slowly being denied and was no longer on the ascendency.

On the Russian front it had been a similar story. After a long and bitter last stand defensive battle over a decimated Stalingrad at the end of 1942, Russia had held on by her fingernails. In the face of certain defeat, Stalin had somehow been able to garner extra resources, men, women, and children, willing or coerced into fighting to defend the motherland. Incredibly they had staged their own daring blitzkrieg movement. Hitler's Axis Forces had been outfoxed and were surrounded on all sides. Then, battered remorselessly for the first weeks of 1943, and seemingly abandoned by their Fuhrer, the encircled Axis Forces were pushed towards starvation in the paralysing bitter cold Winter. Finally, as the noose tightened, ninety thousand desperate men of the Axis army, ignoring Hitler's orders, surrendered to Russia's army of men and women.

It was a major victory for Russia. Along with the American victory at Midway, and the Allies' victories in North Africa around the same time, the tide of the war with Germany and Japan was clearly beginning to change. More hard-fought victories for Britain and the Allies began to follow. With these critical turning points in the war, at last it seemed increasingly possible that Hitler could be defeated. Hope was indeed on the ascendency, but not without enormous cost.

Meanwhile, Maude's husband had been drinking heavily for quite some time now. He knew it, but it was an easy way into oblivion, a coping mechanism to numb mind and soul. It was perhaps a path made all the more inviting by the alcohol addictive genes he could well have inherited. Especially, as some experts today would suggest heritability for alcohol addictions could well be as high as fifty percent.

Certainly, his father, Bob, had turned to drink frequently to escape the horrors of the first World War, leaving Liza to be the wise and steadying influence in the upbringing of all their children. Maude's young man was reasonably intelligent, but Nature sees to it that even the most intelligent of people are no more immune from making their share of foolish mistakes than anyone else.

The war effort work consumed him through the days and sometimes nights, as Britain continued to build more and more aeroplanes. A little time off in the evenings and a rare weekend once in a while offered him some respite, but it was an exhausting work schedule.

Yet, it was not the high demands of his work or even living away from home that was now pushing him mindlessly towards the drink. In fact, in many ways it was during his few free hours away from work that his problems tended to surface and he would be most vulnerable. Then he had time to contemplate not only the dreadful state of his marriage to Maude, but the dreadful state the whole world seemed to be in with the war.

At times he thought there might be a lot of truth in his mother's oft repeated saying that these great wars only reflected the state of mankind, right down to how they chose to live their individual lives. He felt he understood a little better now just what she meant when she said, "Mankind first has to practice kindness in order to be kind."

His mother's sayings often struck a chord with him when he thought of the poor state of his own marriage to Maude. It hurt knowing full well that she was not all to blame, and that he was falling well short in that regard too. His only escape it seemed, was when he totally immersed himself in his work, or drink. It was in some ways an escape from reality, just burying his head trying not to think of it. While his mind was focused totally on his work, it was in some ways a relief, for there was less opportunity for the pain of other thoughts and worries to intrude. The heavy drinking had a similar effect, but then his mind was completely numbed as he escaped into that darker oblivion.

He and Maude seemed to be arguing and fighting a lot when he was home. He knew his drinking probably wasn't helping matters but he enjoyed his nights out, his escape. On more than one occasion Maude had attacked him with the poker or brush handle when he had come back home drunk. He in turn had struck back at her from his drunken stupor. Afterwards he could barely remember what had happened, but he had noticed the signs, the reddish blue bruise marks on her skin. The same signs he had remembered seeing on his own mother as a boy. It made him cringe with guilt and want to avoid Maude all the more.

It is said that war can make people grow up quickly, and time can change them. Both of these may have played their part in Maude's young man's case, but of course there was much more to it than that. One thing was clear, Maude no longer infatuated or held sway over him as she once had done at the outset of their relationship. Far too much had happened since those heady early days when he was swept along by her flamboyant charisma.

Then, of course, there was Grace.

She had changed everything. When Grace had left after their stolen night together, they had agreed to end their brief relationship right there and then. Since that day he had respected her wishes and tried to dismiss all thoughts of her. He had tried to focus on keeping his marriage going, but he knew his life with Maude could never be quite the same again. Grace had awakened something deep within him. Then, just when he had felt truly alive, she had gone. It had left him empty.

He had returned to Maude only to find he was barely going through the motions of marriage. After he had buried his still-born son that day he felt he had also buried some part of the love he had in his heart for Maude, if indeed he ever did have that depth of feeling for her to begin with.

They were husband and wife, but it was now in name only. Between the frequent rows, there were of course times when they would both agree to try to make an effort to be more friendly to each other, at least for the sake of the children. Mostly though, it was like actors on the stage. The ritual greetings and passing of everyday comments seemed meaningless and shallow, almost rehearsed. Beneath the surface, they were becoming more like strangers to each other.

Neither truly felt the call of a soul mate in the other. That innermost call that could help them surmount their differences and bring them together. Instead, neither now felt safe enough or willing enough to truly open their heart again to the other. Always holding back, just a little, just in case, neither giving openly, unconditionally.

Like some universal law, that holding back, that defensive wall, would forever deny them any chance of sharing any real depth of happiness together. For as always when something is held back, it can never be total. A price is paid and something is lost. Both felt it, knew it, but knowing was not enough. So, in their self-imposed isolation, they did little now to try to bridge the wide chasm between them. They had their moments as the play went on, but for them it was becoming merely a façade, an empty ritual of marriage for both of them.

For her part, Maude was still experiencing irrational mood swings. She continued to exhibit the highs and lows of emotions that were typical of what may have been a bi-polar disorder. She was sweeping from the depths of depression one day to the heights of euphoria the next, with external circumstances little changed.

However, one thing that had changed was that Maude had given birth to another child, their third little girl. This time her husband had been a little better prepared as to what to expect throughout her pregnancy, but it had been a tumultuous and fractious journey nevertheless. As before, it had been a difficult time for Maude and she could not hold back from taking her mood swings out on her husband.

For the most part he wore it well enough, but he was at once both apprehensive and relieved to be away from home such a lot during it. This time, especially in the last trimester, he had tried to be at home more to support her. He had even managed special arrangements to be at home again for several days around Christmas, though she was not then due. Despite his caution and uneasiness, Maude had gone through to full term and the birth had gone surprisingly well. In late January of 1943, Maude delivered another healthy baby girl.

They were both grateful that the child, who they named Donna, was strong and healthy and, like their other two daughters, Pearl and Nan, seemed easily contented. For a while it lifted their spirits. Donna filled their every moment. She demanded the full attention of her mother in those first few months, while her father was doing his best to keep his other two daughters entertained during his visits home.

Pearl, now coming up to school age, and Nan, not far behind, were easy to entertain. They were at that joyful and inquisitive young age when life is still full of wonder and everything is an adventure waiting to be explored. Given half a chance, the two older children were also very keen to help look after baby sister Donna, who soon proved to be a constant distraction for them. Indeed, for all of the family it was in many ways an opportunity to build on those joyful times and make happy memories.

Yet, some unpleasant memories seem to cling to us. For some odd reason we revisit them time and time again. Even when we know they are not helpful and it is probably best to let them go, they seem to insist on coming back to cause us pain, especially when still unresolved. It seems then if we find we cannot let such memories go, perhaps we must first try to understand and forgive, if not forget, as much for our own peace of mind, as for the other.

Two years after their still-born child was born, neither Maude nor her husband had managed to forgive or leave that particular memory behind them. It still weighed heavily on both of them. Each remembered the event from their own experience and own perspective of course, and each carried with them the hurt it had caused them.

The same tragic event, experienced differently, remembered differently, but having a similar traumatic effect on each of them. Neither had been able to bring themselves to really talk about it, to attempt to heal the wounds. So there it stayed, captured in raw memory, festering, unspoken and unresolved. A burden for the bearer, still unwilling to be set down, by either of them, driving a wedge between them.

Perhaps that wedge of unresolved issues was only one of a number of things that would impel Maude to choose the path she was soon to take. A path that would inevitably lead her to make that choice that haunted her forever. For in truth, Mad Maude had long ago been shaped by so many complex and extraneous layers. Layers that she herself had not only permitted, but had chosen to make a part of her. So, while Fate may have laid out the awful path before her, it was Mad Maude herself who would choose to take it.

Chapter 20

Abandonment

Everybody is trying to express the love within their nature.
Sometimes this love is subject to attachment.
Sometimes it is subject to delusion.
(Shri Shantananda Saraswati)

Spring 1943 – Autumn 1944

It was in the Spring of 1943 that Maude had met up with one of her old boyfriends from the past. She had been making one of her infrequent visits to meet up with her mother in Portadown, about an hour bus journey from her home.

Her mother lived alone, a frail and cantankerous woman, who seemed to find fault with everything Maude did. Maude's father had passed away just after the first world war, when she was little more than a toddler. He had been another of the vast number of young men who somehow managed to survive the devastation of the first World War only to die soon afterwards with the Spanish flu. Her mother remarried a few years later, and Maude never quite took to her new stepfather, nor he to her. Maude's wild and exuberant youth and the shaping of her character was perhaps due in part to the free rein, if not quite neglect, she enjoyed from those early years.

Portadown, or the town of the little fort as it was known, was not a sea port as such, but sat astride the mighty river Bann. Interestingly, the Bann flowed in two distinctly opposite directions. The upper Bann flowed Northward from its source in the Mourne Mountains through Portadown and on into the great Lough Neagh. The lower Bann flowed Southwards to the Atlantic Ocean, forming the boundary between County Antrim and County Londonderry on its journey.

Like many other towns in Ireland, Portadown had a long history of heated feuds and disputes between Catholic and Protestant through the centuries. Much of the lands around it had been colonised by Protestant settlers brought in by King James I, more than three hundred years prior. In more recent times it had become a busy railway town, but still maintained its long-held reputation for the quality of linen it produced.

Maude had heard the recent reports of two prisoner of war camps for captured Germans being set up in Portadown. She was not at all perturbed by it. Indeed, if anything the reverse was true. She was more than a little excited by it. She had learnt too that a number of Welsh troops had been stationed there to run the camps, and they had often been seen around the town, conversing with the locals and seemingly making themselves very much at home in Portadown.

As far as Maude was concerned, a prison camp or two, and especially an infusion of Welsh troops, all just added to the colourful character of this little railway hub of the North. She was only visiting for the weekend, going through the rituals of sharing her children with her mother, especially baby Donna, the recent arrival.

Uncharacteristically Maude had agreed to go to church with her mother that Sunday morning, and it was there that she had met up with Ewen again after many years. He had come over to talk to her during the morning tea after the service and she was delighted to hear the news of her old friend. She was also surprised to learn that Ewen was stationed there, still unmarried, and more than a little flattered that he still seemed to be interested in her.

The bright conversation and the renewed attention of one of her old flames was like a breath of fresh air for Maude. She felt the memories of her vibrant youth rekindled, easing her back into that carefree playful era of her life. For a short while she felt once more like a lively young woman and less like a haggard struggling mother.

When they were leaving the church Ewen asked, "It's been great to see you Maude, really has. You know I'll be in Portadown a while. Maybe we could catch up again for a drink or two when you are over visiting your mah again? A bit like old times, eh? What do you say?"

Maude saw through the invitation for what it was and could have stopped it all right there, but she didn't. Instead, she agreed to keep in touch with Ewen, telling herself that she needed to get out and visit her mother a little more often anyway. Besides, what harm could it do to see him once in a while? She would just have a bit of harmless fun with an old friend, nothing would come of it.

It was another of those fateful little choices, made at yet another fork in the road of life's meandering journey. It would lead inexorably to another path, and another.

The war was a long way from being over by late 1943, but the Allies were slowly beginning to push back Hitler's Forces. By early 1944, as the Allied Forces drove the Nazis back on all fronts, Churchill was being pressured by both Eisenhower and Stalin to launch an invasion to reclaim France and free some of the other countries of Europe. He resisted, knowing from bitter experience that the Allies were not yet ready and should not underestimate the monumental effort needed for a successful invasion against the might of Germany's still powerful fighting forces.

With Operation Overlord and the landing of the Allied Forces in Normandy later that same year on the 6th of June, Churchill was proved correct in his assessment of just how difficult and massive an operation it would be. Even though the Allies, deploying a host of deceptions, had been able to maintain the crucial element of surprise by landing on the Normandy beaches, rather than the expected Calais, they encountered stern resistance.

When the Nazis were finally driven out of France at the end of August 1944, most of Britain saw it as the beginning of the end for Hitler. At long last there seemed to be an end in sight to this terrible war. A time when the soldiers could start to return home and resume their lives. A time to begin again, to return to some semblance of normality.

For Maude, it was of course great news, but it was something else too. She knew what it meant. She knew she would have to make some decisions about her future, and soon.

Her reunited friendship with Ewen had continued from that chance encounter in the church. Now, well over a year later, it had long since evolved into a secret but full-blown affair. They were seeing each other on a regular basis. Ewen had been asking Maude for some time now to leave her husband and come and live with him.

Although Maude had brought the children along with her in the beginning, Ewen had discouraged it. She had increasingly found it easier to leave them in the care of Liza or a friend while she ostensibly went to visit her ailing mother in Portadown. She was also worried the children might mention something to their father if they accompanied her too often.

With the victory in France, Maude and many others thought that the war might be over soon, perhaps even in a matter of months. From there her life in Ireland would surely fall back into the old predictable pattern. Her husband would return from Langley to her then, the long absences a thing of the past.

From his infrequent visits home, it was already obvious they had little left in common. He was drinking more and they were fighting more. Would they just resume their life together after the war, a fractious relationship, a life of mediocrity and an entrapment for both of them? Inevitably more children, more responsibilities, more suffocation? She realised she did not want any of that. Not any more, indeed, not anything with him anymore. Mad Maude wanted her freedom.

When she was with Ewen, Maude felt she was more able to be like her old self. Ewen was kind to her and more than a little infatuated by her. He was also the sort to fuss and fawn over her and she loved all that attention. She found that she was more often upbeat with Ewen, her depressions not gone, but seemingly more often replaced with happier, carefree times. There was no baggage in their relationship, it felt all fresh and free.

Sometimes the nagging thought occurred to Maude that perhaps she was feeling more like a carefree single woman again because she was almost always on her own now when she visited Ewen. It was like going away on little short holidays every time she visited him, a break from everyday life. She hurriedly dismissed the thought, knowing it was too burdened with other implications. Implications that maybe she was missing something. That maybe too much thinking about it would spoil things.

That old sense of carefree abandon of her youth had enormous appeal for Maude and had no doubt influenced how her relationship with Ewen developed. From the very beginning she had expected that the relationship could not last, could only ever be a temporary fling. However, now she did not want to think of it coming to an end. Especially when she thought of what she would have to go back to again. Nevertheless, she knew she would have to decide soon what she was going to do, before the choice and the opportunity was lost to her.

There was no doubt that Maude loved her children. Of course she did, she was their mother after all. Yet, the children were also a constant reminder of her responsibilities, and her husband. Just thinking of him Maude could feel the emotional claustrophobia descend upon her again. Yes, that traumatic experience with his still-born son had left her scarred and resentful, but it was much more than that now. He had been away so much it would almost be like starting again when he returned after the end of the war. Maude realised she did not want that. They had drifted so far apart that she was not ready or willing to start again with him.

On the other hand, she felt she could still be happy and free with Ewen. He clearly wanted her, but not so much with another man's three children tagging along too. Maude wanted her children and she wanted Ewen. More than anything she desperately wanted her freedom and to start a new life, without her husband.

In the following month, September 1944, the Allies captured Italy. Within a few short weeks Italy had turned on its former ally, joining the Allies in the fight against Hitler. For a while at least it seemed that the Allies advance would continue undeterred through Europe. The end of the war was coming, slowly but surely. Maude felt she had to do something and soon.

The fading Autumn colours clung to the trees and hedgerows as

Maude walked along the familiar country road in the cool morning sunshine. She was on her way to Liza's house with her three children. They were dressed in their Sunday best, a somewhat unusual event as Maude did not usually bother with all that. She was not known for dressing up her children or for attending church, except when it suited her. This time was different however. Maude had scraped together enough money to buy them some smart clothes. In their new outfits, the children had never looked better.

There was a light rhythmic clatter and scuffle of the shoes on their feet as the little group made their way through the lane in the open countryside. That, and the excited chattering of the girls as they walked along, was just enough to prompt little waves of disturbed finches and sparrows to flitter out a short way ahead of them as the group came close. As quickly as they passed, the wave of birds would flitter back into place behind them again, to resume the business of their own little lives.

Lower down in the shuck, and hidden from view, the occasional rabbit, rat or field mouse, played out a similar theme in turn as, unknowing, the group came upon them. The gentle ripple effect of the wave carried on along the lane in tandem with them as they walked along. Unnoticed, Nature was dancing along merrily to their tune as the little party advanced. Once having passed by, it was as if their brief momentary incursion on Nature had already slipped away and was gone forever, which of course it had.

Maude was reminded of that other morning some years before. She and her young husband had walked arm in arm along this same lane to his mother's house for Boxing Day. They had spent the day there with Liza's large family. It was a good memory she recalled. A time when they had enjoyed a few moments of happiness in each other's company. A time when they truly cared for each other, when they were still very much a couple. All that now seemed like a lifetime ago.

She remembered meeting that young woman that day, Grace, wasn't it? Yes, that was it. She remembered the children had clearly taken to Grace, but for some reason she herself had felt just a little strange and uncomfortable in Grace's presence. She had met her just a handful of times again but had not seen her for a long time. Maude wondered what made her think of Grace now, and what had happened to her. There had been rumours, but she had not taken much notice.

The weather was kind to the little group and Maude was pleased to have the opportunity to enjoy this little time in the countryside with her children. Pearl and Nan skipped and danced along and even Donna was walking along beside her, though she had to be carried much of the way. All too soon it seemed, she arrived at the little crossroad close to Liza's house.

Stopping at the side of the road Maude breathed deeply, hesitating for a moment. There was no one around, just the jubilant sounds of Nature. As the girls tugged impatiently at her hands and urged her on, she reminded herself of what she must do. She steeled herself in preparation. The moment had come, there was no going back.

Bending down, Maude hugged and kissed each of her three children in turn, brusquely telling them that she loved them. Pearl looked up at her inquisitively, wondering why they had stopped there and not all gone on to her granny Liza's house. Maude pulled out a bag of sweets and gave them to Pearl, instructing her to take the other two children on to Liza's house without her and share the sweets with them when they got there.

The prospect of sharing sweets was just enough to distract the children. With a few final prompts from Maude, Pearl took hold of Nan and Donna's hands and set off, walking slowly so Donna could keep up.

Maude watched as her three small children walked on up the narrow country lane, hand in hand, to their grandmother Liza's house. Deep down Maude knew she might never see them again. For a moment she was filled with doubt and her eyes started to fill with tears. Her resolve almost gave way. She wanted to run after them, to hold them in her arms and take them home.

As if sensing her mother's emotional turmoil, little Donna glanced back around at her mother and stopped, calling out for her. Maude's heart almost broke on the instant. She was almost on the point of taking a step towards them when Pearl gently tugged Donna's hand and told her to come along with her. As Donna turned to go, the moment shifted yet again.

The beckoning breach in Maude's long-conditioned hard outer shell was hastily remedied and righted itself as she watched them walk away. She clenched her fists firmly down by her sides, staunch, set, as if to keep herself from running after them. With the tears streaming down her cheeks, once again she committed to her awful purpose. "They'll be far better off with him than with me," she told herself grimly. "Yes, they'll be better off, but damn him to hell. Oh, my dear children! What have I done? Oh, damn him, damn him to hell!"

Maude swung around, abruptly turning away from them. Holding herself together, tears blinding her vision and almost on the point of breaking, she forced herself to walk straight ahead along the path that awaited her. The path that she had chosen. Then, in the full knowledge that she was abandoning her children to the care of their father and their grandmother, she walked out of their lives forever.

There were differences of course, given Maude and Grace's

different circumstances. Yet here was a sense of history repeating itself. For it was another bitter trade, another choice, another escape. One that would exact a far greater price from Maude than she could ever imagine. Though she never looked back, or ever again tried to go back, Maude carried with her a vivid image of her three children, walking hand in hand away from her. Walking out of her life.

The image would be forever imbedded in her mind. Even in her new life with Ewen, it would forever haunt her, at times resurfacing to drive her to the verge of insanity. The years would pass and be unforgiving. Unforgiving, until at last, when Maude's youngest daughter, Donna, married and with children of her own, would seek her out. Then, in the face of her daughter's unconditional love, Maude's hard shell would begin to soften and finally she would find some small measure of atonement and escape from her long years of personal perdition.

Hearts Abandoned

Chapter 21

Living In Exile

When in disgrace with Fortune and men's eyes,
I alone beweep my outcast state, and trouble deaf heaven
with my bootless cries, and look upon myself and curse my fate.

Yet in these thoughts myself almost despising,
haply I think on thee, and then my state,
like to the lark at break of day arising, from sullen earth,
sings hymns at heaven's gate.

For thy sweet love remembered, such wealth brings,
that then I scorn to change my state with kings.
(Shakespeare - Sonnet 29)

Early May 1946

Four years had passed since Grace made the escape to Newcastle. The war had ended, life in Newcastle and Ireland had indeed just about returned to peacetime normality, but Grace could still remember that day her parents visited her, as if it was yesterday.

That day when her parents had descended upon her little hideaway refuge with two of her sisters, Wendy and Gwen. The day when her mother, Beth, in a fit of rage, had cursed her and cast her out from her family and her exile had begun. Grace had felt like she had lost everything that day, but Elizabeth had been her saviour.

That awful day four years ago when a dumbstruck Riley had started to make a half apology for Beth, then thought better of it. He had hurriedly told Grace that they had to leave and ushered a protesting Wendy and Gwen out with him. Grace had been left sitting alone, feeling battered, numb and desolate. Against her will, her mind echoed again and again her mother's venomous curse. Fearsome in its might, as if drawing down some supernatural power, it was both a pronouncement and a prophecy. One that Grace felt sure Beth would never recant. For her sins Grace's children would be born black crows and she would forever be cast out from the family she loved.

A confused Grace could not understand how or why her mother would say such things. Thoughts ran unchecked and unbidden through her bewildered mind. Beth knew of Grace's close friendship with Liza and her family living near the Crow's Nest. Perhaps she knew much more than she said. Was it just coincidence or Grace's imagination, or had Beth somehow guessed that Elizabeth's father was the same young man from that family? No, surely not.

When her father and sisters had walked out after Beth that day, there had been nothing to comfort Grace. There had just been the sound of Elizabeth's cries filling the room. The plaintiff wailing of an infant in response to the frightening sounds that surrounded it. Yet it was enough. For a mother it was enough. The anxious sounds of Elizabeth's wailing had pierced the spell that Beth had spun, and once again awoken the maternal instinct in Grace. She had risen to meet the need in both of them.

Isolated from her family, Grace had wept incessantly for what had happened and what must now lie ahead of her. Yet, as she tended to the needs of her daughter and held her in her arms, gradually all crying came to a stop. Grace had looked into the face of her beautiful baby and the infant had smiled. In that moment Grace remembered hope.

She remembered why she had made the decision to leave Jessman, remembered why she had come to live in Newcastle. She remembered her love for the young man and the blessing of this young child, a small miracle. She remembered she had endured before, and now, for her child's sake, she could endure again. It might be difficult, but she would manage.

Slowly but surely the days and months passed as Grace dwelt in Newcastle with her child and the war drew ever closer to an end. After France had been liberated, Hitler's campaign of domination had begun to unravel and he was becoming paranoid after attempts on his life. The intense stress was taking its toll. He was rumoured to be heavily dependent upon drugs and losing his grip on reality.

In mid-December 1944, in what amounted to a major last-ditch gamble, he diverted troops away from the pressing Russian enemy on the Eastern front to spring a surprise attack against the American Allies advance in the forests of the Ardennes in Western Europe.

Recognising the danger, the Allies, under supreme commander and future American president Eisenhower, along with his flamboyant sidekick, Two-Gun Patton, raced to stem the tide with a massive infusion of reinforcements. In a brutal Battle of the Bulge, and aided by clearer skies for aerial bombardments, the Allies regained the upper hand before the year end.

Completely demoralised, the Nazis were a spent force, fighting a retreating battle all the way back to Berlin. The Russians, having taken advantage of a depleted Axis force, quickened their advance from the East. Over the next few months, it became a race to Berlin and the inevitable Victory in Europe Day.

A short while after V.E. Day, the world had been shaken into a frightening new era of warfare when two atom bombs devastated Japan, forcing its inevitable surrender on VJ Day, 2nd September 1945. Finally, six years and one day after it had begun, the second World War was over. Peace, however relative, was bestowed upon mankind once more.

There was much to celebrate at the end of the war as many of the troops started to demobilise and return home. However, as the countless atrocities of the war began to emerge in the months and years that followed, especially the horrendous atrocities towards the Jews, it was clear that while the war was over, the trauma and residual pain it had left behind were far from over.

It seemed that as the war had progressed, for whatever reason that might be used to attempt to justify it, mankind's behaviour towards each other, on both sides, had continued to deteriorate beyond credence. Much would be learnt from the six years of hell. Yet, coming on the heels of the war to end all wars, naturally it had made people everywhere question why it had happened. Worse still, could it happen yet again?

For even amidst the peace that prevailed, new borders, new lines of separation, were already being drawn up. Drawn up, as if it were mankind's eternal destiny to reshape and redraw such temporary lines of possession across the globe to reflect the fluctuating powers of the victors and the vanquished. Though mere brief and temporary tenants of the earth, mankind was still wont to claim sole possession as well as dominion of the lands and seas of that earth. Sometimes with scant regard for the welfare of his own kind or Earth's other occupants.

Wars, it is said, may be fought twice, once in the battlefield and once in memory. Yet how and where exactly do these conflicts start? For the aggressor on the cusp, are they not first fought in the mind? For in a sense, it is there, in the mind, where the real battle first takes place. Where, if in pursuit of steadfastness and inclusiveness, a path of reconciliation and compassion and forgiveness may often be found. Or, where if in pursuit of divisiveness, the path of conflict may be grasped tightly and allowed to dominate.

If that battle in mind is lost, do not the doors of reason then begin to close, quiet truths become ignored, and justifications for conflict become skewed and bent to suit the vagaries of over-zealous egos?

Whether the conflict is at the level of the single individual or on a macro scale, would not the same universal principles apply? And even if a stand must be taken, as it might against fanatics or dictators, might we not often be aiders and abettors, to some degree complicit in creating the fertile ground in which the bitter seeds of discontent more easily take root?

Blissfully oblivious to it all, the child Elizabeth, now aged four, danced along the path in Newcastle without a care in the world. Her movements had that uninhibited graceful flow that comes with the freedom and abandon of the very young. She felt safe in familiar surroundings and routine. Grace strolled on a little way ahead. For some reason she couldn't quite fathom, she felt a little apprehensive that Sunday morning. Perhaps it was nothing, but for some reason her sixth sense seemed to be on high alert.

That Sunday was going to be different, very different. Though Grace had felt some uneasiness about it, she could not have known why. That day Fate would intervene and toy with her life yet again, once more offering Grace another choice to make in response to the circumstances set before her, another path to take.

Looking back, she saw Elizabeth still dancing around and singing to herself as she did so. Grace smiled, confident that Elizabeth would catch her up in her own good time and race past. They had walked this path many times before. It led up to Newcastle's wider promenade and from there they would stroll back along it to complete the loop. Sometimes on special occasions they might have a cup of tea in the little seaside café before returning home. It was a little Sunday morning ritual they both enjoyed after church, and it helped to lift Grace's spirits, especially now that Spring was in the air again.

It had not been easy living in exile. Although not actually living in a different country, Grace felt she might well have been. She could not return home, for what home awaited her, except now here in Newcastle.

Grace had tried to pick up the pieces of her life again after her mother had cast her out that day four years ago. At least now she was free of her abusive husband and living in the beautiful little seaside town that she loved. For most of that first year she had immersed herself in her work with the Down Syndrome child and as housekeeper for her landlord. Her work, and caring for Elizabeth, had filled her days, and she remained busy throughout.

Living in Newcastle certainly helped, but busy days and busy people do not necessarily equate to happy or contented people. In one sense her days were busy and full, yet in another she still felt lonely and empty. Being an outcast from her family was a heavy burden for Grace. She had tried writing to her parents, tried to make the peace, but her letters were returned unopened. Her mother Beth was unmoved, and even after four years the wounds still felt raw.

There had been some good news within those four years of course. It was just less than a year after she had been exiled, when the war was still raging, that she sat alone in her rooms on the morning of

Elizabeth's first birthday. Understandably, Grace would have wanted to celebrate this special birthday with all her family, but she had been denied even that.

As she was getting ready to take Elizabeth out for a stroll in the pram, Grace had heard an uncharacteristic insistent knocking on the door. She had opened it to find her brother and sister, Toby and Wendy, still cold from the journey on the motorbike, but grinning from ear to ear. In unison they leapt on her and hugged her so tightly she could barely breathe. Grace hugged them back just as enthusiastically. Her heart was brimming over with gratitude that her siblings had come to see her, despite their mother's warnings.

Through the excited chattering, Grace learnt that they had broken the curfew imposed by her mother to visit her. They had done so in the full knowledge that they would have to keep the whole thing absolutely secret if they were to avoid reprisals all round. There was much more excited chattering throughout the rest of that morning, as they poured out the news of what had been happening back home. Grace had been delighted and little Elizabeth had been thoroughly swamped with all their fuss and attention. The child seemed none the worse for the avalanche of affection, and did her small part playing along with all the entertainment.

Later they had told Grace that the relationship between Jessman and her parents was still testy at best. However, although he had threatened it, Jessman had not tried to reclaim any of their farm or money they owed him. Much as Toby had predicted, it seemed that after a few months, Jessman had all but stopped searching for Grace and Elizabeth and reverted to his old-style bachelor existence on his farm, aided by ever-willing Sam. He was becoming even more of a recluse, and certainly did not go out of his way to welcome visitors.

Wendy was also excited to tell Grace that she had recently become engaged to be married. She had wanted so much to tell Grace herself, and besides Elizabeth's birthday this was another reason she and Toby had dared visit her in secret. It was to be a short engagement, with the wedding only a few weeks off. Wendy could not hide her disappointment that Grace would be barred from attending. It was to be one of several weddings of her siblings which Grace could not attend, and another of those timeless wedding portraits of family gatherings from which she would be absent. Grace had smiled and given Wendy another hug, but felt again the thousand cuts of being an outcast from her family.

Toby and Wendy had passed the fast-fleeting hours away until the evening, and all too soon it was time to go. There were a few tears shed on their departure, especially as Toby indicated he might again be away for long periods. For just a moment the heavy silence had hung over them. Many young pilots had already lost their lives and though the tide of the war had begun to turn, many more lives would inevitably be lost. Toby reassured them all would be well, and they had readily latched onto his positive approach.

Even though Grace was still ostracised, that visit by Toby and Wendy back then had been a small beginning. One or two of the other older siblings would be able and brave enough to visit again in time. The barriers imposed by her mother's curse were still there, but at least there seemed to be a few tiny chinks of daylight appearing in the dark walls that Beth had erected around Grace to separate her from her family.

At times when she was feeling particularly low and alone, Grace would hold Elizabeth in her arms as if she was clinging on to hope. "We will get through this," she told herself. "We will get through this awful war and we will survive being an outcast from our own family. All this too will pass."

So it was then, after four years of living in exile, in that late Spring of 1946, that Grace and Elizabeth were out enjoying their Sunday morning stroll along the promenade in Newcastle. Momentarily, Grace's thoughts turned again to her brother Toby.

Toby sometimes visited her on a Sunday but she had not seen him for quite some weeks now. When he had returned to Ireland from Germany not long after the war ended, she could see Toby was deeply distressed and traumatised by his experiences. It was not just the horrors of the fighting. He told her he had been appalled and sickened at the numbers of assaults and rapes on German women by the victorious Allied troops, often with senior officers seemingly turning a blind eye.

During the months he had been assigned in Germany he had come to know quite a number of the civilian people there. Despite the initial wariness, he found he had developed a growing respect for many of them and what they too had come through. Toby had taken a strong liking to one attractive young Prussian woman in particular.

Ingrid had been one of many thousands of civilians who had fled from the East in fear of reported Russian atrocities against civilians, in the hope the other Allied Forces would be more tolerant to Prussian women. Toby and Ingrid's friendship had quickly blossomed. They married and Toby brought Ingrid home to Ireland with him. His mother, Beth, had as expected, been outraged when Toby introduced his young Prussian bride. Beth's sharp tongue and outright criticism had spared neither Ingrid nor Toby.

"What business have you got marrying this Nazi and bringing her into my home? Sure, haven't we just fought a war to keep them all out of this country, and now you have the audacity to bring one back with you!"

Toby's efforts to explain Ingrid's situation to his mother fell on deaf ears. Beth would have none of it. So even though Toby had already prepared his wife for Beth's verbal onslaught, it was an unnecessarily painful homecoming. However, in the scheme of what Ingrid and he had already survived, far from insurmountable. Sensibly Toby had quickly found them a separate home when he demobbed, but it was a not at all an easy transition for his young wife Ingrid, an unwelcome visitor in a foreign country.

Grace had sympathised and shown her kindness, knowing something of how it felt to be an outcast. Ingrid was bright and industrious and Grace was glad to see that over the course of the next few visits she and Toby were adapting and getting to grips with their new life.

Grace's thoughts about Toby and Ingrid were interrupted as the wind started to pick up. She and Elizabeth had been strolling along by the sea for a while now. Grace decided they had better not stay out too long in case it started to rain. She called to Elizabeth to hurry up. The child promptly took that as a challenge to race up to and on past her mother onto the promenade. Grace followed after her, more quickly now. Elizabeth, a bundle of energy, was weaving in and out of the benches where people were sitting enjoying the view out to sea. Grace called out to her, not wanting Elizabeth to get too far ahead or disturb other people along the promenade.

It was then, intent on watching Elizabeth and a little distracted, that Grace bumped into the outstretched leg of someone seated on one of the benches. She lost her footing slightly and started to stumble forward. As she tried to right herself, she felt the firm grip on her arm, saving her from falling and then helping her to regain her footing.

It took Grace a few seconds to regain her composure and brush herself off again. A quiet steady voice, so long absent yet so familiar, spoke the words which quickened her heart.

"Are you okay? It's you Grace, isn't it? You once helped me up too when I fell, a long while ago. Do you remember that Grace? Seems it's my turn now."

For a moment the words reverberated in Grace's head as, still a little flustered, she turned to look into the face of the young man now standing before her. It was Elizabeth's father.

Just for them, it was as if time shifted, rewound itself, wiping away the missing years they had spent apart. After that initial surprise, and the warm embrace of friends greeting each other, they sat down together on the seat to talk. Once more they felt so natural in each other's company. There were no pretences, no need for any phoney role playing, it was as if they could just be free to be themselves, without effort. As if it had always been that way with them.

Almost un-noticed, Elizabeth had walked up to stand in front of them, watching them without speaking. The man looked up and smiled, seeing the child properly for the first time. She was of average height and clearly strong and healthy. Her hair was a dark auburn, thick and long, falling around her neck and cradling the fine balanced features of her face. Her grey-green eyes were magnetic, at once observant and inquisitive, yet at the same time sparkling and warm. It all added to her beauty. He saw the likeness of Grace in her features instantly.

"Is she yours?" he asked, barely seeking her confirmation. Grace simply nodded, remaining silent, watching him and waiting. It was enough. The unspoken truth reached out and touched him, and without seeking any further response, he turned back to her. "Is she mine?"

Elizabeth continued to watch them both with a quizzical expression on her young face. Grace recognised the moment. She hesitated then gently took her daughter's hand. "Elizabeth, this man is your daddy. His name is Jacob." Grace felt the flutter in her own heart as she said the words aloud. The child simply smiled and nodded, as if nothing more was needed.

Later, they sat in a quiet corner of the little café together, filling in the missing years, sharing lives lived apart. They had so much to cover, so much had happened to both of them. All the while, even amidst the difficult sharing of the painful times, the easy comfort they found in each other's presence prevailed. For Grace in particular, it helped to make the telling that much more bearable.

With his customary frugal use of words, he explained how it had been between him and Maude. He was married to her and felt compelled to live his life with her, but it wasn't until after he buried his still-born son that he realised it was over between them. When Maude had walked out on him and left their three children at his mother's house, he had felt not just anger that she had abandoned their children, but relief. Relief that she was gone, out of their lives, and he was no longer Maude's man.

Grace had already known that his life with Maude was difficult and that they often fought, but she had not expected Maude to walk out on him and her family. It was rare enough in those times for a woman to leave her husband, almost unheard of, she knew that from her own experience. How could someone walk away and leave behind their own children? Grace was shocked and could not imagine how that was possible.

Yet she also knew from her own experience, that sometimes the truth of a situation does not easily reveal itself. She remembered Liza's words. "Truth sometimes hides beneath an avalanche of convention and lies, conveniently staying out of sight unless we make a real effort to uncover it." Still, Grace could not help but draw a parallel between Maude and herself. Two women, in very different circumstance perhaps, but both making choices that drastically changed the course of their lives.

When she related her own story, Jacob listened carefully and allowed her to talk without interruption. Just as Grace had done for him, he gave her his full undivided attention, this simple gift beyond measure. Once or twice he asked a brief gentle question, following her lead yet without disturbing the flow of her speech. For brief moments it was as if they were so much in tune with each other that there was only the one voice, somehow emanating from each of them in turn. The tense knots, that from time to time arose within Grace as she confronted each difficult part of her story, slowly unravelled and freed her as she spoke it out into the ether.

When they had finished sharing their stories, there was that same easy silence, a natural pause allowing any residual of stirred up emotions to settle down and be at peace. Each of them felt it, but it was more than that. It was as if until those moments of sharing, there had been something missing from their own stories. Now it was not.

Grace looked around her. The little café overlooking the sea was almost empty now, the lunchtime patrons having already left. She looked out to the sea and took in the beauty of the scene. The weather had picked up again and people were strolling along, as if the war had never happened, simply families enjoying a day out in a peaceful seaside town.

Moments together was all it had taken for the flame within them both to rekindle, or more accurately, to burn brighter again never having been extinguished. Grace watched the families stroll by and wondered if, in some other life-time, this might have been them together. The three of them here on holiday, just relaxing in Newcastle for a few days with their daughter before returning to their own beautiful little house somewhere in the country. The little fantasy intrigued her, beckoned her, but she pushed it out of her mind. "Yes perhaps," she whispered quietly to herself, "in some other dream, in some other life-time."

Elizabeth broke Grace's reverie to ask again if they could go home now. The ice-cream, sticks of rock, and two colourful little blow-windmills that the man had bought for her had long since outlived their usefulness. The child was restless, wanting to be on the move again. Grace realised she had already stayed much longer than intended.

Making her apologies she told him that she had to be getting back. He nodded in agreement, and they began to gather their belongings, preparing to leave. Knowing their parting was imminent, they mumbled a few sentiments about how nice, how pleasant it was to meet up again after all this time. The words sounded hollow, inadequate, undermining the depth of their real feelings. They both knew it.

As they left the café and walked along together, Grace was mentally preparing herself for the moment when they would have to part and go their separate ways again. He too had been silent, contemplative. All too soon they reached the junction in the road and Grace slowed, wondering how to say goodbye.

As if reading her thoughts, Jacob stopped and turned to face her. Taking her hand in his, he hesitated a long moment, inhaling deeply before speaking.

"I've nothing to offer you Grace, nothing except three more children who need a mother, a run-down old stone cottage, and myself. I can't even offer you marriage, for you and I are both tied to another, with no hope of divorce. Yet here we both are, alone. If you'll have me Grace, I'll do my best to provide for you and the children, and I'll love you till the end of my days. What do you say? Will you Grace?"

He went silent again, as though having exhausted himself with an unaccustomed flurry of words and emotion. He waited, uncertain as to how she would respond.

Chapter 22

When Speaks The Heart

*Love watches, and sleeping slumbers not; when weary is not tired,
when straitened is not constrained; when frightened is not disturbed;
but like a lovely flame and a torch all on fire, it moves upwards
and securely passes through all opposition.
Whosoever loveth knoweth the sound of this voice.
(Thomas à Kempis)*

*Two roads diverged in a wood and I – I took the one less travelled by,
and that has made all the difference.
(Robert Frost)*

Late May 1946

Jacob drove the borrowed old Ford car slowly and steadily away from Newcastle. Although there was still very little traffic around and these last few days of May weather had for the most part been glorious, still he took his time and drove cautiously. For some reason he had never felt entirely comfortable driving, even though his work mates taught him well at Langley. Perhaps because it felt unnatural to him, or he was unused to the borrowed car. However, the other more important reason was that he carried a very special cargo that day.

Sitting beside him in the front of the car was Grace. Between him and Grace, dangling her feet over the edge of the seat, was a prim faced Elizabeth. Their few belongings were in the small boot of the car and lying on the back seat. The little car trundled onwards, leaving Newcastle behind and slowly winding its way towards Liza's house at the Crow's Nest.

It had been a long two weeks since their encounter on the promenade. Two weeks since he had asked Grace to share a home with him. Two weeks since that day when his stomach had locked waiting on her reply. She had taken so long he thought she was never going to answer him. He was grateful now that he had somehow found the patience to wait.

The silence after he had asked Grace to come and live with him had remained, as Grace, looked at him but paused long and hard before answering. Her mind busily racing ahead. Her thoughts flashing everywhere.

Here it was again, another momentous choice. To be with him, or not? A choice that once again could completely alter the course of her life. A choice that was not without risk. Could she go against her Christian values, step even further outside the norms of society, face scorn and ridicule? In these times surely only a harlot would live in sin without being married. Hadn't her own mother said so in her rage? Hadn't Beth predicted that? Now, in addition, to take on someone else's three children? Surely that made no sense at all?

She had missed him sorely, but she had survived thus far, she and Elizabeth. The realities of war had started to shake loose even the narrowest perceptions of the role of women, especially women with small children and lost husbands. It was far from easy, but she was getting by, she was coping. She had a job, two jobs in fact, and up to a point she had a measure of independence. Even as an outcast from her family she could continue to survive on her own, she knew that now. She could manage without the complication of him coming back into her life. Yes, she could do that.

Yet, if the truth be known, she knew also that even in her beloved Newcastle, even with Elizabeth, her life had felt empty. She could be surrounded by people, but underneath it all she still felt empty and alone.

She looked deep into the man's eyes, torn, searching for her answer. As if to quell the meandering foibles of a discursive mind in turmoil, her inner inviolate heart whispered softly to her to stop, to be still.

On the instant her racing mind fell silent. Relieved of distractions, a new clarity and calm arose within her. Grace realised this could never be a matter of weighing up all the pros and cons, of listing advantages and disadvantages. She would never find her answer there, on some fictitious balance sheet. No ledger could hope to measure or account for the depth of feelings she had for this man, the father of her beautiful child.

A feeling of contentment, even bliss, swept through her then. In that moment of clarity, Grace knew beyond all doubt that she wanted to spend her whole life with this man.

Fate had not offered them some smooth easy path. There would be no crowded church wedding nor happy guests and family to celebrate and wish them well. No, there would be none of that, no ready social acceptance, alas far from it. Yet there was something else here that meant more to Grace than all of that. Hope. Hope that she might not have to go through life alone, hope that she had truly found her soul mate, that they could be together, raise a family together, and happily grow old together.

Fate, so often seemingly unkind to her, had deigned to offer her another path. It was a narrower, more difficult path perhaps, this road less travelled. Yet, there it was, waiting for her response, if she was brave enough to take it. Grace had her answer. Her gaze softened, she drew in another breath, and when she did finally speak, she spoke courageously and from the heart.

At her response he had swept them both off the ground in long joyous hugs. Elizabeth was unsure what was happening but a little hesitatingly she went along anyway with this odd game that adults played.

Afterwards, Grace and he had agreed that she would move in with him in about two weeks, giving them both time to prepare. Grace had told her employers of her departure so that they could be prepared. Meanwhile Jacob had spent the time fixing up the stone house in Balaney in readiness for their arrival, but had visited her again the following weekend anyway. Now, as they neared their destination in the little car, they were due to stop off first at his mother Liza's house. As they all neared Liza's home, Grace was not sure how she would be received, either by Liza or indeed by Jacob's other three children.

She need not have worried. Liza came out to greet them both in a warm embrace as they disembarked from the car. Her son had told Liza of the situation after his return from Newcastle a couple of weeks ago. Liza, not one to be straight-jacketed by the current norms of society, was never going to be shocked nor dismayed at the news. Instead, she had been delighted. Delighted that her son had found a new love and mother for his three children, but most of all, delighted that it was Grace.

Liza had grown to love Grace as a daughter from her visits in the years past. Now, even in the absence of marriage, Grace would be living with her son and welcomed into her family as if, in all but name, she really was her daughter-in-law. Liza knew full well it would not be easy for them, especially with her son's growing drink addiction problems starting to mirror those of his father. That would be a challenge she knew. Then again neither Grace nor her son had come from happy marriages. Perhaps this time there would be opportunity for both of them to learn and have a better life together.

After a warm embrace for Grace, Liza turned to Elizabeth and swept her up into her arms with a beaming smile and a hug to match. Grace, a little surprised by Liza's action, was even more surprised that Elizabeth, normally more reserved, took to Liza on the instant. As she watched them together, Grace was delighted that Elizabeth was seemingly enthralled by Liza. Here was the granny that she had so longed to have for her daughter, loving and caring from the very first moment. A farm, a curse, an outcast, none of that seemed to matter in this moment. Here was the kind granny that had been missing from her child's life, and the mentor that had too long been missing from her own.

Yet the welcoming did not stop there. A short time later, Liza's husband Bob drove up to the house after a little outing. His car was full with their two youngest, Clive and Hazel, and Jacob's three other daughters, Pearl (9), Nan (8), and his youngest, Donna (4). It was a lovely surprise that Liza's daughter, Grace's good friend Valerie, was also with them.

Grace took a moment to greet Bob and Valerie before turning back to the children. It had been some years since Grace had seen the eldest, Pearl, and her sister Nan. Clearly, they did not remember her, being just infants at the time and Grace had not known the youngest, Donna, at all. Liza stepped forward ushering Jacob's three girls up to meet Grace.

"This is Grace, your new mammy," she said. "A bit later on today you'll all be going off to live with her and your daddy in a wee house up the road in Balaney."

It took the three young girls a moment to take in what their granny had just said. They were unsure what to do or say. To Pearl, seemingly having no recollection of Grace, this woman in their midst might as well have been a perfect stranger. Except that to this child there were no such thing as strangers. Just new friends she was yet to meet.

Pearl looked at Grace as if weighing up her future mother in a steady measured stare. Then, mind made up, with the same open-hearted warmth and kindness that her grandmother had displayed a short while earlier, a precocious young Pearl walked right up to stand in front of Grace. As if it was the most natural thing in the world to do, she put her arms around a surprised Grace and gave her a huge hug.

Stepping back a little, and perhaps remembering her granny's training, she took hold of Grace's hand and said formally, "How are you doing my new mammy? I'm very pleased to meet you."

The child's innocent heartfelt welcome took Grace completely by surprise and almost brought her to tears. She looked down into the child's upturned face, an innocent warm and totally accepting face, staring back at her expectantly. Grace, eyes moistening, bent and hugged Pearl in turn. Then, composing herself she went forward to meet the other children, Nan and Donna, introducing her own daughter Elizabeth in the process.

That done, Grace began to relax. In a sense she had come home again. As she sat down in the comfort of Liza's home, Grace noticed again the strange, yet familiar atmosphere that touched her whenever she was in this house. Perhaps it was Liza's influence, but it was almost as if her house emitted a unique ambience all of its own, a place of welcome, where no-one could be a stranger for long.

In short time the house was ringing with the excited sounds of the six young children playing together. Clive, being the eldest and the only boy amongst them, valiantly tried to direct proceedings and usher them all outside to play. He had about as much success as might be expected when five excited screaming and yelling young girls were on the rampage, with scant regard for the instructions of a twelve-year-old boy. They wanted to race around and he was dampening their fun. After a while Clive accepted the inevitable and let them get on with it in whatever way they chose.

Liza had prepared a celebratory lunch and had insisted that they stayed on a little while before going on to their own stone cottage in Balaney. As they set up for lunch, as if on cue, more of Liza's family began to drop in, bringing with them food and gifts for the young couple. Soon the house was full of Jacob's many other siblings and their spouses and children. Liza had organised it all of course. It was just another indication of her understanding and thoughtfulness. A way of letting them know that she, and her family, were all delighted. They had already accepted the situation and, perhaps unlike many, did not intend to treat them any less than if they were just married.

For the next few hours they all relaxed in the warm congenial atmosphere of Liza's home. The house was vibrant, brimming with friendship. Once again it reminded Grace of that family gathering for Boxing Day lunch, just a few years ago, before the war began. Surely all that was a lifetime away. As she looked around to watch them all, laughing and chatting easily with Jacob and each other, so comfortable in each other's company, she reflected on that day. "Oh my, how the big wheel turns," Grace thought. "Who'd have dared guess that I'd be here now with him, welcomed as a daughter into this lovely family and home."

Later, as Jacob prepared to drive them to their home in Balaney, Liza and all the family stood by the front door to wave them off. The car, now full to overflowing with the additional three children and gifts piled into the back, spluttered into life again and slowly began to move off.

Watching them at the doorway, Liza and Valerie could not contain themselves and gave out loud cries of "Wait, wait!"

When the car stopped again, they all came hurrying forward to give all the occupants yet another hug through the wide-open windows and yet again wished them all good luck.

Jacob sighed knowingly and just smiled, waiting patiently for this little ritual of repeated farewells to run its course. For Grace it was unexpected and she felt a little embarrassed. Yet she was grateful for all the fuss and attention they received. She was smiling inwardly. There had been no church wedding, no reception, and yet in the circumstances this little send-off was much more than she could possibly have wished for. She had Liza and her family to thank for that.

The car, groaning under the load, started to trundle forward to begin the last few miles of its journey to their new home. Tied onto each side of the car were balloons of all colours. It was a small token gesture that this was no ordinary journey that they were embarking upon, but a significant beginning and celebratory occasion.

Grace, feeling a little uncertain as they got underway with four children now in tow, sighed deeply. Jacob glanced over towards her and she gave him a nervous smile. Picking up on the slight trace of apprehension in her face, he returned her smile.

"Not long now Grace," he said reassuringly, "We'll soon be home. It'll all be alright."

The man's words were kind and he was at least partially correct in his prediction. They would be home soon, that much was true. And indeed, they would be alright – but just not yet. As they might both have known even then, they were a long way off from being truly alright. Like their car journey, the bumpy road to that particular destination, if indeed it could be called a destination, was still some way ahead for Grace and Jacob, and their new blended family.

There was no fairy tale ending of living happily ever after awaiting them, at least not yet. As any couple setting out on a life together know only too well, it was much more of a beginning than an ending.

Unexpected Celebrations

Chapter 23

New Beginnings, Old Issues

A man is literally what he thinks, his character being the complete sum of all his thoughts. By the right choice and true application of thought, man ascends to the Divine Perfection. By the abuse and wrong application of thought, he descends below the level of the beast.
(James Allen)

Summer 1946 - Summer 1949

At the start of Summer in 1946, when Grace and her man and their new blended family had first arrived at the old stone cottage, her new life began. Jacob had rented the small two-bedroom cottage shortly after the war from two farming brothers who lived nearby. Now it would have to suffice for the six of them, Grace and he, their daughter Elizabeth, and his three girls, Pearl, Nan and Donna.

Like many others during the war years, the cottage had been neglected over the years and was very run down. Jacob had spent many hours working on it and had made some considerable improvements already. He had made sure it was kitted it out well enough for when Grace arrived. Grace appreciated his efforts, but she could see there was still quite a lot of work ahead of them to make this house into a comfortable home. She already had some experience in that area now and gratefully accepted her new little home in the countryside.

Fortunately, Jacob had already found regular work as a coachbuilder craftsman a few miles away. It was a job that, like many just after the war, would have to change for it was becoming another dying art. For now, it allowed him to use his considerable skills working mostly with a variety of intricate wood panelling and framing. He commuted daily by bicycle and returned to Grace and his extended family at the end of long hard days.

Often at weekends Jacob would take out his shotgun and go for long early morning walks over the countryside. Just as often he would bring back the odd pheasant, pigeon, snipe, duck or rabbit, which served as much needed sustenance for him and his family. It would become a very welcome and regular supplement to their weekly food supply over the years, especially as Grace had quickly learnt how to make the most of them.

Some of Jacob's work colleagues persuaded him to join the local pipe band, which he did. As part of the tradition of the bands, he was also encouraged to step up his wayward membership of the local branch of the Orange Order. He was an enthusiastic and skilled piper and soon found himself as their pipe major, leading the piping section of the band.

In just a few years, Jacob would travel with this small-town country band to Scotland and lead them to compete in the prestigious world pipe band championships in Glasgow. Against the odds, their small but excellently prepared band would so impress the judges with their performances that they would become outright winners in their section. They returned home as local legends.

Pearl and Nan attended the nearby country school, while Elizabeth and Donna, being still a little too young, remained at home in Grace's care. On the occasional Sunday, and with the help of one or two of the parishioners, Grace was able to find transport for her and the girls to attend the nearest Protestant church. She was careful of her choice of friends there, knowing only too well that gossip rarely helps anyone. As Liza had suggested, she had adopted Jacob's surname as soon as she moved in with him, and thus had been able to avoid or deflect most of the awkward personal questions. That, her kind manner, and the participation of her girls in church activities, helped her gain gradual acceptance as a member of the little church community.

All in all, that first Summer together in 1946 went well for Grace and Jacob as they began to settle into their lives together. This was quite a test for them, considering it was one of the wettest on record and they were often all cooped up inside the cottage sheltering from the constant Summer rains. The cramped stone cottage was a far from ideal first year of their co-habitation, especially with four young children, but they made do.

Grace improved the look of the inside immensely, but somehow the wet weather always seemed to find yet another leak in the old cottage, no matter how many leaks Jacob fixed. At first Grace had made it a game for the girls to see who could detect the leaks first, then race to place an old saucepan beneath it to catch the drips. By the time it had all been made reliably watertight Jacob had replaced much of the old thatched roof himself.

Grace was particularly happy that the small garden she had planted had survived. Some of her favourites, the lilac shrubs and a few lavender bushes had come on surprisingly well, considering they had developed from a few cuttings she had taken from their landlords' larger tended gardens down the road a bit. On the rare visits from one or other of the two landlord brothers, Grace would remember to smile and thank them, belatedly, for sharing the beauty of I God's Garden, and helping her to establish another of His gardens on her own doorstep. When put like that, it was hard for the two landlords to anything but nod their agreement, especially as Grace and Jacob had already done so much to improve the little cottage rental.

It was in the late Autumn of 1946, that the first early warning signals of that other great challenge in Grace's life began to surface. It would prove to be a challenge that would insidiously creep up on them, tighten its grip and then almost destroy them.

Soon after Grace had moved in with Jacob, Liza had warned her about his vulnerability to alcohol addiction that she thought seemed to run in the men in her husband's family. Grace already knew that Liza's two eldest sons were ardent church goers and abstained completely. However, Liza still had concerns about her two younger sons. She said that binge or heavy drinking occurred more often when people who drank a lot got together. She also cautioned that binge drinking was not confined to young people enjoying themselves and letting off steam, but to people of all ages in Ireland.

In some ways Ireland's post-war drinking culture was perhaps understandable. Many people were still trying to forget the stress and horrors of the long years of war, especially those who actively engaged in the fighting in one form or another. There were multiple reasons for the residual stresses left behind by war of course, but interestingly research in later years would suggest that for many, it was often their own actions during the war that caused them the most grief and guilt afterwards.

Whatever the reason then, getting drunk was a particularly popular pastime post-war in Ireland. Of course, for most people it only amounted to a few nights out socialising from time to time, especially at weekends. They just wanted to have a bit of harmless fun once in a while, and having a few drinks was a way to relax and unwind and enjoy the company of friends. After all, wasn't having a few well-earned beers seen as a working man's right at the end of the week? So what, if they drank to get drunk once in a while, it was not always, and anyway most got over it in time, and most learnt to move on. That was hardly the problem.

However, for some others, perhaps the few unlucky ones, after a while it was not at all about socialising, though it may well have started there. For them, the regular practice of drinking to get drunk quickly turned into an obsession. It became a frequent and entrenched compulsive habit of addiction from which they could not escape. That was very much the problem.

Not many studies had been made of alcohol addiction in that post-war era in Ireland. It would not be until some years later that the government would finally intervene and begin to exert more control over the rich and thriving alcohol industry in its midst.

However, even the early studies confirmed what many families already knew to their cost. That alcohol addiction often led to a culture of violence both in the home and elsewhere. The subsequent research would also show that an astonishing quarter of all deaths of young Irish adults, under forty years of age, were alcohol related.

Even children did not escape unscathed. Many children not only witnessed the traumatic effects of 'alcohol abuse' related violence in their own homes, they were often the recipients of that violence. Sadly, many of those young victims growing up with alcohol abuse, would themselves become perpetrators of the same violent acts. So for some, alcohol addiction was indeed a very serious problem.

Grace was in two minds. She was not sure if there might be an addiction problem with Jacob, but she could not quite ignore Liza's warnings. She was particularly anxious not to have a repeat of the troubles she had with a drunken Jessman.

When she had tried to talk it through with Jacob, he had reassured her that he was already well aware of his so-called family traits.

"Grace, you know full well that my mah had a bit of a rough time with my dah and alcohol after the first World War. Now she thinks we all have the same problem. I know you've had issues too with Jessman. But I'm not like them. I just enjoy a few drinks and a night out with the lads sometimes, that's all."

To be fair, though at times Grace thought he had seemed restless, apart from one significant exception during the 12th July celebration in that first year, it really didn't seem to be any cause for concern.

That exception had been when he had arrived home late in the evening, clearly very tired and very inebriated after a long day out. On that occasion he had barely spoken, but staggered in, dragged off his shoes and slumped down onto the bed, sleeping soundly until the next morning. Grace and the children had been at home that Twelfth day, as little Donna had not been well. Grace had waited up for him but, seeing Jacob's state when he came back, had decided to let him sleep it off. She spent that night in the other room with the children. The next day he had mumbled a brief apology and carried on as if nothing had happened.

Grace had let it pass, not thinking much more about it. After all, nearly half of Northern Ireland Protestants had been out celebrating the 'Glorious Twelfth' and many would have come home a little the worse for wear. Jacob was no exception. Grace felt maybe she was being unreasonable in her expectations, maybe she was looking for problems that weren't there.

However, a few months later, in that late Autumn of 1946, the hunting season opened up again. Jacob accepted an invitation for a weekend's shooting for grouse and partridge in the remote hilly country regions around the Mournes. People tended to know about one another in the country and Grace had been more than a little wary of his friends on that hunting trip. She had good cause to be.

When Jacob returned from the weekend hunting trip away, Grace knew he had been drinking again. With the very wet weather, it had been more of a weekend of heavy drinking than hunting. As it turned out, that weekend of binge drinking, and more that were to follow, would continue to awaken addictive behaviours in him. Behaviours which would resurface again and again.

When Grace confronted him after the weekend away, Jacob dismissed it all as a bit of harmless fun with his pals and refused to see it as anything more than that. Grace had finally decided to let it go, convincing herself it was alright. After all, she had rationalised, many men came home drunk in Ireland, particularly at weekends, and some much more often than that. Didn't other women just accept it as a normal part of life, part of the everyday culture of Ireland? It was not as if it was a common occurrence with Jacob, or indeed any sort of serious problem at all, was it?

A year later, on the 20th day of November 1947, Grace gave birth to her second child. It was another bonny girl. She and Jacob were happy and excited. The girl was healthy and she was theirs, born in their own home. In the lead up to the birth, Grace had been plagued with thoughts of her mother's curse, especially that her children would be born black crows. Jacob suggested it was probably natural to be concerned after all she had been through, but to try to dismiss those awful thoughts and just concentrate on having a healthy baby. It was good advice as it turned out and helped dispel her worries.

In what was a relatively easy birth, for which Grace was extremely thankful, she was assisted by a woman friend who was experienced in helping mothers deliver their new-borns at home. These women were so-called handy women. More commonly they would later become known as mid-wives, because they were 'with the mother' during the birthing process at home. Grace's handy woman friend was part of the growing organisation that in time produced trained and experienced nurses. They were a less expensive way for mothers to deliver their children in the home, especially until the introduction of the National Health service the next year in 1948.

The child was born on the same day that the young Princess Elizabeth married Prince Phillip. As Grace and Jacob wanted to give their child a royal name to commemorate this, and having a child called Elizabeth already, they named her Victoria, or Vicky for short. However, in their enthusiasm they also gave Vicky three other additional Christian names, wanting to include the names of two of Grace's siblings as well as Valerie, Jacob's sister. It was well intentioned, but the child's four names led to quite some confusion when Vicky finally came to be baptised at a multiple baptism ceremony with some other children.

It was a happy day for Jacob and Grace as the children were lined up for the baptismal ceremony. The young Reverend minister, standing in for his senior at late notice, stood nervously by the font. He was still a little new to baptisms and had his head down, reading his copious script. In order to begin the formal proceedings, and with barely a glance up from his script, he asked for the first child to be brought forward and introduced to both him and the congregation. Grace took a step forward and announced Vicky, with her four Christian names in full.

The young Reverend minister, swiftly raising his head from his notes and looking flustered, called out loudly, "No! No! Hold on there now, please! Just one child at a time, just one at a time please!"

As the tittering and nudging rippled through the small

congregation, the confused young Reverend's error was explained to him. He was more than a little embarrassed. However, to his credit he took it exceptionally well, apologising to both Grace and his congregation before continuing. The incident seemed to ease his tension completely, for as he did continue, he began grinning from ear to ear, then burst out laughing at his own mistake, shaking his head in disbelief.

With five young children, all girls, sharing the small cottage, Pearl, Nan, Elizabeth, Donna, and now young Vicky, it was not only crowded, it was rarely quiet. As with other young Irish mothers with growing families, Grace took on the role of keeping the house tidy and clean, preparing meals, washing the endless pile of dirty clothes, and doing her best to keep her children well occupied when they were at home and Jacob still at work.

She was always grateful when Jacob's father, Bob, visited her some weekends to bring them all over to Liza's house. They would all look forward to it as it was always a pleasure to visit Liza. For Grace in particular it was always a very welcome few hours respite. While she was still shunned by her own parents, and could not share her young growing family with them, she took great pleasure in sharing her children with Liza and Bob.

Sometimes in those first few years with Jacob, Grace pondered what her own mother would think of her family and her new life now. Sometimes she still thought of her mother's harsh words and sometimes she had the recurring nightmares of her wedding day. Jacob would try to console her when she did. Gradually they learned to lean on each other a little more when it was needed.

"Well, I may not ever be able to go back to The Liberty Bell again," Grace told Jacob one evening after they had put the children to bed, "but at least all our children are healthy and seem happy. We do seem to be managing well enough Jacob, aren't we?" The question lingered in the air for a moment as Jacob picked up on the tone.

"Yes, all the children are doing fine Grace", he reassured her, "and so are we. Mind you, if Beth and Riley can't take their own daughter back after all this time, then they can stay on that farm of theirs forever, for all I care." On the spur of the moment he added, "And at least we don't have to worry about your mah's curse that our children will be born black crows anymore."

Grace managed a smile in return. She knew he was trying to lighten things up and she really appreciated that. It was just that she wasn't quite as easily convinced as Jacob.

The Harbinger

Chapter 24

The Crow is Born

*We have a secret in our culture
and it is not that birth is painful.
It is that women are strong.
(Laura Stavoe Harm)*

Summer 1949 – Winter 1949

It was early in the Summer of 1949 that Grace found she was pregnant again. Having so little space in the small cottage, they decided to look around for another to rent. They were lucky enough to find one fairly soon that they could afford. It was a slightly bigger stone cottage just a mile or two away in the area of Drombroneth.

The wide-open fireplace dominated the single large room that served as an all-purpose living room, with the kitchen area off to one side of it. The level stone floor was generally cold, some of it being covered by old mats that were worn thin. There were 2 bedrooms and as usual, an outside toilet. As was still the customary practice, such cottages were often whitewashed before Winter. Among other things, the lime-based whitewashing helped protect them against mildew with the onset of snows.

Also typical of the many country cottages, this one had seen better days and was still without electricity or running water. It and two other cottages were situated in a semi-circular open courtyard at the top of a rise, cordoned off by a large unkempt hawthorn hedge running either side of the large iron swing gates. Standing on the rise, facing south, the cottage gave expansive views over the wide-open countryside.

The big old swing gates gave access to the narrow earthy lane that led down the short steep hill to a winding country road at the bottom. Off to the side, at the point where the lane met the road, was a natural spring well, the water shaded by another hawthorn hedgerow that ran along the side of the road. From this small well each family could draw water for all their needs, as long as they were prepared to carry it up the lane in their buckets.

It was into this very same well in a few years to come that a slightly plump young Donna, bending low to scoop up a bucket of water, would find herself taking an unplanned slow motion nose dive into the chilly water. A younger sibling accompanying her had found Donna's sizeable bottom too great a temptation. Without thought for the consequences, the young child gave it an almighty shove from behind. Fortunately, no harm was done and after her unplanned dive, Donna managed to climb out of the well and give chase back up the lane after the escaping perpetrator. Minutes later, a drenched Donna, still intent on completing her original mission, would gamely plod into her home with a bucket of water in each hand and wellington boots full to overflowing!

It was a frugal existence living in Drombroneth, but Grace and Jacob enjoyed the simple country life. The old cottages were basic in the extreme, offering minimal comforts. Yet they sufficed to provide basic shelter for poor families who could not afford better in those post-war years. For some of the people who lived in such places, even amidst their poverty, they were still able to appreciate the beauty of the lush green Irish countryside. Surrounded by open fields and nature, there were times when they were able to enjoy a wealth that could not be measured in monetary terms.

In the slightly larger of the two nearby cottages lived an elderly husband and wife. They had been hard working farmers in times past and had lived there for many years. Their children had long since left home to search for better prospects elsewhere. The old couple remained, surviving on the meagre rent from their two cottages and grazing a few cattle on their remaining acres of land. They also had a few chickens that, being sparsely fed, were literally scratching out a living from the land.

In the other smaller rented cottage was a young couple with two young children. If anything, they seemed to be slightly worse off than Grace and her family. Grace, though she had little herself, would sometimes share a meal with them or give the young woman a few old cast-off clothes for her children.

Grace also made friends with two rather quirky elderly spinster sisters who lived a little way up the country road from them. These two elderly sisters often wore odd clothes. Mostly they wore trousers, which was still a little unusual for women at the time. However, their real mark of distinction was what they wore on their heads.

Bloomers, and colourful ones at that! It seems they may have started to wear a pair of bloomers on their head to protect their hair and keep their head warm when they were working outside in their garden, which was often. In time, this strange headwear became their unique trademark, indoors and outdoors. Naturally it all added to their reputation for being quirky. The sisters clearly didn't care much about fashion, or reputations for that matter. They just did what they thought was expedient, and hang the consequences.

Grace found herself admiring their independence, if not their appearance.

The two sisters seemed to have only a few friends and not many other visitors. Perhaps for good reason. Grace was amused that occasional passers-by who happened to stare a little long at their unusual attire, would often find themselves on the receiving end of the sisters' sharp tongues and witty comments. If the sisters didn't like the look of them, which was fairly often, it was not unknown for them to wave their walking sticks in the air and swear at the passers-by for daring to pause too long near their little cottage.

"Hey! What are you doing there? Have you got nothing better to do than to stand there with your mouth open gawping at us all day? Get on with you now! Move on up that road and mind your own business, before we come out there and mind it for you!"

Needless to say, most people didn't loiter. However, as Grace took the time to find out, beneath all their grumpiness and peculiar appearances, these eccentric old ladies could be as kind and welcoming as any other good neighbour. Their bark was much worse than their bite. Grace's patience and geniality paid off for they soon became good friends. She visited them frequently, taking the children with her and sometimes samples of her fresh baking. Though to be fair, apart from precocious Pearl, her children remained very wary of the odd sisterly duo.

Grace had moved into the cottage in Drombroneth in good time for the birth. Once again, they made the most of the time they had to tidy it up in readiness. It was as her pregnancy entered the third trimester that Grace first noticed the warning signals. She had never experienced anything quite like it in her two previous pregnancies. Her stomach felt so heavy and she seemed to be extending more than ever before. The strong sharp kicks within her surprising Grace with their frequency and intensity. Somewhat reluctantly she plucked up the courage to go and visit her doctor again.

Slim and still with a full head of short greying hair and tightly groomed moustache, doctor Miller was very strict and did not suffer fools gladly. He showed little regard or courtesy for patients whom he felt were wasting his valuable time with only minor ailments. Now, just a few years away from retirement, his manner had become all the more direct, if not caustic. His advice would invariably be accurate, but sometimes he could be blunt, to the point of being obnoxious. Only those brave souls with genuine ailments dared visit him, or if even more daring, requested that he visit them.

Dr Miller could indeed be a bit of a gruff old dragon when he wished, and it seemed he did so wish more often than not. However, his reputation preceded him, not just as the dragon doctor, but also as an expert doctor, if one was courageous enough to go and see him. Yet for all his reputation, he remained polite and deeply caring for those of his patients he deemed were genuinely deserving of his best medical attention. Despite his curt manner, there must have been many who respected him, for his clinic was always full and he was always busy.

Grace had visited Dr Miller just a handful of times in recent times. If the truth be known, she was more than a little afraid of him, but would not let that stop her when she needed his help and advice for her family. She had tried Liza's suggestion to let go of her ideas and worries or judgements about Dr Miller and just meet him as if it was the first time, each and every time she met him. More because of her regard for Liza than the idea itself, Grace had tried it and to her surprise found that it helped. At least she was able to talk to Dr Miller without her mouth going dry, or her mind wondering off when she was supposed to be listening carefully to him.

For his part, Dr Miller already considered Grace to be one of those people who only came to see him as a last resort, either for herself, or for her children, which was not often. He was happy to make time for her. This time as he began to examine Grace, he expressed some surprise, and went through the process a second time. He knew that Grace was not too far away from her time and that she had intended to have a home delivery, again with the aid of a mid-wife. He insisted on seeing her again for another examination a couple of weeks before her due date.

The next visit to Dr Miller went much the same as before, as he again doubled-checked himself on some of the examination process. Although he did not deign to explain the nature of any of his concerns, when he finished his examinations, he sat back down on his chair and was silent for a moment. Then he announced, "Grace, I want you to take advantage of the new National Health service and have this baby in hospital. On no account are you to try to deliver it at home. I will notify the hospital. Now, can you manage that ok?"

Grace was a little taken aback, but she was more than willing to take her doctor's advice. She nodded her agreement and dared to ask him if everything was alright. Dr Miller only added, "I will be on hand to deliver this baby at the hospital, no matter what the hour, and I'll make sure everything is alright. Now, be sure to do what I say Grace."

It was a firm but kind message that could not help but put Grace a little on edge. However, as it turned out, it may just have saved Grace's life.

With just over a week to go before Christmas of that year, Grace had her first early signals of the oncoming labour. Jacob helped her into the back of the car he had arranged to borrow from their landlord and drove off steadily to the hospital. The young woman from next door had already offered to keep an eye on the children. All was set. Grace would be at the hospital in a short time and they would contact Dr Miller so that he could oversee the birth, all as had been arranged beforehand.

Everything was well planned out, what could go wrong? After all, Grace was a strong and healthy young woman who had given birth twice before. There seemed to be no reason for concern, why should there be? Yet, as Grace felt the increasing pangs of labour, she also felt an increasing apprehension, much more so than she had experienced when giving birth to her previous two children. She had her strong Christian faith and she called on it as they journeyed to the hospital. Trying to calm herself, she quietly recited The Lord is my Shepard, a favourite prayer that often helped reassure her that all would be well.

As they neared the hospital and the car slowed, abruptly a particularly painful contraction shot through Grace. She tensed suddenly as, triggered by the pain and apprehension she was feeling about this birth, her mother's words came back to Grace in that instant. She heard her mother speak as if she was there inside her head again. Harsh venomous words, long kept at bay, but never able to be forgotten. Beth's menacing voice reached out across the years to find her once more. Grace heard the words again, as clearly as she had done all those eight years ago, when her own mother had struck her face, then leaned over her and uttered that awful curse.

"With every part of my being, I curse you, Grace! I curse you! May you never find peace, and if you try to find it with him, may your children be born black, black crows!"

Hours later, Grace gasped in agony as the pain of another wave of contractions swept over her, followed soon after by another, and another, and another. She could barely breathe, but now in the hospital bed she heard around her the encouraging urgings of the two young nurses and the firm assertive voice of Dr Miller. The waves of agony seemed endless, the pain unendurable, yet all the while it seemed to be escalating to another level, continuing, on and on, never ending.

Grace had endured child birth twice before, but never before had she felt pain quite like this. Desperately she prayed for it to be over, yet it continued unabated, her pleas and prayers seemingly ignored. Grace was sweating profusely with the effort, oblivious of the bitter cold outside. She sensed something was not quite right with this birth, something was amiss. Nature, all powerful, seemed to be tearing her apart, wreaking havoc on the young mother's body as she struggled to give birth to the thing inside her.

Dr Miller had given Grace some gas and air, a relatively new aid intended to ease the pain of labour, but one which he dared not overuse. It was a delicate balance as she clearly needed help, but he wanted Grace to remain compos mentis so she could retain some measure of control of her mind and her birthing. Though he had said little, he knew this would be a most difficult birth and was not at all confident Grace would survive a caesarean in the circumstances.

The gas and air had the effect of making Grace a little woozy and light headed. Somewhat more unusually, it also made her a little more prone to hallucinate. She closed her eyes and gulped in the gas and air as she struggled to cope with the pain. As the intake of the gas and air took effect, her mother's curse came back to haunt her mind yet again. She tried to dispel them but the words kept repeating in her mind. For a brief moment in her delirium, she imagined she was giving birth to a huge black crow, just as her mother had prophesised.

Sweat and tears ran down Grace's face, as she gripped the hand of the nurse beside her. She was completely drained, her efforts becoming weaker. Exhausted she heard the urging cries of the nurses yet again. Now though, even in the midst of her fatigue, she could hear the rising anxiety creeping into the voices of those around her as they wondered if they would have to perform a Caesarean. Unwittingly their worried voices were now heightening Grace's own sense of concern. Voices that were unknowingly sowing the seeds of doubt that she would be able to give birth.

All except one. Dr Miller's voice was unwavering, unflinching, firm and steady, a solid rock of reassurance to cling to in the swirling sea of doubt and relentless pain that engulfed her.

"Almost there now Grace, almost there. Come on now, you can do this. Take a deep breath then another big push. Now Grace, now, push, come on, come on, one more, that's it Grace. Push! Push!"

Somehow, urged on by his unrelenting firm but reassuring words, Grace found the will within her to try again. Summoning up the last of her energy, she made another effort, then another, and then again. Reaching beyond pain, at the behest of her will, her exhausted body responding, serving her turn long after all else was gone.

Then it was over and for a moment Grace lay still, utterly spent. Her tired mind still swimming, she was only vaguely aware of the sounds all around her. At first it was the cheering of the nurses and excited sounds of relief, as the doctor held the new-born in his arms, wiping away the mucous. Then, as their eyes absorbed the sight, stunned silence. Then rising murmurs of shock and surprise. Full of emotion after the difficult birth and unable to contain her surprise, the voice of the youngest nurse rang out.

"My god Grace, what have you given birth to? Dear love, how on earth did you ever manage to give birth to that? Its half grown and covered in hair!"

For the first time for many hours, Dr Miller smiled broadly as he lifted the wailing child into Grace's awaiting arms. "He's alright Grace, perfectly fine in fact. Just a wee bit big!"

Grace's son was more than a wee bit big, he was enormous,

weighing in at just a fraction under eleven pounds. For a woman of Grace's average build and stature, and in those times, it was truly amazing that she had been able to give birth to such a prodigious baby. Not only that, but his head, shoulders, arms and legs were covered in dark, almost black hair.

The size, swarthy skin, and unusually widespread dark Lanugo hair covering on his body, would come to prompt the nurses to give the child the nick-name of baby Samson. Once again another of Grace's new-born children would draw many of the young hospital nurses to her bedside to see the child for themselves and satisfy their curiosity.

As Grace took the child to her breast and fed him, she felt tired but happy. She had endured this long night. She had given birth to a son. Gone now were the earlier worries. Gone was her mother's voice in her head. Gone was Beth's curse that had haunted her. At least for the moment, they had all been swept away with the birth of this strange child.

It was not long before a healing sleep began to find Grace. Just before it did so, a sleepy fleeting thought passed through her tired mind. Perhaps in the shape of this dark-skinned boy, covered in black hair, she had in a sense given birth to the black crow her mother had prophesied. She would write to her mother Beth and tell her so. She would simply say that the crow has arrived. Yes, that was all that was needed, just those few words, the crow has arrived. The rest would be up to Beth.

Her mind drifting with the pull of sleep, Grace decided to discuss it with Jacob when he was allowed to visit both her and his newborn son. It was worth trying to make the peace again anyway, she told herself, as the soft blanket of sleep wrapped around her.

Once again Grace had found hope within her. At last, after all these years maybe this dark boy-child could be a harbinger of peace. Beth had ignored all Grace's previous letters, but perhaps now, with the birth of this dark crow-child, Grace might at last find a way out of her isolation and exile. Perhaps she might no longer be a disgraced pariah in her mother's eyes. Above all, she hoped she might no longer be an outcast from her own family.

A Wee Nip in the Behind!

Chapter 25

The Cow's Tale

Forgiveness is the fragrance that the violet sheds on the heel that has crushed it.
(Mark Twain)

Autumn 1963 - (13 years later)

Ted, Grace's youngest son, was furious. Rubbing his sore backside at the same time, he was half running, half hobbling along towards the safety of the fowl house, desperate to get out of the way of the big gander that was chasing him and his older brother, Hugh, running alongside him.

Breathlessly Ted shouted out, "If that damn goose bites me in the arse again, I'm going to chop its stupid head off! Granda can go and get his own damn eggs next time!"

Just in time they made it to the fowl house, hurtling through the open door together. All in one movement they slammed the half door shut behind them, as the pursuing gander thumped up against it. Flapping its wings wildly and honking noisily at them, it made fierce stabbing knocks on the door as if to warn them never to return to its domain again. Braving a quick glance at the goose over the bottom door and deciding not to take any chances, the boys slammed the top door closed too, and barred them both shut for good measure!

It was no wonder Grace's two boys had mixed feelings about sleepovers at The Liberty Bell. On the whole they loved their grandparent's farm, despite the one or two hazards such as the gander and the old boar that always seemed to have it in for them. Granny Beth and granda Riley were alright, but they could be strict too at times. Far too strict for the boys' liking.

Anyway, young Ted thought granda Riley was definitely a bit touched, half bonkers at times! However, mostly he liked it when his granda mucked about with them, even if he had an odd sense of humour, even if he was daft. Even so, Ted swore he was going to throw up if granda showed him that awful trick of removing the top of his finger just one more time!

What the boys were not so keen on was when granda Riley lost his temper with them. Like the time they were supposed to be helping to gather the hay but sneaked off to catch field mice instead. His shouting and telling off then was bad enough, but it felt like nothing compared to the events that happened earlier that day. The stupid slip up that led them to where they were now, hiding from a damn goose!

Thirteen years had passed since Grace had been allowed back into her mother's house, The Liberty Bell. Thirteen years since she had given birth to her large hair-covered firstborn son and sent that letter to Beth that eventually brought to an end her eight years of living in exile. The letter had been uncharacteristically brief and to the point.

"Mother dear, your prophecy has come to pass. The crow has

arrived. We have a son. Please, would you like to see him?"

After the birth, Grace had managed to leave the hospital in time to be home for Christmas with her young family. She had prayed that some of that same Christmas spirit might help to melt her mother's heart and that Beth would relent when she received the letter. That at long last she might welcome Grace back into their family once more.

It had not taken Beth and Riley long to get the full story of the birth from Toby. They knew their son and his German wife had kept in contact with Grace over the years, despite their stern warnings. Hearing what Toby described as Grace's extremely difficult struggle with the birth of her son, for the first time Beth's resolve began to waiver.

That night, long after Riley had gone on to bed, she took the letter out again and read the few words over and over. There had been silence except for the gentle tick-tock of the old clock on the mantlepiece in The Liberty Bell, ticking away the seconds and minutes and then the hours as Beth reflected on her decisions and actions of long ago. She had forced Grace to marry Jessman, then cursed her for leaving him.

Back then Beth had thought it only for the best, the best for all of them. Only now, years later, as the clock remorselessly counted out the march of infinite time, with Grace's simple letter in her hands, could Beth begin to realise the toll her actions had taken on her daughter's life. Only now, could she begin to understand how Grace must have really felt. For the first time in years, sorrow surged through Beth, and she wept. Then she said a silent prayer.

When she had shared Grace's letter with her family, the unwritten appeal for peace and reconciliation was plain enough for everyone to see in Grace's simple message.

Riley, and Grace's siblings, had all made passionate pleas on her behalf. Time, that great healer, had dulled the sharp edges of Beth's stubborn resolve just enough. Just enough that this time Beth could listen with a mother's heart. Enough to really hear at last the depth of her family's emotional pleas for peace and forgiveness for Grace.

Finally, after eight long years, Beth had relented. She was aware that Grace's husband, Jessman, who had not enjoyed good health, had long since given up on Grace ever returning to him. Beth knew he would not want her back now anyway. Too much time had passed, too much pain had been endured by everyone. Beth had quietly agreed it was time to bring her outcast daughter and her children home to re-join their family.

Grace's first few visits back to The Liberty Bell after her eight years in exile had not been easy or without tension. She made a conscious effort to forgive her mother and to let the past stay in the past as she tried to rebuild her relationships with both her parents. It was not a one-off effort either. She had tried to remain calm and friendly, even when things did get a little tricky, allowing her mother a little more time to adjust. Grace quickly found that it helped them both having all her children around her, and especially when her siblings also brought their own children along too.

The cousins played together often at The Liberty Bell and when Grace took her children to visit her siblings. Like many families, in time they formed friendships that would last lifetimes. To her credit, Beth soon managed to set aside her initial reservations about Jacob's girls, Pearl, Nan and Donna. They were soon accepted and embraced as family as much as Grace's own children. However, it took a little longer and a lot more patience, but Beth gradually also came to accept, if not openly welcome Jacob into the family clan.

In another couple of years Grace had given birth to young Ted. Eighteen months after that her last child, Joy, was born. All in all,

Grace had given birth to five children, three girls and two boys, though she would also forever love Jacob's three girls as her own daughters. There might have been even more children, but after the birth of Joy, a now semi-retired Dr Miller had given Grace a dire warning that she must not have any more children. He had been treating Grace for increasingly frequent fainting spells and low blood pressure and advised that they were a sure sign that she must take much better care of herself.

When her boys were old enough Grace began to send them off to spend the odd weekend or part of their school holidays at The Liberty Bell. It was ostensibly to help their aging grandparents with work on the farm. Boys being boys, that didn't always work out as planned.

Waiting for an angry goose to go away was not easy. As Grace's two boys waited for the old gander to lose interest in them and wander away again, young Ted was fast becoming impatient. They had already fed the young turkeys and ducks and collected the duck eggs. They were just in the process of collecting a few goose eggs when the big gander had latched onto them and bit young Ted in the backside!

Granda Riley had given them strict instructions to look around the edges of the little pond and bring back as many goose eggs as they could find. Riley didn't want any of the half dozen laying geese to form a clutch of eggs and begin to incubate them. Ted didn't care about all that sort of thing though. He was really hungry and once this angry goose cleared off, he wanted to get back up to the farm for some of granny Beth's freshly made buttermilk and egg on buttered toast for breakfast.

Young Ted had already conveniently forgotten that it was his own fault he and his brother had been sent down to the lower farm for the eggs before breakfast in the first place. Their normal routine was simple enough. Fetch the cows from the fields and help Riley with the milking before breakfast, then return the cows and fetch the eggs after breakfast. However, Ted's antics that morning had made Riley chase them off to fetch the eggs, without the cows or their breakfast.

The boys had brought the half dozen big placid Friesian cross cows up from the fields as usual that morning. It was a long established regular daily routine for the cows. As soon as the field gates were opened, the big animals would start to meander up the lane to the byre for milking to ease their burdensome heavy udders. The boys, trailing behind them, had little to do but chivvy them along, being careful to avoid the many cow-claps deposited on the way. After milking, and breakfast, the boys would take the cows back down to the best pastures in the lower fields again. Then they would carry on a little further to the old cluster of outhouses in the lower meadows to feed the fowl and fetch the duck and geese eggs.

Riley usually did all the milking. He sat on a small three-legged stool, head propped against the side of the tied-up cow, while he kneaded the udder and rhythmically pulled on the cow's teats. This time-honoured practice would usually get things started. Riley would skillfully direct the flow of milk straight into the bucket between his legs, drumming out a regular swoosh, swoosh, swoosh, as he continued the process.

However, for one of the cows in particular, Blasted Bluebell, Riley always insisted that one of the boys keep a firm hold of her tail during milking. This was because big Bluebell had a mind of her own when it came to where her milk should go, and that certainly wasn't into some old enamel bucket! Somehow, she had developed the knack of swishing her dung-smeared tail right around and giving Riley a hard whack on the jaw for his troubles. Hence her extended name, Blasted Bluebell.

That morning it was Ted's turn to hold Blasted Bluebell's tail. It was a mistake from the beginning. Young Ted was preoccupied with the penned calves at the other end of the byre. Literally, his mind was not on the job in hand, being the cow's tail.

Cows cannot produce milk without first giving birth to a calf. It was fairly common practice at the time for most calves, especially bull-calves, to be slaughtered within a few days of birth and sold-off for consumption as veal. Riley generally tried to retain a few of the female calves. He would raise these as heifers, ready to bring into calf and the milking cycle when they were old enough. This allowed him to replace less productive older cows with younger stock.

The female calves were usually removed from their mothers in the first days so that the milk could then be used for human consumption. However, Riley allowed these calves a small share of their mother's milk from a bucket for the next few months. This would continue until they were completely weaned and grass fed. Removal of the calves was an unnatural and difficult process for both man and beast. Despite Riley's best efforts, the mother cows and their calves often had separation issues. Perhaps it was no wonder then that Blasted Bluebell had a tendency to live up to her name at milking time.

As Ted watched his older brother petting the young calves and letting them suck his fingers, his mind was not at all on keeping a firm hold of Bluebell's tail. Sensing the lightness of Ted's grip on her tail, and with one big round eye firmly fixed on Riley's efforts to withdraw her milk, Bluebell yanked her tail swiftly up and away. Before anyone knew what was happening, her long tail went whisking around in a wide arc. Having gained sufficient momentum, she splatted Riley full in the face with a resounding wallop. Things went swiftly downhill from there.

Riley, stunned and blinded by the dung smeared tail, yelled

loudly and jerked his head up in surprise. His yelling and sudden movements startled Bluebell, who promptly shunted backwards in the stall and kicked out. Riley was knocked off the stool, while Bluebell's foot hit the bucket, sending it and its milky contents flying across the floor of the byre.

Young Ted, standing open-mouthed at the rear end of Bluebell, and fortunate not to have been kicked, had barely time to realise what was happening. Then he too was caught on the receiving end of Blasted Bluebell's tail as it came swishing around yet again. The tail flicked Ted around the neck and shoulders, but now standing on the treacherous milk-covered floor, it was enough to send him crashing down onto his backside.

That had been the first of two painful bruises on his backside that Ted received that morning! The gander having added its contribution to his plight a bit later with a well-aimed nip on his behind. Still, young Ted might consider himself very lucky it was not three bruises. Had he been able to get close enough, a very irate Riley would have given him a firm kick in the behind for his troubles in the byre that morning, but fortunately young Ted had enough sense to stay well out of his reach.

With his sight still obscured by the unwelcome deposits from Blasted Bluebell's tail, Riley had to content himself with giving them a stern verbal lashing instead. Then, with a few very direct instructions to Grace's boys to "Get the hell away and go collect the damn goose eggs!" Riley staggered off to wash the dung from his face.

Chapter 26

Fractures

But why is Fantasia dying?
- Because people have begun to lose their hopes
and forget their dreams. So, the Nothing grows stronger.

But what is the Nothing?
- It is the emptiness that is left.

(The Never-Ending Story)

Summer 1965

Like some of her neighbours in the Heights, Grace had recently acquired a small black and white television, though she still preferred to listen to the radio. She had become fascinated by the radio when she had first moved to live in the Heights some nine years before. Electricity had its advantages and in so many ways the radio had become her lifeline. At times Grace was so enthralled with the music and songs that they brought her into a new and different world, alive with the music.

She was so moved with opera singing, especially the Italian American tenor, Mario Lanza, that often everyone in the house would be subjected to a full volume of his radio performances. Interestingly, on one such occasion a young boy sang alongside Lanza during one of his performances of Ave Marie. Grace absolutely loved the performance. The young boy, Luciano Pavarotti, would of course go on to become an even greater international star in later years.

As Elvis, Beatlemania and the new pop genre had been sweeping over the youth of Britain and Northern Ireland, other forms of music like jazz, rock and roll, and even some big band sounds were still clinging onto the older generation. However, while opera had some ardent followers, it would be fair to say that it was not at all a popular pastime or interest for most folk in Ireland. Grace appreciated she was in the minority, but opera seemed to speak to her spirit and she loved it dearly.

She would listen to Mozart, Puccini, Verdi, Wagner, and all the great artists and operas whenever she could and studied them with a passion. They helped bring out the joy that was already present in her, waiting to be expressed. Neighbours in the Heights would not be at all surprised to hear some aria or other soaring up through the airways at full blast, sometimes with Grace giving her all and singing along with it.

Much had happened during the nine years that Grace and Jacob had been living together in the Heights. The three daughters that Maude had abandoned, Pearl, Nan, and Donna had all been raised by Grace, grown up, and married and moved away.

Pearl, now well into her twenties, had already given birth to three fine children. She often brought her eldest girl, Anna, to stay with Grace and her family at weekends. Anna, being a lively and precocious child, became a firm favourite with Grace's children. So much so that the child was considered every bit as much a part of Grace's family as she was of Pearl's.

Donna had also recently given birth to a fine healthy boy, coincidentally on the same day that her sister, Pearl, had given birth to her youngest girl. Grace's eldest girl, Elizabeth, beautiful as ever, had her pick of hopeful young men. However, against the expectations and pressures of society at the time, Elizabeth had chosen to remain single. She was already starting to carve out a promising career for herself in a high fashion shop, and generally only spent weekends at home now. Vicky, who used only one of her four names, had a job in a local shoe shop but was already becoming bored with it. The three youngest of Grace's children, Hugh, Ted and Joy, were still at school.

Grace was worried about the sort of future that might lie in store for all her children. She wanted them to have better opportunities than she herself had, but she knew that worthwhile jobs could be hard to find in Northern Ireland, indeed any jobs. The fervent Presbyterian minister at the church she attended had often preached that the devil finds work for idle hands. Grace smiled at the thought, but she felt he was probably right.

There were too many people unable to find work and that could only lead to more unrest, especially when Protestants were often chosen ahead of Catholics for the few jobs that were on offer. Grace knew of many young men who withdrew their weekly government allowances, only to take it straight around the corner to the betting shops and the public houses. With boredom and unrest, the local youth could easily be drawn into the gangs and more trouble, especially if they had come from difficult backgrounds.

Beneath all her unease, Grace knew that there was a much larger problem. She and Jacob had been having a rough time of it in recent years. They had been getting by after a fashion, but just living together and getting by, was not the same thing as being happy and content. Jacob's drinking habits had been getting worse. She knew that he had made efforts to keep it under control, especially in their first few years. Now however, it was slowly encroaching more and more on their lives. It seemed Liza's early warnings those years ago had not been too far off the mark.

Jacob worked hard and seemed to make it a rule not to imbibe during the working week. However, like so many men of his time, his tendency to go out drinking heavily at weekends had gradually become more frequent, and of late, more habitual.

Many men would return home after a few drinks and resume their family lives. Some would slide past the point of reason somewhere along the way. They would end up staying until the pubs closed and they were obliged to stagger home, generally a bit the worse for wear. Among this number, some prone to unpredictable outbursts. The effects of the excessive alcohol in their systems could make them appear to be completely different people. At those times, these men would become the dangerous few. A danger not only to themselves but to their family and those around them.

Jacob's father had died a few years before in a bad motorbike crash, somewhere out near the Halfway House, a mid-point public house between Dromana and Banbridge. The irony was not lost on Liza. She felt that her husband Bob had been living a kind of halfway life for many years since the events of the Great war changed him, as war often does. He was a decorated war hero who was halfway to being an intelligent loving man, and a wonderful husband and father. Yet he was also half-way to being held captive in his addiction, at times compulsive and unwise, at times neglecting himself and sometimes his family.

Liza had loved her husband dearly and mourned him, but shared with Grace how the post-war depression that led to his addictive drinking had been a constant scourge over the years. She repeatedly warned Grace to keep a safe distance when a man was drunk. They both knew from bitter experience that it was not the time for attempted logical discussions, and certainly not arguments. Any remnants of reason and control were already sacrificed, and alcohol-fuelled memory played havoc, both during and after an argument.

Alcohol abuse in families was not uncommon, and not just something that only happened to other people. It was far more prevalent than society would care to acknowledge. Yet, as often as not, it remained under cover, played down and hidden away, so as not to draw unwanted attention, or bring shame, or worse. So there it stayed and festered.

The more Grace thought about their own situation, the more despondent she became. She had tried talking to Jacob, but in typical response, he refused to see it as a major issue. However, Grace knew he was now associating far more with the sort of friends who had serious drinking problems. She also knew that the more he associated with them, the more he was inclined to follow their lead.

She loved him, but slowly, insidiously, Grace felt her hopes and dreams for the future being gradually eroded. Their relationship was being slowly poisoned by this invasive interloper and Grace felt powerless in its path. Although she resisted, she was starting to lose hope, and hope was the foundation of her life.

Liza had once told her a story about a frog placed in a pot of water. It would immediately jump out of a pot of boiling water, but remain in one of cold water. The frog would happily remain in the pot while the cold water was slowly heated, supposedly finding it comfortable and invitingly warm at first. As the water slowly came to the boil the frog would die. Liza would say that people think it was the boiling water that killed the frog, and of course to an extent they would be right. But no, Liza maintained it was not just that. It was as much the frog's inability to recognise the increasing danger, and its failure to jump out while it still could, that really caused its demise.

Grace could see the moral in the cruel little story, even if Liza had not intended it to apply to Grace's current situation. Being Grace, she had a lot of sympathy for the frog. She felt she could not just ignore their own situation as it was. The water was getting hotter and she did not know what to do.

How could she possibly just up and leave this man that she loved? She had already left one loveless marriage of drunkenness and abuse, been ostracised by her mother from her own family, reared this man's children, and produced children of their own. She had met every storm that had besieged her, somehow survived them, and some might even say had thrived thus far. Still, it was not enough, it seemed there were always more trials to face. Not for the first time Grace wondered if that was just the nature of the waves of life, so often taking us to the brink of our endurance.

Seeing no way out, perhaps it was little wonder that Grace was beginning to lose hope in their future together. Inevitably as she started to lose hope, so the changes began to show in her.

Jacob had begun to sense it too. The laughter and humour had been ebbing away from their relationship for a while now. He had noticed the gradual shift in Grace's attitude from her usual cheery optimism, to one of increased bouts of pessimism and even depression. Increasingly he was reminded of his years with Maude, her volatile mood swings, and how she always seemed to hold him accountable for her unhappiness. Somehow it didn't seem quite right to him that the measure of Maude's happiness should be entirely within someone else's control.

His method of coping way back then had been to spend less

time in the home, avoiding Maude as much as possible. It was an inadequate but not uncommon way that some men had of dealing with such problems. He was not entirely blind to the fact that he had been drifting into similar patterns of behaviour with Grace, or indeed that his self-isolation was in fact exacerbating the situation.

Grace's changing attitude was also impacting him in another more subtle way. To his mind she was losing faith in him. That in turn meant she was also losing faith in the two of them. While he was not one to admit to having much faith in anything himself, he knew her faith underpinned all that was Grace. Yet, he also felt and firmly believed, that they were soul-mates. That Fate had twisted and turned their separate lives in such a way because in the end they were meant to be together. They had come through so much already. That was what made it all the more difficult for him to accept that she now seemed to be losing faith in him, in them.

Ideas and imaginings trickled through his mind. Was she now starting to abandon him as Maude had done? Paradoxically, the idea in itself only made him feel more inclined to keep his distance, so as to be less vulnerable. The strange self-delusion that can be so carefully hidden in the mind clouded his reasoning. If he was somehow less reliant on her support, then perhaps he would be less hurt if she withdrew it.

So, as it had become with Maude, once more he was holding back, closing up, bringing up the drawbridge, getting ready for the siege. His tendency to withdraw, making it more difficult for them to openly acknowledge and deal with their problems.

As we are all wont to do sometimes, he felt the need to justify his more wayward behaviour to himself. That kind of self-justification that often seems to arise when our wants far outweigh our true needs. In Jacob's case it was usually when he was feeling the persuasive urge to have a few drinks, or indeed already having them. At those times he convinced himself that Grace was unjustly blaming him. Blaming him simply because he allowed himself a little time to unwind and have a few drinks with a few friends after a hard week's work.

It was the same old tired logic. So what if he came home a bit drunk once in a while? It was only once in a while and all his pals did that. He was the main bread-winner after all. Grace just took care of the home and their children and had a part-time job cleaning house for a school master up the road to help make ends meet. He was the one who brought in nearly all of the money. Didn't he have the right to have a few hours to himself and a drink on the odd weekend? After all, what else was there to do in a small town like Dromana? After all, it wasn't as if he meant any harm by it, or was causing anybody any harm by it, was he?

When it came to self-examination on that particular topic, or perhaps more aptly self-justification, Jacob was finding it difficult to maintain an impartial jury within himself. A jury within that was not biased. One that would not sugar-coat or seek to distort the absolute truth of the situation. However, for Jacob the time for that unbiased clarity was coming. Coming much sooner than he might have thought.

That Summer of 1965 had not yet passed as Grace sat in the armchair in the living room. She was in her dressing gown, feet tucked up beneath her. She was half asleep, half listening to the gentle sounds of the opera singing on the radio. It was turned down low as everyone else was already asleep in bed. She was just waiting up to make sure he got home safe, then she would help him off to bed to sleep it off. The radio had lulled her into an easy relaxed mood and she was barely staying awake.

With a start, she heard the loud banging on the window pane in the back door. The banging increased incessantly. Then she heard the door being rattled back and forth impatiently on its hinges. As

Grace gathered herself and rose out of the chair to go and answer it, the banging stopped and she heard the back door open.

Suddenly the internal door from the kitchen into the living room burst open and Jacob staggered through. He stood there for a moment, swaying in the doorway, angry that she must have locked him out on purpose, not realising in his inebriated state that he could not have opened the door if she had done so. The angry slurred accusation burst forth from him, directed at this person before him who had tried to deny him access to his own home.

"What the hell did you do that for? Why'd you lock me out of my own house?"

As she sought to bring herself fully awake and understand the meaning of the accusation, Grace first mumbled out a confused denial. He did not hear it properly and repeated the accusation, waving a warning a finger at her as he did so. Grace, gradually taking in his state and beginning to comprehend that he must simply have struggled to open the back door, repeated her denial more loudly this time. Then with a sense of disgust and patience long worn thin, she announced even more loudly, "You're drunk!"

To his alcohol impeded mind and ears, it was both an accusation and a condemnation. He was charged, judged and sentenced all in that one phrase. A verdict that he was both a liar and a fool. He could not see beyond his wounded ego as Grace's next words unwittingly continued to fuel his anger.

"I waited up for you. Where were you? Where have you been till now?"

Grace's questions were little more than rhetorical, a mere reflection of her own annoyance, for she already had a fair idea of which public house he had been in. She had sent her sons to the local Crown public house often enough to find him and tell him to come on home. Alas, this time, in his impoverished and irrational state of being, her questions triggered other pained memories. The questions that he heard were not coming from Grace, but from another source, another voice from his past.

"Where were you? You weren't here, damn you!" Again, those echoes and emotions from his past resurfaced. In his angry stupor he heard that other voice, accusing, blaming. "It's gone and you weren't here, damn you! You left me alone with that thing! I buried it in the bin in the garden! In the bin! You weren't here, damn you!"

The painful image was deeply etched in his mind, never having left. Maude had blamed him for his son's death, then she had abandoned his children and betrayed him. As the all-consuming anger swept up and over him at what she had done, so the big hand swept upwards too, slapping hard into the side of the woman's face.

Grace screamed with the shock and pain, falling away from him. Still blinded by confused memory and anger, he came lurching forward once more. The big hand was raised again, swinging and swiping away the horror of what Maude had done, all now manifest in Grace.

Grace shouted at him to stop as she cowered away into the kitchen, her own hands finding the brush handle, grasping onto it like some kind of weapon, anything to defend herself. She half turned to face him, blood trickling down at the corner of her mouth. The fight or flight instincts welling within her, each wrestling for supremacy. The memory of the years of abuse and suffering at the hands of Jessman resurfaced. She felt the awful long-conditioned fear surging uppermost in her. Why was this same thing happening again now with Jacob? All she could see in that moment was the same old patterns emerging, clinging to her, bringing that same deep-seated fear yet again.

From the very first days of her now broken marriage to Jessman, Grace had suffered abuse. The suppressed anger of the abusive drunkard, the seeping guilt, the escape into an oblivious separate identity, all culminating in a toxic mix. This brew of emotions resulting in mindless assaults on her, the perceived weak, the deserving vulnerable, all in some contorted attempt to make the oppressor feel strong, in control, avenged and powerful.

The fearful flight instinct in Grace gripped her, bid her flee. Run, hide, cower in some dark corner again and lock the door from the inside. There to stay, terrified, hoping she would not be found. "Oh no, oh mammy, mammy, please no!"

Then something else stirred within Grace, something stronger that called her back, and pushed aside her fears. She was tired of being another meek suffering victim, like so many other meek victims waiting to inherit the earth. She could not take any more of this mindless abuse. She had to break free of it. "No, no more." The quiet assertive voice spoke unbidden within her. "This has to stop, now, whatever the cost, for all our sakes."

As he made to come forward again, defiance of long ingrained fear burned in Grace's eyes as she found the strength and will to rise and stand before him. To stand firm against him, not just for her own sake, for that was not enough, but for her children's sake, and even for his sake too. Raising the broom handle, she readied herself for the assault.

"I've had enough of drunken bloody beatings," she screamed. "Enough to last a damn lifetime. No more! Not from him or from you! Do you hear me? No more!"

It was a moment of truth. A declaration of intent. An ultimatum for both of them.

As they stood facing one another, the other screaming reached their ears. The loud pleading sounds were coming from another source, assailing them both. A bewildered Jacob turned to look. His now wakened children had come down the stairs and stood huddled in their nightclothes at the entrance to the living room, staring at their mother and father, crying and yelling at him to stop, to stop hurting her.

Without warning the eldest boy rushed forward, pummelling into him, momentum propelling the man backwards and knocking him off his feet. The drunken man rose angrily, only to see the boy now standing between him and the woman, fists clenched ready and raised, shouting at him.

"Leave her alone! Leave her alone!"

It was another ultimatum, another act of defiance. This time from a boy standing resolute against a man, his own father, in defence of his mother.

Cold dim awareness began to penetrate the man's senses. He stopped, hesitating, hampered mind trying to take in what was happening, trying to discern what was really in front of him. At last Jacob surfaced from the drunken haze, recognising Grace and the boy standing in front of her. He glanced around again, uncertain of this arena, his other children still sobbing, anxiously watching him, in fear of what might happen.

For a moment the numbing effects of the alcohol almost took Jacob down again. It sought to steal his mind away from any semblance of cognition, enticing him away from a painful reality, tempting him back down into the abyss, to obliterate him. With an effort of will, Jacob resisted, refusing to be led there. He stood, shaking his head to try to clear it and turned again towards Grace and the boy. Something familiar in the scene, calling to him.

It was then, pushing its way through the fog of his mind, that another image reached out from the past to find him. There, in Jacob's long-buried memory was another painful image. A memory of another family of children crying, another boy, standing ready to defend his mother against a drunken abusive husband. It was so long ago, but he remembered standing there, just like this boy in front of him now, his own fists clenched in readiness against his own father. He gasped at the memory.

In flashes he remembered he had made vows to himself at that time, vows that he had long since broken. He looked again to see his own family watching him, fearing him, fearing what he might do. Appalled, he turned his eyes again towards Grace, the blood still dripping from her lips. At last Jacob's mind grasped at the enormity of his actions. In that moment he began to see the truth at last and silently began to berate himself. "What have you done? How could you let this happen? Have you become just like him?"

This time there was no easy camouflage of the truth, no self-justification, no rigged inner jury in his mind to excuse his actions. Even in his diminished awareness, the long-overdue questions he dreaded were finally finding their way through to him. Questions that left him nowhere to hide. Questions that begged acceptance of responsibility for his choices and actions. Unable to answer, unable to explain, even to himself, he covered his face in his hands. Unable to cope with more, he forced out a half coherent apology. Without waiting for a response, he turned and headed towards the stairs. As the fog again descended on his mind, it was all he could do to stagger his way up the familiar wooden hill to his bed and oblivion.

Chapter 27

Mourning The Mournes

*We must accept finite disappointment
But we must never lose infinite hope.
(Martin Luther King)*

Autumn 1965

For those familiar with nursery rhymes, the Wee Shoe was aptly dubbed. It was without doubt the smallest caravan for hire in Newcastle. At least young Ted, who was the self-proclaimed authority on such things, had said so. Even this late in the season, it was just about the only caravan they could find that was affordable and available for that week. As it was, they had to sleep top and tail on the bunks, as well as on cushions on the floor.

The Summer had passed into Autumn. They were fortunate to have a few remaining days of fine weather to spend holidaying together in Newcastle in the Wee Shoe. It was tricky enough just getting in and out of it, but being stuck in the Wee Shoe in wet weather for hours on end with four children, two visiting aunts, and Grace herself, would surely have driven even the most patient, least claustrophobic person to distraction. Sometimes we have to be thankful for small mercies, and they were certainly grateful for the fair weather.

Denied the space for their natural yawning and stretching on waking in the morning, everyone was thankful when they could climb out of the Wee Shoe and stretch out cramped arms and legs. These morning pandiculations were Nature's way of gently waking their bodies, readying them for movement, and releasing endorphins and stress on the way. That aside, bailing out of the Wee Shoe was a carefully organised operation, with a strict queueing system, to avoid chaos and blockage at the entrance way. It was quite a challenge for anyone who needed to relieve themselves in a hurry! Which, after late night chats over endless cups of tea, invariably meant nearly everyone!

The morning outpouring and stretching of bodies from the Wee Shoe was quickly followed by a race to the nearby toilet block for yet another outpouring. After a wash up they tucked into a breakfast picnic on blankets on the grass, followed by a trip down to the sea for an early morning paddle, or perhaps in some of the young children's case, a piddle.

Given half a chance, Grace would be out wading around in the water first, with skirts held fast, calling on Wendy and Gloria to join her.

"C'mon you two! Come on, the water's lovely and warm, once you get your backside wet!"

To be fair, her sisters needed little encouragement, though the children were not always so keen to brave the early morning cool waters.

It was much the same when they walked along the pier and came to the playground. As usual, Grace was just as likely to be first to climb onto the swings, defying convention and oblivious to the smiles or frowns from the lookers on. She had long ago mastered the simple art of rocking herself back and forward to gain momentum on the swings and she still loved the feeling of flying freely through the air. Swings were there for all to enjoy, if they could, and Grace was certainly one who still could.

If her enthusiastic efforts to propel herself ever higher embarrassed her children more than a little, well she didn't mind at all. It was only a few moments of uninhibited joy after all, and Grace was sure they would get over it soon enough. Perhaps there was after all a measure of truth in that old saying. "We don't stop playing because we get old, we get old because we stop playing."

The holiday in Newcastle had been Jacob's idea. After the drunken confrontation in their home a few months earlier, he had greatly curtailed his indulgences. At long last he had even voluntarily broached the subject of his drinking habits with Grace. For the first time he seemed genuinely concerned about the problems his drinking might be causing. It was a welcome positive step in the right direction. Gradually they had been able to share how neither of them were happy with where things were heading and had begun to discuss what they wanted to improve or change.

They had both agreed on the need to make a fresh start, as much for the sake of their children as for their own sake. They were aware that some problems tend to follow us wherever we go, until we learn how to deal with them. However, at the same time they both knew it would be harder to step out of unhelpful old habits while remaining in precisely the same environment. If they wanted a different outcome, then they needed to make some significant changes.

Jacob had opened up to share his concerns for his specialist job becoming redundant, and the clamp down on wages that had already taken place. He told Grace of his concerns about the limited opportunities in Northern Ireland, and what all that might mean for the future for them and their family. Not for the first time he also spoke about his long desire to emigrate to Australia and the opportunities that vast new country offered. He suggested that if they made a completely fresh start, especially going to a new country, it might offer all of them a better chance for the future.

When she had considered it afresh, Grace had gradually started to warm to the idea that perhaps they should explore the emigration package to Australia after all. At the very least they could find out what it might have to offer for them. To her surprise, the more they looked into emigrating to Perth, Australia, the more attractive it seemed to both of them.

Jacob was very keen from the outset. For him it was more about the country, the climate and the opportunities for a new and better life for them and their family. He had read up all he could on Australia and loved the idea of the new developing country and the chance to build a future there and grow with it. He knew it would be a wrench to leave behind his mother and his siblings, but he felt he needed to make the move while they were still young enough to do so.

With a clearer insight than he might have had previously, Jacob feared that if he remained where he was, what lay in front of him might be a slow downward spiral, doing the same things he had always done. Whatever happened, one thing he knew for certain, he did not want a repeat of the last drunken episode.

Grace was inclining more towards emigrating too, but she still had lingering reservations. The more she thought about it, the more she agonized over the decision. All the advantages of Australia mattered for Grace too, but for her it was a complete world away. So far away that it would take a ship near forever to get there.

Having been ostracised once from her family, she did not really want to be so far away and parted from them again. So, for Grace, the choice centred more around the people.

Grace loved her wider family, she loved that she could spend precious time with her siblings, and that her children were growing up with their cousins. In many ways they were all growing up as one large extended family of brothers and sisters together. Her children had so many aunts and uncles on both their parent's sides. They had so many cousins, dozens, most of whom they visited regularly. Now, after all she had come through, after all the years apart, perhaps even because of it, Grace felt her close-knit large family was so precious in so many ways. How could she bear to emigrate and part from them yet again?

Her eldest daughter, Elizabeth, was now a very independent career woman with plans for her future. Grace felt that it was very unlikely that Elizabeth would want to go with them. Surely Jacob's daughters, Pearl, Nan and Donna, would not want to uproot their young families and go with them to Australia either? And if Pearl stayed behind in Ireland, what about her daughter, young Anna?

Anna was already more of a little sister than a niece to the rest of Grace's children. The child would be heart-broken if they all left without her, but how could Grace even contemplate taking Anna away from Pearl, her own mother? Then again, how would her own children feel if Anna had to stay behind? They would surely object and no doubt there would be an almighty uproar over that.

Then there were Grace's own parents. Riley and Beth had mellowed with the passing years, but were clearly showing the effects of aging. The same was true of Jacob's mother, Liza. It would be so hard to leave her dear friend and mentor behind. Then of course, there was also Liza's daughter Valerie, Grace's dear friend. All Jacob's other siblings too, all of whom were close to Grace. How could she possibly leave them all behind and maybe never see some of them again?

Last, yet not least, there were also the people of Dromana, and especially, the people of the Heights. Grace had made so many friends in the Heights, some very close friends who were like her family. She wondered how she could possibly just start afresh and leave all those wonderful people behind?

Yes, it was all about the people for Grace.

Once again Grace was faced with yet another difficult choice. A heart wrenching choice, whether or not to leave behind their family, and leave behind the Heights, to go and live in a strange far-away land. Yet a choice that, in their particular circumstances, might just offer a new and better life ahead. Grace knew that whatever she chose, there would be a price of some sort to pay. There always seemed to be a price.

That was when Jacob had suggested Grace take some time out in Newcastle and think about it all before deciding. He had suggested that she invite some of her siblings to join her there for at least some of the time if they could manage it. Grace had welcomed the idea and she felt Newcastle would be appropriate in so many ways.

She knew Wendy and Gloria would probably jump at the chance to join her there for a few days anyway, and some of her other siblings might well make a day trip visit. If it turned out that she did decide to leave Ireland for Australia, then there was no better place than Newcastle to have a last fond farewell.

That was how they had all wound up in the Wee Shoe, holidaying in Newcastle by the Mountains of Mourne, in the smallest caravan in the little seaside town.

In the end it was two very different events that helped Grace to decide which path she should take. The first was the rather amusing sequence of events in Newcastle that served to remind her just how much her sisters meant to her. The second, was a fortuitous visit at Christmas time by one of Jacob's brothers.

They had not long arrived in Newcastle when Bloody Hell descended upon them.

"Oh, Bloody Hell! He's here again!"

Stifling girlish giggles, Wendy and Gloria swiftly tried to turn the corner of the narrow street in Newcastle to stay out of his sight.

Too late, the smiling lounge lizard had already spotted them. With a deep and loud "Well hello again ladies," he was striding over to join them. Still tall and lean with white teeth flashing, fashionable long dark curly hair, bright multi-coloured sports shirt, open just enough to emphasise his hairy chest, he was strutting along towards them in his too tight denim jeans and shiny black winkle picker shoes. Like a colourful farm yard rooster making his early morning calls, he came, the picture of sheer flamboyance and drooling charm. For the moment at least it seemed there was no escaping this persistent would-be, Don Juan.

"Bloody Hell" had introduced himself to Wendy and Gloria as Paul something or other, and began chatting easily to them while they were standing watching Grace and her children riding on the dodgems. He was not called "Bloody Hell" of course. That would follow on naturally enough with Wendy's exasperated repetition of "Oh Bloody Hell, its him again!" on each and every occasion that he seemed to appear out of nowhere to join them, which was often.

Perhaps a little past his prime, Bloody Hell was polite and chatty, in fact very much the suave gentleman. Though they did not actually encourage him, neither did they wish to be rude. Charming and amusing on their first encounter, and indeed on each subsequent encounter, Bloody Hell had clearly taken a shine to Gloria.

Gloria was certainly attractive, but she was already married and politely but assuredly made it clear that she was not at all interested in any silly shenanigans. However, although Bloody Hell finally seemed to get the message, he clearly relished their company and was nothing if not persistent with his flirting!

Newcastle was a small town and frequently 'bumping into' people was easy enough if one was determined enough. Bloody Hell's repeated transparent attempts to do so gave the sisters much fodder for jokes and laughter. Even Bloody Hell may have seen the funny side of it, for he seemed to play along as their likeable rogue and entertainer, regardless. Indeed, he remained the same dashing polite charmer throughout, and they could not help but like and even admire him for that when they came to say their goodbyes. Bloody Hell had added much more adventure and mirth to the sisters visit to Newcastle than even he might have imagined.

For Grace, it was a bitter sweet experience sharing in this odd, amusing little adventure with Wendy and Gloria. She had thoroughly enjoyed their last hurrah in Newcastle with her sisters. The Mourne mountains had once again worked their timeless magic. Spending time in the little seaside town had been so relaxing and such a joy. It had brought back so many memories too of the time she had spent here with Elizabeth, years before when she was living in exile. She felt sad at leaving the little coastal town, and hoped one day to return to this place that she loved so much.

The whole holiday had completely lifted her spirits, but it also reminded her just how much she loved the company of her siblings. If she needed any further reminder, it also helped her to realise just how much she would miss them not being around. The message was clear and simple enough. Grace loved her family dearly. She had to find a way that they would not be shut out of her life by distance, if indeed she went to Australia. However, finding that kind of a solution was not going to be easy.

Fittingly, the little holiday ended on an amusing note too, at least for some of them. On the way home after it, Grace, Wendy, and Gloria journeyed back in the car that Jacob had borrowed to pick them up. They squeezed all the luggage into the car and put the kids together on the bus with a packed lunch and instructions to walk the short journey on up to their home in the Heights as soon as they disembarked in Dromana. Wendy's husband had offered to come and collect his wife and Gloria from the Heights later that evening.

Jacob was still not a regular driver, and was still very cautious, particularly as he was unfamiliar with the borrowed car. After he had picked up Grace and her two sisters, Jacob began to drive very slowly along the long twisty road out of Newcastle. Wendy and Gloria, still buzzing from their most enjoyable holiday, started to take full advantage of the journey back to relive all their adventures.

It started off well enough with Gloria and Wendy in high spirits, excitedly telling Jacob about what a great holiday it had been and what it was like living in the Wee Shoe for a week. When Wendy wisecracked how it was far too small even for a hamster, and how they had to climb right out of it just to turn around, Jacob had barely smiled and just nodded. Wendy could see immediately he wasn't really listening. In stark contrast to their excitement about the holiday, he was intensely focused on driving the heavily overloaded car along the narrow winding road.

Grace had already made it clear to him that the holiday breakaway had been a great idea and was so worthwhile and helpful for her. She sat in the front with him, still a little pensive, leaving most of the excited chatter to her two younger sisters in the back. The constant laughing and loud talking coming from the rear of the car was very distracting for Jacob. He rarely spoke and tried to keep his mind on the driving. Grace's two sisters recognised his discomfort of course, and never ones to miss a chance for a good joke and a few well-intentioned jibes, started to direct their humour more towards him.

At first Jacob suffered in silence as the jibes escalated. Wendy, impishly seeking to goad him a little, began to liken the slow journey to a funeral procession. Always ready to play along with her mischievous sister, Gloria chimed in that even the bus, with all its stops on the way, would be back in Dromana well before them. Jacob grimaced a little when Gloria added that she was sure that at this speed she could run faster than the car. The sisters continued in their high spirits, now all the more determined to get more of a reaction from Jacob.

At a T-junction, Jacob slowed and stopped, taking plenty of time to check thoroughly if any other cars might be coming and if it was safe to cross right over. Wendy pounced on the opportunity. "For Goodness' sake, Jacob, what are you waiting for? Go on over! Sure, there isn't another car within miles and you're still sitting here like some Buddha waiting on a written invitation to cross!" Jacob grimaced again, but smiled and nodded once more as he began to drive onwards.

It was a few moments later, when Wendy reached over to tap his shoulder and ask if he knew the car had more than one gear, that he decided he'd had enough of their mocking and malarkey. Exasperated, he glanced over at Grace and merely raised his eyebrows and gave a deep sigh. She nodded back almost imperceptibly, knowing her man and half suspecting what might be coming next.

Without a word Jacob pulled the car over to one side and stopped. He got out of the car and went around it to open the back door. Holding the door wide open he gave Wendy and Gloria a stern look and beckoned them to get out of the car.

"Come on now, that's it, enough with your wisecracking! Get

out the pair of you! I'm not taking you another yard. You can make your own way back from here. Just collect your luggage from our house when you get there!"

Their smiles faded as they looked open mouthed at him and then at Grace, who sat still and said nothing.

"C'mon! I'm telling you, get out!" he repeated even more sternly. Then added brusquely, "It shouldn't take you two very long to get home on your own since you can run a darn sight faster than this little car."

Jacob's face was deadly serious and Wendy and Gloria realised they might have gone too far. They shot another questioning glance at Grace. She looked straight ahead and held the tense silence. Reluctantly they started to climb out of the car. Jacob closed the door behind them, started the engine and began to drive off. Wendy and Gloria stood on the side of the road watching the car leave and not knowing what to do.

Jacob held on for another long moment before finally stopping again about a hundred yards further up the road. He stepped out of the car and with a wide grin opened the door for them, shouting so they could hear. "Come on you two! I'm not going to wait all day for you. Shall we try that again?" The tension was released as the sisters, realising they'd been played, raced back up to the car and quickly climbed in again before he changed his mind. They were underway again in moments, all laughing, this time Jacob included.

Jacob had made his point and Grace felt sure he would not have left them. Well, fairly sure anyway. Turning to her sisters she said cheerfully, "You two will behave yourselves from now on, won't you?" Gwen and Wendy, nodded enthusiastically, perhaps a little too enthusiastically. Grace turned back around and smiled reassuringly at Jacob. "There you are now Jacob, you heard it straight from the horse's mouth! They'll behave themselves." Jacob smiled back, knowing full well that was never going to happen. How could it? This was Wendy and Gloria after all.

He was right. In a short while they were singing out Ken Dodd's mournful ballad and number one hit, Tears for Souvenirs, having decided it was appropriate for the moment. This was soon followed by a full volume rendition of other songs, all thankfully a little more cheerful. It would certainly take more than a little threat of walking home to rein those two in.

All the same, Grace didn't fail to notice that this time they held back on further jibes and jests until they were very much closer to home. As it happened, the car did beat the bus back to Dromana, though to be fair, it was only by a few minutes!

Letting Go

Chapter 28

Leaving The Heights

*Cherish your visions; cherish your ideals;
cherish the music that stirs in your heart,
the beauty that forms in your mind,
the loveliness that drapes your purest thoughts.
For out of them will grow delightful conditions,
all heavenly environment.
Of these, if you but remain true to them,
your world will at last be built.
(James Allen)*

Christmas 1965 - February 1966

It was a very busy and, in many ways, a very odd Christmas, that December in 1965. In the weeks leading up to and even during it, Jacob had remained sober throughout. He was clearly making a concerted effort to cut back and start afresh. Grace and he had already completed the application forms for them and their family to emigrate to Australia. They had all been through their medicals, been accepted, and had even received proposed sailing dates for mid-February, now just a matter of weeks away. Their final confirmation was all that remained before they set sail for Perth.

There was much to celebrate, much to organise, and so much to be excited about for the future. However, while they were looking forward to their new adventure, Grace, in particular, knew that no matter how well she prepared herself, she would still find it so difficult to leave. It was by now common knowledge that this was probably the last Christmas that Grace and her whole family would be together in Ireland, at least for a long time to come. She did not want to cross her bridges before she came to them, but even so, Grace did try to ready herself mentally for the forthcoming split in her family once again, leaving many loved ones behind.

After her holiday in Newcastle, Grace had returned much refreshed and with a somewhat different perspective. The magic of Newcastle had helped her find a renewed sense of gratitude for all that she already had in life. Somehow it had restored her enthusiasm for life itself. Notably, although it was a most enjoyable break, she had missed Jacob even more than expected.

She felt that they were at a critical point in their relationship. Then again, when was it ever not? Yet, if they were going to make it work better, it was up to both of them to make the effort, not just one or the other. She felt that perhaps he was at last facing up to his problem drinking and was trying to do something about it. He had made clear to her what he felt he needed to do to change things. So, if he was making a genuine effort, she asked herself, was she whole-heartedly with him or not? She felt she was, but did that have to include emigration? Going to the ends of the earth for him?

Grace had learnt that there was no point in seeking to avoid the hard choices that came her way in life. As Liza had often suggested, life has an odd habit of repeating itself, offering the same lesson over and over again, until finally we learn how to deal with it. Seemingly only then can people finally move on. So, Grace told herself that yes, she and Jacob did have to make significant changes in their lives, and yes, there was every possibility that emigration might well be a big part of that.

They had sat down together and gone over the whole emigration package again and again at length, discussing all the implications they could possibly conceive. Even more than before, they had openly shared all their hopes and concerns. This time it had felt like they were both very much on the same side again. They were both more committed to making their relationship work. Both were seeking to understand, as well as to make themselves understood. After much discussion, this time they were more confident it was the right thing to do to emigrate and make the move out of Ireland.

When they had discussed it all with their family, they found that they were mostly supportive. Even their four eldest girls who, as Grace had anticipated, decided they would not go with them but remain in Ireland. Grace's siblings were equally supportive of her emigrating. Though of course, they too shared how much she and her family would be missed and how much they preferred her to remain in Ireland with them. There were tears even then, long before the departure date, when of course there would be many more. So, it was little wonder then that Grace still did not know just how she was going to handle leaving them all behind when it came time to board the ship bound for Australia.

The second something, a rather fateful yet propitious second event, that was to influence Grace's decision process, came about during that Christmas of 1965. It was when one of Liza's other sons, Harry, and his English wife Hattie, came over from Coventry in England for a few days. It was perhaps not so much their timing that was odd, more the nature of their visit.

They had come to spend Christmas in Ireland and catch up with all Harry's family. Harry was a highly skilled chef, who thoroughly enjoyed his work, and his food. He was a rather large well-rounded, kind and affable family man, with an equally large and well-rounded sense of humour to match. He was a staunch Christian, though never one to preach at the drop of a hat. Given the season, Harry could have made a great Father Christmas figure to boot!

With his oversized charm and wit, his disarming frankness, and his genuine larger-than-life laughter, most people took a liking to big Harry on the instant. His easy manner was so like his mother in many ways that those who knew both Liza and Harry, as Grace did, might well have remarked about that particular apple not having far to fall from the tree.

Harry had grown very fond of Grace and all her family and had visited them regularly over the years. He and Hattie were very much liked in turn. However, when Harry had learnt that his brother and Grace were planning to emigrate to Australia, he was not at all impressed by the idea! Having long since left Ireland himself to live in Coventry, he felt he had something worth saying on the matter. In fact, he decided he must have a few words with his younger brother and his wife as soon as possible.

Grace and Jacob and all her family were absolutely delighted when Harry and Harriet dropped in to pay them a visit. They were always very popular, if infrequent, visitors. It didn't take more than a few cups of tea and toasted soda and wheaten farls before the craic turned to the big plans to emigrate to Australia. Harry listened carefully to all that was said about Australia and the opportunities it offered, even nodding in enthusiastic agreement at times.

After he had heard them out, Harry asked Jacob if he and Grace might like to consider an alternative to Australia. They looked a little surprised, but nodded their agreement, both curious to know what sort of alternative Harry might have in mind. Big Harry didn't need a second invitation to tell them. He launched in with unbridled enthusiasm.

"Now look you two, Australia sounds wonderful, it really does, but you'd have to agree, it's a heck of a long way away. Have you not considered going to Coventry yet? Do you not know there's an abundance of opportunities there. Sure, why do you think we're there with our family? It's got a whole range of new car industries and all sorts of expanding business enterprises, it's hard to keep up with it all. I'm telling you, it's growing so fast they can never seem to find enough skilled workers, and they are offering a fair bit of money too!"

Harry described Coventry as the hub of the Midlands. Having been rebuilt after the war, it was now a modern new and thriving city, attracting people to it from all around the world. Among other things, it had a brilliant new cathedral and they had even preserved the old stone one that had been heavily bombed.

He conceded Coventry people probably exaggerated a bit when they said that the newly developed upper and lower precincts were paved with gold! Nevertheless, he was not only enthusiastic but totally convinced that his brother could find any number of suitable jobs there with his intelligence and sought-after skills. Harry's enthusiasm was bubbling over as he described the ready availability of housing, schooling, and all sorts of opportunities for a growing family there, as his brother and Grace listened intently.

Harry had thought a lot about inviting them to try out Coventry as an alternative to going to Australia. It would be their choice, and he would respect whatever choice they made. Nevertheless, like the master chef presenting his range of culinary delights, he had carefully planned how to present his proposal to best effect. Harry, very much the master chef, gave them a moment to digest the tasty verbal morsels he had just laid out before them. Then, like the baker about to add the traditional extra bun to make up the baker's dozen, he leaned forward, ready to round out his alternative proposal.

"Look, here's a suggestion you might like to think about. Why don't you both hold off on Australia for just a little while yet. After Christmas Jacob could come and stay with us and get a job in Coventry for a few weeks, just to see if you might like it there. Jacob, I can get you fixed up with a good job over there as soon as look at you. Then after you give it a wee trial, you can both talk about it and see what you think."

Seeing Grace and Jacob following his every word, Harry quickly took another deep breath, and continued in full flow.

"If you like the place and think it could work there, Hattie and I can help you get sorted out with accommodation and schooling and all that in Coventry. We'd be there on hand to help you settle in, and make it a nice easy transition for you all. Remember now, it would only be a wee trial first, with no commitment at all."

Grace and Jacob said nothing while they digested Harry's tempting proposal. It was well worth thinking about. As Harry pointed out, they could still emigrate to Australia later if that's what they wanted, but at least it could be worth them giving Coventry a try first.

Harry looked directly at Jacob. "If you want to find a place that offers a fresh start and opportunities for you and your family, dear brother, then look no further. Coventry is practically on your doorstep. Sure, I know it still seems like a million miles away from here, but really it's just a wee skip and a jump over the Irish Sea, isn't it?"

Then, with a long pause and his big trademark grin, he transferred his attention to Grace. To emphasise a key point for her, he added that it would be much easier popping back and forth to Ireland from Coventry, to keep in touch with families, than if they went flying off to the other side of the world to Australia!

Harry watched the pensive look on their faces as they took it all in, digesting his final well-timed delivery. It looked like his job might be done for the moment. He was not about to push them into anything, not at all, but he did want to ensure they knew that Coventry might just be a better alternative option. The rest was up to them.

He smiled again and leaned back in his chair, clapping his big hands and vigorously rubbing them together, as if to signal that perhaps another cup of tea and another toasted soda farl would be a fantastic idea right now. He could tell by the thoughtful looks on their faces that, yes, his job was done. Harry waited patiently for their response, his large stomach reminding him that he was still hungry!

Grace of course latched onto the idea enthusiastically and said that she thought it was worth giving it a try. Inwardly she wondered if this could possibly be the alternative solution for which she had been searching. Was it a way to solve her dilemma? A way to have a fresh start, find new opportunities in a new country, but not, as Harry had said, without going to the other side of the world and feeling like she was leaving her family forever?

Grace remained highly curious, while Jacob, although very interested, was more cautious. Over dinner later and for the next two hours he and Grace set about interrogating Harry and Harriet on every detail of life in Coventry and the opportunities there. Harry responded well to all the questions. He had known what to expect from his meticulous brother. Harriet too was well prepared for Grace's barrage of questions about accommodation, schooling and opportunities for the children.

By the end of it they were all but talked out. However, by then

Jacob was convinced it was well worth visiting Coventry to give it a try. So convinced in fact, that in just over a week he was on a flight to Birmingham to meet up with Harry and start a new job there. He was keen to get things sorted out quickly, and find out one way or another if Coventry was a viable option.

When Jacob left the Heights for Coventry, he and Grace arranged to call each other on a neighbour's telephone once a week to find out how things were going. They expected that it might take up to a couple of months in Coventry to decide if it might be the place for them to make a new home. As it happened, it only took a few weeks.

Harry had been correct. Coventry was a rapidly expanding and thriving city. Moreover, he had gone out of his way to help his brother to secure a well-paid job and had begun showing him all around the area. They had even found a very nice terraced house to buy that was fairly close to where Jacob now worked. The mortgage would be hefty, but Harry had offered to help him with the initial deposit until he found his feet.

There were schools nearby, and importantly for Grace, a church. When Jacob rang, he was clearly very enthusiastic from the beginning, with the odd minor hiccups.

"Oh, its great Grace, shaping up really well. The only thing is, they all talk with a funny accent, even worse than Harriet. I thought I'd landed on an alien planet! You'd hardly understand a word they say and they can't understand me either. I have to keep repeating everything!"

He told Grace that the people there seemed to keep to themselves a lot more, minding their own business, and called everyone from Ireland 'Paddy'. However, that aside, they seemed to be an agreeable lot. All in all, he felt that Coventry was very promising and could be just the place for them to make a new life and a new beginning.

Grace agreed, Coventry, not Australia, would be the place where they would make their new home.

For Grace, it seemed that Fate might at last be smiling on them, beckoning them to the land across the Irish sea. She realised too that, even though Jacob had been gone just a few weeks, she was again missing this man that she loved. Here she was, with all her own family and her siblings, friends and neighbours from the Heights, all visiting her regularly because they knew she and her family would be leaving soon, yet she was feeling more alone than ever and missing him. It was an odd situation. Especially after all they had been through, after all the doubts and indecisions about leaving Ireland, surely there was a strange irony in that.

Finally, all the arrangements had been made, caring homes found for their dog and the bantams and all the rest of the children's menagerie. The seemingly endless farewells continued as Grace and the four younger children who were accompanying her to Coventry said their goodbyes. It was a heart-wrenching experience saying farewell to the people they loved. Even though they were all promising to come back within a year or so to visit everyone again, there was no doubt it was the end of an era.

Nothing could ever be quite the same again for those that were leaving. It was the start of a new adventure in a new country. A start of a new way of life. Yet at the same time it was an end to living in the Heights. An end to living in Ireland.

For Pearl, Nan, Donna, and Elizabeth, electing to stay behind, it was still a difficult parting. In their heads they could reconcile that Grace and her family would make a return visit soon, or perhaps they themselves could make a holiday trip to visit them in Coventry, sometime in the near future. Yet, in their hearts, it was far from easy to reconcile the departure of loved ones from their everyday lives. That was the real difference.

For one other in particular, who was given no choice in the matter, it felt in a sense like an abandonment by the people she loved. Pearl's eldest daughter, young Anna, was heartbroken that she could not go with them. Anna could not understand why she would be left behind and pleaded with granny Grace and her family to take her too. Anna was feeling left out, rejected and left behind. There were of course the usual reassurances from well-meaning friends that Anna was still a child and she would very soon get over it in a day or two. In hindsight they were a long way off the mark.

Anna was inconsolable. She had grown so close to Grace's family from almost living with them that she was in a sense the little sister they would have to leave behind. As Grace had rightly predicted, her whole family shared the agony of leaving Anna behind. Yet, they could not possibly take Anna away from her own parents and family.

Perhaps what they failed to see was that for Anna, her family extended well beyond the boundaries of parents and siblings. Just like her mother Pearl, who had been abandoned by Maude years before, the expansive love of this small child could never be limited to just a few.

3rd of February, 1966

It was a cold cloudy grey morning as Gloria took her sister Grace and family to Belfast airport for their flight to England on that first Thursday in February, 1966. The bleak weather mirrored their mood. Grace sat in the front as Gloria drove. The four kids, Joy, Ted, Hugh, and Vicky, all squeezed into the back of the car. Their furniture and luggage had all been packed and sent ahead days before and now they only had a few carry-on bags with them.

Apart from a few last-minute reminders about passing on farewell messages to so and so, they drove almost in silence. Each of them was consumed by mixed emotions and their own thoughts. Even the children were unusually quiet. All of them having said their goodbyes.

As she looked out longingly at the passing Irish countryside, for some reason Grace thought of a poem by Robert Frost that she had read years before. It was something about passing by a little wood, but not having time to stop and explore it because he had promises to keep and miles to go before he could sleep. She felt it was a little like that now for her and her children. They could not linger, and they had all made promises of some kind. Promises to keep in touch, to write, to phone.

Promises to friends and loved ones to remember them, always to remember them. Grace wondered if in the end, for all of them, that was all everyone wanted most. To be loved and remembered kindly, not to be forgotten, not to be set aside.

Still very much in a reflective mood as she travelled towards the airport, Grace was reminded of other journeys she had made over the years. She remembered the short car journey back from her mother's house that Christmas long ago, when she had told Beth that she would leave Jessman. Her mother's reaction then had been a portent of things to come.

Grace remembered the journey to Newcastle in the side-car with her younger brother Toby, as she held her baby Elizabeth in her arms. Toby had been so kind and considerate back then. Not only had he helped make her escape from Jessman possible, he had made sure she could manage in her new life in Newcastle. It was no wonder she and Toby had remained so close over the years.

Then she thought of the journey back from Newcastle, after

spending four years there. Elizabeth's father had driven them to his mother Liza's house, and she'd had that marvellous reception with Jacob's family. What a day that had been. What a start to their lives together Liza had given them.

Then of course there was that other journey back from the recent holiday in Newcastle, when Wendy and Gloria had been making fun of Jacob's driving until he had threatened to make them walk home. She smiled inwardly at the memory. Journeys seemed to be a part of her life in one way or another. If Liza were here, she would no doubt remind her that it's not all about the destination, the journey is important too.

Wiping back the few tears that the memories had brought to her eyes, Grace smiled to herself again. Yes, this was a journey that would lead them to a new life in another country, and to the extent that they would make their new life there, both their purpose and the destination were important too. However, Grace was all too aware that there was another journey involved now. She and Jacob were about to make a fresh start in Coventry and that would require ongoing effort.

It would be a trial for both of them but they would deal with it. He would have to overcome his challenges for she would no longer be the victim. They would make their share of mistakes again no doubt, and there would be many bumps in the road that lay ahead of them. Yet they were on the right path, she felt that in her heart. She was confident now that they had learnt enough to make it work together, for the two of them, and the smaller family that came with them.

Perhaps Fate had intended for them to be together and remain together all along. It was just that Fate enjoyed playing games along the way. Aloud Grace mused, "Well, whatever Fate has or has not ordained, we are all going to be together and we are all going to be happy in Coventry, come what may!"

Her sister Gloria turned her head from her driving to look over and smile at Grace's little outburst and determined words. "Oh yes, for sure you will be happy Grace. Wendy and the rest of us will be over there in the Summer to make absolutely certain you will! You can bet your last half crown on that, big sister!"

As they drove into the airport Grace thought again how much she was looking forward to seeing Jacob again. Yes, her man would be there at Birmingham airport waiting for them with his brother Harry, as he'd promised. She had missed Jacob so much. Being in Ireland was incomplete without him, she knew that now. So, she would go with him to England and live there, the country of her birth, because that was what she and her young family now needed to do.

Oh Ireland, how she would miss it. She knew it was a part of her and her children, and always would be. How they would all miss it. Yet more than anything she wanted to be reunited with Jacob, to embrace this chance to spend the rest of their lives in harmony together. Once more Grace had found enthusiasm and hope in her heart.

As the grey clouds cleared a little, Grace smiled as she saw an aeroplane coming in to land at the airport at the same time as their car drew up there. She had never been on an aeroplane before. She felt elated. This would be a lot more exciting than going on the swings!

What had Harry called it? "A wee skip and a jump across the Irish Sea." Yes, that was it. Surely Coventry would be close enough and yet far enough away that they wouldn't need to go on to Australia.

Yes, surely it would be enough of a wee skip and a jump, for one lifetime anyway.

Chapter 29

To Call Myself Beloved

Well then, what are you? You will find when you have come out of what you are not, that the ripple on the water is whispering to you 'I am That', the birds in the trees are singing to you, 'I am That', the moon and the stars are shining beacons to you, 'I am That'. You are everything in the world and everything in the world is reflected in you. And at the same time, you are That - everything.
(Sri Shantananda Saraswati)

29 July 1984

Nearly twenty years had passed since they had come to live in Coventry.

Grace was in a quiet reflective mood, sitting up in bed that night, as she finished reading her bible. She was so tired these past days, and for some time had been feeling her age. Her hard life had left its mark. Nowadays she usually went to bed quite early as she welcomed more rest.

It was earlier that same evening, sitting dozing in the late afternoon sun in her bamboo chair in the small communal garden by their retirement flat, that she thought she heard a faint whisper on the wind. Maybe it was just her mind imagining it, a nuance perhaps of her advancing years.

Yet it seemed to be there, just very briefly, in the quiet melodic hum of the bees on the flowers, the gentle rustle of the leaves on the trees, a faint murmuring of nature for those who could hear it. A noise, or maybe a word. "Soon", was all it whispered. Somehow though, the sound or word had echoed gently around in her drowsing mind, like a guiding mantra, giving her a feeling of peace and calm. The feeling stayed with her all evening.

As was her way before going to sleep, Grace reflected for a few moments on the day and on her life in general, trying to appreciate the good without it slipping away unnoticed. It had been a glorious Summer's day, she thought, and she had so much enjoyed just sitting and simply relaxing in the garden. The flowers were still in full bloom and there was an abundance of birds and insects coming and going. The fragrances, colours, and sounds, had surrounded her. The whole garden had seemed to open up and come alive all around her as she sat there joyfully, just observing and marvelling at Nature's splendid beauty as it gently bathed her in its warm sunshine. It was a day worth remembering, and long ago she had promised herself she would always make time to remember beautiful days such as this.

As she continued reflecting in her bed, once again she wondered if she had managed to lead a good life. It had certainly not been easy, that much was true. Even so, she had felt much joy, endured much pain too, but met it all as best she could, with love and hope still in her heart. She had raised a fine family, taught them her Christian ways and good moral values from an early age.

As always, she counted all her children as her own, borne of her or not. They were all long grown now and married, all save her firstborn, Elizabeth, still the independent and successful career woman. Yes, all were making their own way in the world. Most now had families of their own too, as was the way of things. Grace so enjoyed spending time with her grandchildren, and hoped there would be more to come.

She looked down at Jacob, the sleeping, now balding man beside her. There had been trials and tribulations, dark secrets and sufferings, but so much joy and love and laughter too. He had been her constant companion and love throughout it all, except perhaps in some of those turbulent early years she didn't care to remember now.

Even after their move to Coventry it had not all been plain sailing for her and Jacob, far from it, but together they had weathered the tempests just the same. They had come through it all and were an old married couple now, still in love and enjoying the twilight of their lives together.

The nightmares were long gone too, a thing of the past. "Maybe all those hard times were given to me to serve some sort of purpose," Grace thought. "Maybe the nightmares too were sent to teach me something. Perhaps to keep me focused on hopes and better dreams, even to live a better life."

"Well maybe," she thought with a wry smile, "but just the same, I think I'd just as soon rather not have had them!"

Leaning over, she sighed deeply and gently kissed Jacob goodnight. "For better or worse," she thought again with another smile, "we've had both, and it's been a difficult journey, but surely it was all worth it."

The past few years they had been especially happy and close, settling into their retirement. They always were close really; it was just that they had finally learnt what it was to live in true harmony together.

She glanced around the room, taking in the many little memorabilia they had collected over the years. Much of it was little gifts from her family, both her offspring and her siblings, who knew the kind of things Grace particularly liked to collect. They were all now treasured mementos of one kind or another in which she found joy.

She thought of Ireland again, her life before, during and after the Heights. All those people she knew, had known, and loved. What a truly amazing adventure her life had been.

The delicate, rarely revealed fragrance of end of season sweet violets wafted up to her from her bedside table. Just like they had been with Napoleon's Josephine, and with the Greek goddess Persephone, violets were one of Grace's favourite flowers. The small bouquet was a thoughtful gift from her youngest, Joy, when she had visited just the day before.

Grace glanced sleepily at the large framed print of the Holy Land on the wall, and then checked the time on her little gold-plated bedside clock from Kuwait. Yet more mementos of her travels far and wide. Travels that she could never have dreamed of as a girl. She was content and grateful for it all.

It was getting late now and she was feeling very tired. As she closed her eyes, her mind began to drift out of the waking realm, and to accept the gift of peaceful rest and the awaiting realm of sleep. Grace's breathing began to slow and her body sank comfortably a little further down into the upturned pillow at her back.

Her glasses slid down onto the tip of her nose, an oft-forgotten adornment of the night. Her well-worn bible was still open at her side, its purpose long since served. For a fleeting moment, the question that had arisen earlier that evening again flickered sleepily across her mind. "Is it ever all lived well and worthwhile, or is there just always more to learn, more to do?"

A short while later, as sleep found her, her body and calm mind glided into a deep contended state. Soon after that, as natural as her breathing had been in life, like the clock that eases down when time is done, Grace's breathing gradually and painlessly slowed. Then, without resistance, it quietened even further and, just as naturally, it ceased.

In that last moment, before the essence of life lifted from her, Grace dimly heard a faint echo of what seemed to be her own voice answering her earlier question.

"Yes," the murmur of the gentle voice inside her head whispered to her. "It was worth it, and it is enough. Rest now Grace. Rest in peace."

And then she was gone.

THE END

*And did you get what you wanted
from this life, even so?*

- I did.

And what did you want?

*- To call myself beloved,
to feel myself beloved on the Earth.*

(Raymond Carver)

Epilogue

Grace's parents, Beth and Riley, lived and died on The Liberty Bell, still struggling to eke out a living on the little farm until their end. Beth continued to mellow with the passing years and their house became an ever-welcoming place, full of their children and many grandchildren.

The old whitewashed outside toilet, a young Grace's refuge, was removed when The Liberty Bell was renovated in later years by Toby, making way for a home for him and his German wife.

Beautiful Elizabeth remained an independent single woman. God's little princess was so moved by her mother's funeral that she became a staunch and passionate Christian. She died of cancer only five years later. Elizabeth said her God had promised she would never lose a hair from her head to the disease. She was right, she never did.

Long after Grace's death, all of her children, including Pearl, Nan and Donna and of course young Anna, came together for a family reunion in Newcastle some 50 years after leaving Ireland. Elizabeth was there too in spirit. The little sea-side town was still magical.

On that same occasion, the people of the Heights came from

near and far and threw a surprise party in Dromana while they were all there. Once the children of the Heights, now a generation of grandparents, they all met up with Grace's family again as very special friends, as if time had been transcended.

Micky, the king of spits from the Heights, became a highly popular postman and still lives in the small town of Dromana. Among his many achievements, he founded a thriving athletic club, appeared on television, and was made a Member of the British Empire.

Jacob was finally able to marry Grace in their later years. He survived her by just a few years and their daughter Elizabeth by just a few months. On his death bed he was asked how he felt about passing into the hereafter. He said that he wasn't exactly thrilled about it, but he wasn't too worried either. Asked why that was, he said he had lots of friends in both places!

Jacob and Maude's offspring, Pearl, Nan, and Donna, remained in Ireland and live there yet. Nan gradually took over the mantle of the family wise woman, after that other grand old lady, Liza, had passed on.

Vicky, who still uses just one of her four names, Joy and Ted, all raised their families in England, gradually moving a little further afield than Coventry. Young Ted, who had begun to hone his negotiation skills in Bill's little shop on the Heights, started his own business and retired a multi-millionaire. Some say he still detests geese and gob-stoppers.

Pearl's eldest daughter, 'little sister Anna,' became a regular visitor to Grace and all of her family in Coventry. She continues to be a big part of their lives. Anna and Joy, were the prime architects of many family reunions over the years and both continue to be the golden glue that helps keep all of Grace's family together.

Hugh, born the black crow, met his future wife in Coventry.

He didn't know it then, but Grace predicted their marriage within minutes of meeting her. After spending some years in the Middle East, they settled in New Zealand. Their family was born some years after Grace's passing, so she never got to know them, or they her. It was one of the many reasons Hugh was prompted to write this book about his mother Grace.

Appendix 1

Acknowledgements

Writing a fictional book, inspired by memories and stories, is such an interesting experience and can take one on an amazing journey. However, it was not a journey that was made alone. I am indebted to many friends and family for their help with this book's creation. To name but a few: -

First and foremost, to my wife, Roberta, who, with the patience of a saint, gave me space to spend endless hours researching and writing this book. Her ideas, guidance, encouragement and support throughout the whole process were invaluable.

To our three children, and daughter-in-law, for always being positive and helpful with useful insights and suggestions for improvement along the way. I hope the story of Grace will be of interest and help you to know a little more about the grandmother you never met.

To our good friends, Brian and Delia, who with sharp eyes and much discussion, helped add perspective and balance.

To all my siblings and especially to our wider family, past and present, of which there were and still are very many.

To the very warm and wonderful people of Dromana and the Heights.

Finally, to 'Grace', for showing us how to love, and for always being there for us.

Thank you all for so many rich and beautiful memories and inspirations, in this your book.

Appendix 2

References

Much of the material from the book is fictional but substantially based on real experiences, some of it my own, much shared by many of my family and friends. Some of the other content was informed or loosely based on:

- Excerpts about WWII were largely informed by a marvellous documentary series, The Greatest Events of WWII, on Netflix, as well as by Wikipedia research
- The Blitz, Belfast Blitz, and London Bombings, Wikipedia
- Battle of Britain, Battle of the Somme, and others, Wikipedia
- Various articles on Alcoholism in Ireland, by Eunan McKinney
- Hereditability of Problem Drinking, by Marlen de Moor and others.
- Alcohol in Northern Ireland, Research and Information Services
- Diagnosis of Schizophrenia (and Bi-Polarism), Wikipedia

- Borderline Personality Disorder vs Bipolar Disorder, by Mary Jo DiLonardo
- The Genetic Lottery, by Cathryn Paige Harden
- Facts & FAQ About Down Syndrome, Wikipedia
- The Life of Reason, by George Santayana, Wikipedia
- History of Northern Ireland, Wikipedia (and others)
- Martin Luther and the Start of Protestant Reformation, Ninety-Five Thesis, Wikipedia
- Williamite War in Ireland 1688-1691, Wikipedia
- Battle of the Boyne, Wikipedia
- Events in Ireland in 1689, and the Siege of Derry, Wikipedia (and others)
- The 1916 Easter Rising, Wikipedia (and others)
- A Century of Women – 1940s – Northern Ireland, Wikipedia
- Women's Suffrages in the United Kingdom, Wikipedia
- Irish Constitution – Formation, Wikipedia
- Ireland in the 1960s, Wikipedia
- Castle Studies Group Journal & Annual Conference, Motte & Bailey
- The Big Snow (1947) and the Great Freeze (1962), Wikipedia
- Timeline of Major Events in WW2, Wikipedia.